BROTHERHOOD PROTECTORS BOXED SET 2

BOOKS 4-6

New York Times & USA Today
Bestselling Author

ELLE JAMES

Cowboy D-Force Copyright © 2018 by Elle James

Montana Ranger Copyright © 2017 by Elle James

Montana Dog Soldier Copyright © 2017 by Elle James

All rights reserved.

No part of this book may be reproduced in any form or by any electronic or mechanical means, including information storage and retrieval systems, without written permission from the author, except for the use of brief quotations in a book review.

BROTHERHOOD PROTECTORS BOXED SET 2

BOOKS 4, 5, 6

BROTHERHOOD PROTECTORS BOXED SETS
BOOK TWO

ELLE JAMES

TWISTED PAGE, INC

AUTHOR'S NOTE

Enjoy other military books by Elle James

Brotherhood Protectors Series
Montana SEAL (#1)
Bride Protector SEAL (#2)
Montana D-Force (#3)
Cowboy D-Force (#4)
Montana Ranger (#5)
Montana Dog Soldier (#6)
Montana SEAL Daddy (#7)
Montana Ranger's Wedding Vow (#8)
Montana SEAL Undercover Daddy (#9)
Cape Cod SEAL Rescue (#10)
Montana SEAL Friendly Fire (#11)
Montana SEAL's Mail-Order Bride (#12)
SEAL Justice (#13)
Ranger Creed (#14)
Delta Force Rescue (#15)
Dog Days of Christmas (#16)
Montana Rescue (#17)
Montana Ranger Returns (#18)

Visit ellejames.com for more titles and release dates
and join Elle James's Newsletter at
https://ellejames.com/contact/

COWBOY D-FORCE

BROTHERHOOD PROTECTORS BOOK #4

New York Times & USA Today
Bestselling Author

ELLE JAMES

COWBOY D-FORCE

BROTHERHOOD PROTECTORS

NEW YORK TIMES BESTSELLING AUTHOR
ELLE JAMES

*This story is dedicated to my readers who keep me writing by buying my books. I love what I do, and I hope you love it, too. Thank you so much for your continued support!
I'd also like to thank my sister and editor, Delilah Devlin, who keeps me in commas.*

Elle James

CHAPTER 1

John Wayne Morrison turned on his barstool and surveyed the occupants of the Blue Moose Tavern in Eagle Rock, Montana, trying to remember how to behave like a civilian.

In one corner of the room, a group of rangy cowboys gathered around the back corner, flipping quarters at a rattlesnake that had the misfortune of finding its way into the bar.

"Here's your beer." The burly bartender banged a mug full of lager on the bar, sloshing some over the top. He glanced at the dusty cowboys and yelled, "Hey, get that snake out of my bar!" Then he muttered under his breath, "Damned fools. Someone's gonna get hurt. You'd think they'd have more sense."

"Are rattlesnakes part of the entertainment around here?" John asked.

The bartender wiped the spilled beer off the counter. "Slow night." His eyes narrowed. "You're new around here. I'm Butch." The man held out a meaty hand. "Got a name?"

"Name's John Morrison, but my friends call me Duke." He gripped the man's hand and shook. Used to strong grips from his former Delta-Force team, he wasn't prepared for the bartender to choke the crap out of his hand. Increasing the strength on his own grasp, he didn't let go until the bartender loosened his grip first and released.

"Duke, huh?" Butch flexed his fingers and went back to filling mugs with beer. "Your middle name happen to be Wayne?"

Resigned to the usual ribbing he got when he gave anyone his full name, Duke nodded. "As a matter of fact, it is. My father was a big fan of old western movies. Stuck me with John Wayne."

"Makes sense to go by Duke."

"Yeah. It's hard to avoid." Duke took a long pull on his drink, letting the cool liquid glide down his throat. The drive from Ft. Hood, Texas had taken two days across some of the most desolate landscape in the country. Now that he was in Montana, he was looking forward to being near the mountains, hunting, fishing and riding horses. Hell, he hadn't been on a horse since he'd joined the army over twelve years ago.

"So, what brings you to Eagle Rock?" Butch asked.

Duke snorted. "Coming home to Montana."

"Coming home? Where ya been?'

"Military." His gut tightened, and his knee throbbed. For the past twelve years, he'd dedicated his life to protecting and serving the nation.

"Branch?" the bartender queried.

"Army."

"Prior marine, myself," Butch said. "Deploy?"

Duke nodded.

"See much action?"

Again, Duke nodded, not offering any more information. Most of his deployments had been Top Secret. Only those with a need to know, and with the requisite clearance, knew about those missions. The last one had been so secret that only the Secretary of State and the President had known of its existence.

"You don't talk much, do you?" Butch raised his hand. "Not that I mind. Most cowboys drink a few beers and expect me to be some kind of free therapist. From difficulties with their bosses, to woman troubles, I've heard it all." The bartender resumed wiping the bar. "You're a freakin' breath of fresh air. You just sit right there and fill a quiet space at my bar."

Duke gave him a hint of a smile and went back to drinking his beer and people-watching.

One of the younger patrons stuck some money in the jukebox, and a cry-in-your-beer song came on. Several cowboys led their ladies onto the small dance floor near an empty stage.

The beer, the music and the laid-back atmosphere soothed Duke's tired soul. After he finished his beer, he'd walk back to the bed and breakfast where he was staying the night. Tomorrow, he'd check in with his new boss, Hank Patterson, at the White Oak Ranch. From there, he'd report to his first assignment as personal security to someone wealthy enough to pay for protection.

As the song ended, so too did his beer. He pushed to his feet and was digging in his pocket for his wallet, when his cell phone buzzed.

He glanced down and grinned when he saw an incoming FaceTime call from Rider, one of his buddies from his former unit at Ft. Hood. He accepted the call. "Hey, dirtbag. Miss me already?"

Blaze, leaned into view beside Rider. "Damn right, we miss you. When are you going to come to your senses and get back to work?"

Rider shoved Blaze away and grinned into the phone. "Just making sure you got there all right. The team isn't the same without you."

His chest tightened. He'd hated leaving the men who'd come to feel like brothers. "Yeah, well, you'll do fine without me. You need fresh meat to pound into shape."

"No, we like the old meat we can count on to have our backs," Blaze said, his face appearing over Rider's shoulder.

"When do you start your new job?" Rider asked.

"Tomorrow," Duke said. "I meet with the head of Brotherhood Protectors, Hank Patterson. Want me to put in a good word for you?"

"Hell, yeah," Rider said. "Never know when this gig will play out. And I'm not getting any younger."

"You'd better check with Briana before you commit to a move to Montana. It gets cold up here in the winter."

Rider nodded. "Will do. You know the gang is due some time off. We might try to make it up there in the near future. I hear the fly fishing is pretty good up your way."

Duke laughed. "What do you know about fly fishing?"

"Nothing, but that's why we keep you around. To show us how to do things"

"Yeah. Well you know I'd always be glad to see any one of you."

"Done," Rider said. "As soon as we can get some leave approved."

"Good. I think you'd like it here. And you're right, the fly fishing is the best."

"I knew it." Rider grinned. "In the meantime, let us know if you get in a bind and need us to bail you out of a bad situation."

"Or a county jail," Blaze added. "And if you find any hot babes in the backwoods, give them my number." He smirked. "As long as they have all of their teeth."

"Will do," Duke said. "I'll be sure to show them that picture I took of you at our last unit picnic."

Rider laughed. "I'm sure the ladies will all want a piece of the cross-dressing, hairy-legged grandma."

Blaze frowned. "I don't suppose you'll ever let me live that one down, will you?"

Duke shook his head. "Not a chance."

"Well, I can mark Montana women off my list as long, as the Duke is flashing his blackmail photo."

"No, seriously, Duke," Rider said, "if you need us, all you have to do is pick up a phone."

"Thanks. It's nice to know I still have friends, even if they're two days away."

"Later," Rider said.

"Later." He rang off with a smile still tugging at his lips and glanced up in time to notice a commotion at the entrance.

A man wearing a windbreaker backed into the room with his camera balanced on his shoulder and aimed at the open doorway.

Curious, Duke handed his credit card over to the bartender and turned back in time to see a blonde strut through the door.

She wore sunglasses, despite it being dark outside and not much lighter inside. She'd gone maybe five steps when she tripped over her own feet, teetered on impossibly high heels and pitched into the camera man.

He fell back on his ass, holding his camera in the air to keep it from bouncing on the hardwood floor.

The blonde, who'd managed to regain her balance, straightened her jacket, tilted her sunglasses and glanced down at the camera man. "Move, you clumsy idiot!"

Two cowboys grabbed the man's shoulders, hauled him to his feet and let go.

"Sorry, Miss Love," he said. "Didn't mean to get in your way." Without missing another beat, he raised his camera to his shoulder and continued filming.

The woman's mouth twisted into a sneer. She planted her hand in the lens of his camera and pushed past the man, nearly knocking him off his feet again.

She made for the bar, dropped her huge, designer

bag on the counter and ordered, "Mango martini. Vodka. Shaken, not stirred." She raised two fingers. "Make that two."

Then she tilted her head downward, looked over the top of her sunglasses at Duke and raised her brows. "Mmm. If the men all look like you, I might learn to like Montana."

Duke saw no need to comment. She wasn't his type—too trashed and too high-maintenance. If he had his credit card back, he would leave the diva and go find a bed to crash in.

"This is the only place I've found to get a decent drink in this godforsaken shithole of a town." She perched one cheek on the barstool and leaned her back against the counter. "I'll be glad to get back to LA in a week." She laid her hand on his arm, digging her nails into his shirt. "Please tell me you're not from around here. I need to talk to someone who hasn't hit his head on the ground so many times he's nothing more than a toothless idiot."

"Sorry. I'm from Montana." Duke's lips twitched. "However, I do have my teeth." He grinned to prove it.

The bartender served the two martinis. Then he leaned close and whispered, "You do realize that's Lena Love, don't you? You're damned lucky, you are."

Duke wasn't feeling all that lucky. The woman next to him hadn't given up her claw-like hold on his arm yet.

Balancing herself against him, she downed first one martini then the other.

"Damned watered-down drinks. Can't even cop a

buzz." She raised her hand. "Two more please, only this time, don't skimp on the vodka." She dug into her voluminous purse, extracted a bottle of pills, shook out two and threw the bottle back inside. "This place smells like sweaty men." She leaned close to Duke and sniffed. "You smell like a sweaty man." She licked his neck. "Mmm, you taste salty."

Duke jerked back, his skin crawling at the woman's behavior. He had the sudden urge to take a shower.

The bartender set her martinis on the counter.

She tossed the pills into her mouth and chased them with the first martini. "That's more like it." Without missing a beat, she chugged her fourth martini and turned toward the dance floor.

"Doesn't anyone know how to party around here?" She shook her head and dug into her purse again. When she couldn't find what she was looking for, she shouted, "Phillip. I need two dollars."

A man dressed in a business suit materialized out of the crowd. "Lena, don't you think we should leave now that you've had your drinks?"

"Fuck no." She held out her hand and wiggled her fingers. "Two dollars, dammit."

Phillip pulled two dollar bills from his own wallet and handed them over.

Lena slapped them on the counter. "Quarters."

Butch glared at the woman, but changed the dollars for quarters, tossing them on the counter.

"Insolent bastard," Lena muttered. She grabbed the change and slid off the stool, nearly falling off her high heels in the process. With one hand on Duke's knee, she pulled herself upright, winked at him and swayed across the floor to the jukebox.

Dropping all eight quarters into the juke box, she bent over the glass top, her bottom, wrapped in a skin-tight skirt that barely covered the necessities, rocking back and forth to the country tune playing. After selecting several songs, she straightened and waited for the first one to begin.

Her head bobbed to the tune, and she looked around the room full of cowboys, who were standing back to see what this woman would do next.

Apparently, she didn't see in any of them whatever it was she was looking for, until she spotted Duke again. Her eyes narrowed, and she stalked toward him, weaving through the array of tables and long-legged men.

"Butch, I'll be needing my credit card," Duke muttered, his pulse picking up, his anxiety level ratcheting to higher than when he'd stepped out in an ISIS-held town. He did not want to be at the bar or anywhere else in the room when the diva made it across the floor. The only thing slowing her down were her high heels and all the alcohol and pills she'd consumed. "Credit card, Butch. Now."

Butch slapped the card and slip of paper on the counter. "She's coming for you, man. That's Lena Love, the actress."

"I wouldn't care if she was bringing me winning lottery numbers. She's trouble." Duke turned away long enough to scribble his name on the bottom line and grab his card. When he glanced up again, he realized he was too late.

Miss Love stood directly in front him, her breasts thrust out, her eyelids seductively lowered and her hand outstretched. "You. Dance floor. Now."

He held up his hands. "Sorry, ma'am. I don't dance." Especially not with women higher than the Empire State Building.

She blinked, the seductive look disappearing and in its place something akin to shock.

Had no one ever said *no* to the woman?

"Excuse me. I was just leaving." He tried to step around her, but she shifted to the side, blocking his path.

"No one says no to Lena Love."

"Life is full of firsts. Get used to them." He tried dodging in the other direction.

For a drunk high on pills and alcohol, she moved fast, again blocking his path.

The cameraman stood to one side, filming the entire exchange.

Duke shot him an annoyed glare and then returned his gaze to the woman. "Look, Miss Love, I've been on the road for two days. I'm tired and not in the mood to play games."

"Just one dance," she begged. "That's all I'm asking."

"Not interested."

"Perhaps you'd be interested in this."

Before he could even guess what she'd do next, Duke

received the full impact of two perfectly matching Double-D sized breasts, naked as the day they'd been implanted, full-on, in front of God and everyone in that bar.

He stood in stunned silence, unable to comprehend what had just happened.

Cowboys throughout the room hooted and threw their hats into the air. Then the chanting started. "More! More! More!"

"That's right, baby! Take it all off," one redneck shouted.

Wolf calls and whistles charged the air, piercing Duke's eardrums.

He took hold of Lena's hands and pulled them down, taking the hem of her shirt with them, covering her boobs. "Seriously, I'm not interested now—or ever. Please, just get out of my way." He gripped her arms and physically lifted her to set her to the side. Then he left her standing there, her jaw hanging, her eyes narrowing into tiny slits.

If he didn't get out of there quickly, the woman might launch herself at him, and he might be forced to break one of the rules his mother had drilled into his head as a young cowboy. Never hit a woman. His vision narrowed and buzzing filled his head. Sweat glazed his palms. He hadn't felt this trapped since he'd been pinned down in a collapsed building in a godforsaken Afghan village.

He made it through the room and out the door. As soon as he was outside, he broke into a sprint toward his truck, climbed in and hauled ass out of the parking lot and away from the obnoxious diva he wanted no part of.

So much for a relaxing reintroduction to his beloved state of Montana. Hopefully, his second day back home would be better than his first.

CHAPTER 2

THE BANGING ON HER JEEP WINDOW JOLTED ANGEL OUT of the nice nap she'd just started. Normally, her boss, Lena, managed to stay longer than thirty minutes in a bar. Angel had been counting on at least that long of a nap.

Except Lena's publicist was pounding the glass, his face a study of desperation. What was Lena up to now?

Angel sighed and lowered the window. "What's up, Phil?"

"She's doing it again. And there's a cameraman inside getting it all on video."

"Get her out," Angel said, rolling the window up.

Phillip clutched the top of the glass as it whirred upward, trying to keep it from closing. "You gotta help me. We need damage control before that video gets out. And she just flashed a stranger. It's all on the god damn video!"

"That's your problem. I'm just the stunt double. I'm not even sure why you brought me along." She shrugged. "Don't really care as long as I get paid an indecent amount of money."

His eyes widened. "Seriously, if you want a paycheck, you have to help me get her out before she kills her chance at any future scripts because she's such a loose cannon."

Angel sighed. Phillip seemed a nice enough guy, but he worked for the bitchiest, most narcissistic woman in Hollywood. Which said a lot, considering Lena lived in Hollywood among hundreds of actress wannabes, who thought they were God's gift to the silver screen. Lord help those who didn't agree.

But Lena was the drama queen to beat all drama queens.

"What's she done now?" How she'd gone from being a respectable stunt woman to Lena Love's body double, on the screen and off, she wasn't sure. Then again, she did know. The money was pretty damned good. Another year and she could afford to buy her own house in the woods and pay cash. Then she could work in a library or an oil change place. Somewhere she didn't have to hurl her body through glass windows or ride motorcycles through flames

"She just flashed one of the customers because he refused to dance with her."

"I like the man already." Angel pulled the keys from the ignition, climbed out of the car and followed Phillip to the door.

She didn't like loud music, and she liked cowboys even less. They usually smelled like horses. And she really didn't like horses. Not since she'd tried stunt riding for Lena. The horse had spooked when one of the booms had fallen to the ground with a loud crash.

Angel had thought she was going to die that day. Three miles later, after jumping a fence, crossing a six-lane highway and crashing into someone's back yard pool, the horse had finally slowed enough for Angel to jump off. How the horse wrangler had gotten the animal out of the swimming pool, she still didn't know. She'd almost drowned along with the animal and had to suffer through a trip to the hospital in the back of an ambulance with a suicidal driver.

She drew her stunt assignments line at horseback riding. And she was about to tell Lena where she could put her big, fat paychecks.

With her blond hair tucked up in a baseball cap, and wearing a baggy hoody and equally baggy jeans, Angel could have passed for a teen from the hood, instead of a woman who, with the right makeup and hairstyle, was the spitting image of Lena Love, multi-million-dollar princess of the big screen.

Lucky her. When she wasn't careful, she was stopped in stores around LA, mistaken for the actress. Having the paparazzi follow her gave her a real understanding of what it was like to be famous.

Lena could have it. It wasn't Angel's circus, and she didn't want anything to do with the publicity.

Unfortunately, she'd been called in on several occasions to "be" Lena when Lena was indisposed and couldn't represent herself—code for stoned out of her mind or passed out cold.

"Damn it, where'd she go?" Phillip stood on his toes,

searching the room for the blonde. "She was at the bar when I went outside."

"I'll check the ladies room," Angel said. "You check outside the back door."

Phillip ran for the back of the building and hopefully a rear exit.

Angel hoped Phillip would find Lena first, and save her from telling the woman what she thought of her troubled life. She wasn't afraid to speak her mind to Lena. Wouldn't matter anyway. When she sobered up, Lena would have no memory of what Angel had said.

She followed the sign indicating the direction for the restrooms and entered a darkened hallway. She'd seen far too many scary movies to like dark hallways. Nothing good ever happened in them.

With a firm mental shove, she pushed her misgivings to the side, pressed on and entered the ladies' room to find the space in complete darkness. Angel ran her hand along the wall, located the light switch and flipped it on.

At first, she thought the bathroom was empty. She turned to leave, but stopped when she heard a slight moan.

"Lena?" she called out.

Another moan sounded. Angel ducked low, looking under the stall doors for legs and feet. In the last one, she found more than legs and feet. She found Lena, lying on the floor in front of the toilet, her back to Angel.

Angel tried the stall door, but it was locked. "Lena, you have to get up and unlock the door."

Another moan, but no movement on the actress's part.

"Jesus, Lena, if you're going to pass out, at least leave the freakin' door unlocked." Angel shot a glance to the ceiling, knowing what she had to do and not liking it one bit. She didn't mind rolling in the dirt, wearing a fire-retardant suit and being doused in gasoline and set on fire, but she really hated touching anything in a public restroom, especially the floors around the toilets.

Yanking several paper towels out of the dispenser, she placed them on the ground in front of the stall door. With a deep breath, she lay on her back and shimmied beneath the stall door, bumping up against Lena's inert body.

The woman moved, groaned and heaved her guts up all over the nasty floor. Now, not only did it smell like urine, the restroom smelled like booze vomit.

Fighting the urge to retch, Angel worked her way into the stall, stood, unlocked the door and flung it open. Then she reached to hook her hands beneath Lena's arms and dragged her away from the toilet and into the middle of the washroom.

That's when she saw it.

"Sweet Jesus, that can't be good." Struggling with the smell and the urge to contribute to it, Angel stepped to the door and opened it. "Phillip, you gotta see this."

Phillip glanced up at the sign over the door. "I can't go into the ladies' restroom."

"Make an exception. We have a problem."

He shot a look down the hallway, and then ducked

through the door. "Make it quick. What's wrong—holy shit! What the hell happened?"

"Apparently, someone didn't like Lena flashing her boobs, or she's got a stalker."

BITCH was written across Lena's forehead in big, black, bold letters. Also, trailing down one cheek were the words, *I'm going to make,* and on the other, *you pay.*

A shiver rippled across Angel's skin, raising goose bumps. She ran to the sink, wet a fresh paper towel and bent to wipe the ink from Lena's face.

The wet paper towel did nothing to remove the ink. She tried adding soap to the towel. The soap had no more effect than the water.

"Sweet Jesus," Phillip said. "What are we going to do now? She can't be seen in public like that."

"Seriously? That's all you're worried about?" Angel pointed at the writing. "That's a threat. And apparently, whoever did it has it in for Miss Love. This ink is not coming off."

Phillip stood, wringing his hands. "She can't leave this bathroom like that."

"As it is, she's not going out on her own two feet anyway. She can't stand up and walk back through the barroom. The woman needs to be carried out."

Phillip tried to lift Lena into his arms, but like a slippery fish, the actress slid through his fingers. "The camera man is waiting to catch anything he can on Lena. She's already had too much negative publicity."

"I thought any publicity, good or bad, was preferable to no publicity."

"Yeah, ask Lindsay Lohan how that worked for her.

Or Brittany Spears. Sometimes it works in their favor, but not always. Talent only gets you so far. Being easy to work with gets you the roles. She's got too much riding on a script she really wants. It's a juicy one that could position her for an Oscar nomination. The studio doesn't want a mess on their hands."

"And she's a mess." Angel murmured. "I've seen her party too hard, but this takes it further. Does she need to go into a rehab center?"

Phillip sighed. "I've tried to talk her into it, but she doesn't think she has a problem."

"Passed out drunk in a bathroom stall is a problem. Whoever did that to her face could have done a whole lot worse."

"She needs a keeper," Phillip said.

Angel held up her hands. "Don't look at me. I'm just a stunt woman, not a bodyguard."

Phillip's eyes narrowed. "You know, you're more valuable as her double than as her bodyguard. This might be the perfect timing to get her into a private rehab facility. She could be detoxing while you're flushing out the jerk who did this to her." His lips spread into a genuine grin and he rubbed his hands together.

"Me? Play the part of Lena Love in real life?" Angel flung her hands in the air and backed away. "Oh, no. I'm all good for taking the hits, driving the fast cars, falling through the windows, but I'm no actress."

"I've seen you mimic Lena's tantrums. That's all you have to do. Please, stay on her ranch for the next two weeks while we clean up her face and dry her out."

Angel frowned. "What about the message on Lena's face? Someone's got it out for her."

"So, you're bait for the nutcase who did this. We'll hire a bodyguard for you, since the world will think you're Lena."

"I'm not so sure I like being bait. And I don't need a bodyguard."

"At least, you'll stay sober. You won't be caught off guard like Lena. And I know you can defend yourself with your military background. But a bodyguard is something Lean would want."

"She has bodyguards. Though, where were they when she was attacked here in the restroom?"

"Something I plan to find out. I'm not impressed with their abilities. Plus, we need one who isn't as familiar with Lena as her own bodyguards. I'll check around the state for someone local."

Angel thought about what Phillip was telling her. "So, all I have to do is play Lena, on her ranch, here in Montana, not LA?"

"Two weeks."

"I'll have full use of the pool and everything, just like Lena?" Angel was warming to the idea.

He nodded. "Everything, even her wardrobe."

"And Lena will be off somewhere in a rehab facility? I don't have to put up with her bullshit?"

Phillip held up two fingers. "Scouts honor."

Angel snorted. "Like you were ever a scout." She made up her mind. "Okay. I'll be Lena for two weeks. Other than an artistic stalker who paints threats on actress's faces, it sounds like the perfect paid vacation." She held out her hand. "Deal."

"Deal." Phillip shook her hand. "I'll have a bodyguard sent out to Love Land tomorrow."

Angel shrugged. "No hurry. I wouldn't want him to get in the way of my downtime."

At that moment, Lena moaned, opened her eyes and said, "Where am I?" Then her eyes rolled to the back of her head, and she passed out again.

"Let's get sleeping beauty out of here," Angel said.

"Yeah, and whatever you do, don't let anyone see us carrying out a passed out drunk Lena Love."

Angel pulled a bright pink camouflage bandana from the hip pocket of her jeans and wrapped it around Lena's signature blond hair.

Phillip tried again to lift Miss Love. "I can't do this on my own. I'm not built to haul actresses around in my arms."

"You carry the top. I'll lift from the lower end." Angel grabbed Lena's narrow ankles. "Ready?"

With a nod, Phillip grabbed the woman beneath her armpits.

"Lift," Angel said. Though Phillip took the brunt of Lena's weight, Angel strained against the dead weight. "Where to?"

Phillip tipped his head toward the rear of the building. "There's an emergency exit at the end of the hallway. We can take her out the back."

"I'm ready when you are," he said, his voice tight.

"Good, let's get her out of here."

Phillip backed all the way down the hall, through the exit, and out into the starlit, Montana sky.

So far, so good. They might get her out of the bar for the night, but how would they get the indelible ink off her face?

Angel figured that would be Phillip's problem to tackle when Lena was in detox.

For the next two weeks, Angel had a date with a swimming pool and fruity cocktails she could slip some whiskey into. Playing the rich and arrogant Lena Love could be fun, as long as her new bodyguard and the artistic stalker didn't rain on her summer sunshine.

CHAPTER 3

Duke pulled up to the gate of the Love Land Ranch and shook his head. He couldn't believe his first assignment was as bodyguard to the infamous Lena Love. The eccentric diva who'd flashed her tits at him the night before at the Blue Moose Tavern. Sure, he'd expected to provide personal security to some rich and famous person, but holy shit.

Not her.

"Is there someone else who can take this one?" he'd asked his new boss, Hank Patterson. Yeah, it might not be the right thing to ask on your first day, but geez, the woman was toxic.

Hank frowned. "I would think you'd be excited to get this gig. Lena Love is iconic in the movie industry."

"She's not the nicest person." Hank's wife, Sadie, entered the room carrying a tiny bundle, their little girl, born only two months previously.

Although he'd just met the man, obviously, in Hank's

book, the baby hung the moon. And the man was extraordinarily loving toward his wife.

Sadie pursed her lips. "I was on the same set with Lena once. I swore I'd never do another movie with her. She's one-hundred-percent diva and a real beyotch." Sadie McClain would know. Having established herself as one of Hollywood's top-grossing actresses, she was Lena's direct competition.

Hank arched an eyebrow. "The assignment is short term. Two weeks. When she goes back to LA, she'll return to using her own bodyguards." Hank fixed his gaze on Duke. "Two weeks. That's all I'm asking. I'd take it myself, but I've got a couple more guys coming on board soon, and I've been out beating the bushes for clients."

"Not to mention, you're on diaper duty this weekend. when I have to be at the premier of my new movie." Sadie stared down at her baby. "Isn't that right, Emma, sweetheart? Daddy has diaper duty."

Hank's lips twisted. "You heard her. I'm tied up this weekend, and all my other agents are assigned. You're the only man I have who can take this one. I have another job coming up, but the client has yet to arrive in country. The timing of this assignment keeps you employed until he arrives." Hank tilted his head. "What have you got against Ms. Love?"

"She made a pass at me last night and gave me a full-frontal exposure of her manufactured breasts."

"She flashed you?" Hank's bark of laughter startled the baby.

Emma cried out.

"Shh, sweet Emma," Sadie sang to soothe the baby back to sleep. "Hank, really," she admonished her husband.

"Two weeks. That's all I ask," Hank said in his inside voice, a smile tugging at his lips.

His first assignment with the Brotherhood Protectors and he already wanted out of it.

Duke stared up at the arched sign and sighed. From bad-ass Delta Force soldier to babysitting a spoiled, obnoxious diva. He'd sunk to a new level of low he'd never expected.

Maybe he would be better off hiring out as a cowboy for room and board on a corporate cattle ranch. At least, he wouldn't have women flashing him.

His mother would be appalled at Miss Love's behavior. He'd just have to keep that little tidbit about the flashing to himself.

Duke blamed his mother for his lack of permanent relationships with the opposite sex. His mother had been the consummate housewife, mother and nurturer. She was the best cook, most accomplished seamstress and the nicest person he had the pleasure of knowing. How could any woman measure up to her perfection?

Yeah, he'd had sex with a number of willing participants, but he'd always found something about them that didn't quite make the cut.

Now. This woman.

Two weeks.

He'd survived for two weeks in the hills of Afghanistan, after being separated from his teammates, living off roots and the wild rabbits he'd snared. Two weeks on a rich woman's resort property would be nothing.

Then why would he rather shoot himself in the foot than face Lena Love again?

He punched in the security code and waited for the gate to open enough he could drive his pickup through.

A wide concrete drive wove through a lodge-pole pine forest and up into the foothills of the Crazy Mountains. The trees thinned, exposing lush green pastures filled with grazing horses and cattle. The road climbed upward and emerged near the top of a hill. A massive structure of rock, cedar and glass consumed his view.

This was a cabin in the mountains?

Holy crap.

If he wasn't being forced to babysit the diva, this would be a plush assignment. Then again, he wasn't on vacation, nor would he be lounging by a pool, drinking Mai Tais and eating bon bons.

A muscular man, wearing pressed jeans and an equally clean and pressed white shirt, strode around the side of the house and waved at Duke. "Hired help parks in the servants' lot behind the barn." He pointed to a drive leading around to the back of the house.

Since he was the hired help, Duke followed the man's instructions and drove around to the back of the house and down a slope to a barn bigger than the high school he'd attended. It was by far the biggest barn he'd ever worked around. It could be a convention center or big-city rodeo arena.

He parked his truck next to several others bearing the Love Land Ranch logo.

Reluctantly, he climbed down from the pickup. With a brief glance at the back seat, he decided to leave his duffel bag until he learned where he'd be sleeping for this gig. He assumed he'd stay in the big house with Miss Love. If his task was to keep her safe, he'd have to be close enough to do that.

"Bodyguard?" The young, muscleman appeared beside Duke.

Duke nodded. "That would be me."

The man stuck out his hand. "Brandt Lucas. Foreman."

Duke gripped the man's hand. "Duke Morrison."

"Miss Love is up at the pool. She asked me to send you to her as soon as you arrived."

"Thank you."

"If you need help with anything to do with the ranch, cattle or horses, see me or my assistant foreman, Lyle Sorenson." He nodded toward an older man in faded jeans, an equally faded blue chambray shirt and a dusty cowboy hat.

The older guy pushed a wheelbarrow full of muck from the barn to a pile at the rear of the massive structure. He dumped the load, glanced up and nodded in Duke's direction.

Duke almost laughed. The difference between the younger, clean, muscle-bound man and the older, wiry, dirty one was too obvious.

Miss Love had probably promoted Lucas to Foreman based on his looks, rather than his abilities.

"How many horses does Miss Love keep on the ranch?" Duke asked, just to test his theory.

Mr. Lucas shrugged. "A dozen or so. If you want exact numbers, you can consult Mr. Sorenson. He keeps the books on the animals."

"And what do you do?" Duke asked.

He puffed out his chest and lifted his chin. "I'm the foreman. I tell the other ranch hands what to do."

Duke swallowed back the laughter threatening to erupt. A real ranch foreman knew, to the head, the number of livestock a ranch had and kept close tabs on additions and losses. He knew how much feed it took to get them through the winter, knew which ones were sickly and which horses got along with the others. He'd never leave it to the ranch hands to manage the herds or care for their health and wellbeing.

Man candy. That was what Brandt Lucas was.

Duke didn't have much respect for a man who didn't earn his keep. But then, he didn't know what Lucas had to do for Miss Love to earn his pay. It might have nothing whatsoever to do with managing the livestock or the crops.

"You can go on up to the house," Brandt said with an easy smile. "Like I said, Miss Love is lying by the pool."

Duke climbed the slope to the big house, admiring the combination of rustic charm and clean, modern lines. He cut through a stand of trees and shrubs that provided a barrier around the stone-paved patio and pool. A rock waterfall graced one end of the pool, and a line of deck chairs stood between the pool and the house. One of which was occupied by a woman wearing a miniscule black bikini and a pair of sunglasses.

He crossed the stone patio to the deck chair and waited for her to acknowledge his presence.

A minute passed and nothing.

Duke cleared his throat.

"I know you're there. You're blocking my sun. Move, please."

He gritted his teeth and forced a smile. "Miss Love, I'm Duke Morrison from Brotherhood Protectors. Hank Patterson sent me over."

"Fine, fine. You can change into a bathing suit and go for a swim for all I care."

"No, thank you, Miss Love. I'm here to work, not play."

She huffed. "I told Phillip I didn't need a bodyguard here on my own ranch. He doesn't listen."

Duke frowned. "Phillip?"

A frown pulled the woman's lips downward. "My publicity agent."

"If it's all the same to you, I'd like to inspect the house and the security system."

She waved her fingers. "Fine. Do what you have to, just do it out of my sunshine."

He shook his head. "Miss Love, are you sure you should be out in the open?"

She tipped her sunglasses low so that she could stare at him over their rims. "And where else but out in the open would I get sunshine? Seriously, couldn't they have sent me a smarter bodyguard?"

Anger bubbled up inside Duke's chest and rose in a heated flush up into his face. He had to remind himself he was representing Hank's business. Going off on a customer wasn't the way to get referrals and additional business. He had to resist his urge to lift Miss Love, chair and all, and dump her into the pool. "I'll just have a look at that security system."

"Whatever." She laid back, sunglasses back in place. "Wake me in thirty minutes. I'll need to flip over and tan my back."

He studied her for another few seconds. Yes, she was beautiful, with a body that didn't quit. Long supple legs, with well-defined muscles and taut abs. Her arms were toned, and there wasn't an ounce of flab anywhere on her. She probably paid her personal trainer a small fortune to get her into that kind of shape. Lying down, her breasts weren't nearly as voluptuous as they'd been when she'd flashed them in his face at the bar the night before.

Apparently, she didn't remember him from the Blue Moose. She'd probably been too plastered to remember much of anything.

Good. He'd rather she didn't remember the encounter. If he was lucky, she wouldn't make another pass at him.

"Oh, and Luke?" she said.

"Duke," he corrected automatically.

"Get me a drink on your way back. Jack Daniels on the rocks with a squeeze of lime."

Babysitter, bartender and waiter. Yeah, he'd come a long way from his calling as a highly-skilled warrior.

"Oh, and Luke?" she called, stopping him again.

"Duke," he said, his ire rising by the second.

"Give me a hand up. I feel like taking a dip in the

pool."

He reached out his hand, gripped hers and yanked her out of her chair a little harder than he'd intended, his anger fueling his muscles. She slammed into his body, her sunglasses knocked from their perch on her nose.

She stared at him through clear, blue-gray eyes, her mouth opened in a silent O. "Was that necessary?"

"You wanted up," he said. "You're up."

Her pretty brows puckered. "You're a rude man, Luke. I've a mind to fire you."

"My name is Duke. And you'd be lucky to have a mind."

She rolled her eyes. "Luke, Duke. What does it matter? You're blocking my sun again. Move." She planted her hands on his chest and gave him a shove, stronger than he'd anticipated and with a little edge to her voice on the last word.

He stepped backward, remembering too late the pool was right behind him. Before he could stop himself, he fell backward. As he went, he reached for anything to grab hold of. It just so happened to be Miss Love's hand.

Momentum sent him into the water. Quick reflexes and a strong grip brought Miss Love in with him.

He hit the water hard and sank fast.

The woman who'd pushed him thrashed and kicked, hitting him with her heel in his war-damaged knee.

Pain shot through his body, stunning him, making the summer sun dim to gray and finally black.

A moment later, an arm came around him from

behind, looped over his shoulder and chest and pulled him to the surface.

As soon as he hit fresh air, he sucked it in, his eyes blinking open. When he realized he was still in the water, he kicked hard and fought the arm holding him.

"Be still, or you'll drown us both," a feminine voice grumbled in his ear.

He leaned back against a warm, soft body, swimming him toward the shallow end of the big pool. When his feet touched the bottom, he stood, getting his bearings and filling his lungs full of life-giving oxygen.

A few steps away in the shallower water, Lena stood, her pretty blond hair plastered to her scalp, her makeup running in black rivulets down her cheeks, her gaze narrowed. "Are you all right?"

For a moment Duke stared at her, trying to comprehend what she'd just asked. Her action, saving him, was so out of character for the diva, she could have been someone else entirely.

Duke wondered if he'd crossed into another dimension where the Lena Love there was actually a nice person, not the spoiled, brat in his own dimension.

"I'm okay," he said, his cheeks heating. His first day on the job as a bodyguard, and his client saved him from drowning. It didn't bode well for the rest of the two weeks.

Angel had been acting full-on diva when she'd managed to send her new bodyguard into the pool. She hadn't expected him to pull her in with him. When she'd surfaced, and he hadn't, she'd panicked for a second. Then the life-saving skills she'd learned when she was a teenaged lifeguard at the neighborhood swimming pool kicked in. She dove down, found Duke and dragged him to the surface, her heart pounding so hard, she could barely breathe. "What happened?"

"Nothing." He waded to the side of the pool and pulled himself up onto the deck.

"Nothing, hell." She followed, determined to get to the bottom of her bodyguard's near drowning. "You passed out."

"Shit happens," he said, then pulled his T-shirt over his head and wrung it out into the pool. His broad, muscular chest had dozens of little scars, some bigger than others. "I'm fully capable of providing protection for you for the next two weeks." He reached down, offering her a hand to help her out of the water.

She hesitated a moment, and then laid her hand in his.

He pulled her out of the water and up onto the deck without slamming her into his chest like he had earlier.

"Thanks," he said, his tone brusque, his eyes sliding over her from head to toe. "You weren't hurt?"

"No. But I'll have to redo my hair and makeup before the camera crew comes to film her—my home." Even that attempt at her boss's waspishness fell flat of the desired annoying effect.

His gaze raked over her wet head and smeared face. "I think it looks fine. More natural."

Without thinking, Angel raised her hand to her damp cheek.

This bodyguard Phillip had hired had come to the pool with a hint of disgust on his face.

Unfortunately, she wasn't at liberty to be herself. She had to play the part of Lena Love in order to convince anyone who might be lurking in the bushes or on a nearby hillside, watching her. Lena needed the break from her real life and the stalker in order to sober up and get her life back on track. The least Angel could do was to put on a great show to hide the fact she was an imposter.

What she hadn't counted on was her bodyguard blacking out in the pool, requiring her to rescue him. She could bet that wasn't something Lena would have done. Lena would have gotten out of the pool cursing about the insubordinate fool getting her hair wet. She'd have stood on the side of the pool railing about her smeared makeup and saying if he drowned he'd be getting what he deserved for causing her to, Lord forbid, break a fingernail.

"Do you even swim?" she asked.

His brows descended. "Of course."

"Then why were you unconscious?"

"It's not important. Whatever happened won't affect my ability to work."

The man wasn't going to give her anymore information than that.

"Fine." She drew in a deep breath and waved her hand toward the house. "Your sleeping quarters are at the top of the stairs, first door on your right. You might as well change into dry clothes. Oh, and let the chef know you're here and to set another plate at the table."

He started toward the barn.

"Where are you going?" she asked.

Duke stopped and faced her. "To get my duffel bag with my dry clothes. I'll be back in just a minute, at which time I'll bring your drink and, in the process, speak with the chef. Will you require anything else?"

She frowned. "Not yet. I'll let you know when I think of something. And next time, don't be so cocky."

He nodded and left, following the path through the surrounding garden and down the hill to the barn.

The man was not what she'd consider handsome, but he was ruggedly appealing. If she was right, the marks on his chest had been caused by shrapnel. And by the slight limp she'd noted as he walked away, his right leg had issues. Probably caused by whatever had peppered his chest with scars.

Her bodyguard bore further scrutiny, not because his touch had ignited a special electrical charge inside her, but because he wasn't very forthcoming with information about himself.

She knew one thing, though. His name was Duke, and it irritated him when she called him Luke. Her lips quirked on the corners. Maybe she was more like Lena than she cared to admit. She found she liked irritating big, hunky men who thought they knew everything there was to know about the women they protected.

Well, Duke Morrison had another think coming. Lena Love was going to have some fun with the big, sexy bodyguard. Angel's lips curved into a sassy smile. Suddenly, two weeks of ranch living on the Love Land Ranch, didn't sound so boring after all.

CHAPTER 4

Duke hurried to his truck to get the duffel bag he'd left there.

Brandt Lucas caught up with him in front of the barn, half jogging to keep up with Duke, a grin on his handsome face. "I take it you met Miss Love."

"I did," Duke said through gritted teeth.

"She push you in the pool, or did you decide to cool off?"

"I misjudged my footing." And the woman's mean streak. Yeah, he'd witnessed it the previous night, but hadn't imagined she'd stoop to pushing him into the pool fully clothed.

What had him baffled was that she'd saved him from drowning when he'd blacked out. This was a side to Miss Love that was incongruous with everything he'd witnessed and heard about the actress.

For a few moments, she'd been very real and undeniably attractive. Not in the movie star, glossy, superbly-put-together way. She'd almost been a girl-next-door, tough-but-caring woman his mother would have liked.

He liked that version of Lena almost enough to want to stay for the full two weeks. Too bad her mouth had kicked in again after she'd nearly redeemed herself by saving him.

"I don't know why Miss Love needs to hire a bodyguard," Lucas said. "There are plenty of staff members who live here fulltime to look out for her."

"You all have your jobs. I have mine. Perhaps she likes having someone dedicated to securing her well-being." Duke reached his truck, unlocked it and pulled out the duffel bag. When he turned, he almost bumped into Lucas.

"Are you sure that's the only reason she hired you?" The man stood in front of Duke with his arms crossed over his chest, his chin raised, his eyes narrowed.

"What other reason would she have?"

The pimped up cowboy looked down his nose and raked his gaze over Duke. "She usually prefers her lovers to be...better dressed, for one." He sniffed. "You're not her usual type."

Duke almost laughed in the man's face, but Lucas was blocking his path and irritating him more by the second. "And you're more her type?"

Lucas's smirk was as irritating as his words. "I don't like to kiss and tell, but yes."

Heat burned inside Duke's chest. He clenched his fist around the handles of the duffel bag to keep from throwing it in Lucas's face. Duke's mother would have washed the asshole's mouth out with soap for talking badly about a girl or woman. Though Ms. Love hadn't earned his respect, she was female, and he wouldn't stand by while a prissy man who dressed like a cowboy impugned her character. "Get out of my way."

"Don't say I didn't warn you. Miss Love will use you and discard you like every other male she's brought to her ranch. And if you think pleasuring her will convince her to give you a part in one of her movies, you're going to be disappointed."

"I said, *Get. Out. Of. My. Way.*"

Lucas raised his smooth, manicured hands. "Fine. Have it your way. I'll save my 'I told you so' for when she has you pack up and—"

Duke dropped his bag and plowed his fist into Brandt Lucas's perfect nose.

The man screamed like a girl and fell flat on his ass, getting dirt all over his freshly pressed jeans. Blood spurted from his nose, staining his clean white shirt. "You animal. Why'd you go and do that?"

"I felt threatened," Duke said, his tone flat and bored. "I had to defend myself from your aggression." He fought to keep from laughing.

"Did you have to punch me in my nose?" he whined, tears rolling down his cheeks. "Oh, Lord, I need to see a doctor. No, I need a plastic surgeon. You could have broken it. Oh, my beautiful, perfect nose."

"Don't say I didn't warn you to get out of my way." Duke grabbed his duffel bag, stepped over the man and marched up the slope to the main house, feeling just a little better for having punched someone. Though he felt a little guilty he'd hit someone who was clearly no match for him. It was like kicking a stupid dog. The dog couldn't help he was born stupid. And kicking a dog was just wrong in every way.

But the man had talked trash about his client. For that reason alone, Lucas had deserved Duke's response.

Back through the garden, Duke made his way toward the house, slightly disappointed he didn't see Lena lying in the lounge chair where he'd originally found her. She was nowhere to be seen on the back patio.

Entering through the rear glass door, he stopped to stare at the three-story, cathedral ceiling made of rough-hewn cedar beams arching high over his head.

A bank of windows stretched from the floor all the way up to the impossibly high ceiling, giving a view of the Crazy Mountains most people could never afford in their lifetimes.

Plush leather furniture surrounded a massive stone fireplace, and a thick sheepskin rug lay in front of the hearth. Perfect for a midnight tryst of writhing, naked bodies making love into the early hours of morning.

He could imagine Lena's beautiful body stretched out on the sheepskin, her back arched in the throes of a mind-blowing orgasm.

His groin tightened, and he adjusted his damp jeans. Now was not the time to get a hard-on. Especially for the client. If she lived up to her reputation, she'd have him deliver crackers and cheese to her bed and expect him to share the snack and more.

Before he'd gone for a swim, he'd have said an emphatic *Hell No*.

After she'd saved his ass from certain drowning, his opinion had altered. He saw an entirely different side to the mouthy Miss Love. No, he wasn't naïve enough to think she was cured of her bitchiness in the space of five minutes, but she bore watching. Something wasn't ringing true about the woman.

He headed for the stairs and climbed them one at a time, the injured knee telling him about every step by sending a stab of pain through his leg. The therapist had said he'd have to work the knee daily to get it anywhere near to what it used to be. He'd also said it would never be the same. Duke would have to adjust to a new normal.

Just like his job. He wasn't one of the prestigious Delta Force team anymore. He'd have to adjust to the new normal lifestyle of a rent-a-bodyguard. There was no shame in making a living in an environment where people weren't shooting at him.

Then why was he missing the sound of gunfire and the rush of adrenalin it gave him when he charged into battle?

Most of all, he missed his brothers. Fort Hood seemed a very long way from the Love Land Ranch.

He found the guest room at the top of the stairs, first door on the right, and entered, placing his duffel bag on the floor. The bed was a giant, king-sized, four-poster with thick wooden cannon balls on each corner post. The mattress was covered in a white duvet and piles of feather pillows. A man could lose his women in a bed that size.

Duke unzipped his duffel and fished out a pair of

black trousers and a gray polo shirt Hank had given him with the Brotherhood Protectors logo embroidered on the left breast. He figured the outfit would be dressy enough for a bodyguard, without going into the over-the-top stereotype of men dressed in black suits, wearing mirrored sunglasses. He'd ask Miss Love what kind of uniform she expected. Not that he'd necessarily agree to wear it, if it was too hot or too stiff. He needed the ability to run fast (well, as fast as his knee would take him) dive, roll, leap and fight his way out of any situation. Constrictive clothing wasn't conducive to most of those activities.

A door at the side of his room led into an ensuite bathroom with a man-sized shower and a claw-foot tub. Again, he imagined Miss Love bathing naked in the tub, bubbles barely covering the tops of her breasts as she leaned back her head and smiled.

And again, his cock hardened and caused him distress in the still-damp denim.

Trying without much success to put Miss Love's gorgeous body out of his thoughts, he peeled off the wet clothes and slung them over the side of the tub. Then he stepped beneath the showerhead and turned on the cold water, full blast. If he had any hope of chilling his desire, the water would have to be icy cold. His client had a body that could stop a Mack truck. Slim in all the right places, taut enough to bounce a quarter off her belly and smooth, silky skin stretched over firm muscles.

No matter how long he stood under the shower, his desire refused to abate, and her royal pain in the ass wouldn't wait forever for him to get over his hard-on.

She'd want that drink he should have gotten her before they both had gone for a swim.

He shut off the water, dried his body and dropped his towel. A knock on the door of the bedroom startled him into grabbing the towel from the floor and wrapping it around his waist.

"Yeah," he said, loud enough whoever was on the other side would hear.

"Phillip and the camera crew are here." Lena said. "Look alive. I need you downstairs ASAP."

The woman sounded more like a drill sergeant than an actress. The firm tone of command lingered in the air and spurred Duke to hurry into his clothes, pull on a dry pair of shoes and head downstairs.

Lena stood by the front entrance, a forced smile stretching her lips across her teeth. Her publicist stood by her side, holding the door as half a dozen men and women entered, passing by Miss Love in their hurry to get inside the famous actress's personal domain.

One by one, the journalists and the crews wandered room by room. Miss Love enlisted the assistance of the housekeeper to explain the layout of the house and the names of each of the suites.

Keeping a close eye on the guests and the camera man, Duke edged closer to Lena, ready to leap in front of her should someone get too close.

At last they worked their way into the master suite. Everyone was suitably impressed with the beautiful, modern king-size bed with its soft cotton-candy pink comforter.

Lena led the crew into the bathroom, and they all came to an abrupt halt.

"Damn!" Lena cursed. "How the hell did he get in here?"

Duke's adrenaline spiked, and he squeezed between her Publicist and the wall, breaking through to the open interior of the massive master bath.

Lena stood staring at the wall of mirrors, her lips pressed into a thin line.

Written in garish red lipstick were the words:
The predator thrills not in the capture
But in chasing the prey
He revels in the scent of fear

ANGEL HAD to give the author credit for writing that much in lipstick. She'd have given up after the first line.

Despite her flippant outlook on the message, a chill rippled across her skin. The message drawn on Lena's face was playing out. Whoever had it in for Lena was on a roll. She wondered how far he'd take it.

"Everyone out," Duke commanded.

Lena started for the door, but Duke hooked her arm and pulled her against his body.

Electric current zapped through her, heating her where she touched him and spreading that warmth throughout her body. The man was like an igniter switch on a gas burning fireplace. Every time he touched her, her blood burned.

Not a good thing when she needed to keep her secrets and her distance.

Most of the men and women backed out, with the exception of Phillip. The publicity agent's eyes took on an excited glow. He snagged the cameraman as he attempted to fit through the door with the camera on his shoulder. "Where are you going? You need to get a shot of that."

Angel nearly laughed when Duke glared at the two.

"I said get out," Duke said in his lowest, most dangerous and absolutely sexiest voice.

Places farther south inside Angel throbbed to the tone.

"Are you kidding?" Phillip ignored Duke and directed the cameraman. "Get the mirror from this angle." He turned to Lena. "Stand closer to the mirror and look terrified. This is good stuff. It might even make national news."

"Out!" Duke said.

Phillip jumped and finally seemed to hear Duke. The man really was irritating. Angel didn't know how Lena put up with him.

"You don't understand," Phillip whined. "This is an opportunity to get Lena into the public eye, gain sympathy and show how vulnerable she can be. The studios will eat this shit up."

"You'll have to schedule another show. As long as I'm her bodyguard, this chick's my responsibility." Duke pointed to the door. "Get out, before I throw you out." He stood between Phillip and Angel, his arms crossed over his chest.

Standing behind him, Angel had the best view of all those rippling muscles. As a stunt woman, she was around some pretty ripped dudes. But this bodyguard had alpha magnetism in spades. She could swear he'd been in the military at some time in the recent past. He carried himself with the dignity of a man who'd worn a uniform for his country. Having served herself, she could pick them out in a crowd of civilians.

Angel leaned around him to see if Phillip was actually going to get smart and get out while he still had all of his teeth.

Phillip frowned. "You're supposed to be guarding her, not interfering in her publicity."

"I'm guarding her from you." He grabbed Phillip's arm and dragged him toward the door.

The cameraman scurried out, bumping his big camera against the doorframe in his hurry to escape the wrath of Duke.

"I'll have a talk with Mr. Patterson about your behavior," Phillip said.

"Do that. In the meantime, don't piss me off." He gave one last shove, sending Phillip stumbling out of the bathroom. Then he slammed the door in the man's face.

Angel couldn't help it, she had to give the man props for taking matters in his own hands and doing what he was being paid to do. "Bravo. I've wanted to do that from the moment he arrived."

Duke turned back, a frown cleaving his forehead. "Then why didn't you?"

She shrugged. "I guess he knows what he's doing. He's the publicist. I'm just the talent." She tipped her head toward the mirror, remembering to play her Lena part. "What a shame."

"What do you mean?"

Her lips twisted. "That was my favorite lipstick." She fought to keep from laughing at the look of disgust on Duke's face.

He shook his head. "Ruining a tube of lipstick is the least of your worries."

"You don't know how hard it is to find a color you simply love." She raised a hand to fluff her hair and stared past the smears on the mirror to study her reflection like Lena would have, every chance she got.

"Sweetheart, that message is a threat."

A shiver of awareness slipped across her skin at his endearment. Not that he'd meant it as such, but on his lips, it sounded kinda sexy. Especially as laced with sarcasm as it was. She wondered what the word would sound like if he spoke it in a low, intimate voice. Another shiver of awareness swept across her and culminated low in her belly. She had to get over the strange attraction she was feeling toward the rugged bodyguard.

"Miss Love, whoever wrote that message there intends to continue his little game. To what end result, I don't know, but it can't be good."

"This place is wired for security. How did he get all the way to my bathroom in the short time between when I greeted my guests and when we arrived back up here?"

"I don't know." He searched the counter and floor.

"What are you doing?" she asked.

"If we could find the tube, we could send it off for latent print analysis. Our trespasser might be in the AFIS system."

"A hardened criminal?" She forced a fake shiver. "Mmm, how deliciously dangerous."

Duke straightened, gripped her arms and stared down into her eyes. "You don't get it. This guy is playing a predatory game with you."

Oh, she got it all right. She was the bait. But Lena wouldn't know any better. She thought she was invincible. "He's just trying to scare me." She propped a hand on her hip. "I'm not impressed."

"He's a predator. Like a cat playing with his food before he kills it. What if that's his ultimate end game?"

She frowned. "You don't know that."

"True. But I'd rather be safe than sorry. I didn't hire onto this gig to lose my first client because she wouldn't take her own safety seriously."

She dipped her lashes low over her eyes. "That's why I have you, isn't it? I'm paying you to keep me safe."

"If you want me to keep you safe, you have to play by my rules."

"Rules?" She opened her eyes wide and then batted them like she'd seen Lena do on numerous occasions. "Oh, I don't like following rules."

He let go of her and backed away a couple of steps. "Then find yourself another puppet to play with." Duke turned on his heel and started for the door.

Crap. She hadn't wanted him to quit. She was just playing Lena. Apparently, too well. If not Duke as her bodyguard, who else would she get? Better the one she knew than a gamble on someone else.

Angel lunged for him, grabbed his arm and yanked him around. "Wait. Don't go. I'll follow your stupid rules." She rested her hand on his chest. "Just don't leave me." Leaning up on her toes, she brushed her lips across his. "Please."

He remained stiff and unbending. "My rules?"

She nodded. "Your rules."

A knock sounded on the bathroom door. "Lena?" Phillip said.

Angel released Duke's arm. "Yes, Phillip. What do you want?" she asked, her gaze never wavering from Duke's.

"The camera crew wants you to do a short interview out by the pool. Preferably in one of your designer swimsuits."

She cringed inwardly. Lena might be used to parading around in next to nothing, but Angel liked to keep her clothes on in mixed company. And she'd never expose her entire body unless it was behind closed doors and they were about to make love.

Her core tingled and her gaze slipped down the angular lines of Duke's torso and lower to his narrow hips. Yeah, getting naked with someone like him in private...she could do.

Getting naked in front of a camera and a dozen members of a production team...not no, but hell no.

"An interview by the pool?" She raised her brows in question. "Would that violate your rules?"

"Not so long as I'm nearby," Duke said.

"Then we need to get going." She started to go around him.

He grabbed her wrist and dragged her body up against his. "One other rule."

She looked up into his brown eyes, her heartbeat fluttering against her chest. "Rule?" she repeated, her brain misfiring with the electric currents frying her nerve endings.

"No more of this." He brushed his lips across hers.

Unlike his hard-muscled body, his mouth was soft, his lips full and sensuous. Angel pressed into him, rising up on her toes to get closer to that incredible mouth.

He leaned back just a hair and said, "And never any of this." Duke claimed her lips, crushing his mouth to hers. He pushed his tongue past her teeth.

Angel opened to him and met him halfway, tangling her tongue with his in a frenzied caress that set her entire body on fire with a need she'd never known existed.

His hands swept down her back and cupped her ass.

She raised her hands to caress the back of his neck, deepening the connection, wishing there weren't so many barriers between them. She wanted him…naked…in bed…driving deep inside her.

When at last he set her away, she swayed, her knees feeling more like jelly than bone. She wiped the back of her hand across her throbbing lips and wondered what had just happened. But then she knew.

She'd just experienced a kiss like none she'd had before. The kind that defined souls and knocked off her socks.

He stared down at her, his eyes narrowed. "Am I perfectly clear?"

"Huh?'

His lips twitched. "The rules?"

She blinked, trying to remember what they'd been talking about. Was he saying they couldn't kiss like they'd just kissed? Inside, her body wailed at the unfairness of such a rule. How could anyone promise not to kiss like that when surely it was as critical to her life as her next breath?

"You're kidding right?" she whispered.

"I never kid," he said. "You're my client. I'm your bodyguard. Anything sexual between us is strictly off limits." His mouth firmed into a straight line, and his eyes narrowed.

Anger jolted through her lust-crazed senses, flushing out all thoughts of kissing this man ever again. She forced a smile to her lips and lifted her chin. "That should be no problem whatsoever on my part." She raised her brows. "Now, if you'll excuse me, my public awaits."

He stepped to the side, allowing her to pass him. As she did, he leaned close and whispered, "Liar." He cleared his throat. "By the way, they expect you in a swimsuit."

Heat burning her cheeks, Angel marched to Lena's dresser where the actress kept a colorful array of new swimsuits. She grabbed a bright pink one and turned to face Duke, her eyebrows cocked. Then she stepped into the suit bottoms and dragged it up her legs rucking the skirt as she pulled it up over her thighs and buttocks.

Duke's face didn't change, but for the tick in his jaw and the slight narrowing of his eyes.

When she had the bottoms in place, she turned her back and pulled her dress over her head. Slipping her arms into the straps of the suit, she pressed the cups of the bra to her breasts and faced Duke. "Hook me."

Angel presented her back. Yes, she was playing with fire, but the man needed to suffer, too.

He grabbed the straps and hooked them, his knuckles grazing her skin, sending fire shooting through her veins. Her little ploy to make him hot and bothered had backfired.

Forcing a haughty look to her face, she marched out of the bedroom and down the sweeping staircase to the main level.

Angel couldn't get away from him fast enough. The arrogant, conceited man thought he could kiss her like that and remain unaffected. Well to hell with him. She'd show him it was no skin off her nose to ignore him and his ruggedly attractive body. Men! Who needed them?

If her knees were weak, it wasn't because of Duke. If her heart still pounded like a base drum on steroids, maybe she needed to see a doctor. If her core throbbed, aching for more than a single kiss, she'd just have to get out her sex toys and take care of her own needs. She'd be damned if she slept with Duke Morrison. He was strictly O. F. F. limits.

Angel stepped out onto the back patio where the group who'd come to interview Lena was patiently awaiting her reappearance.

She fielded a few pre-approved questions with the

canned answers she'd gone over with Phillip. When they'd finished the interview, Phillip handed her a martini, told her to tilt her head toward the sky as if she were enjoying her vacation and the fresh Montana air.

Ready for them to be done, she did what was asked and held the glass in her hand, a martini the last thing on earth she wanted.

As the camera crew filmed, she counted the seconds until she could kick them out and go back to relaxing like she'd been doing before Duke showed up and disturbed her like no other.

She suspected that even if he left the house, he wouldn't leave her mind or senses nearly as quickly.

"One more pose," Phillip said. "With the martini glass for the still shot for the Better Living magazine article."

With a sigh, Angel lifted the glass and pasted a smile on her lips.

The glass exploded in her hand, showering sticky mango martini all over her scantily-clad body.

CHAPTER 5

Duke flew through the air and landed on top of Lena, covering her body with his.

The camera crew scattered.

Phillip hit the deck and crawled beneath a lounger.

Duke wrapped his arms around Lena and rolled off the lounger onto the concrete, taking the brunt of the impact on his right shoulder.

"What are you doing?" Lena asked, writhing in his arms.

"Getting you out of the line of fire." She elbowed him in the gut, and he grunted. "Woman, stop struggling and let me get you out of range."

"Why didn't you just tell me to move? I'm perfectly capable of getting myself wherever it is I need to go."

"Are you getting this?" Phillip yelled to the cameraman.

"Yes, sir," the cameraman responded from behind a brick outdoor kitchen. He squatted down on his haunches, his camera trained on Lena.

"Really?" Duke glared at Phillip. "Miss Love could have been killed and you're still filming?"

"It's great promo," Phillip said. "And the public will love it. I can see the film offers rolling in already."

"Phillip, go to hell," Lena said, and low-crawled like a veteran soldier across the concrete to the door into the house.

Duke followed, using his body as a shield for hers in case the shooter decided to take another shot.

Once through the door, they weren't in the clear until they moved past the huge picture window into another room.

Finally, Lena rose to her feet, a frown denting her forehead, scrapes on her knees and elbows from her crawl across the stone and concrete. "How am I supposed to relax and vacation when some redneck stalker is taking potshots at me?"

Phillip crawled through the back door and stood as soon as he entered the huge living area.

The idiot probably didn't realize he was still silhouetted against the windows.

Duke wasn't going to tell him. As far as he was concerned, the publicist deserved a bullet to the head. The man was going to get Miss Love killed. "Tell your publicist to take his crew and go away."

"Phillip, take your crew and go back to the hotel." Lena wiped her hands together.

"Okay, okay. We'll leave for now. But we need to come back and get more footage of the outside of the house tomorrow."

"No." Duke shook his head. "You're done. Until we

find out who's leaving threatening messages and shooting at Miss Love, no one will be allowed on the estate who doesn't already belong here."

Phillip crossed his arms over his chest. "You can't tell me what to do."

Duke took a step toward the man.

The publicist's eyes widened, and he stepped backward. "Miss Love hired me. She's the only one who can tell me to leave or stay." He turned to Lena.

She narrowed her eyes and let the silence stretch between them. "I didn't agree to an interview in the first place. This was supposed to be a two-week vacation. I can't get any R&R with all of these people around." Then she jerked her thumb over her shoulder. "Go."

Phillip glared at Duke, and then shifted his anger to Lena. "You're only here because of me."

"And I'm only alive because of him." She tilted her head toward Duke. "I plan on staying alive, long after you vacate this house. The sooner you leave with your entourage, the better chance I have, and the better chance Mr. Morrison has of finding the person responsible for the attacks."

Phillip stalked toward her and paused when he came up alongside her. "We'll discuss this later."

"There's nothing to discuss. I'm only here for two weeks. I don't want this fanatic following her—me back to LA, do you?"

Phillip's lips pressed together, and his eyebrows descended. Finally, he responded, "No." He turned to Duke. "Do what you have to do to find out who's doing this."

Duke dipped his head briefly. "That's why I'm here."

The publicist marched through the house and out the front door, ducking low as he exited into the open.

Lena followed the man, closing the door behind him. Then she peeked through the window, without putting herself in view of anyone who could be targeting her.

Duke had to give her credit for staying out of the line of fire. She might be a diva, but she wasn't as stupid as he'd originally pegged her.

The parking area outside the house emptied of all of the vehicles, including the cameraman's van.

Duke walked up beside her. "You did the right thing."

"He only has the best interests of her—my career in mind."

"You won't have a career if you're dead."

She snorted. "Good point." She sighed and glanced around. "What am I supposed to do for the next two weeks if I can't go outside the house? That's not much of a vacation."

"I don't know. Have you tried reading a book?"

She looked around. "I suppose I could."

"Do you happen to know where the security system hub is located? Do you store the recordings?"

She shrugged. "I have no idea. You could ask the foreman. He might know."

"Brandt Lucas?" Duke snorted.

"Oh, right." Her cheeks flushed a soft pink, making her more adorable and vulnerable than the usual spoiled movie star. "How about the assistant foreman?"

Duke nodded. "I'll check with him. For now, I need you to come with me as I search the entire house for any intruders." He pulled his handgun from his side cargo pocket and checked the safety.

Lena frowned. "You think he might be inside?"

"If there is more than one person involved, one could be inside while the other is set up as a sniper."

"And I need to go with you on this tour because...?"

"I can't keep an eye on you and protect you if you're not with me at all times." He captured her gaze. "Are you going to argue with me every step of the way?"

She smiled. "I might. What would be the fun of having a bodyguard if I can't argue with him?"

"As long as you follow my instructions implicitly when the shit hits the fan."

She nodded. "You've got it." Lena waved her hand. "Lead the way."

"You know, you're not half bad when you're not drinking."

She rolled her eyes. "Then I'm not doing my job as a diva. I'll be sure to ratchet up the bitch. Now, shut up and search."

"And she's back." Despite himself, he chuckled at her return to the Lena he expected. Somehow, he couldn't find it in his heart to completely dislike her. Not when he knew how good of a kisser she was, and how sweet her body felt against his. Hell, his lips still tingled from their encounter in the bathroom.

He'd held women to his mother's high standard for a very long time, thus the reason he hadn't married or landed in a permanent relationship. And Lena was not the kind of woman he'd write home about.

But she had a body that didn't quit. If she wasn't his

client, he might consider sleeping with her. He could imagine she would be wild in bed.

His groin tightened at the mental image of her naked in his bed, calling out his name as he thrust deep inside her.

Duke gave himself a firm mental shake. He really had to pull himself together, or he'd end up another notch on Lena Love's bedpost.

Angel followed Duke through the house, getting to know it a little better and getting to know it from the perspective of having to defend herself within its confines.

Someone had entered, trashed the mirror and left without being seen. How could that happen?

Now she followed her bodyguard around, knowing the more she was around him, the more her body responded to his. Sheesh. It wasn't as if she'd gone a long time without sex or anything.

She paused and thought about it. How long had it been? One month, two? She thought back to her last date and bit down hard on her lip. That poor excuse for a date had been over a year ago. She'd been so busy on movie sets and working directly for Lena that she hadn't bothered to have a life of her own. No wonder she was so hot for the bodyguard. She was suffering sexual withdrawals of the worst kind. Trying to think of anything but how she wanted to run her fingers across his bare chest and down the highly defined six pack he carried on his abs, she blurted out, "So, what's your story?"

"What story?" he asked, raising an eyebrow.

"Huh. You're going to play it that way? I'm going to have to pull it out of you?" She nodded. "Fine. Start with how long have you been a bodyguard?"

"Counting today?" he said, tipped his head to the side and squinted into the distance before answering. "Half a day."

"What?" She stepped back. "You aren't even a bodyguard? What's this dude, Hank Patterson, sending out?"

"He hires former military to man his security business."

"So you're former military?" She smirked. Yeah, she'd known it. He had the bearing and the discipline. "What branch?"

"Army."

"MOS?"

He stopped in the middle of the study, and turned toward her. "What do you know about military occupational specialty codes?"

She shrugged and glanced away, her cheeks turning red. "I read." She really had to remember who she was supposed to be. Lena Love wouldn't have a clue what an MOS was. She would barely know there was a difference between the Army, Air Force, Navy and Marines.

"My MOS in the army was 11B, Infantry."

Throwing on her Lena act, she wrinkled her brow and slid her gaze over his muscular form. "Really? I would have thought you were a SEAL or Delta Force like in the movies." She touched his arm.

"SEALs are Navy. Delta Force is the Army's Special Operations Detachment–Delta. Their primary mission is counter-terrorism."

Angel digested his words, a thrill of excitement rippling across her skin. "You say that like you know first-hand."

He nodded. "Maybe I do." He moved through the study, checking beneath the desk, behind curtains and in the small closet. "Right now, we have the mission of searching this house. I take my work seriously."

"You were Delta Force." Angel stared at him with new respect. "Only the best of the best from green beret and rangers are invited to become part of the D-Force team."

He tested the knobs on the French doors before turning to face her. "Yes. I was Delta Force."

"What happened? Why are you working as a bodyguard when you should be countering terrorism?"

He shrugged. "Took one too many hits from IEDs. The Medical Review Board retired me as of a week ago." Duke's jaw was tight, his lips pressed into a thin line. He hadn't wanted to leave the military. Angel could see it in every groove etched into his face.

She touched his arm. "I'm sorry."

"For what? I got to come home for the first time in years. Some guys aren't that lucky. Some don't come home until they're brought home in a body bag."

Angel could tell leaving the military had been hard for him. She understood. After she'd been injured in a firefight, she too had been processed out, leaving her unit, her brothers and sisters in arms, behind.

To combat her loneliness, she'd returned to her home state of California and had been discovered working at an auto repair shop by a talent agent who'd recognized the startling resemblance she had to the mega-star Lena Love. When he'd discovered she rode a motorcycle and wasn't afraid of fire, taking a punch, or falling through windows, he'd gotten her the gig of playing Lena's stunt woman for the action adventure movies she was known for.

"How does it feel to be back in Montana?" she asked.

He shrugged. "I've barely been outside much to tell. I got in late last night and came straight here after meeting my boss."

Her heart squeezed in her chest. He had to be missing his team. Being an alpha man, he wouldn't let on. Hell, she hadn't, but anyone with eyes would have known her hell-for-leather death-wish wasn't normal for her.

Another thirty minutes searching the premises brought Angel and Duke to the conclusion only the maid, the chef, Angel and Duke were inside the house. Lyle Sorenson, the assistant foreman let them know the security footage was stored on the provider's server, and unless someone had the password to log on, they weren't getting in until the following day during office hours.

The scents of food cooking in the kitchen made Angel's belly rumble. "Supper will be served shortly and Le—I like to dress for dinner." She studied him with a critical eye. "I don't suppose you have anything but jeans with you?"

"I have a pair of trousers and a button-up shirt." His eyes narrowed. "Why?"

"You'll have dinner with me." She lifted her chin, daring him to argue.

Duke shook his head. "That's not necessary. I can wait outside the dining room while you eat."

"You said it yourself. The only way you can protect me is to be with me at all times." She tipped her chin higher and stared down her nose, putting on her full-Lena affect. "I insist." There were advantages to being a pushy, rich bitch. She got her way.

She also presented a target for unwanted attention for the paparazzi and fanatical stalkers. Angel only had to deal with the hassle for two weeks. Lena dealt with it on a daily basis. Yes, she was a pain in the ass, but she never got a minute to herself. That would make Angel nuts, too.

Angel climbed the stairs ahead of Duke and left him at his room to change for dinner. She jumped into the shower, rinsed off the sticky martini and washed her hair.

Quickly blowing it dry, she went to Lena's closet and picked through the dresses, bypassing the leopard prints, loud colors and sheer fabrics, and opting for a simple, floor-length gown of a butter-soft material Angel couldn't name, having never owned anything nearly as nice. The French vanilla, crème-colored dress dropped down over her body like a sensual caress, firing up her blood and making her want to walk back to Duke's room and have him run his hand over the incredible fabric and, of course, every part of her body.

Shaking herself out of the thought, she looked through the jewelry in the built-in drawers of the walk-in closet and selected a pearl necklace and matching earrings.

With her hair down around her shoulders, she glanced at her reflection and gasped. The image wasn't the Angel Carson she knew. What people said about clothes "making the man" was true. She felt like a completely different person. She slipped on a pair of strappy sandals and hurried down the stairs, following the aromas coming from the kitchen.

Duke stood at the bottom of the staircase, dressed in tailored black trousers, a crisp white shirt and black cowboy boots. He'd slicked back his damp dark hair from his forehead and looked like he could model as the Marlboro man. Still rugged and handsome, even in semi-formal attire.

His smoldering gaze swept her length. "Beautiful," he said in that deep tone that made butterflies flutter in her belly. He offered her his arm and led her into the dining room.

Heat rushed up into her cheeks over the compliment. Yeah, he was the bodyguard and he was paid to keep Lena happy, but it still felt good to be noticed and appreciated.

The table had been set for two people, with a candle arrangement providing intimate lighting. Obviously, the chef had assumed Miss Love was entertaining a male guest and probably had plans to seduce the poor schmuck.

Empty wine glasses were set in front of the plates along with napkins and flatware.

Duke pulled out her chair. "Shall we take our seats?"

Angel slipped onto the chair. "What I've had of the chef's meals have been beyond exquisite."

"I'm sure you insist on the best," he said.

Having seen Lena rip a cook a new one for serving a less than stellar hamburger of all things, Angel knew the truth of Duke's statement. "I work hard and make a lot of money. I deserved to spend it the way I like."

"Yes, you do." Duke agreed, taking the seat across from hers.

The maid served the meal one course after another, and was there to collect their empty plates and replace them with the next set without missing a beat.

The meal was a delicious perk of playing Lena Love. The woman really did demand the best from her staff, and they delivered.

Angel ate every last morsel, including the dessert of tiramisu.

Duke shook his head. "How do you stay so thin if you eat that much?" He held up his hands. "Not that I'm judging. It's just that most women eat like birds to keep from gaining so much as an ounce."

"I work it off," Angel said. Granted Lena did pick at her food, but she also worked to keep her body beautiful when she wasn't sucking down the alcohol and drugs.

Duke sat back, holding his cup of coffee in his hand. "You know my background. What about you? Did you always know you wanted to be an actress?"

Angel nodded. She knew Lena's story, having studied her autobiography to know more about the woman she worked for. "I started out in commercials until my agent set me up for an audition for a movie. Sh—I was eight years old." She shrugged. "The movie hit big and launched my career. I never looked back."

That was about all she knew about Lena's life, other than what she'd witnessed and what the tabloids reported. After a long day of pretending to be the actress, Angel wanted nothing more than to go to Lena's bedroom and be herself behind closed doors.

"I'm tired," Angel said. "It's been a long day. What do you say we call it a night?"

Duke nodded. "I have to admit, I'm pretty tired myself. After driving for the past two days, I could use some real sleep." He rose and held her chair, while she stood and moved away from the table.

Again, he offered his arm.

She took it, knowing that being so close to him was not conducive to sleep. The electric stimulus made her want to strip the clothes off his body and hers and have wild monkey sex in the middle of the living room.

Her best course of action would be to get to her room as soon as possible, and take another shower. Cold. And go straight to bed.

With a plan in mind, she climbed the stairs and hurried forward, ready to leave Duke behind.

Only he didn't go to his room as she'd expected. "I need to check your room once more before we call it a night."

"Is that necessary?" she asked. "You checked the door

and window locks in every room of the house not long ago. Do you think someone could slip in that easily?"

"Locks can be picked," he said.

She rolled her eyes. "Okay. Do your thing. The sooner you're done, the sooner I'll get to sleep."

He made a quick pass through the master suite, checking beneath the bed, the closet and the bathroom where the mirror had been scrubbed clean. "All clear," he reported.

When Duke finally left the room, Angel let out an exasperated sigh and stripped out of the dress. Standing in nothing but a pair of lace panties, she didn't want to get dressed for bed after all. Being near the big D-Force man, she'd learned she was not unaffected by him.

With the man in her thoughts out of the room, the walls seemed farther apart, the cavernous room bigger than her entire first apartment.

Her pulse still hammered against her veins, and she couldn't stay still for long. She needed to get out and run for a couple miles to burn off the calories. Unfortunately, that wouldn't be an option.

Angel paced the length of the room and back several times. Nothing seemed to calm her nerves. A glance at the clock indicated it was getting late. What she really wanted to do was go for a swim.

Surely the shooter wouldn't be out this late at night looking for another opportunity to ruin her day.

She replaced her gorgeous dress with a blue and white LA Dodgers jersey, and then waited another fifteen minutes. The house was quiet, and she didn't hear any movement from the room down the hallway.

Angel eased open the door and peered out into the hallway.

A wash of relief warred with disappointment. Duke wasn't in the hallway or on the stairs as she descended to the bottom floor. Knowing she was taking a huge risk, Angel couldn't resist. She needed some space and fresh air to clear her head. Careful not to make a noise, she pushed open the French doors leading out to the pool deck. The lights had been turned off and nothing but the moon lit her way to the water's edge.

Angel stood in the shadows beneath the awning and scanned the vicinity for movement.

Satisfied she was alone, she stripped out of the jersey and walked into the pool in nothing but her panties. Soon she was cleaving through the water, from one end of the pool to the other. The more she pushed herself, the better she felt. By the time she slowed to tread water in the deep end, she was truly tired and ready to go to sleep.

A splash startled her and made her lose her rhythm. She sank beneath the surface and came up spluttering. "What the hell, Duke?" She turned toward the intruder as he surfaced. "Brandt?"

He swam toward her, a smile stretching across his face. "I waited for a long time, but you never sent for me, so I decided to come looking for you."

Angel tried to cover her naked breasts and tread water at the same time, failing miserably with both. "Uh. Brandt, I didn't send for you for a reason. I don't need your services, or whatever you call it."

His brows furrowed, but he didn't slow his advance

on her person, moving through the water in an easy breaststroke, his lips curving into a sexy grin. "Playing hard to get? You know that turns me on."

"Seriously, Brandt," she said in her sternest voice. "I'm not in the mood. Don't come any closer.

His grin broadened. "Your mouth is saying no, but your eyes and your body are saying yes."

"Dude, you need an interpreter. My eyes and body are most certainly not saying yes." She gave up covering her breasts and used both arms to swim backward, away from the advancing foreman.

"We usually make love the first night you're back. When you didn't call for me, I thought it was because you were too tired from your trip." He kicked his feet, following her to the deep end. "Why else would you be out here swimming in the nude, if you didn't want to get it on?" He captured her in his arms.

Angel reacted by bringing her knee up sharply, hitting him in the groin.

Brandt swore and curled his body into a ball, but he didn't let go of Angel's arm. "Why'd you go and do that?"

"I told you not to come closer. Now, let go of my arm before I hit you again."

"I don't understand."

Another splash made them both turn toward the latest occupant to the pool.

A dark form shot beneath the surface like a missile from a submarine, a blur of motion, headed straight for Angel and Brandt.

Brandt jerked downward, his head disappearing into

the water. With his hand still on Angel's arm, he pulled her under with him.

Angel pried at his fingers, but he managed to get his other hand on her arm and clung to her, in effect, pushing her deeper into the pool.

Her lungs burning, Angel fought, kicked and slammed her hands on his grip, praying he would let go soon, or she'd drown.

CHAPTER 6

Duke had been in the shower when Lena sneaked out of her room. If he hadn't performed one last check before calling it a night, he wouldn't have known until too late. He'd gone into her room with the intention of securing any unlatched windows and asking if she needed anything. When he'd found the bed empty and her missing, his pulse had quickened, and he'd run from the room.

Damn, the woman didn't know what was good for her. She couldn't just go traipsing around her huge house in the middle of the night. Whoever had left the message on her mirror had managed to get inside her security system. If he'd done it once, he could do it again.

Duke had been halfway down the stairs when he'd spotted her through the huge picture windows, swimming laps in the pool. As she'd turned to backstroke in the opposite direction, the moonlight had glinted off her naked breasts.

Duke had been captivated by the perfection of her body, the slim, sleek lines and tight muscles of her arms and legs cleaving through the water. He'd stood transfixed longer than he should have.

Then another figure had dived into the pool and swam toward Lena.

Duke had flown down the steps and across the living area to the back door.

The man had made it across the pool before Duke reached the edge.

And, sweet Jesus, Lena was struggling.

A red flush of rage washed over Duke as he launched himself into the water. Within seconds, he had the perpetrator by the ankle, pulling him under.

Unfortunately, he still had his hands on Lena, dragging her down with him.

Duke climbed up the man's body and hooked his arm around the guy's neck, squeezing hard enough to choke him.

Eventually, the perpetrator released his hold on Lena. She pushed off the bottom and shot to the surface.

Duke swam backward, toward the shallow end where he set the attacker on his own feet and shoved him toward the side. "Get out. And get the hell off the property."

The man who turned to face him was Brandt Lucas.

"Are you insane? You nearly killed me." Brandt coughed, slogging his way through the shallow end to the steps leading out. "I wasn't attacking her. I was trying to make love to her."

Duke shot a glance toward Lena where she clung to the side of the pool, breathing hard. "Is that true?"

"Oh, he was trying," she said, "but I wasn't buying."

When Brandt stood on the deck, he pushed the wet hair off his forehead and sneered at Lena. "You are one crazy bitch. You promised me you'd get me into the movies. I've wasted my time working as your foreman when I could have been working in LA as a model."

Lena shrugged. "Guess you'll have to jumpstart your own career instead of flying on my coattails. Don't let the gate hit you in the backside as you leave."

Brandt grabbed his jeans, jammed his legs into them and dragged them up over his hips. "Should have listened to my agent," he muttered. "Nothing to do out here but listen to the cows bellowing." Finally, he left the poolside, heading toward the barn and the bunkhouse.

Duke raked a hand through his damp hair. "Need a hand getting out of the water?"

She shook her head. "No. No thank you." She had one arm covering her breasts, the other holding onto the side of the pool. "You can go back to bed. I was just finishing up. I'll head inside in just a minute."

His lips quirked. He knew she was naked, and after she'd nearly been mauled by her former foreman, he wasn't letting her off easy. She'd been careless. "I'll wait to make sure you get back to your room safely."

"No need. I can get there on my own."

"Miss Love, you know I can't leave you out here alone," he said, deepening his tone. "Whenever you want to take a swim, you need to let me know. I'll come with you."

"I didn't want to make a big deal of it. I was careful and looked for anyone lurking around, before I got into the water."

Duke's jaw tightened. "But you need someone to watch your back when you can't possibly pay attention. You put yourself at risk." He held out his hand. "Come on inside. You shouldn't be out in the open anyway. The shooter might be watching as we speak."

"I'll take my chances."

Duke walked toward her, the water getting deeper around him. When he couldn't touch the bottom anymore, he swam, moving slowly, giving her the option to get out on her own, or deal with him.

"Don't come any closer," she said.

"I'm getting you out of the water."

"Damn it, Duke! I'm naked. I'm not getting out until you get out first and turn your back."

He chuckled. "I know you're naked. I was watching you from inside the house." He stopped in front of her and he held out his hand. "I won't do anything you don't want me to do. Just come inside where you don't present a target to your stalker." He didn't look down at her breasts, though it took all of his control to resist. Instead, he captured her gaze with his and waited.

She sucked her bottom lip between her teeth, meeting his glance unwaveringly. A moment or two passed. Then she placed her hand in his.

He drew her against his body, treading water with one arm.

Her breasts pressed against his bare chest.

Duke swallowed hard on the groan rising up his throat and said, "Ready?"

"Yes," she said, her voice a breathy whisper. Her thighs bumped into his beneath the water, sending heat blasting through his system straight to his groin.

He swam with her to the shallower water until he could put his feet on the bottom. For some reason, he couldn't force himself to move further.

The moon cast a pale blue glow over her head and shoulders. With her hair lying flat against her scalp, every feature on her face was exposed, from the high cheekbones, to her full, luscious lips.

Perhaps it was the magic of the moonlight that made him bend to touch his mouth to hers. He had to do it, just like he had to breathe.

She met his lips with a soft sigh, leaned into him and wrapped her arms around his neck, her mouth opening to him.

He plunged in, his tongue sliding along hers in an intimate caress. She tasted of tiramisu and coffee. Two of his favorite flavors.

When he had to come up for air, he pressed his temple to hers. "Come on, we need to get inside."

Before she could protest, he swept her naked body into his arms and carried her up the steps, trailing water across the concrete and tile decking.

She reached for the door handle, turned it and let them in the back door.

Duke kicked it shut behind them and let her twist the deadbolt to lock the door.

"You can put me down now."

He shook his head. "Not until I know you're in your room for the night."

She raised her brows. "Have it your way. I'm not that light, and you have a damaged leg. Good luck getting up those stairs."

"No offense, Miss Love, but shut up." He crossed the smooth, custom oak floors and mounted the stairs, carrying her all the way. He started out fast, but by the time they reached the top of the staircase, Duke was breathing hard, and his leg ached like a motherfucker.

With her arms crossed over her chest and an expression that said, *I told you so,* Lena stared at him. "Uncle?"

He gritted his teeth, dragged in a deep breath and then strode down the hall. At her bedroom, he kicked open the door, entered the huge room and dumped her ass on the king-sized bed.

"Hey! That wasn't very nice." She righted herself and pulled the comforter over her nakedness. "You, Mr. Morrison, are no gentleman."

"And you, Miss Love, are no lady. Didn't your mother teach you to wear a swimsuit when you go swimming out in the open?"

"It's my place. I can walk around stark naked wherever the hell I please." She tilted back her head and stared down her nose at him. "Besides, a polite gentleman would have looked away."

"Since we've already established that I'm no gentleman, it's a moot point." He strode to the windows, checked the locks, double-checked the bathroom and ducked to glance under her bed.

A slim, bare foot shot out hitting him in the shoulder, knocking him backward.

He grabbed the ankle attached to the foot as he went down, dragging her off the bed. They landed in a tangled heap on the sheepskin rug.

Lena tried to scramble out of reach.

Duke wasn't having any of it. "Prepare to reap what you sew." He flipped her onto her back on the rug, straddled her hips and pinned her wrists high above her head. Then he stared down at her flushed face.

"I don't think pinning your client to the floor is in your job description." She wiggled beneath him, igniting his desire for this mess of a woman.

"I'm guarding your body." His gaze slipped lower. "And since you seem to enjoy strutting around in your birthday suit, I assume you have no problem with your bodyguard seeing you nude." His glance slipped to the breasts he'd seen last night, flashed fully in his face. Only this time, there was something different. On her left breast, just below the nipple was a tattoo of a heart surrounded by two doves in flight.

He froze, studying the tattoo.

"Hey, you can quit staring now," she said, her cheeks turning redder by the minute. She arched her back in an attempt to dislodge him.

Still holding her wrists with one of his hands, he pointed at the mark. "This tattoo, when did you get it?"

She stopped struggling. "When I was eighteen. The year my parents died."

For a moment, her words hung in the air, as if they

didn't quite belong anywhere. Then it all came crashing down around Duke.

He glared down at her. "Who the hell are you?"

Her eyes widened as she stared up at him. "Wh-what do you mean? I'm Lena Love. Who else would I be?" Her gaze slipped to the corner of the room.

"The woman in the bar who flashed me last night was Lena Love. She didn't have a tattoo on her breasts. You, however, do."

She set her jaw in a tight line. "Get off of me."

Duke shook his head. "Not until you tell me what the hell is going on."

Angel could tell by the dark look in Duke's eyes he wasn't going to buy any more of her bullshit.

"I'm Lena Love, and I'm ordering you to let go of me."

He shook his head. "Nope. Try again."

She fought to free her wrists, finally giving up. "Fine. Let me up, and I'll tell you what you want to know."

For a long moment, he continued to hold her wrists above her head. Then he abruptly released them and rose to his feet.

Angel covered her breasts with her hands, glad she at least still wore panties. Though, even with everything covered, she felt completely exposed to his all-seeing gaze.

He reached a hand down to her.

She ignored it, rolled to her side and pushed to a standing position. With her back to him, she crossed to a dresser, pulled out a leopard print nightgown, threw it down in disgust and found a plain gray T-shirt. Pulling it over her head, she turned to confront her bodyguard.

"Come with me." She led the way into the bathroom with its bright white walls, brushed chrome fixtures and muted lighting

Once she closed the door behind him, she turned on the water in the shower. "Just in case anyone is listening in or recording our conversation," she explained, even though he hadn't asked. Nervous now, she tugged at the hem of the T-shirt, noticing too late that her nipples poked into the fabric making little tents.

"Start talking," Duke ordered.

"I will. I will. Keep your britches on." She turned away and pushed her wet hair out of her face. "Last night when Lena was at the bar, she consumed too much alcohol and did things she would never do sober." At least Angel hoped she wouldn't flash someone when she wasn't high or drunk. The truth was that Lena was a loose cannon, on a one-way trip to cratering her career if she didn't get sober. "We found her in the ladies' room passed out on the floor. Someone had written a message on her face in indelible ink."

"What was the message?"

"Bitch. I'm going to make you pay."

Duke shook his head. "Did you ever consider that information might be important to a bodyguard?"

"I suppose it would have been nice to know."

"So, who are you?"

"I'm Lena's stunt woman and body double."

Duke snapped his fingers impatiently. "Do you have your own name?"

"Angel Carson."

"Background."

"Prior military, currently a stunt woman."

"Branch and specialty?"

"Army Ranger."

"Seriously?" He stared at her, as if seeing her for the first time. "Not many women have made it through Ranger training."

"I know. I was in the second class that allowed female trainees."

"Why did you get out of the Army?"

"Not because I wanted to." She glanced away. "TBI – Traumatic Brain Injury." She touched a finger to her head. "My team got caught in an explosion. I survived, but the impact scrambled my brain enough the Medical Review Board processed me out."

"And you thought being a stunt woman would improve your brain injury?"

Angel shrugged. "What else was I fit for? I trained to go into dangerous situations, to shoot and be shot at."

"How did they know you had a TBI?"

She snorted. "I was in a coma for a week. When I came to, I had temporary amnesia and situational amnesia of the attack."

"That's normal. The brain protects you from reliving the trauma."

"Not completely. I had terrible nightmares, but couldn't remember them when I woke. At first my sense of taste and smell were off. I had dizzy spells and really bad headaches. Those symptoms faded as time passed."

"I'm sorry you had to go through all of that."

"I was sorry I lost my team, my career and everything I knew." She shrugged. Three years had passed since then.

"How did you land a job as a stunt woman?"

She gave a short smile. "It's one of those Hollywood stories you always hear about. A scout spotted me at an oil change place. The rest, you could say, is history."

"Where is the real Lena Love?"

"Phillip was supposed to get her checked into a rehab facility to dry her out and clean up her face. Meanwhile, I'm the bait for her attacker." She drew in a deep breath, glad to get all of that off her chest. "I never was a good liar. I'm glad you know. But you can't tell anyone. In order for Lena to get the privacy she needs, I have to put on a convincing act as the real Hollywood diva." She gave him a crooked smile. "So, was I convincing?"

Duke chuckled. "At first, yes. But I think I knew deep down, you weren't the same woman from last night. For one, Lena Love would never have pulled me out of the pool. She probably would have let me drown before she called for help."

Angel nodded, her lips twisting into a wry grin. "You're probably right."

"The question is, where do we go from here?"

"Nowhere," Angel said. "I'm here for the remainder of the two weeks, making the staff nuts and being a pain in the ass to anyone and everyone with whom I come in contact."

"I don't like that you're putting yourself up as the target. The bullet that hit your martini glass this evening could easily have hit you instead."

She nodded. The thought had occurred to her, and she hadn't been all that happy about it.

"Who has Lena pissed off enough to want to cause her a whole lot of grief and possibly even kill her?"

"Hell, who hasn't she pissed off?" Angel sighed. "The possibilities could be too many to calculate."

"Any rivals vying for the same parts?"

"She is up for a really big part in a movie. Phillip has been waiting on pins and needles for the call."

"Who else is being considered for that part?"

"You'll have to ask Phillip. He knows all of the ins and outs, and the actresses and actors who are anybody in Hollywood." Angel sighed. "I'm just the stunt woman. Nobody of consequence in the grand scheme of the big studios."

"Except you look like Lena Love, which has put you in the unlucky position of being the decoy to draw out a potential killer." Duke frowned. "We have to find this person before he makes good on thinning the talent pool."

"We don't know he's out to kill Lena." Angel perched on the edge of the bed and tugged at the T-shirt's hem.

"No, but that bullet today made it an entirely different game. One we want to win. If we're serious about luring him out into the open, we need to take the game to a new level."

Angel frowned. "And how do we do that?"

"Ever been camping in Montana?"

Her frown deepened. "No. Sounds cold and uncomfortable."

"If we stay here at the house, you're nothing but a sitting duck. If we lead him up into the hills, we can switch the hunted to the hunters."

A slow grin spread across Angel's face. "I like the way you think."

"Yeah?" He chucked a finger beneath her chin. "I like the way your nipples poke at your T-shirt. I suggest you go to bed and get some sleep. Tomorrow we head into the mountains."

She frowned. "Hey, you're not supposed to be so obvious about your lascivious observations."

He gave her a lopsided grin. "Yeah, well we've already established I'm no gentleman."

Angel's lips twisted. "Your mother would be so proud."

"Leave my mother out of this."

She rose from the bed and poked a finger into his chest. "Leave my nipples out of this." Angel jutted out her chest, parading her pointy breasts as she headed for the door. When she reached it, she flung it open and tipped her head. "Goodnight, bodyguard."

"Goodnight...Lena." As he passed her, he leaned close, captured her head in the palm of his hand and whispered, "Angel fits you so much better."

Her body quivered. "Just so you know, my teammates called me the Angel of Death." She shot him a challenging glance.

"I can see it. You wouldn't be where you are today, if you were any other way."

Angel frowned.

Duke shook his head. "I meant that in the best, strongest way." With his hand still cupping her head, he bent and captured her lips with his. When he raised his head again, he smiled that sexy smile that turned her knees to melted butter. "Oh," he said, his voice deep and husky. "I'm sleeping in your room, tonight."

She had been leaning toward him, her entire body drawn to him like a moth to a flame, when his words sank in. She jerked back. "Like hell you are."

He patted her cheek like a parent pats a child's. "Get used to it. We're going to be spending a lot of time together over the next couple of days. Or however long it takes to flush out your stalker."

Her pulse thundered through her veins, and her palms grew moist, along with another place farther south. How was she going to resist this man if he insisted on being right beside her? Day and night? A normal, sexually deprived woman could only take so much before she conceded defeat and begged to join the other side.

CHAPTER 7

Duke lay on the chaise lounge in Lena Love's bedroom, trying not to think about the tattoo on Angel's breast and the fact that, since she was a decoy for Lena, she really wasn't his client. Lena was.

Which meant the separation between client and bodyguard didn't apply to him and Angel. Why that gave him a sense of joy, he didn't know.

He really should consider Angel off limits as well. She wasn't his type. Nothing about her was like his age-old image of the perfect woman. She was as different from his mother as night was from day.

His mother had stayed home and raised her sons, helped with homework, sewed, cooked cleaned and made their lives better with her loving, nurturing nature.

Despite her name, Angel didn't strike Duke as the kind of woman who could sew curtains to frame a window, or sauté onions and make a roast that would melt in his mouth. She had a smart mouth and a hard knee that hit with a wicked determination to end an attack before it got ugly. She had proven herself in her training as an elite Army Ranger and then she'd faced combat head-on. He'd never met a woman who'd willingly walked into a war-torn area, knowing she could get killed or maimed, and still function without launching herself into a fit of hysterics.

The woman probably didn't know a saucepan from a skillet. Cook a roast? Probably not.

But he had the feeling if he handed her a rifle, she'd know how to disassemble and assemble it in under a minute. And he'd bet his favorite nine-millimeter pistol she was an expert marksman. The Army Rangers only graduated the best of the best. They didn't cut the women any slack to fill a quota. If anything, they had to work harder than the men to prove themselves.

"Are you asleep," her voice said in the dark.

"No," he answered.

"I've laid on that lounge. It's not very comfortable."

"No. It's not." He rolled onto his back and nearly fell off the narrow chaise that was barely big enough to hold him.

A long pause stretched between them.

"It's ridiculous for you to sleep there when this bed is sufficiently large enough for two people. We would never touch each other."

That's where she might be wrong. If Duke slept in that bed with her, he wouldn't have the ability to resist touching her. "I'll sleep here."

Silence stretched between them.

"Seriously, you should take the other side of this bed.

I'll feel bad if you don't get any rest when we're about to go days without sleep."

"I'm not likely to get any sleep if you keep talking," he said into the darkness.

She snorted. "See if I try to be nice again."

"I know it's a stretch."

"Damn right it is."

"Geez woman, if I move to the bed, I can't guarantee I won't touch you." There, if she didn't already know he was attracted to her in a big way, she did now.

"I said we wouldn't *have* to touch." Her little pause lengthened. "Unless we wanted to," she said, her voice fading into the shadows.

"Don't ask, unless you really mean it. Once I've tasted the honey, I won't be able leave the hive."

Angel burst out laughing. "You didn't just liken my lady parts to a beehive, did you?"

A smile played at Duke's lips. "I did." He pushed to his feet and crossed the room to where she lay in Lena's big bed, covered in that damned cotton-candy-pink comforter.

Still chuckling, she shook her head. "I'm sorry, but that's about the most unromantic thing a man has ever said to me."

He tipped his head to the side. "Scoot."

She moved over to make it easy for him to slide onto the mattress.

"How's this." He lay on his side and leaned up on one elbow. "Your lips are as soft as my dog's belly."

"Not even close," she said, staring up at him in the little bit of moonlight streaming through the window.

"No?" He pushed a strand of her hair back behind her ear. "I really loved my dog."

"You're going to have to do better if you want to stay with me tonight."

"Mmm, I know just what to say."

She shook her head. "I'm almost afraid to ask, but here goes. What would you say?"

"I knew there was something different about you this morning. In many ways, you look very much like Lena, but you're not like her at all. I couldn't put my finger on it until just now. Where Lena is all about Lena, you care about others." He tapped her chest. "You have a heart. Otherwise, you wouldn't have saved me from drowning and you wouldn't have agreed to be the bait to draw out her stalker."

"What else have I got to do in my life?" she asked, her voice not much more than a whisper. "I'm not married. I don't have kids. I don't even have an impressive career."

"You have all of your life to live the way you want. And you deserve to make it happy."

"Life's not the same when you have no one to share it." She touched her fingers to his bare chest.

"You need to stop living Lena's life and make one of your own."

"Now, that's pretty romantic," she said, cupping his cheek. She leaned close and pressed her lips to one of his little, hard brown nipples. "I think you might have potential."

"For what?"

"Well, not as a gentleman, but then I never stated a

preference for gentlemen. I kind of like my men to be a little more rugged."

"I can be rugged," he leaned over her and nibbled on her earlobe, nipping just a little harder to make his point.

"Ow." She raised her hand to her ear and laughed. "But gentle when he needs to be."

He slipped his hand along her arm and down to her waist, stopping to balance on her hip. "How am I doing?"

"I don't know. There appears to be too much getting in the way of this lesson in what this lady wants and what you have to offer."

"Like?"

She slid her hand into the waistband of his boxer shorts and snapped the elastic. "Getting the idea, cowboy?"

"I think so. I might be a grunt, but I can be taught." He slipped her T-shirt over her head and tossed it to the floor.

She helped shove his boxers down over his hips and thighs, her fingers trailing across his skin, making him crazy with need. This slow, steady, getting-to-know-you dance they had started couldn't get moving fast enough. He longed to take her, to slide into her warm, slick wetness. But first, he wanted her to reach the level of insanity she was inspiring in him.

He slid a finger along the smooth line of her jaw and down the long, slender column of her neck. Moving lower, he skimmed the rounded swell of her breasts, stopping to tweak the nipple and circle the tattoo. "What does the tattoo stand for?"

"The kind of love that brings two people together for the rest of their lives. The kind of love my parents have for each other."

"That's beautiful." He kissed the bead of her nipple, and then flicked it with the tip of his tongue. "Like you."

"Wow," she said, her words catching on her indrawn breath. "Now, you're getting the idea."

"I told you, I can be taught. But it's easy when the recipient inspires me." He circled her nipple several times before sucking it into his mouth and pulling hard.

He was quickly falling into her, without a care as to how to disengage and walk away when the two weeks were up, or the stalker was found and carted off to jail.

Duke had no intention of leaving Montana any time soon. Living in LA was not even a consideration. But then, he and Angel had only just met. They'd known each other for such a short amount of time. Dreaming of a future with her would be insane.

Then why was he thinking about how many more times he'd like to make love to this woman? That implied a future that couldn't be.

Angel closed her eyes, pretending she and Duke weren't in Lena Love's bed but on some tropical island in the middle of the ocean, away from everything that could get in the way of this moment. She ran her hand across his rock-hard shoulder and down over his chest. "What about you?"

He brushed the tip of her nose with his lips and then took her mouth in a long, soul-tugging kiss that left her breathing hard and wanting so much more.

"What about me?" he asked, his fingers feathering over her hip and sliding down to the tuft of hair over her sex.

"What made—" her words caught in her lungs as he parted her folds and flicked the nubbin between, "—you want to be Delta-Force." There, she'd gotten it out, now she could draw in another breath.

He flicked her again, and her insides tensed, squeezing her lungs, her core, her senses. She couldn't think past what he was doing to her down there.

"I love my country. I like being all I can be, and Delta Force was that."

"Were you processed out for medical reasons, too?" He hit the right spot, and she gasped. "There. Oh, sweet Jesus. There!" She arched her back off the bed.

Duke's hand followed, cupping her sex until she settled, and then he resumed teasing that bundle of nerves to a fever of excitement.

"Yes. Medically retired," he answered.

"Leg?" She managed to push the word from her lungs as another wave of sensations rocked her. Angel drew her knees up and let them fall to the side.

"Leg."

"Does it keep you from…" God, he flicked her there again. She was so close to a full-on orgasm she couldn't finish her sentence. Hell, she couldn't remember what she had been saying.

"Keep me from making love to you?" He chuckled. "Oh, hell no."

"Good. Because I want you."

"Then show me how much." He parted her legs and lay down between them, skimming a trail of kisses and nips down her abdomen to the place that was already so sensitized she was almost afraid she'd come apart into a million pieces if he touched her there with his tongue.

And then he did.

Angel rocketed to the heavens, her body exploding with sensations, until she couldn't remember what was earth and what was sky. She rode the wave through to the very end, her hips pumping, her hands buried in his hair, fingers flexing into his scalp.

When she came back to the earth long enough to breathe, she tugged on a handful of his hair. "Now. Inside me. Hurry."

He crawled up her body and pressed his cock to her entrance, and then stopped.

"Holy crap, Duke," she wailed. "Why are you stopping now?"

He grinned, though his mouth appeared strained as if he could barely hold back. "Protection?"

"Fuck!" She slammed her fist against the mattress. They couldn't get to the door and not go in. Then she thought about Lena. "She has got to have a stock of condoms. Check the nightstand."

Duke leaned over, pulled open the top drawer of the nightstand and laughed. "You were right. She's got everything. A year's supply of condoms, sex toys, lubricant and even several varieties of whips."

"Stop talking," Angel commanded. "Am I the only one turned on here?"

He selected a condom, his face splitting into a grin. "Impatient much?"

"Fuck you." She snatched the package from his hand, tore it open and rolled the item over his rock-hard cock. "Now, get busy. I'm riding an orgasm I don't ever want to stop."

"Mmm." He bent to take her mouth with his, sucking her bottom lip between his teeth where he bit down softly before releasing it. "You're so romantic when you curse like a sailor."

"Like a Ranger. Get it right." She clasped his ass in her hands, done with the chatter and ready to take him all the way home.

Once again, he positioned himself at her entrance and gently dipped in.

Her muscles contracted, as if to pull him deeper inside her channel. Past patience, and so hot she could spontaneously combust, Angel grabbed his buttocks and slammed him home. "Oh, sweet Jesus. Now we're headed in the right direction."

Duke slid out, the movement excruciatingly slow.

Angel wrapped her legs around his waist and dug her heels into his backside, wanting him inside again, filling her to full and fucking her like there was no tomorrow.

Finally getting the hint, Duke moved in an out, increasing the pace and the intensity until he was pounding, hard and fast.

"Yes!" Angel yelled.

She dropped her heels to the mattress and dug in, lifting her hips to meet him thrust for thrust.

His body tensed, his jaw hardened and he slammed into her one last time, driving deep and holding there, his cock pulsing against the walls of her channel.

Angel came, her sex convulsing around his, her body shaking with the power of her release.

A minute passed, maybe two, before Duke lay down on her, wrapped his arms around her and rolled her and him onto their sides without disturbing their intimate connection.

Angel lay spent, her heartbeat slowly returning to normal. "Wow," she said when she could get enough breath to form a word.

"Wow, yourself," Duke managed. "I didn't expect sex with Lena Love could rock my world so completely." He winked.

"Hey. Lena's got nothing on me."

"Damn right. You're one in a million."

She snorted. "Remember that."

"I'm not likely to forget for a very long time." He cupped her cheek and stared deep into her eyes.

Angel's thoughts clarified in that instant and shook her even more than the most incredible orgasm she'd ever experienced.

Her gut bunched into a tight knot.

I could fall for this guy. I mean, really fall.
Hard.

CHAPTER 8

Duke packed a shirt and a pair of jeans into a backpack, and then threw in a handful of condoms he'd grabbed from the stash in Lena's nightstand. Not that they'd have time or the opportunity to make love in the mountains. But he could never be too prepared.

"Look at this." Angel carried a lightweight laptop into the room and set it on the bed beside his backpack. "Lena Love dumped Myles Crain a week ago after the media got hold of some pictures of his trophy hunts in Africa." She scrolled through several photos of a handsome man in khaki slacks and shirt, standing beside the carcass of a slain elephant. The next was Myles Crain smiling for the camera beside a dead giraffe, its neck folded over neatly to fit in the picture. The last one was of Myles and a lion. He held the head up, the lion's jaw had dropped open, exposing razor sharp teeth that had been no match for the hunter's long-distance rifle.

"He's a real sweetheart, isn't he?" Duke commented.

"Seems like the kind of guy Lena would go for. One who likes to shoot caged animals."

"That's just it. She didn't want to dump him." Angel closed the laptop. "I called Phillip to get the story. He told her she had to dump him. Myles was getting so much bad publicity, it threatened to impact her career. If she didn't dump him, he'd bring her down with him." Angel's lips twisted. "She dumped him publicly, through a television interview on a major talk show. Phillip said Myles was livid. He even called Phillip and threatened to kill him."

"A regular Prince Charming and a potential suspect."

Her brows twisted. "Another thing I found out about him that might put a damper on our trip into the mountains…"

"What? He likes to shoot women holding martini glasses?"

"No. He's big into predator games. He belongs to a league of hunters who pay men to be human prey."

"Like laser tag?" Duke's stomach knotted.

"Like laser tag on steroids. It's on a much grander scale. The course is over a thousand acres. The hunters have to track the individuals. The runners who stay 'alive' the longest are paid top dollar."

"So he's had some experience tracking humans as well as animals in a pen." Duke laid out an array of weapons on the comforter. "I'm liking this guy more and more." He held up a military-grade rifle. "Know how to use one of these?"

She lifted the weapon, pulled back the bolt, peered

inside, and then closed it again. "Of course. It's an M4A1 with a SOPMOD upgrade. We used these in my unit. Pretty damned accurate." She hefted it in her arms. "This one mine?"

He nodded. "And this." Duke handed her an M9 Beretta and holster with a belt.

"Where did you get all of this?"

"I have my conceal carry license."

She snorted. "This is enough stuff to supply an army."

"My new boss has connections."

Angel shook her head. "We're up against one man."

"And you've been in combat. One man can cause a lot of damage."

She nodded, her lips pressing into a thin line. "You're right." Squaring her shoulders, she dipped into the duffel bag he was loading with all of the guns and ammo. "Good, the magazines are loaded."

Duke grinned. "Not much good if they aren't."

"When are we leaving?"

"In ten minutes. I spoke with the foreman about hunting cabins on the ranch."

"The foreman?" Angel cocked her brows.

"Not Brandt Lucas. He was a figurehead."

"More likely a Lena fuckbuddy," Angel commented.

"He's long gone. Packed his shit and left last night."

Angel shivered. "Good riddance."

"Sorenson said there's a hunting cabin on a peak a couple of miles into the mountains. He gave me the general directions. We should be able to get there in an hour or two."

"I'm packed and ready when you are. I'll be in the kitchen loading some staples in case we're there for longer than a day or two."

"I'll be down in a couple of minutes. Stay away from the windows. Don't present a target."

She shook her head. "I'm not a newb."

"Yeah, but you haven't been in combat for several years." He grabbed her arm, pulled her against him and kissed her lips. "Humor me, will you?"

She smiled. "Okay. But only because I like your weapons." With a wink, she turned and left the room.

Duke called Hank Patterson and let him know what they'd discovered about Lena's ex-boyfriend and what had been going on since Duke had taken on the assignment as Lena's bodyguard.

"It's a good thing she has you to look out for her," Hank said. "Shooting a glass out of her hand is far too close for comfort."

"Yeah, well, I have a plan." Duke laid out his plan to lure the stalker away from the ranch and up into the mountains.

"Are you sure you want to do it that way?" Hank asked. "I can bring in my other agents from their current assignments to back you. But you'd have to give me at least a day. I can come with you now and we can have the others join us when they get in."

"I'm afraid if I take an army up into the mountains, our stalker won't come out of hiding." He glanced at the arsenal of weaponry he was taking with him. Knowing Angel could handle a gun as well as he could, made it easier for him to say, "I'm pretty confident I can manage this on my own." He wouldn't be on his own with the real liability that was Lena. Angel would be a member of his team, an asset to the upcoming fight.

"I can't say that I like the idea of you and Miss Love going up into the mountains without more support."

"Remember, I'm from Montana. I know my way around the mountains."

"You might know your way around, but does Miss Love?"

"I'll take care of her." And he would. But she'd also be fully capable of taking care of herself.

Hank sighed. "Okay. I'll give you two days, and then I'm coming up after you."

"Fair enough," Duke agreed. "I hope it won't take two days. I'm aiming to be back at Love Land after only a night."

"I admire your conviction. I just hope it's not misplaced."

"Give me two days."

"Okay." Hank ended the call.

Duke tossed the phone on the bed and sifted through the magazines and pouches.

When his cellphone rang, he spent a few seconds looking for it amid the magazines, ammunition and pouches scattered across the bed. When he found it, he noticed the caller ID and hit the talk button. "Hey, Rider. You guys really must be missing me."

"Not at all. We're just jealous as hell that you're having all the fun in Montana without us."

Duke snorted. "Fun. Right."

Rider's tone grew serious. "What's happening?"

"You could say I'm missing my brothers about now."

"Protecting a movie star more than you can handle?"

"She's got a psycho hunter after her. He's only been playing with her to begin with, but he took a warning shot at her yesterday."

"Damn," Rider said. "And here we all thought bodyguarding was a boondoggle."

"Me too, until it got too close to home, and a lot more dangerous."

"Well, don't tell the guys I was the one to blow the surprise, but me, Blaze and a couple others packed our fishing gear and chartered a plane leaving today."

"For?"

"Eagle Rock, Montana."

A wave of relief washed over Duke. He'd have his team as backup if the shit hit the fan. "How soon will you be here?"

"We leave in fifteen minutes," Rider said. "Flight time is under five hours. Think you can hold out until we get there?"

"I think so. I told my boss I didn't need help, but you can never have too many Deltas on a mission."

Rider chuckled. "Got that right."

"We're heading into the mountains to see if we can force his hand."

"Send us the coordinates. We'll be there."

"Roger." For the first time since he'd left Fort Hood, Texas, he felt like he had a mission. Something to fight for. "Hopefully, by the time the team gets here, it'll be that cake walk you mentioned and we'll get in some fly fishing."

"Yeah." Rider paused. "Stay safe, buddy."

"Will do."

If all worked out as planned, they'd lead the stalker into the woods, turn the game on him and the predator would become the prey.

Between a former Army Ranger and a Delta Force soldier, they should be able to flush out the bad guy and give him a little of his own medicine. His hunting days would soon be over.

And if all else failed, the cavalry was on its way for some fly fishing, and other duties as required.

"I HAVE to admit I feel a little better wearing body armor," Angel said softly, so only Duke could hear. As she stood in front of the barn, she adjusted the Kevlar vest beneath the oversized blouse she'd found in Lena's closet. She glanced around. "What vehicle are we taking?"

Lyle, the recently promoted ranch foreman led two horses out of the barn and handed the reins of a big black one to Duke.

As he led the bay toward Angel, she held up her hands, shaking her head. "I'm not riding that."

"Why not?"

Angel bit her lip, about to say it was in her contract that she didn't have to do any stunts requiring her to ride a horse. But even though she'd told Duke who she was, no one but Phillip knew she wasn't the real Lena.

And Lena rode horses. Damn. "I just don't feel like riding a horse today." She glanced around. "Don't we have four-wheelers or something?"

"Some of the trails up to the cabin are really narrow. A horse has a better chance of getting around," Lyle said. "Miss Love, you know you feel safer riding horses than four-wheelers. Besides, it's been weeks since you've taken Hollywood for a ride."

The horse danced away from Angel. Though humans couldn't tell the difference between Angel and Lena, the horse obviously smelled a difference. It was probably the fear Angel was sweating out of every freakin' pore.

Without making a big fuss and revealing her lack of horse-riding skills, Angel gritted her teeth and stuck her foot in the stirrup.

The horse danced away again.

Angel held onto the side of the saddle, hopping along beside the horse.

"Don't know what's gotten into that animal." Lyle held onto the bridle and steadied the beast while Angel mounted, swinging her leg over the top of the saddle and landing with a jarring thump on her ass.

Sweet Jesus, I'm going to die!

Forcing a smile to her face, she said, "Let's ride!" If her voice was shaky and her grip on the reins wasn't right, well, fuck it. She was doing what she'd always sworn she wouldn't—riding a goddamn horse!

Her legs cinched around the horse's belly.

As soon as Lyle released the bridle, Hollywood danced sideways.

Angel bit down hard on her tongue to keep from crying out. Her feet flapped in the stirrups, and her heels touched the horse's flanks.

Hollywood leaped toward the gate, nearly leaving Angel behind.

By the grace of God and her hold on the saddle horn, she barely managed to remain in the saddle.

Hollywood stopped at the gate and waited for Lyle to open it.

Lyle stared up at the horse and scratched his head. "Don't know what's wrong with that horse. He never acts this way around you."

"I've been a little off kilter. Maybe he senses it," Angel bit out between her gritted teeth. "We'll work the kinks out on the trail. See you in a couple of days." She lifted her hand briefly in a little wave.

"Enjoy your stay in the cabin. I was up there a week ago. It's all set up with canned goods and firewood."

"Thank you, Lyle," Angel said, before she remembered Lena wouldn't have been as nice.

Duke rode up beside her, his horse stopping close enough Duke's leg touched Angel's.

A flash of desire raced through her at his nearness.

"Ready?" he asked.

Oh, yeah. She was ready to go back up to Lena's bed and make a repeat performance of last night. She sighed. Alas, they had a dangerous job to do. Hopefully, her stalker was watching and already planning to follow them up into the mountains. "Ready as I'll ever be," she said, her eyes narrowed. She was ready to take out the bastard bent on making Lena's life hell and ending it in a fantasy hunt to the kill.

Angel called bullshit on that. She and Duke would turn the tables on the bastard and bring him down.

Duke led the way, following the directions Lyle had given, along with the GPS device he'd brought in his gear.

After they had ridden out of sight of the barn and house, he'd slowed for Angel, snapped a lead rope onto Hollywood's bridal and led the animal behind his horse.

"You didn't tell me you couldn't ride."

"It never occurred to me that we'd take horses up in the mountains."

"Sweetheart, we're on a ranch…with horses and cattle. It's what you ride on a ranch."

"Or four-wheelers. I understand a lot of ranchers use them in lieu of horses, nowadays." She snapped her fingers in a Lena show of temper. "Get with the times, cowboy."

He chuckled. "I assume that's the Lena we all know and love."

Angel smirked. "I was just getting into the part when you figured it out."

Duke started up a trail that led through a pass between two hills. The path grew narrower and the slopes steeper, falling off to the right.

Angel held onto the saddle horn. "I sure hope this horse knows what the hell he's doing."

"They're sure-footed. The thing to remember is to stay in the saddle."

She snorted. "Easy for you to say. I have a feeling this horse has a mind of his own. And he doesn't seem to like me on his back."

Hollywood blew out a whinny and shook his mane.

Angel nodded. "See?"

Duke glanced back over his shoulder, his brows furrowing. "If you're that uncomfortable riding, you can ride double with me."

"No, thank you. I like having my own saddle horn to hang onto and stirrups to stand in."

THEY RODE for the next hour without speaking.

Duke glanced back often, worried about Angel. Hell, he hadn't been riding for a long time, and his ass was getting sore in the saddle. He could imagine how tired Angel would be when they reached the cabin.

Around noon, he stopped at the creek Lyle had said he'd find. He dismounted and reached up to help Angel down from her horse.

She swung her leg over and dropped down into his arms.

For a moment he held her, letting her get her feet under her, and well, really just held her. The woman hadn't complained since they'd left the barn. She was tough and willing to do things the hard way. "How are you holding up?"

"I'll let you know when we get there." She glanced around. "Right now, I'm as hungry as a horse." She patted Hollywood's neck. "I think we're starting to bond."

Hollywood tossed his head and backed away a step.

"Fine, we're not bonding. At least he hasn't tried to dump me off the side of a cliff and run back to the barn. I call that progress."

Duke chuckled and slapped her bottom.

"Hey!" She rubbed her backside. "Why don't they make saddles cushioned?"

"They wouldn't last very long."

"Yeah, well they should."

With a smile on his face, Duke pulled out sandwiches he'd packed in the saddle bags and handed her one.

She ate standing, refusing to settle onto a nearby boulder.

"Have you seen any signs of a tail?" she asked.

Duke shook his head. "No signs yet. I'm hoping he won't be that close behind us. It will give us time to get to the cabin first and set up some early warning devices.

She nodded, chewing as she looked around. "This would be nice if we weren't on a mission."

"Perhaps when this is all said and done, we'll be allowed to come back for a real vacation." As soon as the words were out of his mouth, Duke realized what his words implied. He wanted and expected to continue to see Angel after his two weeks of bodyguard duty ended. But that might not be the case.

"Are you headed back to Hollywood at the end of the two weeks?" he asked.

Angel finished off the last bite of her sandwich and

wiped the crumbs off her hands onto her jeans. "I don't know. I'm not sure how many more stunts my body can withstand." She smiled at him over her shoulder. "I'm not getting any younger."

Duke stepped behind her and circled her waist with his arms, pulling her back against his front. "You make yourself sound old. What are you, twenty-seven?"

"See how much you know. I'm twenty-nine. I'll be thirty in three months."

"Ever think of staying in Montana?"

She leaned her head on his shoulder. "Hadn't crossed my mind. But I can see why people like it here. It's beautiful."

"Yes, it is." He kissed her temple. "Beautiful—"

The sound of a branch snapping made Duke freeze.

Hollywood whickered and tossed his head.

Duke's horse answered and pulled against his reins tied to a tree limb.

Duke shoved Angel behind him and drew his pistol from the holster on his hip.

Angel drew her weapon, too, and backed toward a tree. She held on to Duke's shirt, leading him back with her until they were both near enough to duck for cover.

"Are we being paranoid?" She stood beside him, facing the opposite direction.

"Hell, no." Now that they were out in the woods, just the two of them and one sick bastard preying on them, Duke was rethinking his assertion that he and Angel could handle this guy on their own.

At least not yet. They weren't in a defensive position, nor could they see the enemy coming. Until they had a clear field of vision and fire, they were still on the prey side of the equation.

Silence reined, and the horses settled. Nothing moved but the swish of the horses' tails.

"Ready to move on?"

Angel nodded. "Ready."

"Think you can mount on your own?"

She bit her bottom lip, and then squared her shoulders. "Yes. Remember Hollywood and I have an understanding."

"Then let's get moving. I want to get set up long before dusk."

"Agreed."

"I'll be right back."

Angel waited while Duke strode quickly across the clearing to the where the horses were secured. He untied both sets of reins and walked the horses back to the trees. He looped the reins over Hollywood's neck and held the bridle while Angel mounted. Once she landed in the saddle, he swung up on his horse. "Lean over the horse's neck. You'll make less of a target."

She nodded.

He nudged his horse into a gallop and raced to the path.

Hollywood followed, easily keeping pace.

Angel held onto the saddle horn, leaning close to the horse's neck.

Once they rounded a bend in the trail, Duke slowed his horse to manage the winding trail to the cabin.

Within another hour, they arrived at the cabin,

quickly dismounted and unloaded the duffel bag from the back of Duke's horse.

Angel managed to dismount on her own and led the horse to a small corral several feet away from the cabin.

Once inside, Duke pulled all of the cans off the shelf and handed them and a can opener to Angel. "Open them halfway and empty the contents."

While she did that, he hurried to a nearby creek, with one of the cooking pots and scooped up pebbles from the creek bed.

When he got back to the cabin, Angel had all of the cans empty and had started poking holes in the sides with a pocket knife.

His heart swelled. He hadn't had to tell Angel what he was doing with the cans. She'd instinctively known.

Duke strung them together with long lengths of fishing line. Angel poured a few pebbles into each can and bent their lids closed.

When they were done, they carried their makeshift, early warning system out twenty yards deep into the woods around the periphery of the camp. Crouching in the brush, they watched and listened for several minutes for sounds of movement.

When Duke was as certain as he could be that they were alone, he strung the cans between the trees, setting the fishing line just high enough off the ground it would catch a foot passing through.

Once they'd strung the lines all around the perimeter, Duke and Angel returned to the cabin.

"You know we can't stay here, right?" Duke handed her a radio headset and settled one on his head.

She slipped the radio on and tapped the mic. "I know."

He could hear her voice through the radio in his ear and it made him feel a little better about positioning themselves on either side of the clearing.

He whispered into the mic, "There are bears and wolves in these woods."

Angel nodded, acknowledging that she could hear him through the radio, and then patted her handgun and lifted one of the M4A1 rifles. "We'll be ready. The early warning system will inform us about two and four-legged creatures."

He held up a hand for a high-five. "Let's do this." When she slapped his hand, he grabbed hers and pulled her close. "Don't be a hero, and keep your head down. It's not often I find a woman who speaks my language and looks as good as you do in body armor."

"You're not so bad yourself. I don't suppose you'd consider going out on a date with me when this is all over?"

Duke closed his eyes and heaved a sigh. "There you go, being all macho. I'm supposed to ask *you* out."

"We're in a bit of a hurry, and you took too long." She held his hand up to her cheek. "It was a yes or no question."

"Yes."

Her face blossomed in a smile. "Good. Now that we have that settled, let's catch us a bad guy."

Duke shook his head. "I'm glad I never had a problem taking orders from a woman. In fact, I kind of like it when you order me around." He pulled her into his arms, guns and all and kissed her.

She returned the kiss with equal force and passion.

When they broke apart, she stared at him, her smile gone. "Do me a favor and don't die on me, will you?"

His heart pinched hard in his chest at the look in her eyes. "I'm going to be around for a long time. I have a date with a pretty girl. I refuse to disappoint her."

CHAPTER 9

Duke left the cabin through the front door. Angel waited a minute or two and sneaked out the back door, and then ducked into the brush. Once in the shadows, she stuck leaves and strands of grass into the back of her shirt and in her hair and smeared dirt on her face.

When she was sufficiently camouflaged, she worked her way around to the position she and Duke had agreed would be hers. There, she burrowed into the leaves and brush, careful not to point her weapons in Duke's direction. "In position."

"In position," he responded.

Angel lay with her rifle ready, her pistol within easy reach and waited.

Minutes passed into an hour. She shifted slightly several times, to keep her arms and legs from falling to sleep. Just when Angel began to think the joke was on them and their stalker wasn't that interested in following them into the mountains, Duke spoke in her ear.

"I'm going to the cabin to light a lantern."

"I've got your back," Angel said.

Duke slipped around the edge of the perimeter to the trail leading in from the creek. He emerged as if he'd been at the creek all along and was on his way back to spend the night in the cabin.

Angel held her breath until he entered the cabin. She released her breath, thankful he'd made it into the cabin and no shots had been fired.

A minute went by, then another.

Alternating her attention on the cabin and in the direction of the path leading up the hill to the clearing where the cabin stood, she almost didn't see the arrow until it arched toward the cabin roof.

For an instant, she wondered what the hell an arrow was going to do against a solid wood cabin. Then it hit the roof and an explosion blew out the windows and knocked the door off its hinges. Smoke and flames rose from the structure, billowing into the air.

Angel gasped and started to rise.

The rattle of pebbles in cans alerted her to movement near her.

She swung her rifle in the direction of the noise in time to see what appeared to be a shaggy bush hunkered low, moving through the brush fast, heading toward her position and zigzagging back and forth.

With her heart lodged in her throat, not knowing whether Duke had made it out of the cabin before the explosion, Angel zeroed in on the bastard and pulled the trigger.

As the bullet left the barrel, the attacker dodged right, raised a camouflaged rifle and aimed at her.

Angel fired again, hitting him in the arm as he fired a round.

A bullet whizzed past her ear and hit the tree behind her, sending chunks of bark showering down on her.

The man hit the ground with a grunt, rolled over with his weapon and aimed directly at Angel.

She flung herself to the left at the same time as a shot rang out. Landing hard on the butt of her rifle, she gasped as pain shot through her rib. For a moment, she thought she'd been hit, but she didn't care. The bastard had to die, or he'd kill her.

She rolled over several times to get away from her previous position and behind a log lying on the ground. When she stopped, she glanced over the top of the log.

Her attacker had assumed a kneeling position, his weapon aiming toward the log behind which she hid.

"You're nothing but a cold-hearted bitch, Lena Love."

"Is that right, Myles?" Angel called out, betting on the attacker being Lena's ex-boyfriend. "You think you're some big bad hunter, but all you've ever done is kill caged animals."

"You hired a bodyguard to protect you, but I killed him, too."

Angel's stomach knotted. She refused to believe Duke was dead. He'd promised to go out on a date with her. A Delta Force soldier's promise was sacred. He'd keep it, damn it. She blinked her stinging eyes. For a moment, silence filled the air. In the distance, the hum of an aircraft engine echoed through the mountains, and smoke drifted through the air.

Duke had yet to turn up, leading Angel to believe he could be dead or dying in the burning cabin. She had to do something to force Myles's hand and get this over with so that she could find Duke.

"Hey Myles, were you afraid my bodyguard was better in bed than you? Is that why you felt a need to kill him?" she taunted. "Because he *was. So* much better... and *bigger.*" In Angel's mind, a man who had to kill defenseless, endangered animals purely for sport, had to have a little dick.

"Bitch." Myles fired at the log, knocking a notch in the top, far too close to Angel's head for her comfort.

"That's my date you're calling names," a voice shouted in the distance and into Angel's headset.

Her heart leaped with joy.

Duke!

She heard the shot and looked up in time to see Myles fall to the ground. He rolled over to his side and reached for his rifle lying in the dirt not far from where he'd landed.

Another shot rang out hitting Myles again, this time in the gut. Lena's ex-boyfriend lay groaning in the dirt.

Angel left the cover of her log, ran toward Myles and grabbed his rifle, flinging it away.

Not that he would need it anymore, he wasn't going far with three bullets in him.

Duke appeared beside her. "Did you shoot that last shot?"

"No. I thought you did." She flung her arms around him. "I thought you were dead."

He chuckled and hugged her to him. "Deltas don't die that easily."

She leaned back and stared up at him. "How did you get out of the house?"

He grinned. "Same way you did—through the back door. And none too soon."

She rose on her toes and kissed him. "You scared the crap out of me. I didn't know whether or not you were in that cabin when it blew."

A shadow fell over Angel and Duke.

They glanced up at the same time to see a man dangling from a parachute, a rifle in his hand. As he neared the trees, he adjusted the pitch of the chute, angling toward the clearing near the smoldering cabin. He landed on his feet, gathered his chute and moved out of the way as another man and parachute spiraled downward toward the clearing, and still another.

Duke grabbed Angel's arm and hurried her toward what ended up being four men, folding their chutes, all carrying military-grade rifles.

Angel dug her heels in the dirt, refusing to step out into the clearing "Are you sure they're friendly?"

"Friendly?" Duke laughed out loud. "These men are my brothers."

Her frown eased only slightly. "Brothers? I assumed you were an only child."

He dragged her toward the one who'd landed first,

and whose bullet had been the one to end Myles's hunting expeditions permanently.

"Rider!" Duke dropped her arm and engulfed the man and his parachute harness in a bear hug.

The man he'd called Rider pounded him on his back. "And to think, we almost missed the party." He glanced over Duke's shoulder at Angel. "Aren't you going to introduce me to your client?" His gaze went to the rifle she carried and the sticks and twigs she'd stuck in her hair. "Since when did movie stars start carrying rifles and shooting bad guys other than on sets with blank rounds?"

"Rider, this isn't Lena Love, though she's the spitting image of the movie star. This is her stunt double and former Army Ranger, Angel Carson."

"Should have known Duke was having way too much fun without us. We got here just in time." Rider held out his hand to Angel.

"Nice to meet you." When she placed her hand in his, he didn't shake it. Instead, he pulled her into his arms and hugged her.

Duke grabbed Rider's shoulder and pulled him away from Angel. "Hey, get your grubby hands off my girl. You have Briana, now."

"And I don't want any other woman. But I'm happy you found a woman who can hold her own in a gunfight." Rider grinned at Angel. "I can't wait to introduce you to Briana. She's going to love you."

Another man joined them. "Duke, what's this? You've only been here a couple of days, and you've already found a woman?" He turned to Angel and held out his hand. "By the way, I'm Blaze, this dirt bag's teammate. I guess Duke's joined a different kind of team altogether." He winked. "A better looking team."

Duke's cheeks reddened.

Angel loved that Duke was embarrassed and couldn't help giving him even more hell than his buddies were. "Hey, don't I have a say in whose woman I am?"

All five men turned toward her.

"You mean you're not Duke's?" Rider asked. He looked past her to the man lying on the ground, moaning. "Tell me that's not your guy.

Angel and Duke replied as one. "No!"

Duke slipped an arm around Angel. "Give us a chance. I owe this woman a night out. Now that we've taken care of Lena's ex-boyfriend, we might just get to go on that date. Then she can decide whether or not she wants a man, and if that man could possibly be me."

"Well, don't let us get in the way of true love. We've each got a date with a fishing pole. Point us to the nearest stream, and we'll get out of the way."

"Be happy to," Duke said. "After we put out the fire and get Lena's ex off the mountain."

"Oh, so now we have to work for the right to fish?" Blaze shook his head. "Fine. Let's do this and get to our mini vacation before we have to head back."

Duke's friends helped load Myles onto Hollywood's saddle. Then they loaded their parachutes onto the other saddle and headed down the mountain, leading the horses.

Duke walked beside Angel, trailing behind the

others. "The guys are just kidding about you being my woman."

"Oh, that's too bad." She leaned into him. "I was kind of liking the idea."

"Yeah?" Duke's face brightened. "It's never wise for a man to assume anything, especially about a woman who can fire a rifle almost as well as he can."

She jabbed him in the gut. "*Better* than he can."

"You nicked the guy in the leg," he reminded her.

Her lips quirked on the corners. "I was *aiming* for the leg."

"You win." He pulled her into his embrace and lifted her chin. "But in the end…I win."

"How so?"

"I got the girl."

"You did?" she said, her voice barely a whisper, her gaze sinking to his mouth.

"Yup." Then he kissed her, claiming her, making her his with that single caress.

When she pulled away, she said, "You'll get no argument from me, as long as you keep kissing me like that."

"Deal." And he kissed her again. Under the big sky of Montana, on a trail in the Crazy Mountains, in front of his band of brothers, Duke had staked his claim on Angel.

She couldn't have been happier. And he owed her a date. She would insist on the location. A place that had a king-sized bed with a cotton-candy-pink comforter and a drawer full of protection.

They still had the majority of the two weeks to enjoy

Lena's hospitality. She planned on making the most of it...with Duke.

MONTANA RANGER

BROTHERHOOD PROTECTORS BOOK #5

New York Times & USA Today
Bestselling Author

ELLE JAMES

MONTANA RANGER

BROTHERHOOD PROTECTORS

NEW YORK TIMES BESTSELLING AUTHOR
ELLE JAMES

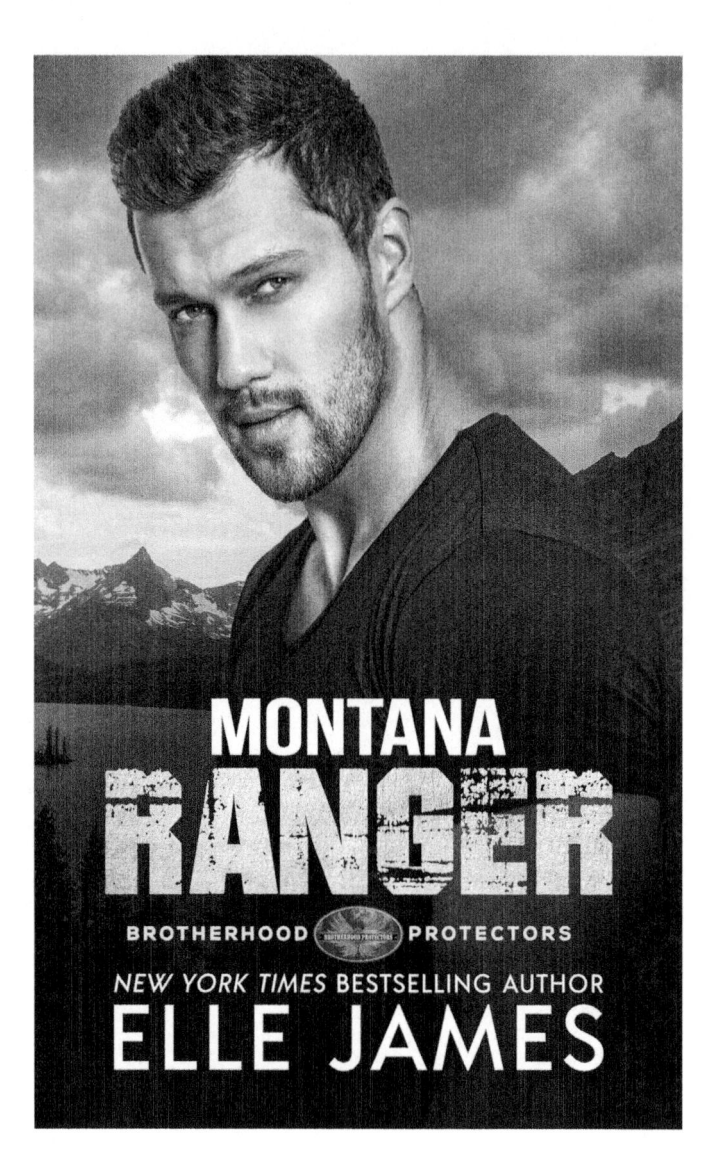

This story is dedicated to military men and women who separate from active duty and find it hard to fit in with the so-called real world. You are loved and appreciated for all you have done to protect this great nation!

Elle James

CHAPTER 1

Axel Svenson, or Swede, as he preferred to be called, flexed his hand before he stuck it out. He found the scars were less disconcerting than proffering his left hand to shake. "Nice to meet you, ma'am."

"You can call me Allie. Ma'am makes me sound old." Alyssa Patterson took the hand without flinching. "No offense, but I can't say that I'm as thrilled to meet you. I really don't need a bodyguard, despite what my brother says."

"Yes, you do," her brother, Hank 'Montana' Patterson, said.

His first day on the job with the Brotherhood Protectors and Swede's first client didn't want his services. It wasn't exactly the way he'd pictured his initial assignment. From the way Montana had described the work, he'd expected to be allocated to a helpless rich person who needed someone to chauffeur, him or her, around. All he'd have to do was look big and tough. With the scar on the side of his face, he had no doubt he could intimidate the hell out of most people.

Instead of a rich socialite, Montana had tasked Swede with protecting his kid sister. And she wasn't thrilled with the idea.

"If your sister doesn't want a bodyguard, why force one on her?" Swede asked.

Allie's eyes narrowed. "Wait, you're taking my side?"

Swede shrugged. "You're a grown-ass woman. If you don't think you need a bodyguard, you shouldn't have to accept one."

Allie turned to her brother and flashed a smile. "I might like this guy after all."

Sadie, Montana's wife, laughed.

Montana shot a brief frown at Allie and Sadie, and turned to Swede. "After several suspicious events, Allie's fiancé is concerned about her. And frankly, so am I."

"I have too much to do between now and the wedding to have someone on my heels slowing me down," Allie argued.

Montana gave her an "I'm the big brother" look. "You already agreed to Swede tagging along. Just shut up and let him."

Allie crossed her arms over her chest. "I'm going to a fitting, having my nails done and shopping for lingerie for the wedding night. That's when I'm not hauling hay, cleaning stalls and checking fences not only on the Bear Creek Ranch, but on the Double Diamond." She gave Swede a look that sized him up and found him lacking. "What do you know about any of those activities?"

He shrugged. "Nothing."

Allie rolled her eyes and turned back to Montana. "Let me guess, he's never been on a ranch, and doesn't know one end of a horse from another?"

Rather than allow himself to feel inadequate, Swede stiffened his back and straightened to his full six-feet-four inches. "I might not know my way around a ranch, but I'm good with a gun, I learn fast, I'm quick on my feet and highly observant."

She opened her mouth.

Swede pressed a finger to her lips. "Let me demonstrate." He gave her the same assessing stare she'd given him. "You came straight from the horse stalls you spoke of because you smell like manure, and you're tracking it into the house. You didn't take time to brush your hair this morning, likely because you had to clean the stalls and take care of the animals. Your hands are shaky, probably because you drink too much coffee. You haven't slept well in days, if the circles under your eyes are any indication. The lack of sleep has everything to do with all of the things you mentioned, plus you're worried your brother might be right and you might be in danger." He crossed his arms over his chest, much like she had. "Did I miss anything?"

"Great. And he's a smartass." Allie glared at her brother.

Montana raised his hands. "Hey, don't look at me. Take it up with your fiancé. He was the one who thought you needed protection. Maybe if you'd decided to marry one of the locals instead of a rich man who just bought a ranch in Montana because he could, you wouldn't be in any more danger than getting thrown by a horse."

"Do you hear yourself?" Allie asked. "You sound like our father."

Montana scowled and his jaw tightened.

His wife, Sadie, touched his arm. "Sweetheart, Allie has the right to choose her partner. Let her take up the bodyguard issue with Damien. He's the one who thinks she might need one. He can better explain his concerns."

Montana slipped an arm around Sadie's waist. "You're right." He turned to his sister. "I'm sorry. You can marry any rich jerk you want. I don't have to like it, and I'll tell you so, but if this is what you want, I won't stand in your way."

"Damn right, you won't." She lifted her head.

"At least let Swede tag along. If Damien is set on hiring a bodyguard, perhaps he can convince you." Montana held open his arms. "You know I love you, kid. I only want what's best for you."

Allie sucked in a deep breath, let it out and stepped into her brother's hug. "I guess that's your job."

"Yup. I wouldn't be a big brother unless I told you how I see it." Montana sniffed. "And Swede is right. You do smell like manure."

Allie punched him in the belly. "Thanks. Love you, too." She hugged her sister-in-law and patted her stomach. "Take care of my niece."

Sadie laid a hand over her flat abdomen. "I will." She hugged Allie. "Let Swede take care of you. I want our baby to know her Auntie Allie."

"I'll be around. I might be marrying a rich man who

travels all over the world, but my life is here in Montana."

"Don't forget..." Sadie touched her arm. "We have the final fitting for your dress the day after tomorrow."

Allie sighed. "I don't know why I had to have it altered. It fit just fine."

"The dress was too loose around your waist and too short," Sadie reminded her. "And no, you can't wear your favorite cowboy boots under it."

"Why?" Allie protested. "Nobody will see my feet."

"Because they'd smell like you do now. Like the inside of a horse stall." Montana turned her around. "Go on. Talk to Damien before you go back to the ranch."

Swede's chest tightened over the back-and-forth arguing between the siblings. Montana was lucky. He had a wife, a baby on the way, his sister and his father. For Swede, one of the hardest things about being processed out of the military was losing the only family he had. His SEAL team. The soldiers he'd met during his recovery had family members come visit them. Not Swede.

The whole recovery process would have been a lot harder but for two things: the Australian shepherd he'd rescued from the animal shelter, and the Delta-Force soldier he'd met during his physical therapy sessions. Bear Parker had been in the same boat as he was. No home to go to, no family to greet him when he got there. They'd gone out for a beer several times after therapy sessions. Which reminded Swede...

He hesitated before following Allie. "You know,

Montana, when you start getting more business, I know another man you might want to hire."

"Yeah?" Montana's brows rose. "Tell me."

"He's not a SEAL, but he's former Delta Force."

"I might have work for him. Is he available now? Or do we have to wait until his enlistment is up?"

"Available now. I met him in Bethesda during my recovery. I'm sure he'd be interested."

"Pass on his details, and I'll contact him."

"And Montana, thanks for the opportunity." Swede held out his hand.

Montana took it and pulled the big man into a bear hug. "We're in this together."

Swede hugged him back. "Once a SEAL, always a SEAL."

"Right. We just have to find out where we fit now that we're not fighting wars in foreign countries."

"If you're going to follow Allie, you'd better get going," Sadie said. "She's pulling down the drive now."

Swede sprinted from the room, feeling only a slight twinge in his thigh from the shrapnel wounds. He hurried to his truck, parked in front of the house. Ruger barked a greeting and moved out of the driver's seat.

"Good boy." Swede started the engine and spun the truck around, spitting gravel in his wake.

ALLIE WAS furious Damien hadn't asked her first before contacting her brother about a bodyguard. She'd made it perfectly clear to her fiancé that she was a very independent woman who liked doing things her way. If he wasn't okay with that, he shouldn't have dated her or asked her to marry him. She wasn't changing for any man.

A glance in her rearview mirror made her smile. She'd left without waiting for Swede. If he was to be her bodyguard, he'd have to do a whole lot better at keeping up.

He didn't catch up to Allie until she slowed to turn onto the highway.

Yes, she was driving like a bat out of hell, racing along the highway like she was actually trying to lose him. Maybe she was. Having someone follow her around like she needed a babysitter wasn't her idea. Why make it easy on the man?

Apparently, Swede wasn't so easily deterred. He caught up and rode her tail, even though she was breaking the speed limit.

The gate to her current home with her father at Bear Creek Ranch came and went. She didn't slow down until she reached the grandiose stone and wood monstrosity with the words Double Diamond Ranch seared into the cedar archway. Unlike most gravel ranch roads, the Double Diamond road was paved all the way up to a huge mansion of a house, spreading across the top of a knoll.

Damien had purchased it from a movie star who'd gotten tired of the cold winters and moved back to sunny California to retire. The drive was lined with trim white wood fencing and trees spaced perfectly along the way. Horses grazed in the pastures if they weren't being cared for in the massive stable. The stable was magnificent with twelve stalls, a spotless tack room and an office for the foreman.

Allie had a love-hate relationship with the ranch. She loved what wealth could buy, but, at the same time, hated the waste of so many dollars on things that weren't necessary to have a working ranch in Montana. But, this wasn't a working ranch. It was a gentleman's retreat where riding was done for exercise and fun, not out of the necessity of managing cattle.

When she married Damien, she hoped to change that. She wasn't the kind of woman who sat around the house eating bon bons with servants who tended to her every need. *Bleck!* She got the sour taste in her mouth, and felt the need to spit to clear it.

Allie pulled to a stop in front of the mansion and slid out of the driver's seat. Without waiting for Swede, she marched up to the front entrance and pounded on the door, her anger fueling her fist.

Footsteps sounded on the steps behind her. The bodyguard was getting faster. Darn it all.

A man in a uniform opened the door. "Ah, Miss Patterson. Mr. Reynolds is out at the stable. Perhaps you'd like to come inside and wait for him?"

"No, thank you, Miles. I'll find him." Allie turned and ran into Swede. Beside him was a blue merle Australian shepherd with ice blue eyes much like his master's. "Why are you standing so close?"

He stepped aside with what could only be regarded as a sarcastic flourish. "Maybe if you looked before you rushed headlong into things, you wouldn't have a problem with where I stand."

She snorted. "This your sidekick?"

"You could say that. His name is Ruger."

Her expression softened, and she reached down to scratch the dog's ears. She had a soft spot for dogs, especially working dogs, which she was almost sure this one was not.

Ruger leaned against her leg, his tail thumping against the stoop.

Allie could get lost in eyes so blue. Her jaw hardened, she straightened and gave Swede a narrow-eyed glare. "Just stay out of my way, will ya?" She ducked around him and marched across the manicured lawn toward the stable. "Damien!" she called out. "I need to talk to you."

Her fiancé, dressed in freshly pressed khaki slacks, a dark polo shirt, and black leather jacket emerged from around the far side of the stable, his brows pulled into a deep frown. "Alyssa, what are you doing here?"

Not *'Alyssa, darling, I'm so happy you came to see me'*. Was the honeymoon over before it had even begun? And without the requisite sex? That was another thing she would take up with Damien when she had a moment alone with him. Why hadn't they gone all the way yet? This waiting for the wedding bullshit was positively archaic. What if he was lousy in bed? Worse yet, what if she was lousy in bed with him? She wasn't a virgin, but it had been a while since she'd slept with someone.

Frustrated by all she had to do before the wedding and adding the aggravation of having to put up with a shadow following her around, she launched her attack.

"What's this about you going behind my back to hire a bodyguard for me?"

He glanced back in the direction from where he'd come. "Darling, I think it's best. It appears that I've made a few enemies along the road to success. Some would like to steal away my good fortune."

"What kind of enemies?" Swede asked, stepping up beside Allie. He held out his hand. "I'm the bodyguard you hired. Axel Svenson. Most people call me Swede."

Allie crossed her arms over her chest as the men shook hands.

"Damien Reynolds. I'm glad to meet you. Let me show you the latest in what has me concerned." He hooked Allie's elbow, turned and walked around the side of the stable. He stopped and waved his hand at the wall. Splashed across the side of the well-maintained structure were bold letters spray-painted in red.

TAKE WHAT'S MINE
I'LL TAKE WHAT'S YOURS

A chill slithered down Allie's spine at how the red paint resembled blood, with long trails dripping from the letters down the side of the stable. She shuddered and straightened. "Damien, it's just paint."

His mouth pressed into a thin line. "It's a threat. A promise to take what I've accumulated here. Whoever did this might also target the people I care about."

Swede turned to Allie. "Didn't your brother say something about cut brake lines on your truck?"

Damien's brows dipped. "Have you had anything else happen since then?"

Allie shot a narrow-eyed glare at Swede. "No. And that could have been a fluke."

"I'd rather be safe than sorry. Less than a week remains until our wedding. Then we'll get away on our honeymoon, and leave all of this behind."

"If there really is a problem," Allie pointed to the stable wall, "which it seems there is, we'd only delay dealing with the issue."

Damien shoved a hand through his immaculate hair. The gesture barely ruffled the dark locks.

Sometimes that irritated Allie, considering she looked like she needed to brush her hair the minute she stepped outside.

"How about us tackling one challenge at a time?" He lifted her hand and pressed a kiss to her callused fingers. "Let Mr. Svenson get you to the wedding on time and intact. When we get back from the honeymoon, we can deal with whoever is causing the problems."

"I can take care of myself," Allie insisted. "I have a gun, and I know how to use it."

"I know you do, darling. But you can't always be watching over your shoulder. I know you have last-minute preparations for the wedding. You don't need to worry yourself about some lunatic stirring up trouble. Leave it to your bodyguard."

Allie bristled, biting hard on her tongue. One of the things she liked about Damien was also one of the attributes that really pissed her off. He treated her like a lady. As a hardcore rancher, it was a nice change to be seen as a woman, not just another ranch hand. But then,

Damien sometimes took it a little too far, treating her like a woman who didn't know one end of the gun barrel from the other. Rather than call him on his patronizing attitude, and show any discord between them to the hired bodyguard, Allie swallowed the words she wanted to say. "Okay, I'll let him tag along."

"Good, because I have to go out of town for the next few days."

Allie frowned. "Our wedding is in less than a week. You promised you'd be here to help with last-minute details."

"Now, Alyssa, I still have a business to run. I can't just let it go." He glanced at the stable wall. "Some emergencies have come up and I need to handle them."

"Fine," she said. "Just be sure to make it to the church on time for the rehearsal and the actual ceremony." She'd be damned if she got stood up at the altar like some pathetic female in a romance novel. In this case, she'd have to get in line behind her father and brother to shoot him. "When are you leaving?"

"This evening. I'm catching a flight out of Bozeman." He cupped the back of her head and bent to kiss her.

As soon as his lips touched hers, an explosion rocked the earth beneath Allie's feet. Damien dropped where he stood.

Swede grabbed Allie and threw her on the ground, covering her body with his as a second explosion blasted through the side of the stable, shooting splintered boards over their heads.

Fire shot up from the far end of the stable, and

smoke filled the air. Horses screamed inside the remaining walls. Ruger barked in response.

Allie bucked beneath Swede. "Let me up!"

Swede rolled to the side, and pushed to his feet.

As soon as his heavy weight was off her, Allie jumped up and ran into the burning building.

CHAPTER 2

Swede raced after Allie, his body shaking, the explosion having thrown him back to his combat days. Only this wasn't Afghanistan or Iraq. His primary job was to protect a woman hell-bent on running headfirst into danger.

Seeing Allie run into the burning stable, Swede had no other choice but to chase after her into the smoke-filled structure. Ruger tried to follow, but Swede pointed his finger at the dog's nose. "Stay." He could only pray the dog would remember the one command long enough for Swede to get Allie out.

Inside, the smoke hit him immediately, burning his eyes and lungs. He pulled his T-shirt up over his mouth and blinked to clear his eyes. Hunkering below the bulk of the smoke, he hurried toward the pair of legs encased in blue jeans, standing in front of a stall, struggling to throw open the latch.

A horse on the other side pawed at the gate, its eyes rolled back, nostrils flaring.

Swede brushed aside Allie, slammed the lever to the side and jerked the door open.

With a shrill scream, the horse pushed through and raced toward the exit.

Allie had gone deeper into the smoke-filled stable and threw open another stall.

The horse inside reared, thrashing its legs.

Swede grabbed Allie and dragged her out of the way of the deadly hooves.

"Let go of me!" she cried, struggling to be free.

"Get out, now." Swede coughed and ducked low. "I'll take care of the rest of them."

"No way." Allie's eyes streamed with tears, making tracks in the soot clinging to her face. "One person can't get them all." She pushed away, and ran to the next stall.

Rather than fight her, Swede pitched in and helped her free the remaining horses from the stable. When the stalls were empty, he waved to Allie. "Get out. Now!" The heat from the fire bore down on him, but he wouldn't leave until she was out.

Allie ran for the door and Swede fell in behind her. At the last minute, just before he passed through the open door, a movement caught his eye. He reached between two feed barrels and snagged a cat by the scruff of its neck. With the feline clawing at his arm, Swede dove for the door. Once outside, he didn't let go of the cat until he was far enough away from the stable the cat wouldn't run back inside. When he set the creature on the ground, it ran back toward the stable. Ruger blocked its way, growling fiercely. The cat changed directions and ran toward the house.

. . .

ALLIE'S LUNGS burned with every breath. She knelt on the ground fifteen feet from the barn, coughing so hard her entire body shook with the force.

Swede dropped down beside her, his lungs burning, and coughing equally as hard. "We need to get you to a hospital," he said, between fits of hacking. "Smoke inhalation can be fatal."

She raised her hand, swallowed hard and shook her head. "I don't need a hospital. I just need fresh air." Her gaze went to the stable. "What kind of monster targets a stable full of horses? What did the horses ever do to him?"

"Some people have no respect for life," Swede said. "Animal or human."

"People like that need to die a really terrible death." Her chest still tight, Allie lay down on the ground and closed her eyes. A moment later, she sat up straight when a thought came to her. "Where's Damien?"

Swede shook his head. "He wasn't in the stable. I made a final sweep before we got out."

Allie glanced around. "Thankfully, all of the animals survived. When the fire burns down and the horses can be gathered, we can assess injuries."

"Alyssa!" Damien came running from the direction of the house. "Thank God, you're okay. The fire department is on its way."

Allie wanted to ask him where the hell he was when the horses were trapped inside their stalls. The call to the fire department could have waited until all the animals were safe. She stood, brushing the grass and dust off her jeans.

Damien opened his arms for her, but she didn't step into them.

"I'm covered in soot. I wouldn't want to mess up your jacket with the smell."

He glanced down at the garment. "I don't care about the jacket." And he pulled her into his arms. "I'm just glad you're all right." He tipped her face up to him, pulled a cloth handkerchief out of his pocket and dabbed at her lips. Then he kissed her. "You shouldn't have gone into the stable."

"I wasn't about to let those horses burn in the fire."

"But you could have died." He kissed her again and then set her to arm's length. "Now, do you see why I wanted to hire a bodyguard?"

Witnessing the tender moment, Swede turned away from the couple. He'd have to get used to disappearing if he wanted this bodyguard gig to work out. He imagined the first rule of being a bodyguard was to keep one's mouth shut. A good bodyguard was there all the time, but not to be seen or heard, except when necessary. Or at least, that's how he figured it should be. He wondered if Hank had drafted a set of standard operating procedures for the company. He made a mental note to ask the next time he saw his friend.

Ruger leaned against his leg, a low whining sound rising up his throat. Swede bent to pat the dog's head and scratch behind his ears. "It's okay, boy. You did good."

"So, it's all settled then?" Reynolds was saying.

Swede turned back to Allie and her fiancé.

"Mr. Svenson, you're in charge of my bride's safety," Reynolds said. "I expect you to guard her with your life, and make sure she gets to the church for the wedding." He glanced down at Allie. "From what your brother said, this man is one of our nation's finest. A navy SEAL, a combat veteran skilled in almost every weapon imaginable. Who better to guard my precious Alyssa?"

Swede fought to keep from rolling his eyes or snorting. In the brief amount of time he'd known Allie, he could imagine she was fighting not to gag. The woman had spunk and valued her independence. *Precious* wasn't one of the words Swede would use to describe her. It was too frilly.

Allie stepped back. "You be careful, too. You're in more danger than I am. Whoever is mad at you blew up *your* stable, not mine."

Damien nodded, his jaw tightening. "I hope to find out who it is while I'm away, but it pays to be overly cautious, especially after we've seen what he might do. Now, if you'll excuse me, I have to pack a bag and get to the airport. I trust you can answer any questions the fire department might have." Without waiting for a response, the man turned and left Allie and Swede standing in front of the burning stable.

Less than five minutes later, Reynolds drove away in a white Land Rover, before the fire trucks could arrive.

Swede shook his head. The man had narrowly missed being blown up in an explosion, his fiancée had almost died in the ensuing fire, and he'd been willing to let his expensive horses die. Swede violated his first rule of being a bodyguard and opened his mouth. "You're engaged to him?"

"Don't judge." Allie turned and walked away.

"Right. I'm just the bodyguard," Swede muttered under his breath and followed her. "Where are you going?"

"The horses need to be caught and put out to pasture before the fire truck spooks them and they run out onto the highway." She walked up to a horse standing in the corner of a fence, its eyes wild, its feet dancing in the dirt, stirring up a small cloud of dust.

Allie spoke in a calm voice. "It's okay. That big bad fire won't get you." She slowly reached for the animal's halter.

The gelding reared, pawing at the air, nearly knocking over Allie.

Swede grabbed her around the middle and pulled her out of reach. Only thing was that, once he had her out of harm's way, he didn't want to let go. The woman tried his patience and had a mouth on her, but she cared about the horses and risked her own life to save theirs. He admired that in the infuriating woman.

"What are you doing?" Allie demanded, struggling to free herself from his hold.

When he realized he'd held on too long, he abruptly let go.

Allie broke free and backed away in a hurry. Her movement startled the gelding. Again, the animal rose on its hind legs.

And, once again, Swede grabbed her and pulled her

away from the flailing hooves. This time, she was facing him and her hands rested on his chest.

For a moment, she froze, her fingers curling into his shirt. Her gaze rose from his chest to his mouth.

For a brief, unexplainable moment, Swede had the undeniable urge to kiss the woman.

Her eyes widened, and she pushed against his chest. "Let go of me."

"The horse is understandably afraid. Let me try to catch him." Swede held her a moment longer. "I'm going to release you. Please don't make any sudden moves."

"I know what I'm doing," she insisted with a glare. "I grew up around horses."

"Just let me do this."

"How many horses have you been around?" she asked.

"Counting the ones we got out of the stable?" His lips twisted. "Five." The total number of horses they'd rescued from the fire.

"My point, exactly." Allie pushed her sleeves up her arms. "You'll get hurt."

"Give me the benefit of the doubt," Swede said. "Stay here with Ruger. He's never been around farm animals, that I know of. Keep him from coming after me."

Allie waved an arm. "Fine. Go ahead. Get yourself killed. Then I won't have you following me around." She dropped to her haunches next to Ruger. "Poor dog. What did you do to deserve him?"

"I'll have you know he was on death row at a dog pound when I rescued him." But, if Swede was telling the whole truth, Ruger had been the one doing the rescuing.

Standing in front of the frantic beast with the heat of the still-burning fire behind him, Swede studied the animal. Having grown up in the city, he'd never really thought much about horses. Like most kids, he'd always dreamed of living on a ranch and riding horses, but the opportunity had never presented itself. Now that he was in Montana, he would make a point of learning how to ride and care for a horse.

Starting now.

He eased toward the horse, maintaining eye contact with the beast. When he'd brought Ruger home, he'd treated him with kindness and respect, he noticed how the dog responded to the tone of his voice even when he talked nonsense. If that worked with a dog, perhaps it would work with a horse. He spoke in a low, steady, monotone, advancing slowly, holding out his hand, praying the horse didn't take a bite out of it or trample him in his crazed state of mind. This horse was like most creatures when they were scared, it needed reassurance and comfort.

Swede inched toward the horse, and it whinnied and pawed at the dirt, but it didn't rear. Hoping the smell of smoke wasn't still clinging to his skin, Swede let the horse smell his hand and touch his fingers with its big lips. The sensation was new and exhilarating to Swede. The horse was like a big dog. When he thought of it that way, he relaxed and smoothed his hand over the nose and up to scratch behind his ears, wrapping his other hand around the halter.

Allie hated that Swede, a greenhorn who'd never been near a horse, had walked up to one who was so clearly spooked and calmed him.

She snorted. "Beginner's luck. We have four more to catch. You better get cracking." She walked with Ruger over to a gate and held it open.

Swede led the animal through and released it on the other side.

The horse galloped across the pasture, moving as far away from the smoke and flames as it could get.

The other four horses were easier to round up, and they soon had all of them in the fenced pasture. Just in time, too. The wailing of sirens grew louder, and soon the driveway filled with a pumper truck, a paramedic's vehicle, and a sheriff's deputy. Several ranchers' trucks arrived, all part of the volunteer firefighters who served the county.

Swede and Allie moved back as the fire-fighters made use of the nearby pond and pumped water onto the flames. Unfortunately, the stable was a complete loss, but the firefighters kept the blaze from spreading to the house and grassy fields.

After the paramedics checked out both Swede and Allie for smoke inhalation, they gave them a blast of oxygen. The pair was released, with the recommendation that they go to the clinic in Eagle Rock.

But, that would have to be later. The sheriff and fire chief had questions. Allie answered them as best she could. Someone had left a threatening message on the side of the building, and then the building exploded. She had no idea who the perpetrator might be. The only person who might have the answer to that question had left to catch a flight out that afternoon. Yes, he should be back within the week. He had a wedding to attend, after all.

What else could she say? Less than a week out from her wedding, and this incident hit her full in the face. How well did she know her fiancé? She knew so little about his business and why someone would want to hurt him. She swore she'd grill Damien thoroughly before the wedding. How had she been so caught up in her own life she hadn't bothered to get to know her future husband's? Had she thought the man was independently wealthy just because his parents were rich?

For the first time since she'd agreed to marry Damien, Allie started to get cold feet. Up until now, the relationship had seemed like a fairytale. She'd met her prince charming at a local fundraiser for charity. He'd taken her out on several dates, and then flown her in his private jet to have dinner in Seattle. Yeah, he'd swept her off her feet, and shown her a life so foreign she couldn't help but be dazzled. Best of all, he treated her like a woman, instead of another one of the guys.

When he'd popped the question less than a month ago, he'd been so romantic. He'd gotten down on one knee and asked her to marry him. Just like in the movies. It was every girl's dream. Allie had been no different. She couldn't say no to the man, or the life he promised. And his ranch was something she had only fantasized of. She couldn't wait to dig in and make it all it could be, not just a show place.

Hell, was she more in love with the ranch than the man? She shook her head. No. Damien might not know how to be a rancher, but that wasn't why she was marrying him. She cared for him. When she'd had disagreements with her cantankerous father, she'd turned to Damien, who'd been there to just hold her and let her vent. He hadn't offered advice, presumably because he trusted her judgment on how to handle her family.

He was an excellent horseman, having ridden in competitive dressage since he was a teenager. His parents had spared no expense in his education, sending him to private schools and then Yale. As a child, he'd traveled all over the world, and then again for the business he'd built for himself in contracting.

The tension slowly released from her shoulders. Maybe she knew more about him than she thought. So, she didn't know the particulars about his contracting business, only that he made a lot of money doing it. He had building projects all over the world, with a concentration in the rebuilding efforts going on in Afghanistan. He'd been there twice already that year, and maybe he was headed there now. When he called to check in, she'd ask.

A pickup pulled in behind the fire truck and emergency vehicles. Will Franklin got out, his eyes rounding. He walked up to where Allie and Swede stood near the sheriff and the fire chief. "What happened?" he asked.

Allie filled him in on the explosion.

Will started toward the stables. "The horses?"

Placing a hand on the man's arm, Allie answered, "Swede and I got them out." She turned to her bodyguard. "This is Will Franklin, Damien's foreman. Will, this is Swede Svenson. A…friend of mine."

Will shook hands with Swede and then glanced around. "Where's Mr. Reynolds?"

"He left shortly after the explosion," Allie said. "Apparently, he had to take care of business before the wedding."

"I'd better check the horses."

"I'll help." Allie followed Will through the gate to the pasture.

Swede followed with Ruger trotting alongside.

The horse he'd sweet-talked came trotting up to him.

Grinning, Swede held out his hand, and the horse nuzzled his open palm.

"Has he been around horses much?" Will asked Allie.

"No." Allie shook her head.

Will's lips twisted and he shook his head. "That horse doesn't usually come up to anyone."

Swede held the gelding's halter while Will and Allie looked over the animal. Other than smelling like soot, he seemed to be okay.

They performed the same inspection on the other four horses. When Will and Allie were satisfied they hadn't suffered any lasting ill effects, Allie checked in with the fire chief and sheriff once more.

"If you need us for further questions, we'll be at the Bear Creek Ranch."

Without waiting for her escort, she crossed to her truck, climbed in and left the Double Diamond.

Swede, with Ruger, stayed right behind her all the way to the ranch house.

As Allie drove up to her family home, she wondered what sleeping arrangements she'd have to make for her new bodyguard. She snorted. Her father would be thrilled to know she was bringing a man into his house. As her bodyguard, he couldn't sleep in the barn. Nor could he sleep in the foreman's quarters, as that was already taken. Unlike larger ranches, they didn't have a bunkhouse for ranch hands. It was up to her, her father, and Eddy, their foreman, to manage the herd. During cattle roundup days, they hired extra hands who slept in the barn, and Mrs. Edwards cooked for them.

No, Swede would have to stay in her brother's old bedroom. A tingle rippled down her spine at the thought of the big SEAL sleeping in the room next to her. But then, he was a bodyguard. What good was a bodyguard if he wasn't close to the body he was guarding?

She parked the truck beside the old house with its wide porches. Yeah, the paint was peeling and the steps needed repair, but the place was her home. At least, for the next week. Allie's heart squeezed in her chest. It wasn't as big and fancy as the mansion at the Double Diamond, but it had a helluva view of the Crazy Mountains, and it had been the house where she'd lived for the past twenty-seven years.

Allie supposed she'd get used to living on the Double Diamond. She'd be with Damien, when he was home from his trips. She'd have Miles, the butler, and Barbara, the cook, to talk to in the big house. She'd spend most of her time outside, tending horses and the cattle she hoped to bring onto the three-thousand-acre ranch.

She opened the door to her truck, pushing aside thoughts of her future home. First things first. Her father couldn't know Swede was her bodyguard. He'd flip if he knew Damien was having trouble. Her father would find out soon enough when word got around about the explosion and fire that consumed the stable at the Double Diamond.

Swede parked beside her, got out and rounded the front of his truck with Ruger.

"I think I can get a room in the house for you, but my father isn't keen on dogs inside."

He glanced at the porch. "Which room is yours? I can toss a sleeping bag outside your window."

"Seriously?" Allie shook her head. "I can't ask you to do that. I'll see what I can do to bend my father's rule."

"I'm not here to cause you more problems. I'm here to keep you safe. And I've slept in worse places than on a porch."

As a SEAL, he probably had. Still... "You can have Hank's old room. Grab your stuff, you can stow it inside." Allie started up the steps. When she realized Swede wasn't following, she turned back to him. "You and Ruger can have Hank's old room. There. Are you satisfied?"

Swede walked around to the side of his truck, grabbed a duffle bag and an old blanket and followed her into the house.

"Georgia?" Allie called out.

A gray-haired woman wearing jeans and a short-sleeved plaid shirt stepped into the hallway. "Allie, I'm glad you're here. I heard there was a fire out at the Double Diamond, and I was worried you might be there." She studied Allie before hurrying forward and hugging her. "Oh, dear. You were, weren't you? You're all covered in soot and smell like smoke. I'm glad you're okay. What a terrible thing."

Allie almost laughed. News traveled fast in small communities. She should have known it had already made it home. "Do Dad and Eddy know?"

"Not yet. They've been out repairing fences all day. I haven't seen them since breakfast."

Good. She'd get Swede installed before they got back. "Georgia, this is Swede Svenson, a friend of mine from college, who came early for the wedding. He was going to stay in Eagle Rock, but I told him we had room here for him and his dog."

Georgia smiled at Swede and held out her hand. "Nice to meet you. There are fresh sheets on the bed in Hank's old room." Her smile wrinkled into a bit of a frown. "As for the dog, well, you'll have to take it up with Mr. Patterson. He doesn't like animals in the house."

Allie nodded. "I'll take care of it. Could you show him to the room so he can toss his bag? I need to ride out and check on that sick heifer."

"I'm coming with you," Swede insisted.

Allie sighed. "Fine. I'll wait." Again, she didn't want everyone to know Damien had hired a bodyguard. In order to keep that little bit of information on the down-low, she had to play the hostess to her "friend."

This bodyguard business was going to be a big pain in the ass. And having a hunky SEAL following her around might be more difficult than she ever imagined.

CHAPTER 3

Swede followed Georgia up the stairs and across a landing to the first door on the right.

"You can use this room. The one next to it is Allie's, and at the end of the hall is Mr. Patterson's." She opened the door and stepped aside. "The bathroom is across the hall. If you need anything, let me know. Dinner is at 6:30. Mr. Patterson doesn't like folks being late." She smiled. "Where was it you met Allie, again?"

"In college," he said.

"At Montana State University?" she queried.

He swallowed hard. "Yes, ma'am."

"How did you like Missoula? I have a sister who lives there."

He shrugged. "It's okay," he said, hating that he was lying to a very nice woman. But, Allie had started the lie and he wouldn't be the one to spill the beans.

"Uh-huh." Georgia's eyes narrowed. "And what was your degree?"

"Engineering," he replied. At least this was the truth.

Working on his degree online and in a classroom the semesters he was Stateside, he'd earned a degree in engineering. He dropped his bag on the floor and turned to leave the room, only to find Georgia standing in the doorway with her arms folded over her chest.

"How long have you known Allie?" An eyebrow cocked high.

"Five, maybe six…If you don't mind, she's waiting for me." He started toward the woman.

She didn't budge for a moment and then snorted. "Uh-huh." Georgia stepped out of the way. "Remember, supper's on the table at 6:30."

He hurried past her and down the stairs. Ruger fell in step beside him as he pushed through the door onto the porch where he found Allie.

"Is there a reason you lied to Georgia about who I am?" he asked, his voice terse, anger simmering low in his belly.

Allie glanced at the house where Georgia stood in the window of the kitchen, watching them. "I didn't want them to worry about me."

"Well, you need to tell me more about yourself before you commit me to being an old school chum. In what city is Montana State University?"

"Bozeman."

Damn. "Not Missoula?"

"No. That's University of Montana."

He winced. "You'll have to do some damage control with Georgia. She's on to me." He left it at that and walked down the steps.

"I'll square up with her before dinner."

"Which is at 6:30 sharp. She told me twice. I take it that you don't want to be late."

Allie caught up with him and fell in step. "Welcome to the Bear Creek Ranch. My father likes things the way he likes things."

"And he likes the man you've chosen to marry?"

Allie's steps faltered for a moment. "That's none of your business."

"While I'm your bodyguard, everything about you is my business."

"The hell it is." Allie walked faster. She reached the barn first, and turned to face him. "Remember, it wasn't my idea to hire you. If I had my way, I'd have you sent back to the White Oak with Hank, looking for some rich celebrity to follow around like a lap dog." She shot a glance at the animal beside him. "No offense, Ruger."

She spun toward the door and reached for the handle.

Swede slammed his palm onto the wood, keeping the door from budging. "Look, princess, as long as I'm being paid to protect you, I'm following you around like a lap dog. Only, this lap dog bites. So don't push me."

She turned in the small amount of space between the barn door and his chest and stared up into his eyes. "I'm not a princess, and if you call me that again, I'll show you just how not a princess I can be. Now, move your arm." Her green eyes flashed and color rose in her cheeks.

God, she was beautiful and fearless. Swede had scared newbie SEALs with his full-on glare. Not this ranch woman with fire in her eyes and bright auburn hair. He held his ground for another second, his pulse pounding and his breath mingling with hers, fighting that sudden desire to kiss her.

Her eyes widened and she licked her lips.

As though she could read his mind.

As soon as the thought struck, he dropped his arm and moved away.

Allie lifted her chin, turned and ducked into the barn.

Swede followed at a slower pace, wondering what the hell was wrong with him? Bodyguards weren't supposed to kiss their clients. Especially one who'd told him multiple times she didn't want him around. He found her in the tack room, a blanket and bridle over one shoulder as she hefted a saddle from a wooden stand.

"Here, let me," Swede said, because his mother had raised a gentleman, and gentlemen lifted heavy objects for ladies.

He reached for the saddle.

But, she jerked away. "You'll need to get your own."

He glanced around the room at the seven saddles resting on stands. "Which would you suggest?"

Her lips twitched, and she tilted her head to get a look at his backside. "One big enough for your butt."

His groin tightened at her playful look. Immediately, he turned away before he started thinking about her as anything other than the person he was assigned to protect, who happened to be engaged to the man who'd hired him. At first glance, the saddles all looked pretty much the same. Upon closer inspection, he selected a dark brown one he hoped would fit, grabbed a blanket from a stack and hurried out of the tack room.

Allie had her horse tethered outside a stall. She'd already placed the blanket and saddle on the horse and was reaching beneath the horse's belly for the girth.

Swede knew what these were because, as a kid, he'd dreamed of learning to ride and studied what he could find in his grade school library. He watched carefully as she looped a long leather strap through the metal ring on the girth, pulled it tight, and then looped it again. When she'd used most of the strap, she tied the remainder in a single knot. Then she let the stirrup down.

"Is there a particular horse you want me to ride?" he asked.

She gave him an assessing glance. "Little Joe. Last stall on the left. You get the horse and I'll get his bridle."

Swede walked to the last stall on the left and opened the gate. The horse nudged his way through and would have taken off, but Swede slipped his hand through the animal's halter before he'd gone two steps and brought him under control. He spoke to the horse like he'd done with the spooked one at the Double Diamond. Within seconds, he was able to walk him to the spot next to Allie's horse where a lead rope was tied to a metal loop. He snapped the lead on the halter and quickly laid the blanket and saddle in place. Then he reached beneath the horse and pulled the girth up, looping the leather through the ring, like he'd seen her do.

"Make sure you get it tight. Little Joe likes to blow

out his belly while you're saddling him. And you'll need to adjust the stirrups to fit your longer legs."

Following her advice, he tightened the girth and adjusted the stirrups, while Allie slipped the bridle into the horse's mouth.

Once they were out of the barn, Allie led her horse to a gate, opened it and waited for Swede to walk his horse through. She followed and closed the gate behind them.

Then she swung up into the saddle from the left side of the horse. As he'd told her, he was very observant. He mimicked every one of her moves until he found himself up in the saddle. Then the horse danced sideways, whinnied and took off running as fast as the goddamn wind. Where were the damned brakes?

Swede held onto the reins and the saddle horn and sent a desperate prayer to the heavens. He'd almost rather be shot at by a dozen Taliban than be at the mercy of a crazed horse. Over the thunder of his horse's hooves and blood pounding in his ears, he heard a shout.

"Whoa!" Allie, atop her mare, raced up beside him, leaned dangerously toward Swede, grabbed the rein closest to her and pulled back. "Whoa!"

Both horses slowed until they came to a halt. Allie handed back the rein and shook her head. "You really haven't ridden a horse before, have you?"

His heart still pounding, he shook his head. "Never." He wiped the sweat off his brow and breathed. "But I learn quickly."

"Tap the flanks with your heels, gently, to make him

go. Pull back on the reins to make him stop." She demonstrated as she spoke. "If pulling back on the reins doesn't do the trick, the horse might have the bit between his teeth. Then you pull back on one side only and make him turn in a circle until he stops."

Swede nodded. "Got it."

"Now, I really need to check on that heifer." She tapped her heels against her horse's flanks, and the animal lurched forward.

Swede did the same.

Little Joe leaped after the other horse.

Swede slipped backward in the saddle, but he righted himself and rode after Allie. Several times, he slowed the horse by pulling back on the reins. The animal didn't like being left behind, but he slowed. Feeling a little more confident, he settled into the rhythm of the horse's gallop. Thankfully, Little Joe was perfectly happy following Allie, giving Swede the opportunity to relax and look around.

The Crazy Mountains were undeniably beautiful, with towering trees and jagged peaks capped with remnants of winter snow clinging to the higher elevations.

Allie led him through a narrow valley, across a stream, up and over a ridge, and then stopped near a copse of trees overlooking a grassy valley.

Swede rode up next to her, pulling back on the reins.

She nodded toward several cows grazing in the field beyond. "She seems to be doing better today. At least she's up and eating."

They all looked pretty healthy to Swede. "Which one is she?"

"The brown and white Hereford at the edge of the others." Allie pointed to one that was a bit smaller and not as filled out. "She's okay, for now. I'll check on her tomorrow."

Allie glanced across at Swede. "How are you?"

"Fine." He shifted in the saddle, knowing he'd be sore later. But he'd never admit it to her.

"Trotting is the hardest gait on the butt. If you stand up in your stirrups every other bump, you won't be beaten to death. It's called posting. Like this." She tapped her horse's flanks and the animal took off at a trot. Allie rose and fell in rhythm with the horse's steps.

Swede nudged his mount and the horse broke into a trot. He tried what Allie demonstrated, but ended up standing in the stirrups the entire time, not quite getting the rhythm.

"When you get it right, it stops hurting," she said. "Then the movement becomes natural."

"How long have you been riding?" he asked.

"Since I was big enough to sit up on my own, so my father says. I think I was about four years old when my father put me on a horse by myself." Squinting in the sun, Allie turned back in the direction from which they'd come. "It's getting close to dinner time. We'd better get back."

They crossed the ridge and eased down the other side into the narrow valley with a stream winding through. Everything seemed so peaceful and different than the hills of Afghanistan, filled with Taliban fighters waiting to blow off his head.

Just when Swede thought it couldn't get more placid, the roar of a small engine echoed off the hillsides.

Swede looked around for the source, but the echoes made it hard to determine. Then a four-wheeled all-terrain vehicle erupted out of the tree line and raced straight for Allie.

Swede urged his horse forward, creating a barrier between the oncoming vehicle and the woman he was supposed to protect. He reached beneath his jacket and pulled out the nine millimeter Glock he'd purchased before he'd left the military and aimed for the man on the ATV. He'd give him five more seconds to turn away.

Five. Four. Three. Two. One.

Just as Swede pulled the trigger, he saw Allie's horse rear, throwing her from the saddle. Spooked by Allie's horse and the oncoming ATV, Little Joe bucked.

Swede's shot went wide of its target.

The sound was enough to make the rider swerve to the right and cross the stream, heading up into the hills.

Swede yanked the reins, turned the horse and trotted back to where Allie lay on the ground, her own horse long gone.

The woman lay perfectly still, her eyes wide open.

Swede started to dismount when Allie said, "Don't move."

"Why? Are you okay?"

"I will be, as long as you don't move a muscle and keep Little Joe from coming any closer."

Then he heard the telltale buzz of a rattlesnake's tail.

Wound into a tight coil, lying in the dirt near a rock, lay the biggest rattlesnake Swede had ever seen.

The slightest move on Allie's part could make the snake strike her in the face.

"Be very still," he advised.

"Duh. You think I don't know that?" she said, barely moving her lips and whispering softly so as not to disturb the creature.

"I'll slide down off the horse."

"Any movement could make him strike. I'd rather you didn't."

"What do you want me to do?"

"I don't know. Feed him a mouse. Wait until he leaves. Shoot him. Something." Her voice was soft and calm for having a huge snake in her face.

Little Joe appeared unfazed by the snake lying nearby. He stood still, waiting for Swede's next command.

Still holding the nine-millimeter in his hand, he raised it and aimed down the barrel at the snake.

"What are you doing?" Allie said, through gritted teeth.

"Close your eyes," he said.

"Oh, no, you are not…" She squeezed her eyes shut and tensed.

Swede pulled the trigger. The bullet hit the snake in the head, flipping it over in the dust.

Little Joe danced to the side, but didn't bolt.

Allie rolled away and jumped to her feet. "Are you crazy?"

Swede holstered his weapon and dropped down out

of the saddle. Holding onto the reins, he approached Allie and gripped her arm. "Are you okay?"

"I'm fine, despite the fact you could have killed me."

"But, I didn't." He looked into her eyes, checking her pupils. "Did you bang your head against the ground?"

Allie rubbed her bottom. "No, I hurt my pride more than anything else. I haven't been thrown from a horse in years." She glanced at the snake lying still on the ground. "I guess Major had a good reason to spook." Brushing the dust off her jeans, she looked out across the stream and up the hill on the other side. "Who the hell was on the ATV?"

"I was hoping you could tell me."

"It wasn't one of our vehicles."

"He was aiming for you. And I was aiming for him when your horse reared."

Allie frowned. "I guess I should thank you."

"No need. I was just doing my job."

"Okay, so you aren't a great horseman, but you did shoot the snake without killing me." She drew in a deep breath and let it out. "Thanks."

"You're welcome."

"Now, we'd better get back to the house before we're late for dinner."

Allie balanced her hands on her hips. "Since my horse is halfway back to the barn by now, we'll have to ride double. I'll drive. But you'll need to mount first."

Swede swung up into the saddle, removed his foot from the stirrup and reached for her hand.

Allie placed her toe where his had been, and Swede

pulled her up in front of him. For a moment, she was sitting in his lap. Her auburn hair drifted into his face.

Inhaling a hint of strawberry and the fresh, outdoor scent clinging to her, he closed his eyes and tried not to think of her sitting where she was, or that his groin was reacting naturally and hardening.

His eyes snapped open and he pushed backward, over the lip of the saddle and sat on Little Joe's rump.

He tried holding onto the saddle, but as soon as Allie nudged Little Joe's flanks, the animal leaped forward.

Swede slipped backward and almost fell off the horse. He wrapped his arms around Allie's waist and held tight all the way back to the barn.

When they arrived in the barnyard, Swede slipped off the back of the horse and landed on his feet.

Allie swung her leg over Little Joe's back, and dropped to the ground. "You didn't do badly for your first ride on a horse."

The insides of his thighs ached, but it was a good ache. After months in a hospital and physical therapy, getting out into the open, clean air of Montana felt good.

Now, if he could keep Allie safe from whoever just tried to run her over, he'd feel even better.

ALLIE HURRIED into the house to get cleaned up and dressed for dinner. Her father believed in punctuality. As children, if they weren't at the table on time, they didn't eat. Of course, when their mother was alive, she'd sneak a snack into their rooms, later. After she'd passed away, Georgia continued the tradition.

When Allie got married and had her own house, she wouldn't be as strict. She might even have dinner at different hours other than 6:30pm every single day. She ran up the stairs, calling out, "I have the shower first."

A low chuckle sounded at the bottom of the stairs, warming her from the inside.

When she made it to the top, she glanced over the banister.

Swede stood at the base of the staircase, his hand resting on the banister, staring up at her, his mouth tipped upward in a smile.

Allie stumbled, recovered and ran for her bedroom, her cheeks burning.

The man had no right to be so very handsome when he smiled. And how different from Damien. Not that Damien wasn't handsome. He was. Like a prince. Not like a rugged navy SEAL with boundless muscles and a wicked grin.

Grabbing fresh jeans and a soft green pullover blouse, she entered the bathroom, locked the door and ducked under the shower's cool spray. By the time she'd rinsed off the dirt, smoke and sweat from her body and shampooed her hair, she had her head on straight. Without wasting any time, she was out of the shower, dried and had combed the tangles out of her long hair, thinking for the hundredth time she needed to cut it short. But she couldn't bring herself to do more than trim it. Every time she looked into the mirror, she saw her mother, the parent who'd given her the auburn hair and green eyes her father had fallen in love with.

Dressed and brushed, she ducked back into her room, pulled on socks and a pair of clean boots and ran down the stairs to see if Georgia needed help getting the food on the table. She didn't run into Swede, figuring he was in his room unpacking.

Georgia stood at the stove, stirring gravy in a pot. "You can take the roast out to the table."

Allie did, and returned to the kitchen. "Mmm. That smells good."

Having been the housekeeper since before Allie's mother passed, Georgia was like a surrogate mother. She lifted the pot off the stove and poured the gravy into a bowl. "Before your father comes down, you want to tell me why you lied to me, your father and Eddy?"

With a spoonful of gravy halfway to her mouth, Allie grimaced. "I'm sorry I lied."

"I wasn't born yesterday." Georgia planted a fist on her hip. "Swede didn't go to school with you, did he?"

Allie had hated lying to Georgia. It gnawed at her belly, making her feel nauseated. "No. I met him this morning, at Hank's."

"So, why did you invite a complete stranger to stay in the house?"

"He's a buddy of Hank's from his navy SEAL team. Damien hired him to be my bodyguard until the wedding."

"Bodyguard?" Georgia's brows furrowed. "Does this have anything to do with the fire at his place?"

Allie nodded. "And my cut brake lines. Someone is

mad at Damien and is taking it out on him. Damien thinks he might be targeting me, as well."

"And what do you think?"

She hated to admit it, but… "I think he's right. When I went out to check on the sick heifer, I was almost run over by someone on an ATV. Swede kept that from happening." Allie didn't add that Swede had shot a snake next to her head as well. No use worrying Georgia any more than she already was, based on her deepening frown.

The older woman took her hands. "What has that fiancé gotten you into?"

"I don't know, but he's working on it." Or so she assumed. Why else would he take off before the sheriff and firefighters arrived at his place to put out a fire?

Georgia held her at arm's length. "You know you can back out of the wedding any time between now and the actual ceremony."

Allie smiled at her. "I'm okay. The wedding is going on as planned. Just a few more days, and I'll be a married woman with a house of my own to run."

"You hate household chores."

"Yeah, but I'll have people to do them for me. The way I like them done." Allie pulled Georgia into a quick hug. "Not that you haven't done a terrific job taking care of us all these years. Have I ever said thank you?"

"Yes, dear. You have." Georgia hugged her tight. "We're going to miss you around here."

"I'll only be a couple of miles away."

"Maybe so, but it will seem like a long way to me. I'll be outnumbered by the men."

Allie laughed. "I'm sure you'll keep them in line."

"Are you two going to stand around gabbing or come eat?" Eddy, the ranch foreman and Georgia's husband, entered the kitchen, sniffed and rubbed his belly. "Something smells good."

Georgia stepped back, dabbing her eyes with the hem of her apron. "Did you wash up?" she said, her voice brisk as she turned toward the stove and retrieved a pan full of corn.

"Yes, I did." Eddy sneaked up behind her, pulled her back against his front and nuzzled her neck. "You smell good enough to eat."

Georgia smacked his hands playfully and giggled. "Oh, go on with yourself."

"Not until I get me some sugar."

She set the pan of corn on the stove, turned in his arm and kissed him. "Now, go set the table."

Eddy grinned and smacked her bottom.

"Dang it, Eddy!" Georgia waved a wooden spoon at him. "I'm not above spanking you with this."

"Promises, promises." He fished silverware from a drawer and laid them on the table, whistling as he did.

Allie was used to their playful antics. The childless couple had always been loving and unabashed at showing it in front of others.

"It's 6:30, are we eating or not?" Allie's father entered the big country kitchen, pulled back the chair at the head of the table and sat.

Allie carried the bowl of corn while Georgia brought a basket full of fresh-baked rolls.

"It's 6:25, not 6:30. Remember, Daddy? You always

set your watch five minutes ahead." Allie shot a glance toward the doorway, wondering what was keeping Swede.

Just as she looked that way, he entered the room.

"Pardon me if I kept you waiting."

Allie's father frowned at Swede. "Who the hell are you? And what are you doing in my house?"

For the next hour, Eddy and Mr. Patterson grilled Swede about everything from letting Ruger in the house, to what he knew about horses and cattle, to the types of weapons his team used on special operations.

With admirable patience, Swede answered every question. Eddy and Allie's father seemed satisfied with the man's answers, even when he owned up to knowing nothing about livestock. When the meal was over, he got up like the inquisition hadn't fazed him a bit.

Allie, on the other hand, felt like she'd been run through the wringer. And the worst part was, she'd seen another side of Swede she hadn't wanted to see. A proud military man who'd served his country and now had to figure out how to fit into a life without the SEALs.

He even helped clean the table and wash dishes.

Damn it, if she wasn't careful, she might end up liking the exasperating man.

Tired from a long day, full of stress and trauma, she trudged up the stairs and brushed her teeth. When she exited the bathroom, she ran into Swede. He'd shed his shirt and boots and wore only jeans.

The moisture in Allie's mouth dried as she stared at his broad, muscular chest.

"Are you okay?" Swede asked.

Dragging her eyes upward, she couldn't make her gaze quite reach his eyes, stopping on his full, sexy lips. "I'm fine," she managed to squeak out. Then she dove into her room and slammed the door behind her.

This just would not do. The man was far too attractive to be a bodyguard.

Allie stripped, pulled on an old MSU T-shirt from her college days and crawled into bed, reminding herself that her wedding was only a few days away. Closing her eyes, she tried to picture Damien in a tuxedo, standing at the altar. But the face she saw wasn't Damien's, it was Swede's.

Double damn.

CHAPTER 4

Swede woke early the next morning after a crappy night's sleep. Thankfully, he hadn't had any of the dreams that had plagued him since he'd left the service. He dressed in sweats, a T-shirt, and tennis shoes and took Ruger outside. Staying within sight of the house, he performed his morning calisthenics—pushups, sit-ups, leg-lifts and more. It paid to stay in shape. Even while he'd been recovering from his wounds in the hospital, he'd done everything he could.

Today, his hand and thighs ached from riding the day before. He stretched his legs and ran to the end of the driveway and back several times before he finally reentered the house.

The smell of bacon lured him to the kitchen where Georgia cooked breakfast. "This will be ready by the time you're out of the shower," she promised.

"Thanks," Swede said. "It smells good." He took the stairs two at a time, grabbed a pair of clean jeans, and hit the shower.

When he was done, he stepped out of the tub, toweled dry, and tossed the towel to the floor. He was reaching for his jeans when the door swung open. Swede straightened as Allie started in.

When she saw him standing there naked, she widened her eyes and her mouth dropped open. For a long moment she stared. Then her cheeks turned a brilliant red, and she backed out of the doorway. "Pardon me." She pulled the door shut. Through the panel, she said, "Oh, my God."

Swede laughed out loud, and then tried to pull on his jeans over a rock-hard erection. He waited a minute, thinking of everything that could douse his desire, from babies to grandmothers. Nothing seemed to work when the image of Allie's face kept coming to mind. Carefully tucking himself in, he pulled his T-shirt over his head and let it hang down over the ridge of his fly.

He found Allie downstairs in the kitchen with Georgia. Allie didn't look him in the eye, her cheeks still a pretty shade of pink. "My father and Eddy are out cutting hay, so I'm working the barn today. Have you ever mucked a stall?" Finally, she glanced his way.

Swede shook his head, feeling a little inadequate for the job of ranch hand. "No, but I'm game." *As long as I'm near you.*

"I know the task is not part of your job description, so don't feel like you have to."

Swede shot a glance toward Georgia.

The older woman nodded. "I know. I'm just glad someone is looking out for our girl." She held up a coffee pot. "Coffee?"

"Please," Swede said.

"I still think you should tell Eddy and your father what's going on." Georgia gave Allie a stern look as she poured the steaming brew into two mugs and carried them to the table. "They could be looking out for you, too."

"Absolutely not," Allie said. "My father would do his best to call off the wedding. I've spent too much money on everything, and the event is only a few days away. I pick up my dress tomorrow, and everything is downhill from there."

Georgia raised her brows. "Downhill?"

Allie rolled her eyes and took one of the plates of food from the kitchen counter. "You know what I mean."

"All the preparations are nothing but money and time," Georgia said.

Swede stood quietly, watching the interaction between the two women.

Apparently, Georgia didn't want Allie to marry Damien. Swede wondered why.

Allie ignored Georgia's comment and focused on Swede, her color back to normal, her jaw set in a tight line. "The sooner we get done cleaning the stalls, the sooner we can exercise the horses. After that, we can call it a day. I have to tell you, though, it'll be a long, hard day."

"I'm up for it."

Allie handed him a plate full of eggs, bacon and biscuits. "Eat up."

After breakfast, Swede followed Allie out to the barn. She handed him a pitchfork and pointed to a wheelbarrow. "Tie the horse up outside the stall and start shoveling."

Swede worked through the morning, glad for the physical labor that flexed his muscles and the rich, earthy smell of manure. It beat the scent of diesel smoke and gun powder any day.

Ruger stood guard outside the barn, lying in a patch of sun, watching as Swede and Allie wheeled barrels full of soiled straw out to a pile behind the barn. By noon, they had all the stalls cleaned, the horses brushed, and the chickens and pigs fed.

Georgia had sandwiches waiting when they came inside. Then they were right back out in the sunshine to exercise the horses.

Allie lunged a couple of mares in the corral and then had Swede take over. She watched him, giving tips on how to handle the animal and the lunging rope.

Swede was glad the horse knew what to do. The work wasn't hard. In fact, it had a certain rhythm that bred a sense of calm.

Georgia shouted from the house that Allie had a call from the caterer.

"This horse is about done. You can turn her out into the pasture and then bring out another horse. Just stay clear of Diablo, the black gelding in the last stall. He's a work in progress, and he hasn't quite got the hang of anything."

"Who rides him?"

"No one, yet. Like I said, he's a work in progress. In other words, he's too wild to handle easily." Allie waved at Georgia. "I have to go. No need to follow me. You can keep an eye on the house from the corral, and I really doubt anyone will attack me there."

Swede nodded. She was right. He had a good view of the house and the road leading to it from the corral.

As Allie hurried inside, Swede couldn't help but follow her progress. He told himself it was part of his job, but the truth was the way her hips swayed in her jeans was completely mesmerizing.

The horse he held on a lead tossed her head, pulling Swede back to the task at hand. He walked her through the gate into the pasture and unhooked the lead.

She pranced away and joined the other horses already grazing.

Glancing back at the house and drive, Swede returned to the barn and walked along the stalls, most of which were empty now. One mare stood placidly, watching him as he passed her and walked down the line of stalls to the end.

When they'd been cleaning, Allie had led Diablo in and out. She'd also taken charge of brushing him.

As Swede neared, the animal stuck his head over the top of the gate and nickered.

"So, you're a real ball-buster, are you?" Swede spoke softly and reached out a hand to rub the gelding's nose.

Diablo nuzzled his hand.

"Do you want out?"

The horse pawed at the dirt and tossed his head as if saying *yes*.

"How hard can it be to walk you around a corral?" Swede snapped the lead onto Diablo's halter and opened the stall.

As soon as the latch was free, Diablo hit the door, knocking Swede backward. He staggered and held on tightly to the lunging rope, while being dragged out of the barn by the bolting horse.

When Swede got his feet under himself, he dug his heels into the dirt and slowed the horse.

Diablo reared and jerked the lead, but Swede held steady and started talking. Soon, the horse stopped fighting and settled on all fours.

Ruger stepped up beside Swede as if to show his support.

Diablo lowered his nose to the dog, and the four-legged creatures sniffed each other.

"You're not so bad, just a little spirited." He raised his hand slowly to stroke the horse's nose. "See? I'm not here to hurt you." The gelding tossed his head as if to disagree. "Ruger wouldn't be beside me now if I hurt him. He trusts me because he gave me a chance. I gave him one, too." Swede continued to talk to the horse as he led him into the corral and closed the gate behind him. Still holding the lead close to Diablo's halter, Swede walked the horse around the outer circle. He kept a running monologue going, to calm the animal.

Ruger stood outside the pen. Every time they passed the dog, the horse looked his way.

After walking around the pen for five minutes, getting the gelding used to the environment, Swede picked up the pace and settled into a slow and steady jog.

Diablo matched his pace and trotted alongside Swede. Slowly, Swede lengthened the lead, still running with the horse, but putting more distance between them. Whenever Diablo slowed, Swede clicked his tongue and jogged faster, encouraging the horse to keep moving. When the lead was long enough and Swede was standing in the middle of the corral, the horse slowed. Swede clicked his tongue, and Diablo broke into a trot.

After several more circles around the corral, Swede let Diablo come to a stop. He pulled in the lead until he could rub the horse's nose. "You're a good boy," Swede soothed, running his hand across the horse's nose and up to scratch his ears. Then he swept his hand along the gelding's neck to his back.

Diablo pawed the earth and whinnied, swaying on his hooves.

Swede scratched the animal's back, side and around to his belly. He moved his hands up to the horse's back again and laid his arms over the top, scratching the other side, while leaning his weight on the animal.

Diablo tossed his head, but didn't move away.

Holding onto the lead rope, Swede grabbed hold of a handful of Diablo's mane and swung his leg over the top of the horse. He leaned forward and wrapped his arms around Diablo's neck, speaking to him the entire time, fully expecting to be thrown, but hoping it wouldn't happen.

Diablo backed up and then moved forward, whinnying.

Ruger whined behind the rails of the corral, capturing the gelding's attention.

Diablo trotted to where the dog stood and lowered his head to sniff.

Swede molded his body to the horse, still rubbing his neck and speaking softly.

Seeing Diablo and Ruger greeting each other with their noses, Swede slipped off the horse's back and patted his neck. "See? It's not as bad as you think."

When Swede straightened, he noticed he had an audience.

"Damnedest thing I've ever seen." Eddy leaned against a corral panel, his arms resting on the top rail.

"That horse doesn't like anyone," Lloyd Patterson said, scratching his head.

"And to beat it all, Swede never rode a horse until yesterday." Allie joined the two men at the fence, a smile tilting the corners of her lips. "You're lucky he didn't take you for a ride."

Swede rubbed Diablo's neck. "I think he just needed a friend." He tipped his head toward Ruger. Diablo and Ruger sniffed at each other. Ruger's tail thumped the ground.

"The man we bought him from said he had another gelding raised with Diablo," Mr. Patterson said.

"You might want to check and see if he still has him," Allie said. "Seems Diablo needs a friend."

"Why? Swede's dog seems to be doing the job," Eddy said.

"And why feed another horse?" her father added. "It's cheaper to feed a dog."

Allie's smile slipped. "Swede and Ruger are only here until after the wedding." She opened the gate. "I think we have one more horse to exercise. Dad, is there anything else you want done before we call it a day?"

"Not a thing. We could use a little help hauling the first cutting of hay the day after tomorrow. It should be dry enough, and we need to get it in before the rain."

As he walked Diablo though the gate, Swede glanced at the bright blue Montana sky. "Is a rainstorm expected?"

Lloyd flexed his shoulder. "I can feel it in my bursitis. If not tomorrow, then the next day. By the end of the week for certain."

"Great. It'll probably rain on my wedding day," Allie muttered

"You can always put it off," her father said. "No need to rush into marriage."

"I'm getting married on Saturday," Allie said, her tone flat but firm.

Mr. Patterson faced his daughter. "If you're going to get married, why Reynolds?"

"Because he asked me, and I said yes."

Lloyd nodded toward Swede. "Why not marry a real man—like a war hero?"

"Dad!" Allie's face burned a bright red. "You don't even know Swede. Besides, who said he wanted to get married in the first place?" She threw her hands in the air. "What did Mom see in you? All I'm getting is a grumpy old man who is stubborn and insensitive."

Her father's face grew rigid, his eyes a stormy gray. "I loved your mother and would have done anything for her. And she loved me, too." He lifted his chin. "Can you say that about Reynolds?"

Swede could feel the tension between father and daughter, as palpable as electricity singeing the air.

"I'm getting married on Saturday. You can come to the wedding and wish me well–or not. But I don't want to hear another negative word about Damien." She stomped into the barn, leaving the men outside, scratching their heads.

"Women," Lloyd grumbled. "Can't live with them… and can't live without them."

"Guess you'll find out in a few days." Eddy pounded Lloyd's back and turned to Swede. "Good job with Diablo. You might have a knack for ranching after all, city boy."

Swede nodded. "Thanks."

Inside the barn, Allie had grabbed a lunging rope, snapped it onto the last mare needing exercise, and led her past Swede and Diablo. "Don't say a word."

Swede grinned. "I wasn't going to."

"My father raised me, but he doesn't know anything about me, or how I feel."

"Maybe he just wants you to be happy."

Allie raised her hand. "I said, don't say a word." She walked out, leading the mare, her lips pressed into a thin line.

Swede chuckled.

"No laughing, either," Allie's voice sounded from just outside the barn door.

Swede fed Diablo and brushed his coat. Ruger lay nearby. It seemed the dog's mere presence had the same calming effect on the horse as it did on Swede. *Go figure.* All Swede knew was that if not for Ruger, he'd still be suffering the effects of his nightmares and breaking out in cold sweats over loud noises. Yeah, he'd pulled Ruger off death row at the pound, but Ruger had pulled Swede out of a life of misery, suffering from PTSD.

Now, if only the dog could perform miracles and dampen the increasing urge Swede felt to kiss the feisty Miss Patterson.

AFTER THE LAST horse had been exercised and all the animals fed, Allie trudged back to the house and sat on the steps to remove her boots. "Thanks for the help."

Swede dropped down beside her and pulled off his boots, as well. He smelled of sweat, hay and manure. Not the kind of smell Allie associated with Damien. Her fiancé never seemed to sweat. Even when they rode horses together, he came back smelling like his aftershave, not the leather and dusty scent of being in the great outdoors.

Allie should prefer the clean scent of aftershave, but leather and dust, to her, was more manly and satisfying.

She drew in a deep breath, trying not to be too obvious. Yeah, Swede smelled like how Allie considered a man should. But then, she wasn't marrying Damien because of his scent.

Then why was she marrying him?

Because he'd asked, and she didn't want to marry any of the local men she'd grown up with. They were too much like brothers, who didn't even consider going anywhere else but Montana or the nearest stock show or rodeo. Some didn't even want to cross the border into Canada, preferring to remain on their ranches where they'd been born, lived all their lives and where they'd die.

"Do you like to travel?" Allie blurted out without thinking.

Swede shrugged. "I do. But some day I hope to have a place to call home. Traveling is all well and good, but roots help you appreciate where you're going. You're lucky you have a place to call home."

"You don't?" Allie wanted to travel, but like Swede said, she liked to have a home base to come back to.

"Not since my folks died. The closest I came were the apartments I rented near the bases where I was stationed. I rarely saw the insides of those places, having deployed often."

"I'm sorry." She pulled off the second boot and set it beside the first. "Where did your parents live?"

"In Minneapolis, Minnesota."

She smiled softly. "So you have a vague idea of what cold winters are like."

"I do. Not as cold as it gets in Montana, but I know my way around snow."

She gave him an assessing glance. "Ever play hockey?"

Swede nodded. "That's how I got this scar." He pointed to the one on his chin."

"And I thought you'd gotten that working as a SEAL."

He shook his head, his glance shifting to his hand, which he lifted to the scar that ran along the side of his face, from his hairline to his cheekbone. "I got this one in Kandahar Province, on my last mission in Afghanistan."

Allie took his hand in hers and studied the jagged scars between his thumb and forefinger. "And these?"

"Syria."

"Does it still hurt?" she traced the jagged scars with the tip of her finger.

He clenched his hand, only closing it halfway. "A little. I haven't gotten full range of motion yet, but don't worry. I can fire a weapon accurately with either hand."

Her eyes widened and she stared into his. "Holy hell. It didn't even dawn on me that you shot that snake with your left hand. Are you even left-handed?"

Swede shook his head. "Not naturally, but I've learned to be since I joined the navy and became a SEAL. It was a challenge to learn to shoot with both hands. Now, I'm glad I did."

Allie felt warmth filter from his hand into hers and up her arm. She let go of him, grabbed her boots and stood. "You can have the shower first."

"You're not going back out?" he asked.

"No. I thought I'd feed Ruger for you, if you like." She bent to scratch the dog's ears. "He's proving to be useful around here."

Swede's lip quirked up in a half-smile. "He's smart and learns quickly."

Allie chuckled. "Like you?"

"I like to think I can do anything I set my mind to."

"I'll give you that. From what I've seen or read about SEAL training, anyone who can make it through to graduation has to have a lot of stamina and fortitude." She glanced toward the house. "You better get going. I'd like to wash the stink off me, too."

Swede grinned. "I never thought I'd say this, but horse manure smells pretty good on you." He winked and held the door open.

She twisted her lips into a crooked smile. "Thanks. I think."

"Ruger's food is in the mud room," Swede said. Then he turned to the dog. "Stay."

Ruger sat on the porch and whined softly.

"I'll be right back with food and water for you," Allie said, and followed Swede inside.

Swede set his dirty boots inside the mudroom door and headed for the stairs.

Allie set her boots on the floor and straightened, her gaze following the man up the stairs. He had a great butt that looked exceptional in jeans. And he didn't wear fancy, expensive jeans like Damien. Swede wore the kind most of the cowboys around Eagle Rock wore. Plain, serviceable and tough. Like the man. Well, he wasn't exactly plain.

His face wasn't classicly handsome like Damien's, with all his features completely symmetrical. Swede's nose must have been broken more than once and didn't sit exactly straight on his face. He had the scar on his chin, and the one on the side of his face, marring his otherwise rugged good looks. It was the breadth of his shoulders, the trimness of his waist, and the thickness of his thighs that made Allie's heartbeat flutter.

Damn! There she went again. Thinking about the SEAL, rather than dreaming about her future husband.

She picked up Ruger's water bowl, strode into the kitchen and filled it. When she came back out on the deck, the dog sat exactly where Swede had told him to stay. His tail thumped against the porch boards.

Allie set the water in front of Ruger and went back inside for his food. When she came out, she saw he'd lapped up every drop of the water. Then he wolfed down the food she put in front of him, and looked up at her expectantly.

"More?" Allie laughed and gave him more.

When he was finished, she let him into the house.

The telephone rang on the stand in the hallway. Allie answered. "Bear Creek Ranch."

"Allie, Hank here."

"Hey," she said, always glad to hear from her brother since he'd returned from the war in Afghanistan. "What's up?"

"Sadie and I are going out to the Blue Moose Tavern tonight for some drinks and dancing. We thought you and Swede might want to join us."

Allie frowned. Not *you and Damien*. But then, Damien was out of town, and Hank knew it from the fire. She sighed. "Sounds good." She arranged for the time and place to meet and then ended the call.

She'd almost said no. After a hard day's work, she wasn't sure she had the energy to drink and dance. But, it did break the monotony of ranch life. Allie sniffed. First, a shower.

Allie headed upstairs.

Ruger followed and plopped down in front of the bathroom door to wait for Swede. "Traitor. I fed you, he didn't."

The dog stared up at her through soulful blue eyes.

"Fine. Stay here. See if I care."

The door opened, and Swede stood there with a towel looped around his bare shoulders, his wet hair slicked back and wearing nothing but blue jeans, half buttoned up.

The air caught in Allie's lungs, and she fought to push some past her vocal cords. When she finally did, she said, "Fed your dog."

"Thank you. I'm sure Ruger appreciated that." Swede smiled with that melt-me-to-the-core twist of his lips. "Your turn."

Allie had to really focus to make sense of what he was saying. When she did, she nodded. "Great." Then she spun on her socks and ran for her bedroom, where she pressed her palms to her burning cheeks. "What is wrong with me?" she whispered. Then she remembered.

"Oh, Swede?"

The man leaned into the doorway. "Yes, darlin'?"

Don't do that!

She gulped to swallow past the constriction in her throat. "I'm going to meet Hank and Sadie at the Blue Moose Tavern for drinks after dinner."

"Sounds good. What's the dress code?"

"Dress code?" Allie laughed. "We're in Montana, not

the military." She laughed, shut her door and leaned against it. She never laughed like that with Damien.

Why was she suddenly comparing everyone to Damien?

Not everyone. Just Swede.

Damn.

CHAPTER 5

Swede dressed in clean jeans, a white, button-down shirt, and his best cowboy boots he'd purchased before moving west to work in Montana. He didn't know why he hadn't owned a pair before. They were comfortable and easy to get into.

He stood at the bottom of the stairs waiting for Allie to come down. They'd had dinner with Lloyd and the Edwards. After dinner, Allie excused herself to get dressed for their night out with her brother.

Swede didn't see anything wrong with the jeans and T-shirt she'd worn. And her hair, though wet from her shower, was neatly combed and smelled like strawberries. Nope. He didn't see anything wrong with that.

Ruger would remain out on the porch until they returned from the bar. No use keeping him up with loud music. Besides, they might not allow dogs inside.

Georgia stepped into the hallway, wiping her hands on her apron. "My, don't you look nice?"

"Thank you, ma'am," Swede said.

She untied the apron in the back and lifted the strap up over her head. "I was about to leave and go to our house. Is there anything you need before I call it a night?"

"No, ma'am," he answered.

Georgia glanced up the staircase. "There you are. You've kept this man waiting long enough." The older woman smiled. "I'm sure he'll agree it was worth it."

Swede followed Georgia's gaze, his eyes widening, a low whistle escaping from his lips. "Wow."

Allie wore a short white dress that caressed her body perfectly, the skirt brushing against the middle of her thighs with every step she took. She'd dried her hair and it lay in big, soft curls around her shoulders, framing her face. The makeup she'd applied naturally enhanced her cheeks and made her green eyes stand out.

"Wow," he repeated.

Her lips quirked. "You said that." She came down the steps in strappy sandals that drew attention to her toned and tanned calves.

Swede struggled to pull his jaw off the floor and act like a bodyguard, not a teenager on his first date. He couldn't help but look at her several times as if she weren't real, but a figment of his imagination. She was stunningly beautiful in a fresh, girl-next-door way.

"Well, I must say that dress is you." Georgia took her hands and smiled, her eyes misting. "Isn't it one you bought for your honeymoon to the Cayman Islands?"

Allie shrugged. "I felt like wearing it. After all, I'll be out in public with Sadie McClain. Not that I can compete with her. She's amazing."

"Sweetie, you don't have to compete," Georgia said. "You're beautiful in your own way."

"Thanks." Allie hugged Georgia and then turned toward Swede, her shoulders thrown back, making her breasts rise. "Ready?"

Swede was almost certain he wasn't ready to take Allie for a night on the town. Thankfully, it was only to Eagle Rock, a village with a population of maybe a thousand, counting all of the outlying ranch owners, ranch hands and hound dogs. Surely they'd roll up the sidewalks by 9:00.

"I'll drive." Swede hooked her elbow and guided her to his truck, opened the door and handed her up.

He couldn't get over the transformation from the sweaty, dirt-covered ranch girl to the sexy redheaded temptress. His gaze swung her direction several times on the drive into Eagle Rock.

At least two dozen trucks lined the parking lot and the street around the Blue Moose Tavern. The thumps of drums and a bass guitar could be heard all the way out into the street even before Swede opened his door.

"I see Hank's truck," Allie said. "He and Sadie must already be inside." She waited for Swede to get out and come around to open her door. He reached in to capture her around the waist and helped her to the ground. He held on a moment or two longer than he should have, but he couldn't get his fingers to loosen their hold on her body.

"Ready to go?" she asked.

Oh, hell no. "Yes."

From the outside, the bar didn't look like much.

Inside, it was a lot bigger than the exterior storefront indicated.

A three-man band played country-western music, and several couples were two-stepping their way around the dance floor.

"I see them." Allie grabbed his hand and led him, weaving between the tables, saying hello to almost everyone in the room. Several cowboys whistled when she walked by. One reached out to touch her leg, but a hard stare from Swede made him back off and turn his reach into a wave.

Hank and Sadie sat at a table facing the front entrance, with a broad-shouldered man seated in front of them with his back to the room.

Swede and Allie arrived at the table and the stranger turned and jumped to his feet, with a smile and a wince. "Swede. You son of a bitch. Good to see you." Bear, the Delta Force friend he'd made during rehab, pounded his back and hugged him so hard it hurt his ribs. The guy didn't know his own strength. The leg wound had done nothing to diminish his arm strength.

"And this must be your assignment." Bear winked. "Hi, Tate Parker. But call me Bear."

"Alyssa Patterson, but you can call me Allie." She shook his hand, but was pulled into a hug similar to the one Swede had endured.

Bear set her to arm's length and raked his gaze over her. "Allie, wearing a dress like that, you need to be on the dance floor. Care to dance with me?" He held out his arm. "I can't promise I won't step on your toes. The docs said I'd never dance again. But I fooled them. I never could dance, but what I lack in skill, I make up for in enthusiasm."

Allie laughed and followed Bear to the dance floor.

Swede stepped aside, wanting to punch his friend for taking off with his girl. Then he had to remind himself Allie wasn't his girl. In fact, she was Reynolds's girl, soon to be wife.

"What's wrong, Swede? You look like you swallowed a lemon." Hank nodded toward Bear. "I thought you would be happy to see your friend. He got in an hour ago and insisted on coming with us, even though he's been up since four this morning."

"Bear's a force to be reckoned with. I swear, he knows no limits to his physical abilities." Another glance Allie's way and Swede turned back to Hank. "I take it Bear will fit in with the team you're building?"

"Perfectly. I talked with him on the phone yesterday evening and had him on a plane first thing this morning."

"Great." Swede really was glad for the friend who'd been at his side through his own physical therapy and re-introduction into the civilian world. But did he have to hold Allie so close?

"I spoke with the fire chief. They found evidence of C-4 explosives and a detonator similar to the ones used by the military."

"Great. That tells me that whoever set that charge probably knew what he was doing."

Hank's lips firmed. "Afraid so."

Sadie leaned forward. "What I don't understand is how Damien could walk away from it all and leave his fiancée to answer to the sheriff and fire fighters." The pretty actress frowned. "If I were Allie, I'd dump his ass and call off the wedding."

"Before the explosions, he said he had a business emergency he had to deal with and the plane was waiting," Swede said. "But no business emergency is enough to leave the woman you love behind with the lingering threat of someone trying to blow you and her away."

Sadie smacked her palm on the table. "Damn right. I've got half a mind to tell her that."

Hank slipped his arm around Sadie. "That's what I like about you. Your passion." He kissed his wife. "Our baby is going to be hell on wheels when he's born."

Sadie lifted her chin. "She."

Swede smiled at the happy couple, glad his teammate had found the woman of his dreams. But they still had a big problem on their hands. One involving Hank's sister and her fiancé. "What do you know about Damien Reynolds, and any of the people who work for him?"

Hank retained his hold on his wife's hand, but he turned his attention back to the case. "I searched the web, looking for anything linked to Damien and found an article about him and his corporation being awarded a big government construction contract. I have a call in to a friend of mine who works in procurement in D.C. I'll let you know what I find."

Swede nodded toward Bear. "What have you got for Bear to work on?"

"I take it you haven't heard about the national guardsman who was attacked in Bozeman last night?"

Swede swung his gaze back to Hank. "No, I didn't. What happened?"

"I don't have all of the details. What I do know is that he was cut up pretty badly. Fortunately, someone found him shortly after the attack, and he was rushed to the hospital. Whoever did it sliced him open, basically eviscerating him."

Sadie gasped and covered her belly. "That's terrible!"

Swede's own gut clenched. "And he survived?"

"The guy who found him performed basic first aid, applying pressure to the wound. The first responders were able to get to him before he bled out, and the surgeon put his intestines back together. He's in ICU. He's not good, but they're hoping he makes it."

"Why would someone do that?" Sadie sat back in her chair, her face pale, her hand resting over her flat tummy.

"I don't know, but I'm putting Bear on it. The investigation doesn't pay, but the victim is a fellow serviceman. I feel we owe it to him to do something. He's a twenty-year-old kid, just back from deployment and only been home a day."

Swede's fists clenched. He wanted to kill the bastard who'd hurt the kid. He'd seen his share of stomach-turning atrocities, but that was in the Middle East where the Taliban and ISIS rebels had no regard for life. But this…Hell, they were on American soil with baseball and mom's apple pie. "Things like that shouldn't happen here," he said.

"Agreed."

"What do the Bozeman Police Department have to say about it?" Swede asked.

"They don't know what to think. As far as they could tell, they have no suspects, and they couldn't find a motivation for the attack. The guy's wallet was still on him, and he had five hundred dollars inside. For now, they're calling it a random act of violence."

"Bullshit." Swede's fists bunched. "It's just another way of saying they don't have a suspect or a clue as to who might have done it."

"Exactly. I want Bear to talk to the kid's family and his CO. I'm sure the police will be doing the same, but I won't feel right unless we do something to help find the bastard. In the meantime, you need to stick to Allie like glue. I don't think the two incidents are related, but I'd rather not take any chances. I love my little sister and don't want anything bad to happen."

"I'm on it." Swede pushed to his feet as the song ended. He crossed to the dance floor and tapped Bear's shoulder. "Mind if I cut in?"

Bear backed away, grinning. "Yes, I do mind, but I guess since it's you, I won't protest too much." He turned to Allie and raised her hand to press a kiss to the backs of her knuckles. "Thank you for the two-step lesson."

She nodded. "You're a quick study. Thank you for the dance."

Swede took her hand as the music transitioned into a slow, heart-breaking, belly-rubbing song.

Allie glanced up at him. "We can wait for a faster song, if you were hoping to two-step."

"No, this one is perfect." Perfect if she wasn't engaged to another man. Perfect to hold her close and sniff the strawberry scent of her hair. Perfect if she wasn't the body he was supposed to guard, and wasn't a woman getting married on Saturday.

Allie melted into Swede's arms, her body pressing close to his. She fit against him like they were made for each other. God, she had to stop thinking that way. On Saturday, she was supposed to marry the man of her dreams. What she was feeling was only pre-wedding jitters. Damien was the man for her, not Swede.

Then why was she leaning into his body, resting her cheek against his chest and wishing the song would never end?

With their hips touching, Allie knew immediately that she wasn't the only one feeling whatever it was building between them. The hard ridge of his fly pressed into her belly, the slow song lending itself to false dreams and dangerous passion.

As if of their own volition, her hands slipped up his chest and wrapped around the back of his neck.

Swede cupped her face, turning it up to his. "Do you know what you do to me?" he whispered.

"I have an idea," she said, her voice breathy. Allie couldn't seem to breathe normally. Not with Swede so close and the heat building between them.

His head dipped lower, and his lips hovered over hers. If she leaned up on her toes, they'd kiss. It would be wrong. So very wrong. But…

As she bunched her muscles, she heard the music end, and the band announce a fifteen-minute break.

Swede straightened. "We should go back to the table."

"Yes, we should." Allie couldn't make her feet move.

"Look." Swede gripped her hands and squeezed hard. "Whatever this is, whatever we're feeling right now, isn't real."

Allie's chest tightened, and her eyes stung. "Of course, it isn't," she agreed, though her body felt otherwise.

"You're getting married on Saturday, and I'll move on to my next assignment. Let's not make this any harder than it has to be."

She nodded, knowing what he said couldn't be truer, even though she still wanted to feel his lips against hers. "You're right."

Swede stepped back, his arms falling to his sides.

Allie pasted a smile on her lips and forced air past her vocal cords. "Thank you for the dance. If you'll excuse me…" She made a beeline for the ladies' room. Once inside, she stood in front of the mirror, staring at the face of a woman who was engaged to one man and lusting after another. Her mother and father had raised her better than that. She ran cold water from the tap, stuck her hands beneath the spray and then splashed her cheeks with her wet hands.

"Hey." Sadie entered behind her and slipped an arm over Allie's shoulder. "Are you okay?"

Too disturbed to come up with a lie, she shook her head. "I don't know."

"You look a little flushed." Sadie ripped a paper towel from the roll, wet it and squeezed out the excess before patting Allie's face with it. "For a moment out there, I thought you and Swede were going to kiss."

Allie met Sadie's gaze in the mirror. "The bad part about it is that I wanted to," she admitted.

Sadie sighed. "Baby, are you sure Damien's the right man for you?"

Throwing her hands in the air, Allie spun and paced all three steps across the room and back. "I'm getting married on Saturday. No man I just met is going to derail my plans."

Sadie held up her hands. "Okay. You're getting married on Saturday." She tossed the wet paper towel in the trash and tore off a dry one. "If it's Damien you're determined to marry, then you have to stop drooling over your bodyguard."

Again, Allie's gaze met Sadie's in the mirror. Her shoulders slumped, and she nodded. "You're right. It's not right. I need to go home, get a good night's sleep and wake up with the right frame of mind."

"Don't forget, tomorrow we pick up your wedding dress," Sadie reminded her.

Allie's chest pinched. Instead of being giddy with excitement, like a bride should be, she dreaded going. She needed to call Damien. Maybe hearing his voice would help get her back on track. He was the man she was going to marry on Saturday. This was only a case of cold feet. Straightening her shoulders, she stepped out of the bathroom and ran into a wall of muscles.

Sadie squeezed by them and darted back into the bar room.

Some friend she was.

Swede's arms came up around her and crushed her against his chest. "Are you all right?"

"Yes." She nodded, and then shook her head. "No. I need to go home."

"We've only been here twenty minutes. Are you sure you don't want to stay and visit with your brother?"

"No. I'm tired and have a big day ahead of me." She stepped back. "If you want to stay, I can see if Bear will take me back to the ranch."

Swede's jaw hardened. "I'll take you." He hooked her elbow in a tight grip and led her back to the table where they said their goodbyes and then left the tavern.

Once outside, Allie sucked in deep breaths, hoping the fresh Montana air would clear her head.

Swede opened the truck door for her and handed her up into the passenger seat. The touch of his fingers against her elbow shot electric currents throughout her body and left her tingling. This couldn't be. Maybe she'd had too much to drink. Then she remembered, she hadn't had a chance to order a drink.

As she watched Swede walk around to the driver's side, Allie moaned softly. She needed to talk to Damien. What she was feeling was lonely and neglected. That was all.

Swede climbed into the driver's seat and shifted the truck in gear.

Allie stared out the side window, refusing to look his in direction. How he must be laughing at her, thinking she was a two-timing woman, eager to cheat on her fiancé while he was out of town. Allie wanted to tell him that wasn't the case. That she wasn't that kind of woman. But she'd had those feelings. And feeling it was almost as bad as actually doing it.

They'd driven past all the houses and continued onto the highway leading to the Bear Creek Ranch when headlights flashed brightly in the rearview mirror.

Swede squinted and tipped the windshield mirror upward. He decreased his speed a little, but the vehicle wasn't interested in passing.

Allie watched through the side mirror and finally turned in her seat to glance through the rear window. "What the hell is he trying to prove?"

Swede lowered his window and waved the guy on.

The headlights seemed to get larger as the vehicle sped up. Instead of swerving to go around, the SUV rammed into the back of the truck.

Allie jerked forward. The seatbelt snapped tight, keeping her from slamming into the dash.

"Hang on!" Swede yelled. "He's going to hit us again."

Allie braced her hand on the dash, her body already bruised from the first attack.

The trailing vehicle rammed them again, hitting at a bit of an angle.

Swede's truck fishtailed. He fought to straighten it before it ran off the road into a ditch. Just when he had it under control, the attacker raced up beside them and slammed into the driver's side.

The truck ran off the pavement onto the gravel shoulder.

Allie held onto the oh-shit handle above the door as Swede fought with the steering wheel to bring the truck back onto the blacktop.

It was hard to do with the attacking vehicle pushing him further off the road.

Swede changed tactics and slammed on his brakes. The truck skidded in the gravel but slowed faster than the attacking full-sized SUV. His maneuver bought them a few seconds, allowing Swede to drive back up onto the highway.

No sooner had he righted the truck, something hit the front windshield dead-center between the driver and passenger sides.

Allie's heart plunged into the pit of her belly. The hole in the windshield was perfectly round. "They're shooting at us!"

"Get down!" Swede shouted. He spun the steering wheel and hit the accelerator at the same time. The truck did a complete one-hundred-eighty-degree turn.

Another bullet blasted through the back windshield, through the headrest of the passenger seat and exited through the front windshield. If Allie hadn't ducked when Swede told her to, she would have been hit in the back of the head. Her stomach flipped, and she remained low in her seat.

"Switch places!" Swede yelled.

"What? Are you insane?"

"They're coming around. Hurry. Switch places."

Swede shifted the seat back and slammed his foot on the accelerator.

Allie slid across the console and into Swede's lap. Once she had control of the steering wheel, he crawled out from under her and lifted his foot off the accelerator.

He fell across the other seat, righted himself, lowered the window and poked out his handgun.

The other vehicle had performed a slower version of the turnaround Swede had executed moments before and was now quickly catching up.

Her heart pounding against her ribs, Allie slammed her foot all the way down on the accelerator, while Swede leaned halfway out the window and fired.

The trailing SUV swerved, but kept coming.

Swede fired again, hitting one of the headlights.

Another bullet hit the back windshield, spraying glass fragments throughout the truck's interior.

Allie kept her head low and her gaze on the curving road ahead. Reaching town meant the guy behind them might veer off and leave them alone.

Swede fired again, but the SUV kept coming.

Allie rounded a curve, reaching out to grab Swede's belt to keep him from flying out.

He stayed with the truck and fired again on the SUV.

After flying around another curve and over a rise, Allie nearly cried out in relief when the lights of Eagle Rock twinkled from below. She drove faster, refusing to slow for the curves leading into town. The lights behind her disappeared as she made the last turn, drove onto

Main Street and straight toward the local sheriff's office.

Swede dropped back into the passenger seat, still holding his handgun in one hand, while his other covered his right shoulder.

Allie pulled into the parking lot of the county jail and sheriff's office, honking the truck's horn. She shoved the shift into park, dropped down out of the driver's seat and ran toward the door.

Sheriff Joe Barron stepped outside, his hand resting on the handle of his service weapon. "What the hell's going on?"

Allie stopped in front of him, breathing hard and shaking from head to toe. "Someone tried to kill us." She turned back to look at the road leading into town, happy to see it empty of traffic. Especially the kind of traffic that fires bullets.

Swede dropped down out of the truck, having holstered his handgun beneath his jacket. He held his hand over his right arm. "You don't happen to have a first aid kit in your office, do you?"

"I do."

"Good." Swede pulled his hand away from his arm. His palm and fingers were drenched, and the sleeve of his black leather jacket shone with wet, sticky blood.

Allie swayed, and her heart leaped into her throat. "Damn, Swede, you've been shot."

CHAPTER 6

Within minutes, the volunteer firefighter paramedic, local doctor, Hank, Bear and Sadie converged on the sheriff's office. Between all of them, they insisted on moving Swede two buildings down to the only medical clinic in town.

Swede shook his head, insisting the injury was nothing but a flesh wound. Upon closer inspection, the doctor and paramedic agreed, but it had nicked him deep enough to cause a significant amount of bleeding.

"Did you get a look at the license plate?" Sheriff Barron asked.

Swede shook his head. "I didn't."

"Me neither," Allie confirmed. "It all happened so fast, and bullets were flying. We didn't have time to breathe, much less jot down a license plate." She hovered near Swede, offering to hold the adhesive tape or hand them a bottle of rubbing alcohol when needed.

Swede let the doctor treat the wound. He'd seen what happened when soldiers didn't take care of themselves. Infections could be lethal, or cause the loss of a limb. But he drew the line at stitches. "Just slap on a butterfly bandage. It'll heal."

The doctor flushed the wound with water and alcohol and then pressed a couple of bandages across it. "Change the bandage daily, or if it gets really dirty. Other than a nice scar, you'll probably live."

"Thought so."

"But not if that guy is still running loose." Allie held out Swede's jacket. Sadie had rinsed the blood out of it as best she could and dried it with towels and a blow dryer while the doc worked on him.

Sheriff Barron shook his head. "I don't know what's going on around here, but we have to get to the bottom of it. We can't have the good citizens of the county afraid to come outside."

"So far, Reynolds and Allie seem to be the targets," Hank said.

"Yeah. We're trying to track down the source of the C-4 and the paint used to deface the stable before it burned to the ground. The state forensics lab is working on it, and a hundred other hot cases." The sheriff drew in a deep breath and let it out. "In the meantime, to make sure you get home safe, I'll escort you to the Bear Creek Ranch, personally."

Allie smiled at her friend. "Thank you, Joe."

He draped an arm over her shoulders, and hugged her. "I'm sorry this is happening to you, but I'm glad you had someone like Mr. Svenson with you. Your own personal SEAL to keep you safe when the crap hits the fan."

Allie nodded, her gaze seeking and connecting with Swede's.

Swede felt a warmth flooding through him that had nothing to do with the jacket he'd shrugged into. The arm felt fine, but he'd like to get back to Bear Creek Ranch where Allie was surrounded by people who loved and looked out for her. After the attack that evening, Swede wasn't sure his skills were enough to keep Allie safe.

"You know, Allie," Sheriff Barron was saying. "You really might consider postponing your wedding. With the way things have been going, it would make too big a target for these yahoos to pass up."

Allie's eyes narrowed and her lips thinned. "I'm getting married on Saturday. Scare tactics aren't keeping me from my wedding."

The sheriff raised his hands. "Just saying, it might not be safe for you or your guests."

Her brows furrowing, Allie seemed to chew on Joe Barron's words. "I don't want anyone else to get hurt because of me." She looked up at her friend. "I'll think about it. But as far as anyone knows, the wedding is still on."

Swede's stomach bunched at the determination in Allie's voice. What did he expect? She was engaged to a wealthy man and had been, well before Swede showed up in Eagle Rock. Besides, he wasn't in the market for a long-term relationship. Not with his hang-ups. Hell, he was barely satisfactory at his new job. A man who was at one hundred percent would have taken out the attackers. But he'd missed, allowing the bastards to live.

Sheriff Barron waved toward the door. "Allie, if you're ready to go, I'll escort you two to the ranch gate."

Allie glanced at Swede.

Swede nodded. "We're ready."

"Call me when you get home." Hank pressed a kiss to Allie's forehead. "I like to know you're okay."

Sadie hugged her. "I'll see you tomorrow."

"Do you want us to swing by and pick you up for the trip into Bozeman?" Swede asked.

Hank shook his head. "No. We will all drive in at the same time. Sadie and I will meet you at the gate to the Bear Creek Ranch."

"And I'll bring up the rear," Bear said. "I want to swing by the hospital and check on the soldier, and then I'll go by his unit to talk to his commander."

Swede had wondered how it would be as a civilian, without the support and camaraderie of his SEAL team. Not much had changed. With Hank and Bear nearby, Swede knew they had his back. He hoped, between the three of them, they could keep Allie safe.

Allie insisted on driving Swede's truck back to the ranch. With the sheriff's SUV behind them, they had no repeat performances from the earlier attacker. The sheriff parked at the entrance to Bear Creek Ranch and waited until Allie was halfway to the house before he turned to go back to town.

"You have some good people here in Montana," Swede noted.

Allie snorted. "Except the ones trying to kill me?"

"With that exception. I think the good people outnumber the bad."

She nodded. "You're right. I love living here. I love the people I grew up with and the sense of community. Although, sometimes they can get into your business when you don't want them to. But for the most part, everyone looks out for everyone else."

"You're lucky to have them." Swede's hand rested on his pistol. Even though they were on the Bear Creek Ranch, he couldn't let down his guard for a moment. He had done so earlier, and it had almost gotten them killed. All because he'd wanted to kiss Allie.

And still did.

He sat in silence as Allie drove up to the house and parked.

"What will you tell my father about your truck?" Allie asked, staring at the holes in the windshield.

"I'll tell him I got behind a gravel truck."

"What about the dent in the door?"

"It could have been a rude driver in the Blue Moose parking lot, backing into me and driving off."

She nodded. "He might buy it."

"You need to talk to Damien," Swede said.

She stared at the house in front of her. "I know."

"He has to know more than he's telling us about this threat. If we could talk to him about it, we might have a better starting point in our search to locate the attacker."

"I'll try to get in touch with him tonight. If he's on the other side of the world, it might be difficult to contact him." Allie unbuckled her seatbelt and reached for the keys in the ignition.

"Why are you marrying Reynolds?" Swede asked

before he could stop himself. It wasn't the kind of question a bodyguard asked his client. But there it was.

Her hand froze on the keys. "Why do you ask?" she countered. She didn't glance his way. Instead, she stared at the keyring.

Swede studied her face, looking for a reaction, a clue to her feelings about the man she had promised to marry. "I don't know him well, but you two just don't seem right for each other. Like you don't fit." Again, as soon as the words left his mouth, he wished he could have taken them back.

Allie's fingers curled around the keys, and her mouth pulled into a tight line. "You're right. You don't know Damien. And, for that matter, you don't know me." She pushed open the door, stepped down on the running board and dropped to the ground.

Swede rounded the front of the truck and took the keys she held out to him. "You didn't answer the question. Why are you marrying Damien?"

Allie pushed back her shoulders and met his gaze. "That's none of your business. You're just the bodyguard my fiancé hired to protect me. After the wedding, I'll be on my way to the Cayman Islands, and you'll be on to your next assignment. What does it matter?"

Swede gripped her arms, wanting to wring the truth out of the woman. But, he knew she was right. It wasn't his business. Still, he didn't understand the relationship between Allie and Damien, and one thing was bugging the hell out of him. "You never said you loved him."

Allie stared up into his eyes, her hands pressed to his

chest, neither pushing him away nor bringing him closer. "I don't have to say the words to you."

Swede pulled her closer until their bodies touched, hip to hip, breasts to chest. "Do you want to kiss him when you're dancing?"

"Why are you doing this?" she whispered. "You said you aren't into relationships. Why are you interested in mine?"

"Answer my question." He leaned closer, his mouth moving nearer to hers.

Allie licked her lips, sending a burst of flame through Swede's system. He couldn't go back now that he'd started down this path.

Swede's voice dropped lower, his groin tightening as the ridge beneath his fly rubbed against Allie's belly. "Does he make you want to fall into bed and make love to him with only a glance?"

"You don't know what you're doing," she said, her gaze slipping to his mouth, her tongue sweeping across her lips again.

"*Me?* I think *you* don't know what you're doing. Or what you really want."

"And you know me well enough to know what I want and need?" she challenged.

"No, but I know what *I* want." His hands slipped down her arms and around to rest on her lower back. "I want that kiss." Then Swede broke all the rules he associated with being a bodyguard and kissed the woman he was sworn to protect. Not only did he kiss her, he branded her with his mouth, taking everything she would give and sweeping past her teeth to take even more.

Their tongues danced a sensual tango, thrusting and parrying.

Allie's hands slid beneath Swede's jacket, curled over his chest and locked behind his neck, pulling him closer.

Swede knew what he was doing was wrong, but something drew him to Allie. Something he found irresistible. Unfortunately, one kiss would never be enough. With her imminent marriage to a man who didn't care enough about his fiancée to be with her when someone was out to kill her, looming, Swede's stomach knotted and his heart hurt. He tore his lips away from hers.

"No." Swede lifted his head and stared down into her face. "No."

Allie looked up into his eyes, her green ones glazed, her breathing coming in labored breaths. Her body still pressed to his, her hands flattened against his chest. She blinked and the glaze cleared. Her eyes widened, and she gasped. "Damn you." Allie stepped back and swung her arm, her palm connecting with his face in a resounding slap.

Swede's cheek stung with the force of the blow. He stood there, unmoving, knowing he deserved every bit of it. "I'm sorry. I shouldn't have done that."

Through gritted teeth, she said, "Don't. Ever. Touch. Me. Again." She spun on her heels and ran in the house.

If he wasn't mistaken, Swede could swear he heard a sob before the door closed behind Allie.

. . .

She didn't stop running until she reached the sanctuary of her bedroom. After she shut the door, Allie leaned her back against it and slid to the floor. Tears rolled down her cheeks. Allie touched her fingers to the tears. What was wrong with her? She was never this emotional. The last time she cried was the day her mother died. Since then, her father insisted crying was only for babies. She wasn't a baby; she was a grown woman with a wedding ahead of her.

For a minute more, she allowed herself to sink into the depths of despair, sobbing quietly so that her bodyguard couldn't hear her break down. Then she got up, stripped out of the pretty dress, wadded it into a ball and stuffed it in the very back of her closet. If she never wore the dress again, that was just fine with her.

Pulling a T-shirt over her head, Allie peeked out into the hallway. Nothing moved. A light shined beneath the door of Hank's old bedroom, her father's room was dark and the bathroom door across the hall was open with the light on. She crossed to the bathroom, closed and locked the door, then brushed her teeth and scrubbed off the little bit of makeup that hadn't washed away with her tears.

Allie brushed her hair and secured it in a ponytail on top of her head. Looking in the mirror, she appeared much like the little girl who'd lost her mother. Right now she missed her mom more than ever. When she opened the door, she half-feared, half-wished she'd run into Swede in the hallway. Again, it was empty.

After trudging across the corridor to her room, she closed the door and collapsed on the bed. She lifted the phone, dialed Damien's number and waited. She heard one ring and his phone rolled over to voicemail.

Damn.

Tomorrow she really needed to talk to Damien. That kiss had only made matters worse. Now, not only had she cheated in thought, she'd cheated in deed. How could she go into a marriage with the guilt of that kiss weighing on her mind? Then again, how could she tell Damien without hurting him?

Allie curled up on the bed, hugging a pillow to her chest. For a long time, she lay still, willing herself to sleep, hoping everything would appear brighter with the morning sunshine.

After tossing and turning until the wee hours of the morning, Allie finally drifted to sleep.

It was her wedding day. She wore the dress she had picked out, and had her hair piled high on her head with ringlets falling down her back. Her father walked her down the aisle very slowly, his face grim. As they passed the rows of guests, people whispered and pointed. They knew. Her face heated and her belly churned.

When Allie finally reached the altar, she turned to face the man who would become her husband until death should they part. But Damien wasn't the one waiting for her. The man in the tuxedo stood taller and straighter. A man of military bearing and discipline. Waiting to marry her was the man who'd been hired by her fiancé to protect her.

Swede.

Pounding on her door woke her at 8:00 the next morning. Her father's voice boomed through the paneling. "If you want to eat, you need to come down, now.

Georgia is cleaning the kitchen, and she's waiting on you."

"I'm coming," Allie responded. One glance at the clock made her throw back the comforter and leap out of the bed. "Why didn't anyone wake me earlier?"

"Swede said you didn't get to bed until late. We decided you needed your beauty sleep."

Allie crossed the room to her dresser and selected a pullover blouse. "Are you saying I'm looking more like a hag lately?" She ripped her sleep shirt over her head, put on a bra and dragged on the clean shirt she'd wear to town.

"I wouldn't say that," her father said. "But you have had dark circles beneath your eyes. I think you work too hard."

Allie stuck her feet into her jeans and pulled them up, securing the zipper. "Well, that plays right into my plans for today. I'm going to Bozeman to pick up my wedding dress. That means I won't be around to help out in the hay field until late this evening." She grabbed a pair of walking shoes and the high heels she'd wear under her wedding dress and opened her bedroom door.

"The hay won't be dry enough to bale until tomorrow. Take your time."

"Thanks, Dad." She glanced at her father, sensing he wanted to say more, but couldn't come up with the words to express the emotions playing across his face. Well, as much emotion as Lloyd Patterson ever expressed. The man was taciturn and rough around the edges, but Allie knew deep down he loved her and Hank, and only wanted the best for them.

Her father stared at her for a moment longer. "I heard what happened last night."

Allie's fists clenched. She shouldn't have slapped Swede for kissing her, and she sure as hell shouldn't have kissed him in the first place. Today, after she picked up her wedding dress, she'd call Damien and confess that she was confused and scared and…well… she'd come up with a good reason for kissing her bodyguard. Although, she couldn't at the moment, other than she'd wanted to more than she wanted to breathe. "Look, Dad, what happened last night won't happen again."

His brows furrowed. "How do you know it won't happen again?"

She squared her shoulders. "Because I'm not going to let it."

Her father shook his head, his gaze narrowing to a slit. "I don't see how you can keep it from happening again until they catch the guy who did it. From what Sheriff Barron said, you didn't even get a look at the license plate. How will they find the shooter if you didn't even get that?"

Allie almost laughed out loud at her father's words. Holy hell, she'd thought he was talking about the kiss. Thank goodness the people who knew about that would remain the only two. Until she confessed to her fiancé. *If* she confessed. "You're right, Dad. It could happen again. We just have to hope it doesn't."

"I'm just glad your friend Swede was with you. I

can't imagine what would have happened had you been alone." He took her hands. "With the wedding so close, and this shooter still on the loose, don't you think you should consider postponing?"

What was with everyone trying to convince her to postpone or call off her wedding? "It was probably a random act. I'm getting married on Saturday. I've spent too much money on everything, and it's non-refundable."

"That's no reason to get married. Here you are in trouble, and your fiancé isn't anywhere around to keep you safe." Her father dropped her hands, a scowl making deep grooves in his forehead. "What kind of man doesn't take care of his woman?"

"He'll be back before the wedding. You can ask him then." Allie stepped past her father. "In the meantime, I have a wedding dress to pick up at the bridal shop."

"I really wish you'd stay here at the ranch. I don't want to see you hurt."

"I'll have Sadie, Hank and Swede with me. If I need help, they have offered to provide it." She didn't wait around to argue further. Allie hurried down to the kitchen.

"You'll have to hustle if you want breakfast before you leave for your appointment at the dressmakers." Georgia held out a plate of fluffy scrambled eggs. "Hank called. He and Sadie will be at the gate in ten minutes."

"I'm not hungry. But thanks." Allie aimed straight for the coffee pot, poured half a cup and downed it, burning her tongue. With her father's words and the images of her dream still rattling around in her head, Allie braced herself and stepped out on the porch.

Swede sat on the porch steps, scratching Ruger behind the ears. When he heard the door open, he stood and faced her. "I've been thinking."

Allie marched down the steps and out to her truck, her keys in hand. "That's nice."

"What happened last night—"

"It didn't." Allie turned to face him. "Nothing happened last night. Get it?"

Swede pressed his hand to the cheek Allie had slapped the night before. "Sure felt like it happened."

"Don't ever let it happen again."

"I wasn't the only one kissing." He grabbed her arm and forced her to stop and look at him. "You weren't fighting me."

Allie glared and looked back at the house. "Shh. Whatever happened cannot happen again. On either side."

"Trust me. I won't kiss you again." He let go of her arm, walked to her truck and stopped next to the passenger side. "Not unless you ask me." His lips twitched on the corners.

Allie contemplated hurling her keys at him. How dare he laugh at such a huge mistake? She refused to rise to his bait. Instead, she climbed into the driver's seat, fit the key into the ignition and started the engine.

Swede tried the handle on the passenger side. "Hey, unlock the door."

For a moment, Allie considered driving off without the infuriating man. One glance at the bullet holes in his truck changed her mind. She popped the locks and waited for him to climb in.

"I thought you were going to leave without me."

"Believe me, I almost did." She slammed the gear into reverse, backed up and turned around, heading for the gate.

As agreed upon, Sadie and Hank were waiting in Hank's pickup. Bear, in one of Hank's White Oak Ranch trucks, waited behind them.

Allie waved as she passed the two trucks and drove all the way into Bozeman without saying another word to Swede.

"Stop at the hospital. Hank, Bear and I want to talk to the kid who got cut up."

With a nod, no words, Allie turned and headed for the hospital, pulling into a visitors' slot.

Allie turned off the engine but made no move to get out. "I'll wait out here."

Swede was halfway out of the truck. "Like hell, you will." He rounded to the other side and grabbed her door handle.

Moving quickly, she hit the door lock. Her gaze went from the lock to his eyes.

Swede frowned and tried the door handle. "Allie, don't be ridiculous. You can't stay out here by yourself. Please, unlock the door."

She stared at him for a long moment and then sighed. Who was she kidding? She might as well paint a big red bulls-eye on her and the truck.

She tapped the button releasing the locks and slid out of the truck.

CHAPTER 7

Swede let out a long breath and touched her arm. "I'm sorry for anything I've said or done that makes you not want me to protect you. I promise not to touch you or make you uncomfortable. But please, don't lock me out."

Allie shook her head. "No, that was childish of me. I won't do it again." She held up her hand. "I promise."

The other two trucks pulled in and parked nearby. Sadie joined Allie and took her hand. The men surrounded the women as they entered the hospital.

At the information desk, Bear asked for Thomas Baker, the soldier brought in with knife wounds.

The volunteer keyed something into the computer and waited a moment. Then she looked up and smiled. "He's in ICU."

"How is he?" Bear asked.

The gray-haired lady shrugged. "You'll have to speak with the nurses in ICU. They'll be able to tell you more."

They rode the elevator up to ICU.

Nurses hurried from room to room, tending to seriously ill patients, taking vital signs, administering medication and trying to make their patients more comfortable in an uncomfortable situation.

Hank approached the nurses' station and asked to see Thomas Baker.

"Are you a relative of Mr. Baker?" the head nurse asked.

"No," Hank responded. "I'm a war veteran, come to pay my respects to the young soldier. He deserves a whole lot more than what he got from the low-life who did this."

The nurse nodded. "Agreed. But rules are rules. Only relatives are allowed into the room. Unless Mr. Baker requests to see you."

"We'd like to talk to him about the attack, in case there is anything we can do to help, or keep this from happening to others."

"Isn't that what the police are doing?" asked the head nurse. "They were in an hour ago, after Mr. Baker woke."

"I imagine they are doing a fine job of finding the attacker," Hank said. "But we'd still like to help."

The woman behind the counter stared at Hank for a long moment and finally said, "Get the family's permission to visit with Mr. Baker, and I'll bend the rules for you this once." Her eyes narrowed. "But, if you do anything to upset my patient, you'll be thrown out of here so fast you won't know what hit you."

Hank held up both hands. "We're here to help, not hurt."

"His mother and father are in the ICU waiting room. You can catch up with them there. They must agree or you're not getting in to see the young man."

"We understand," Bear assured her.

As they walked away from the nurses' station, Allie asked, "What if you can't get in to see Baker?"

"Bear will be making an appointment to visit with the soldier's commander," Hank said. "Maybe he can shed light on what happened."

In the ICU waiting room, the only other people present were a man and a woman appearing tense and exhausted.

Hank stopped just inside the door. "The rest of you should find a seat. I'd like to talk to Baker's parents with just me and Bear, so as not to overwhelm them."

"Right." Swede followed Allie to a seat on the far side of the waiting room. He sat on one side, and Sadie sat on the other.

A few minutes later, Hank, Bear and Baker's parents left the waiting room.

Swede wished he could be a fly on the wall in Thomas Baker's room, but he was content to be next to Allie. With all of the attacks on her and then this one on Baker, he wasn't comfortable leaving her alone here in the hospital. Forget about leaving her out in the parking lot.

Allie turned to Sadie. "Have you had any morning sickness, yet?"

Sadie shrugged. "A little, but nothing unmanageable. I still can't believe we're having a baby in seven months."

Allie grinned. "I can't wait. Hank's going to make a

great father. And I'm over-the-moon about being an aunt."

Swede listened to the ladies talking, a little envious of Hank. The man had a family and a baby on the way. Wow. Nothing could be more grounding than having a child and a wife. A glance at Allie made him wonder what it would be like to be married to a woman like her, and to have children. He could picture an auburn-haired little girl running through the yard, her curls bouncing on her shoulders. She'd laugh and play with her mother, beautiful and carefree.

Too bad that child wouldn't be his. That thought caught him by surprise. He'd never considered himself good husband material, especially after all the operations he'd been on. Shooting other people and being shot at did something to a man. As if the nightmares, ducking at every loud noise, always easing around corners and looking behind you for the enemy weren't enough, trying to fit into a society at once familiar and yet foreign was a challenge in itself. Most people Stateside were only worried about what they were cooking for dinner, not whether they would live to see their next meal.

Like so many other combat veterans, Swede found the transition hard and didn't wish his problems on anyone. Especially an attractive, independent woman like Allie.

Sitting with Allie and Sadie, hearing talk of renovating a room for the baby reminded Swede that his buddy Hank was getting on with his life. He'd been through everything Swede had, and more. If he could move on and give himself a chance at a real life with a family and children, why couldn't Swede?

He glanced at Allie.

Reynolds didn't know how good he had it. His fiancée was amazing. She'd make a great aunt, and an even better mother.

Hank and Bear entered the waiting room five minutes later, their faces grim.

Swede stood. "What did you learn?"

"Baker is lucky to be alive," Bear said.

Hank pushed a hand through his hair. "From what his parents and the nurse said, his attacker gutted him and left him to die."

"Was he able to give a description of the attacker, or any kind of motivation?" Swede asked.

"No," Hank said.

"He wasn't involved with a girl, so no ex-boyfriend issues." Bear's jaw tightened. "The kid was jumped walking home from getting a lousy hamburger yesterday evening. He didn't provoke anyone or start a fight. Hell, he'd barely said two words to the server at the hamburger joint."

"Bear is headed to Baker's unit," Hank said. "Since it wasn't a robbery, and he just returned from a deployment, maybe his commander can tell us whether or not he'd had any troubles with other unit members."

"I'll be with the ladies all afternoon." Swede nodded toward Hank and Bear. "Let us know what you find out."

"Will do." Hank glanced at Allie and Sadie. "You two stay close to Swede. If there's a nutcase walking around stabbing people, we don't want him taking a crack at you."

Sadie and Allie stood and edged a little closer to Swede.

"We'll stay with him," Sadie said, giving Swede a sad look. "Poor guy. He'll have to put up with sitting in a bridal shop while we try on our dresses."

"I can handle it," Swede said. Better to suffer through a female shopping trip than to worry whether or not they'd make it home alive.

Bear smirked. "Better you than me, buddy." He winked at the women. "Not that spending an afternoon with two beautiful women sounds bad at all, it's just all that talk about fabric and lace makes me itch."

"Same here," Hank agreed.

Sadie pointed toward the exit. "We could do without your negativity. The final fitting of the bride's gown is supposed to be a happy, optimistic time. We're better off without the two of you."

She hooked Swede's arm. "Come on, Swede, we'll have a nice afternoon, despite those two."

Hank snagged Sadie around the waist and hugged her to him. "Kiss me, you ornery woman, before I turn you over my knee and spank you."

She laughed up at him. "Not in front of the others." And she kissed him, long and hard, melting into his body.

Swede shifted uncomfortably, bumping into Allie.

"Disgustingly mushy, if you ask me," Allie whispered.

"I heard that," Sadie said, breaking off the kiss.

They walked to the elevator together, returned to the ground floor and exited the hospital.

Hank left in Bear's truck. "I'll have him drop me off at the bridal store when we're done poking around."

Sadie drove Hank's truck while Allie and Swede rode together the few blocks to the bridal shop.

Inside the building, the attendant hustled Sadie and Allie to the dressing rooms. Another attendant showed Swede to a cushioned seat to wait. Around him were full-length mirrors and more seats. He chuckled quietly. If his SEAL teammates could see him now, they'd howl with laughter. Badass SEAL surrounded by tulle and taffeta, or whatever it was they made wedding dresses out of.

Sadie was first to emerge from the dressing room in a pretty sky-blue dress. She lifted her skirt and walked toward Swede. "What do you think?"

He shrugged. "It's nice."

"Allie wanted sky-blue to remind her of the Montana skies. I like the sentiment." She turned away and stared at herself in the mirror. "Although, it's a good thing she's getting married Saturday. I don't know how much longer I'll fit in this dress." She ran her hands over her belly. "It won't be long before I start showing." She smiled, her eyes glazing with tears. "I'm going to be a mommy. And Hank's going to be a father." Sadie glanced at Swede in the mirror. "It's a big change from fighting the Taliban and ISIS, huh?"

Swede nodded.

"Ta, da!" The attendant who'd disappeared with Allie

opened the dressing room door and stepped aside with a flourish. "And we have the bride. Isn't she beautiful?"

Allie stepped out of the dressing room, her cheeks a rosy red, her gaze locked on Sadie.

"Oh, Allie." Sadie clapped her hands together. "You look amazing."

Swede swallowed hard past the constriction in his throat.

Allie, the cowgirl who could ride like she was born in a saddle, who loved ranch life and getting her hands dirty, had transformed from girl next door to…Oh, hell, a radiant and beautiful princess in a lacy white dress that hugged her body from the strapless neckline all the way down past her hips where it flared out, ending in a long train. The attendant had swept up her hair on her head and fixed it with a pearl comb.

Allie's gaze shifted from Sadie to Swede. She didn't say anything.

Swede could only stare. This woman was preparing to marry another man. How could he comment when all he wanted to do was say *No! Don't marry Reynolds! He doesn't deserve you.*

To keep from uttering those words, Swede had to get outside. Fast. He pushed to his feet and walked out of the viewing room, out of the building and into the fresh Montana air. There he sucked in a long, steadying breath. Then another. No matter how many breaths he took, he couldn't seem to get enough air into his lungs to ease the pressure.

One thing became very clear to him. He didn't want

the bride he was sworn to protect and get to the church on time to marry Damien Reynolds.

"WHAT THE HELL JUST HAPPENED?" Allie stood with her hands on her lace-covered hips, staring at the empty doorframe Swede had just passed through.

"He's a man. They can't handle all this girl stuff." Sadie tilted her head to the side and tapped her chin. "Or, is it that he didn't like seeing you in a dress you'd be wearing to marry another man?"

"Don't be ridiculous." Allie turned her back to Sadie. "Unzip me. The dress is fine. We can leave as soon as you're ready." She couldn't wait to get out of the dress shop. Really, she couldn't wait to ask Swede why he'd run out like a cat with his tail on fire.

"What's up between you and Swede?" Sadie asked.

"Nothing," Allie replied, a little too quickly. She took a deep breath and answered more slowly. "Nothing. I'm marrying Damien on Saturday." *Come hell or high water.*

"Look, Allie, you don't have to go through with this wedding."

"I accepted his proposal. I'm marrying Damien on Saturday." She refused to be a wishy-washy bride. Having made her decision, she should stick to it.

Sadie finished unzipping the back of the dress and turned Allie to face her. "You don't have to marry him."

"I keep my word."

"This is a case where you can break your promise, if it doesn't feel right." Sadie squeezed her hands. "From the look on your face, it doesn't feel right, does it?"

"I don't know." Holding the front of the dress up, Allie turned to the mirror, trying to see what Sadie saw in her face. But all she saw was a cheater who'd kissed her bodyguard. "I need to see Damien. Everything will be okay once he's back in town."

"Will it?" Sadie rested her hands on Allie's shoulders.

"This is all pre-wedding jitters. I'll be fine as soon as Damien is back in town."

Sadie planted her hands on her hips and stared at Allie in the mirror. "Okay, assuming you really love Damien, and you still want to marry him, tell me why. What's so great about him that you can't see yourself with any other man?"

That was the problem, Allie *could* see herself with another man. *Swede.* Hell, he'd been the groom in her wedding dream. What was the matter with her? Damien was everything a woman could want in a husband. "He's handsome," Allie started. In a preppy, businessman way. Not in that rugged, outdoorsy way, like Swede.

Not helping.

"So? Handsome isn't everything. I work around extremely handsome men in Hollywood." Sadie snorted. "Trust me, handsome isn't everything."

"He's a very successful businessman," Allie stated.

"So, he knows how to make money. How important is that to you? You and your father haven't wanted for anything. What can money buy that you don't already have?"

"I can travel more. See the world." *Damn was she that materialistic?*

"With a man you're not sure you're in love with?"

Sadie crossed her arms over her chest. "I'd rather stay home. I've been on sets in different countries. Without someone you love to share the excitement of exploring a foreign country, the trip is just sad and lonely."

"Damien's a fine horseman. Swede never rode a horse until he came to Bear Creek Ranch."

Sadie's eyes widened, and she pointed a finger at Allie. "Ah ha! You're comparing Damien to Swede. You *do* feel something there, or you wouldn't."

"I don't feel anything where Swede is concerned." Allie hiked up her skirt with one hand and marched into the dressing room, slamming the door. "You're reading way too much into my relationship with my bodyguard. He's just the hired help. Nothing more. He said so himself."

"But you wish it was more, don't you?" Sadie's voice was soft, barely audible through the door.

Allie let the dress fall to the floor like her heart sinking into her gut. *No.* She didn't wish Swede could be more than the hired help. It would mess up everything. "I'm marrying Damien."

"Allie, the big question is, do you love him?" Sadie said through the door.

Her chest tightened, and her throat constricted. Did she love Damien? Or had she been in love with the idea of getting married? "I'm not getting any younger," she whispered.

"You're only twenty-seven. You have years of dating and meeting more men in front of you."

"I know all the men in Eagle Rock and the surrounding ranches. I don't want any of them."

"Do you want Damien because he's not from Eagle Rock, or because you love him?"

God, why was Sadie pushing her into saying something she didn't want to say? Allie leaned against the door, tears filling her eyes. "Please, Sadie, stop."

For a long moment, silence reigned.

"I'm sorry, Allie. I won't say anything else other than I love you like the sister I never had. I don't want to see you marry someone you don't love. Marriage is hard, even when you *do* love your spouse. It's harder when you have nothing in common, and you don't love one another." She paused. "I'm going to be a mother. I can't imagine letting a child of mine enter a loveless marriage. That would be so unfair to him or her. Think about it, Allie."

Allie stepped out of the dress as several warm tears slipped from the corners of her eyes and rolled down her cold cheeks. She dressed quickly, left the room and handed the wedding gown to the attendant who'd stood patiently and discreetly out of the way during the whole conversation.

"Will you be taking the dress, today?" she asked.

"Yes." Allie didn't want to make another trip to town for it.

Sadie hugged her. "Ready to go home? I'm sorry if I upset you."

Allie shrugged. "I'm okay. I need to get a good night's sleep. We're hauling hay tomorrow."

"Seriously?" Sadie shook her head. "Your wedding, should you choose to go through with it, is in a couple of days."

"Wedding or not, the hay has to be baled and loaded into the barn." The hard work and long day would keep her occupied so much that she wouldn't have time to think. If she was going through with the wedding, the chores had to be done before the big day.

If.

Damn. Now she was thinking *if*, not *when*.

CHAPTER 8

Swede held the door for Allie as she hung the wedding dress in the back seat of the truck and then climbed into the passenger seat. The ride home from the bridal shop was uneventful, and completely and painfully silent.

Hank and Bear had returned from their visit to Baker's unit, arriving as Swede and the ladies left the bridal shop. The commander wasn't in, having gone to Wyoming earlier that morning. They expected him to be back the next day.

Bear had stayed in Bozeman to run by the police station and see if he could get any information from them about the stabbing. Hank and Sadie followed Swede and Allie to the gate of Bear Creek Ranch. As they pulled off the road at the entrance, Hank waved at Allie. "I can be by in the morning to help with the hay."

"Thanks. I'm sure Dad and Eddy can use all the help they can get," Allie said.

When they left, Swede turned to Allie. "I take it we're

hauling hay tomorrow?" He didn't like that he'd been left out of the conversation until now.

"You don't have to. It's not part of the job description."

"If you're out hauling hay, I'm out hauling hay."

Allie opened her mouth for a moment and then snapped it shut.

Dinner was much the same. Mr. Patterson and Eddy talked about baling and loading the hay the next day.

Swede wasn't clear on all the terms they used. He nodded when he thought he should.

"Allie, are you driving the truck for us? Or should I get Georgia to drive?" Eddy asked.

"Since Swede will be here, why not let him drive? I can help load the hay," Allie suggested.

Georgia's brows furrowed. "Don't be silly. Your wedding is in a couple days, you can't go out and get scratched and bruised. You want to have perfect skin and no sunburn for the big day. I'll drive the truck, and you'll stay at the house and cook dinner."

"No, ma'am." Allie said. "I want to help with the hay, and you know I can't boil eggs without burning the water."

"Then you'll drive, and Swede can help load," her father said. "Since that's settled, why don't you get some sleep? We have to be up by dawn to get this cutting done in a day."

"But—"

"No buts. Go to bed." Her father left the table and climbed the stairs.

"You'd think I was a little girl," Allie mumbled. "I'm a

grown woman, with a mind of my own," she said louder. "I don't need my daddy telling me when to go to bed."

"I heard that," her father said.

Swede's lips twitched, but he fought the smile.

Allie stared at him through narrowed eyes. "Don't laugh. It only encourages him."

Unable to hold back, Swede laughed out loud.

Eddy clapped a hand on his back. "She's as stubborn as her father."

Allie glared at Eddy. "I'm in the room."

Georgia patted her back. "Yes, dear, you are. Now, go to bed. Maybe a good night's sleep will improve your disposition."

"My disposition is just fine, thank you very much." But she rose from her chair, carried her plate to the sink and climbed the stairs to her room.

Swede waited thirty minutes before going to bed, giving Allie enough time to get through the shower and back to her room. He didn't want to bump into her in the hallway. He was afraid he'd try to kiss her again. And that wouldn't do.

SLEEP WAS A LONG TIME COMING, and dawn arrived too soon.

The sound of boots on the stairs woke him. He hurried to dress and get downstairs before the others left without him.

Lloyd and Eddy were just finishing breakfast when Swede walked into the kitchen.

"You two can join us at the barn when you're done here," Mr. Patterson said. "We have to connect the trailer and fuel the tractor."

"I won't be long," Swede promised.

Georgia set a heaping plate of food in front of him.

He stared down at it. "Looks good, ma'am, but I can't eat all of that."

She laughed. "You'll burn it off before noon. Eat."

Allie entered, dressed in jeans, a long-sleeved shirt, boots and a cowboy hat. She tossed another cowboy hat on the table next to Swede. "That's one of Hank's old hats. You'll need it today. Try it."

Swede settled the hat on his head. It fit perfectly.

Allie sat across from him, but never lifted her head to look him in the eye.

Georgia kept up a running commentary about some of the local gossip, seemingly unaware of the tension between Swede and Allie.

By the time Swede choked down half of the food Georgia insisted he eat, he'd had enough. He pushed back from the table, lifted his plate and carried it to the counter. "Please cover that, and I'll eat the rest for dinner tonight."

"Are you sure?" she asked.

"Positive." He kissed the older woman's cheek. "Thank you for all you do."

Georgia blushed and waved a hand at him. "Get out of here. You'll have Eddy jealous if he catches you kissing me."

Allie stood as well and carried her plate to the sink. "Thank you, Georgia."

"I'll bring sandwiches for lunch," Georgia promised.

Swede walked out of the house first and scanned the vicinity, not expecting trouble, but keeping aware was an essential part of his job. They hadn't expected trouble at Reynolds's stable, and it had exploded in their faces.

Hank arrived as Swede and Allie joined Eddy and Mr. Patterson at the barn. Eddy would bale the hay while the other men loaded the bales on the trailer.

Allie drove the truck through the hayfield, inching along at a snail's pace. Ruger walked along beside the truck, occasionally chasing a rabbit or digging for a prairie dog.

Swede considered himself in pretty good shape since rehab, but the work was hard, the hay was itchy, and the sun beat down on them throughout the day. By noon, Swede and Hank had shed their shirts, their bodies covered in sweat and hay dust.

"It's been a while since I've hauled hay," Hank said. "Now I remember why I disliked it." He ran his hand through his hair, loosening the stray straws. "But, you always feel good about what you accomplish when all the bales are neatly stacked in the barn."

Swede tossed another bale on top of the ever-increasing stack. Hank's father manned the top of the pile, stacking the bales in an overlapping pattern to keep them from falling off. "It's good, hard work." And it helped him keep his mind off Allie. Except she was driving the truck. Every time he glanced up, he could see her face in the side mirror.

As her bodyguard, it was hard not to focus on her.

Even out in the hayfield, he had to be on his toes. Whoever shot at them from the vehicle the other night, could be hiding at the edge of the pasture with a high-powered sniper rifle.

Swede glanced around again, his gaze coming back to Allie in the mirror.

"Did Bear hear anything new from the police?" Swede asked. Anything to take his thoughts off Allie.

"Nothing we didn't already know from talking to Baker and his parents." Hank tossed a bale up onto the back of the trailer. "Bear would have come to help here, but he's headed to Baker's unit to wait for the commander to return from Wyoming."

"I'd like to get my hands around the throat of the guy who attacked the kid."

"You and me both." Hank wiped the sweat from his brow and walked to the next bale in the field. "It's bugging the crap out of me that I can't come up with a single motivation for the attack."

"It's some crazy son-of-a-bitch who happened by at the same time Baker felt like having a hamburger."

Hank shook his head. "My gut tells me the attack is more than that."

"I'd like to help with the investigation," Swede said.

"You are, by keeping an eye on my little sister. She's got enough problems." Hank shot a glance toward Allie. "I tried to call Reynolds last night. He didn't pick up. I left a message, but he didn't get back to me."

"Allie doesn't even know where he went on his business trip," Swede said. "What kind of guy leaves his fiancée a few days before his wedding and doesn't share where he's going?"

"Maybe he's having an illicit affair with one of his clients." Hank's jaw tightened. "In which case, I'll have to kill him for hurting my sister."

"Get in line." Swede's fists clenched. He flexed his injured hand, the ache building with each bale. But he didn't stop to cry about it. The ache reminded him to keep focused on what had to be done.

Protect Allie.

"Has Allie said anything about what she'll do if her fiancé doesn't show up for the wedding?"

"Not at all. She keeps repeating that she's getting married Saturday." Swede chuckled. "I believe if Reynolds doesn't show up for his wedding, she'll kill him."

Hank laughed out loud. "Sounds like Allie. She's a very determined and stubborn woman. She gets it from our father."

"What does she see in Reynolds?"

"I haven't a clue, and I really don't know him well enough to judge him. Except that he's not here when shit's hitting the fan with my sister. That's a really big strike in my book." Hank glanced up at his father on top of the stack of hay. "Does my father know why you're here?" he said in a lowered voice.

Swede shook his head. "Allie insisted on calling me a friend from college, here for her wedding. Mrs. Edwards knows."

"It's probably just as well. My father might go off half-cocked with both barrels loaded, looking for the crackpot taking shots at his little girl. And I don't think he approves of this marriage."

"Does anyone, except Allie?" Swede chose that moment to glance at the mirror.

Allie was staring back at him, her eyes narrowed. Had she heard him mention her name?

Swede switched sides of the truck. Seeing Allie in the mirror only made him want to shake her. Why was she insisting on marrying a man who clearly didn't care enough about her to be there when she was in trouble? Trouble that could have been brought on by his own business dealings, and her association with him.

When Reynolds returned from his business trip, Swede wanted to have a few words with the man.

THE DAY CRAWLED by at the pace Allie drove the pickup pulling the hay trailer. She counted the minutes until all of the hay was loaded into the barn. Then, and only then, could she get away from the sight of a shirtless Swede, muscles bulging with the weight of the bales as he tossed them like toys into the air. Every time she glanced into the side-view mirror, he was there, looking back at her. How was she supposed to quit thinking about him when he was larger than life and freakin' gorgeous in all his sweaty glory?

Her call to Damien the night before had gone unanswered. Same with the voicemail she'd left, asking him to return her call. He was probably in some far corner of the world where cell phone reception was as crappy or non-existent as it was in the rural areas of Montana.

Still, the man was getting married in two days. The least he could do was call his fiancée each night to whisper sweet nothings in her ear and tell her how much he loved her.

Allie frowned into the mirror at the same time Swede glanced up.

Come to think of it, Damien hadn't said he loved her since the day he'd proposed. Sure, the occasion had been romantic. He'd taken her to one of the most expensive restaurants in Bozeman and then they'd walked along the city streets afterward, arm-in-arm. When they'd come to the city park, the almost-full moon overhead gave just the right amount of light so they didn't need flashlights to see their way.

Damien had stopped, pulled her into his arms and stared into her eyes.

No man had ever held her like that. Most men she knew treated her like one of the guys, until Damien came along and reminded her that she was a woman, with all the needs and emotions most women had.

Then he'd dropped to one knee and asked her to marry him, and she'd been thrilled that a man thought she would make a good wife. But, was that enough to commit her life to a man she still barely knew?

The more she thought about it, the more she realized she might have made a huge mistake by saying yes.

If only she could talk to Damien. Maybe she'd get back that spark of excitement and be happy about the upcoming nuptials instead of feeling like Saturday would be one big disaster.

She was glad she'd insisted on a small wedding with family and a few friends.

The sooner she spoke to Damien, the better. Waiting until the actual wedding would be too late.

In the meantime, Allie drove a few feet forward at a time, gnashing her teeth, counting the bales until they were done. And they wouldn't be done until all of the hay was neatly stored in the barn.

Could this day get any longer?

By late afternoon, the last bale had been stacked in the barn. Though it was late, the sun wouldn't set for another hour or two. The men shook hands and parted, Hank heading home, Eddy heading for the foreman's house for a shower, her father and Swede for the main house.

Allie entered behind the two men and stopped in the kitchen.

Swede stopped, too, turning back toward her.

"Go ahead," she said. "You can have the first shower. I didn't sweat as much as you did." She wandered into the living room, and waited until she heard the water running.

Georgia had run over to the foreman's house for a few minutes, and Allie's father was in his own room showering.

With no one watching her, and her need to talk to Damien so important to her future, Allie decided to make a break for it. Perhaps Damien was back at his ranch and she could corner him for answers to all the burning questions she'd stored up since he left. Number one being, *why the hell did you ask me to marry you?*

She left the house and hurried to the barn. Catching and saddling a horse would take too long, so she pushed the four-wheeler out behind the barn and pressed the start button. The Bear Creek Ranch and the Double Diamond were both large spreads, but they adjoined on the southern border.

Allie had made the ride on horseback several times, and once on the four-wheeler. The terrain wasn't too challenging, and she could get there and back in less than an hour. Surely Damien would be home by now.

She sped away, hoping no one saw her leave. Since her decision wasn't planned, hopefully that attacker wasn't watching. If he had observed her all day, maybe he'd think she was done for the night when she'd gone inside the house. Either way, she was pretty good on the four-wheeler and confident enough in her skills to elude the bad guys. She hoped.

The trip across the ranch took twenty minutes and wouldn't have taken that long if she hadn't had to dismount, open three gates, drive through and close them behind her. Soon she was driving up to the mansion that could be her home in just two days. The broad columns and huge windows were stunning. But, would she fit in that house? Would the place feel like home? Could she be the kind of wife a businessman like Damien needed?

Did she want to be that kind of wife?

The sight of the burned-out hull of the stable and the scent of charred lumber made her want to gag. Nothing had been done to clean up the mess or start building a new stable to house the fine horses Damien kept. Perhaps that would be her first goal as the new wife of the owner. Allie dismounted, climbed the stairs to the front entrance and rang the doorbell.

Miles opened the door. "Miss Patterson, so nice of you to stop by. But I'm afraid Mr. Reynolds hasn't returned from his business trip. Would you care to come in for a cool beverage?"

Not really. Allie needed to talk to Damien.

Miles opened the door wider and Allie entered, wanting to see again what she was getting into by marrying the most eligible bachelor in the county. Hell, maybe in the whole state of Montana. How had she landed a catch like that?

The entryway floors of marble tiles stretched all the way into the main living area at the back of the house with twenty-foot ceilings and windows stretching the full height and length of the room. She could see from the front to the back of the house and through the windows to the snow-capped peaks of the Crazy Mountains.

"Miss Patterson, if you'd like to have a seat, I can get you that drink. What would you like?"

Allie stared around the room, feeling like an interloper, a stranger, a square peg in a round hole. This place didn't fit her personality. She'd be afraid to put her feet on the coffee table or wear her boots inside.

"Nothing, Miles. I'm sorry, but I can't stay." Though it never had in the past, the pure ostentatiousness of the decor threatened to overwhelm her now that she stood in the middle of the living room without Damien at her side. She'd mistaken the way he belonged for her belonging there, as well. Now she couldn't get out of there fast enough.

Allie turned and started for the door.

"Miss Patterson, Mr. Reynolds asked me to give you a piece of luggage from the set you two will be taking with you to the Cayman Islands on your honeymoon. Would you like to take it with you now, or would you like me to deliver it to your house tomorrow?"

She didn't want it at all. But she couldn't tell Miles she was getting cold feet. And she didn't want him to make the trip to the ranch, wasting his time if she decided to chicken out at the last minute. "No need to deliver it, Miles," she said.

"Then I'll collect it and bring it out to you in just a moment."

Before Allie could correct Miles and tell him she really didn't want the case, she watched him disappear into the cavernous house.

Great. Now she'd have one more thing to lug back to the ranch, and it would get dusty on the cross-country trip. Feeling like a fool, Allie left the house and walked out to the ATV. From where she'd parked, she stared at the shell of the stable, wondering who would have been heartless enough to destroy such a lovely building, nearly killing the animals inside.

Miles hurried out of the house, carrying a medium-sized, brown leather suitcase. When he noticed she was on the ATV, he stopped and frowned. "I thought you had arrived in your truck. Perhaps I'll deliver this tomorrow, after all."

"No worries, Miles. I can strap it to the back of the

four-wheeler. It won't get any more roughed up than it would by the baggage handlers at the airport."

"If you're sure." Miles held the case clutched to his chest.

Allie reached for the bag, and Miles handed it over. She strapped it to the rack on the back of the four-wheeler and climbed aboard. "If Mr. Reynolds makes it in tonight, tell him it's imperative that he call me immediately."

"I will," Miles promised. "Stay safe, Miss Patterson."

Allie rode out across the pasture, her heart heavy, the suitcase banging against the rack behind her. The closer it came to her wedding day, the more convinced she became that it wouldn't happen. But, she couldn't call it off without first speaking with Damien. Doing so was only fair. She refused to be a bride who jilted the groom at the altar. A day early was better than when all the guests were seated and waiting.

Halfway back to the ranch, she crested a hill and started down into a valley. So wrapped up in her own miserable decision and the consequences she faced, she didn't hear the other engine over her own until an ATV roared up beside her and rammed into her back tire. Her four-wheeler lurched and swerved toward a drop-off.

Heart thumping, she managed to straighten the steering wheel. She thumbed the throttle, sending her vehicle racing ahead. Fortunately, she was back on the Bear Creek Ranch and she knew every inch of the place like the back of her hand.

Speeding across the rocky terrain, she topped a rise so fast her wheels left the ground for a second and then slammed to the earth on the downward slope. She cursed herself for riding out without carrying the requisite shotgun. Too far from the barn to make it back quickly enough, she had to go in defensive mode. If she could put enough distance between them, she knew of a place she could hide until the attacking rider gave up and went away.

Now would be a good time for her bodyguard to discover her missing and come looking for her.

After only five minutes in the shower, Swede walked out, his towel slung over his shoulders, wearing only blue jeans. He stopped in front of Allie's open bedroom door. Nothing moved inside. He stepped in and looked around. "Allie?" No answer.

Not too worried, Swede entered his bedroom, pulled a clean T-shirt out of his duffle bag and dragged it over his head.

Allie had been downstairs when he'd gone for his shower. He'd let her know it was her turn. Pulling on a pair of boots, he hurried down the stairs, his feet moving faster each step he took, a niggling feeling creeping across his skin. "Allie?"

The back door creaked, and footsteps sounded in the kitchen.

Swede headed that direction only to find Georgia checking the contents of the oven. "Have you seen Allie?" he asked.

Georgia straightened. "I thought she'd gone for her shower."

At that point, Swede's belly clenched. "She's not in her room, nor in the shower. I just came from upstairs."

"What's for supper?" Lloyd entered the kitchen and sniffed. "Something smells good."

"Mr. Patterson, have you seen your daughter since we came inside?" Swede asked.

He shrugged. "Not since I went up for a shower. She might be out at the barn. Although, Eddy said he'd feed the animals. Maybe she decided to help."

"Eddy was in the shower when I left our house," Georgia said. "He didn't say anything about Allie."

"I'll check the barn," Swede said.

"I'll check around the house," Georgia said.

"Why the worry?" Lloyd asked, following Swede out the back door. "She's always fiddling around the barn."

"I just want to make sure she's all right," Swede said.

"Why wouldn't she be?" her father asked.

Swede didn't answer. He opened the barn door and entered. All the horses were in their stalls. Which meant she hadn't taken one out to exercise or ride, she wasn't anywhere around the barn and her truck was in the driveway.

Mr. Patterson stood near the rear of the barn, staring into an empty corner where a four-wheeler had been parked the day Swede and Allie had mucked the stalls. "You don't suppose Allie took the four-wheeler out to check on that sick heifer, do you?"

Damn. Swede walked out the back door of the barn.

As he suspected, he found fresh tire tracks in the dust. Allie had gone out alone on the four-wheeler.

"Sir, do you have another four-wheeler?" Swede asked.

"Nope. Just the one."

"Please, go get Mr. Edwards while I saddle up. We need to find Allie."

"Why are you so worried about her? She does this all the time."

Swede wanted to leave and find Allie, but he owed it to her father to let him know what was going on. "Mr. Patterson, I'm sorry, but we didn't want to worry you. I'm not Allie's friend from college. I was hired by Mr. Reynolds to be her bodyguard. Several attacks have occurred around your daughter. We need to find her before someone else does."

"You mean to tell me that shooter from the other night wasn't just a random act?"

Swede shook his head. "Not only did someone take a shot at us on our way back from the Blue Moose Tavern, he tried to run us off the road. And the day we went out to check on the heifer, a man on an ATV tried to run your daughter over. We need to hurry."

CHAPTER 9

Allie rounded a rocky corner, ducked between boulders, and rode down the middle of a stream for a short distance to hide her tracks and then climbed up the bank into a stand of trees surrounded by low brush. Behind the trees rose a bluff with several caves carved out by centuries of water flowing through the rocks. If she could make it to the caves, she had a chance of hiding inside one she and Hank used to play in as teenagers.

She ditched the ATV behind the brush, jumped off and ran, ducking to avoid low-hanging branches, leaping over medium boulders and glancing over her shoulder every four or five steps.

The sound of an engine nearby made her run faster. She had to make it to the cave before he saw her. The biggest challenge was once she started up the rocky path, she could be visible from below. She clung to the bottom of the bluff for as long as she could until she stood almost directly below the cave entrance. To get there, she had to climb over huge rocks. Eventually, she'd rise above the treetops and scoot along a ledge to enter. A thin waterfall ran out of the mouth of the cave, dropping one hundred feet to a stream. One slip on the climb upward and she could make that same fall and, like the water, splatter all over the river rocks below.

As long as her attacker was still on the ATV, he might not be able to see her climbing up the side of the bluff. He'd have to have a clear line of sight from the bottom of the bluff through the branches of the trees.

Allie took a step, slipped and caught herself before tumbling over the side. Her heart pounded so loudly in her ears she could barely hear anything else. She stopped, crouched low in the rocks, and listened. She could hear nothing but the whoosh of the wind through the trees.

Sweet Jesus. She had to move even faster. If the man had found her ATV, he might figure out she'd gone up the bluff to the caves.

Her muscles ached and her lungs burned with the extra effort to pull herself up the side of the bluff. Finally, she arrived at the cave and fell inside, crawling deeper into the shadows.

She lay still for several minutes, filling her lungs with the cool, damp air, straining to listen for the sound of someone climbing up after her. Allie pushed to her feet, her knees wobbling, her body drained.

Why had she ducked out on Swede? All she had to do was ask him to take her to the Double Diamond Ranch. He would have. If she'd found Damien there, Allie could have taken him aside, out of earshot of

Swede, and told him how she was feeling. Yes, the discussion would have been awkward. But she wouldn't be in the situation she was in now.

The sound of a pebble bouncing off other rocks made her freeze. Allie shrank into the back of the cave near a tunnel that led even deeper. She didn't want to go much farther without a light, but she would, if she had to.

A shadowy silhouette appeared in the mouth of the cave.

Allie swallowed a gasp and slipped deeper into the tunnel.

SWEDE TIED Little Joe to the hitch, ran to the tack room and grabbed the saddle he'd used the last time he'd ridden. Blanket, saddle, girth… he fumbled, trying to remember how Allie had looped the leather strap through the girth. Once he had it tight enough, he ran back to the tack room for the bridle.

"We have to find her, Little Joe," he said to the horse, slipping the bit between his teeth.

Outside the barn, Ruger waited patiently for Swede to give him permission to go with him.

"Come on, Ruger, we have to find Allie."

The dog tipped his head.

Mr. Patterson and Eddy came running from the house.

"We had a call from Miles, Damien Reynold's butler. He wanted to know if Allie had made it back to the house all right."

"She rode an ATV all the way over to the Double Diamond? It's over five miles."

"By the highway," Mr. Patterson stated. "She probably went cross-country. She knows the way and can get there and back fairly quickly on an ATV."

Then why wasn't she back already? Swede didn't say it, but he could see the same question in Lloyd and Eddy's faces.

"We'll saddle up and be right behind you." Eddy pointed across the pasture. "Head toward the gap between those two hills. You're armed, right?"

Swede patted the handgun beneath his jacket. "I am."

"Good. We'll catch you as soon as we saddle the horses."

Eddy had already disappeared into the barn. Lloyd followed.

Swede nudged the horse's flanks with his heels, and Little Joe sprang forward. God, he wished he'd had the ATV. He wasn't sure he'd be of much use on horseback. Going on foot wasn't an option. He might not reach her in time.

"Come, Ruger!" he called out.

The dog shot ahead of the horse, racing across the pasture like he knew where he was going.

Swede hoped he did. He hadn't trained Ruger to track a person, nor had he given the dog something of Allie's to sniff. But Swede felt more confident with the animal by his side, especially with Little Joe eating up the pasture beneath his feet. Galloping was much easier on the seat than trotting any day, and the gait got him where he needed to go faster. He just hoped when it came time to slow down, the horse would know what to do.

Riding on wings and a prayer, he charged across the pasture, aiming for the gap between the hills. As he topped a rise, the vista changed. On the other side of the hills were more hills, some rocky with steely gray bluffs. This was a different route than Allie had taken him two days before. As he raced through the divide, he hoped Eddy and Lloyd would catch up to him soon before he compounded the problem by getting lost.

Little Joe slowed, the ground beneath his hooves getting rockier and more treacherous. As Swede neared the base of one of the bluffs, he saw movement out of the corner of his eye. At first, he thought it might be a bird flying up the side of the cliff. When he turned and glanced up, he saw a figure in black entering a cave.

Swede pulled back on the reins so hard Little Joe reared and nearly trampled Ruger. Swede held on to the saddle horn and dug his heels into the stirrups, praying the horse didn't tip over backward.

Finally, Little Joe came down on all four hooves.

"Hey!" Swede shouted.

The man in the cave paused and glanced down. He had one hand braced on the wall of the bluff, and he held something in the other hand. Something small and dark...like a handgun.

Swede nudged Little Joe and leaned forward as the horse plowed through brush and trees, crossed a creek and stopped in front of the rocky escarpment.

Even before Little Joe was completely stopped, Swede swung out of the saddle to the ground.

The man at the mouth of the cave turned toward Swede and fired a round.

Swede ducked behind a boulder and waved at Little Joe, afraid the idiot above would hit the horse.

Little Joe spooked and ran, probably headed back to the barn. Ruger crouched next to Swede.

If Swede guessed right, that man up there was after Allie and might have her trapped. He didn't know how deep the cave went. All he knew was the man was armed and had fired on him first. That gave him the right to defend himself, and Allie. However, in order to be effective with a handgun, he had to get closer.

Taking a deep breath, Swede eased out from behind the boulder, spied the next big rock he could use as cover and made a dash toward it, zigzagging as he ran. Ruger ran with him, arriving at the same time as Swede.

Another shot ricocheted off the top of the big rock they ducked behind. Swede performed this maneuver, again and again, moving higher up the side of the bluff, picking his way through the rough terrain as best he could. Within minutes, he was within a reasonable range to fire.

The figure disappeared into the cave.

Damn. Swede took the opportunity to race as fast as he could, stepping over stones, climbing over boulders and pulling himself higher up the trail.

Still, the man didn't appear, making Swede even more anxious, his heart banging against his ribs.

Ruger, on four legs, had much better balance and nimbly climbed the rocky terrain.

"Get 'em, Ruger. Get 'em," Swede said.

The dog raced the remaining yards up the incline and ran into the cave. A shot rang out.

Swede held his breath, praying Allie or Ruger hadn't taken that bullet. Using the remainder of his breath and strength, he heaved himself up over the rocks and ran into the cave.

Though Ruger was only considered a medium-sized dog, he'd tackled and pinned the gunman.

But not for long. The man knocked Ruger to the side, lurched to his feet and dove for his gun.

Swede reached it first, kicking it out the mouth of the cave. The man switched directions and flung himself at Swede.

Barely inside the cave himself, Swede wasn't in a position to take the full force of the man's weight. In a split second, Swede fell to the ground. It was that, or be knocked over the ledge.

The gunman didn't have time to slow his forward momentum. He tripped over Swede's body, stepped in the middle of the waterfall flowing out of the cave's entrance and tumbled over the edge.

He cried out as he plummeted to the base of the falls, landing with a dull thump.

Wasting no time on the dead man, Swede entered the cave, calling out, "Allie? It's me, Swede."

Ruger disappeared into the darkness and whined softly.

"Allie?"

"Swede?" She materialized in front of him, Ruger at her side, his tail wagging a thousand times a minute. For a moment, Allie stared at Swede, her bottom lip trembling.

His heart swelled and he opened his arms.

Allie rushed into them. "I prayed you'd come," she said into his shirt, her voice catching on a sob. "I don't think he would have found me back in the tunnels. But it was really dark, and I've never gone in very deep without a flashlight."

"You're okay, now." Swede smoothed a hand over her hair, speaking to her like he did to the animals in a slow, calming tone, though nothing inside him was calm. He'd almost lost her. She'd been so close to taking a bullet from that man's gun or falling over the ledge to her death on the rocks below.

Swede buried his face in her hair and inhaled the strawberry scent, mixed with the evergreen fragrance of the trees. "You scared the hell out of me."

"I'm sorry." She stared up at him. "I had to go to see Damien."

"I would have taken you."

"I know, but I needed to go by myself."

"And?"

She snorted. "He wasn't there."

Without releasing her, he leaned back enough to cup her cheek. "What was so all-fired important you had to go without me to escort you?"

She stared up at him, her green eyes darkening. "You."

God, he wanted to kiss her. Every beat of his heart urged him to do it. "Me?"

Allie nodded and reached up to touch his face, her

fingers tracing the scar along his cheek. "I can't stop thinking about you."

"Funny," he said. "There must be something in the water." He bent his head, no longer capable of resisting those very tempting lips. Before he took them, he asked, "Are you going to slap me again?"

She chuckled, wrapped her hand around the back of his neck and said, "Not a chance." Then she met his lips with hers, kissing him as long and hard as he kissed her.

Swede slid his hands down her back to the base of her spine and lower, pressing her hips to his. Nothing could stop him from claiming this woman's mouth.

Except the shout echoing off the walls of the bluffs.

"Allie! Swede!" Lloyd Patterson's voice boomed through the gathering dusk.

Swede was first to step away. He stared down into Allie's eyes. "Are you okay?"

Allie nodded, pressing the back of her hand to her mouth. She squared her shoulders and nodded again. "We need to call in the sheriff and an ambulance."

"Or a coroner," Swede said. "I'd be surprised if he survived the fall."

Her jaw tightened and her eyes narrowed. "It's wrong of me to say it, but I hope he's dead."

"Not wrong." He slipped his arm around her waist and eased toward the opening of the cave. "In this case, it was us, or him."

Allie tipped her chin. "I choose us."

"His own actions sent him over the edge. The landing did the rest." He gripped her hand. "Come on, your father will be beside himself until he sees his darling daughter."

She shot a glance his way. "He knows?"

Swede nodded. "You turned up missing, so I had to tell him. He was well on his way to figuring it out by then."

Allie sighed. "He'll be mad at me."

"Probably," Swede agreed. "But he'll be happy you're alive and well."

"After we get down from here safely." She peered over the edge. "If I remember correctly, it's easier climbing up than going down."

Swede winked. "We'll help each other."

Picking their way over the rocks, they eased their way down the bluff.

Eddy and Lloyd were at the bottom of the waterfall beside the body of Allie's attacker.

"We heard the gunshots and followed the sound," Eddy said.

Lloyd stared hard at Allie.

"I'm sorry, Dad. I didn't want to worry you."

"My ass," he bit out. "Being a target of someone bent on killing you is a no-brainer. You tell me and everyone else around you. That way we're all looking out for you."

Allie pushed her shoulders back. "You're right."

"And don't go running off alone." Her father nodded toward the body on the ground. "He might not be the only one gunning for you. I'm gonna have words with Mr. Reynolds."

"I went over to his place to have a talk with him, myself," Allie said. "He's not in town."

"After what's happened, I want to take a bullwhip to the boy."

Allie touched her father's arm. "Then you'd end up in jail."

Patterson scowled. "It would be worth it. Any man who skips out of town when his fiancée is in trouble deserves to be whipped. Hell, he doesn't deserve the fiancée, and she'd be smart to tell him so."

"Daddy…" Allie glanced around. She nodded toward the body, lying face down on the rocks. "Who is it?"

Eddy stepped across the rocks, checked for a pulse and shook his head. "Didn't think he'd survive that fall." He grabbed the man's arm and turned him over.

Allie gasped. "That's Will Franklin, Damien's foreman." Her brows drew together. "I'll bet he was also the one who blew up the barn."

"The bastard was conveniently in town when it happened," Swede agreed.

"If he wasn't already dead, I'd shoot him myself." Allie glared at the corpse. "That explosion and fire almost killed five horses."

Swede was so relieved Will hadn't succeeded in killing Allie, he almost laughed at her statement. The image of Will with a gun in his hand, so close he could have fired into the cave and hit Allie, stole all the humor out of the situation.

"How did you guys get here?" Allie asked, looking around.

"Horseback," Swede responded.

Allie's brows rose. "You? Out here?"

Swede nodded. "Little Joe did good. But, he's not above leaving me here to head back to the barn."

Turning to her father and Eddy, Allie asked, "And you two?"

"Our horses are tied to a branch near the creek," Eddy answered.

Allie clapped her hands together. "Then let's get back to the ranch."

"Swede, you can ride double with me," Eddy offered.

"Allie can ride with me," her father said.

She shook her head. "I ditched my four-wheeler in the brush. As long as it starts, I can make it back to the barn on my own four wheels."

"And I'm going with you," Swede said.

"Tell you what," Lloyd said. "You three head on back and call the sheriff. I'll stay out here until Eddy brings him out. Don't want the wolves destroying evidence."

Eddy nodded.

Swede followed Allie to the stand of brush where she'd hidden her ATV. It was still there, untouched and undamaged, with that damned suitcase strapped to the back.

Allie climbed on and started the engine. Then she turned to Swede. "Hop on."

He slid his leg over the seat and settled behind her, wrapping his arms around her waist.

Being a bodyguard had its perks, but Swede was sure kissing the fiancée of the man he was working for wasn't supposed to be one of them.

Allie revved the engine and took off. Ruger followed, easily keeping up with the pair on the ATV.

Though he was relieved Will Franklin wouldn't be a threat anymore, Swede wasn't sure Allie was out of the woods yet. What beef could Will have had against Allie? Was he afraid she'd usurp his control of the ranch? Or had someone hired him to carry out the threat that had been painted on the side of the stable?

Swede didn't have the answers and, at that moment, he didn't care. What he did care about was the woman in front of him. The one who smelled like strawberries and evergreen forests. She even had a few twigs sticking out of her wild auburn curls.

God, she was beautiful. The more he was with her, the deeper he fell.

It would be tough delivering her to the wedding and letting go. But, he had to. His job wasn't to steal the bride, it was to protect her and give her to another man in two days.

Pressure threatened to squeeze the air out of Swede's lungs. All those bodyguard rules had flown out the window on his first assignment. He wondered if this was really the job for him in the wilds of Montana, or if he should do something less stressful and go be a deckhand on a charter fishing boat.

A strand of auburn hair floated back on him, brushing across his face, touching him in a way he'd never considered as poignant. It was like a finger stroking him, teasing him urging him to continue to follow this woman, no matter where she led him.

CHAPTER 10

Back at the house, Georgia met Allie and Swede in the barnyard.

Eddy had beat them back, riding fast and hard to get to a telephone and call 911.

"Oh, thank God!" Georgia wrapped Allie in a bear hug that nearly crushed her bones. "You had us all so worried. I think I lost a couple of years off my life and gained a few more gray hairs."

"I'm sorry," Allie said, her teeth chattering. Darkness had settled in and the night sky, clear of all clouds, had already begun to release the heat of the day.

The older woman clucked her tongue. "Never mind the scoldin'. The important thing is that you're okay." She stared at Allie. "Oh, baby, you're cold. Let's get you inside."

"Really, I'm okay. Nothing but a few scratches and bruises. I could use a hot shower, though." Things for her could have ended a whole lot worse. At least she wasn't dead, like Will Franklin. A twinge of compassion flickered across her consciousness over the man's death, immediately followed by the strengthening of her will. He had tried to kill her on multiple occasions. Swede might have been collateral damage. "I'll be upstairs if anyone needs me."

Allie marched up to her room, gathered clean underwear and a pair of pajamas, a change from her usual oversized T-shirt. Once in the shower, she turned up the heat and stood under the spray until her insides were as warm as her outsides. When she stepped out of the shower to dry off, she started shaking and couldn't seem to stop.

Never had she been more afraid than when she'd been trapped in the cave with a man wielding a gun. That was the stuff Wild West movies were made of. Thinking a cup of hot cocoa would help, she left the bathroom and padded down the stairs to the kitchen.

Through the kitchen window she could see half a dozen vehicles in the barnyard. An ambulance, a couple of sheriff's deputy's vehicles, and a small first-responder fire truck. Allie glanced down at her pajamas. Maybe she should get dressed to speak to the authorities. She debated going back upstairs, but decided she was fully covered and wanted the hot cocoa more.

Once she took the mug out of the microwave, she pulled on a pair of boots and a jacket, grabbed her cocoa and stepped outside.

Half a dozen people surrounded her, all asking questions at once.

Swede worked his way through the small crowd and slipped an arm around her.

Allie leaned against him, grateful for his solid strength and willingness to stand beside her during the questioning. By the time they'd loaded Will Franklin's body into the ambulance and everyone departed, Allie was mentally and physically exhausted.

"Come on, let's get you inside." Swede touched a hand to her lower back and guided her back to the house.

Instead of going directly inside, Allie stopped on the second step up to the porch. "I'm tired, but too wound up to go right to sleep. I think I need to stay out here for a few minutes. The cool night air helps clear my mind. Go. Get your shower. I won't go anywhere." She held up her hand. "I promise."

"I can't leave you outside alone," Swede said.

"Go," a voice said behind him. "Get your shower. I'll sit with my daughter." Her dad walked out onto the porch, carrying a steaming cup of coffee.

"I'll only be a few minutes," Swede said.

"Take your time." Her father lowered himself to the porch step and patted the space beside him.

Allie sat. She couldn't remember a time since her mother died that her father had sat beside her on the porch steps. Tears welled in her eyes, and she fought to keep them from sliding down her cheeks. What was wrong with her? She wasn't usually this emotional.

Since her mother died and Hank joined the Navy, Allie had tried to be everything her father needed, sometimes forgetting what she needed. Which was probably half the reason she'd accepted Damien's proposal of marriage. He'd seen in her a woman. Not a daughter or a rancher. She'd felt special for a brief moment, the typical female with dreams of a fairytale wedding to a handsome man. But she'd been blinded by the wedding planning. Now she had a big mess to clean up, and she was so tired.

Her father reached out and took her hands in his big, callused fingers. "Allie, I don't say it enough, but I love you to the moon and back."

Tears slipped from her eyes and rolled down her cheeks. Once they'd started, she couldn't hold them back. "Oh, Daddy." She leaned into his shoulder. "I've missed you."

"I'm sorry, I haven't been much of a father since your mother died. I miss her so badly some days I don't know if I can go on."

"Me, too."

"She should have been here for you, to talk with you about all the woman things I can't begin to understand."

"You haven't done so badly. And I've had Georgia to lean on."

"What have I taught you, other than how to be an old grouch? Hell, I ran off your brother."

"He wouldn't have made it through SEAL training if not for the way you toughened him up. He told me so himself." She squeezed his hand.

"Tonight, I realized just how close I came to losing you." He looked down at their joined hands. "It scared me. Bad. I don't want to lose any more of my family. I'll fight to keep you safe. So, please, if you're in trouble, let me know."

No matter how independent she was, she still needed her father. "I will, Daddy."

He kissed her forehead like he used to when she was a little girl. "If Damien makes you happy, then I'm all for your wedding. But if he hurts you or you want out, I'll have my shotgun ready."

Allie half-chuckled and half-sobbed. "Thanks, Dad. I'll remember that."

A sound behind them made Allie turn.

Swede stood in the doorway, dressed in clean jeans and a blue chambray shirt, his hair wet, his feet bare.

God, he was the most ruggedly gorgeous man Allie had ever seen.

Her father stood. "I need to hit the sack. We have another load of hay to haul in tomorrow."

"I'll help with that," Allie offered.

"Don't you have to get your nails, hair or some such nonsense done for the wedding?" her father asked.

She smiled. "That happens the day of the wedding." If she went through with it. She needed to talk to Damien. Soon.

Again, her father bent and pressed a kiss to her forehead. "Whatever makes you happy, makes me happy." He entered the house, closing the door behind him.

Swede sat in the spot Allie's father had vacated moments before.

Ruger dropped onto the porch directly behind him and laid his head on his paws.

"Are you okay?" Swede asked.

"I am, now." She wiped the moisture from her cheeks and stared out at the moon, shining high above the Crazy Mountains. "I'm sorry about taking off."

"Yeah. About that..." He leaned his elbows on his knees. "Having a bodyguard necessitates a two-way commitment. I can't do my job if you run away."

"I wasn't running away. I needed to see Damien." She shoved her hand through her wet hair, lifting it off her shoulders. "Alone."

Swede nodded. "And he wasn't there."

She shook her head. "No."

"You could have called ahead and saved a whole lot of trouble."

"I know. I called but no one picked up. And, frankly, I wasn't thinking clearly." *I was thinking of you, you big galoot.*

"Would it help if you got a different bodyguard? Bear and I could switch assignments."

"Is that what you want?" she asked, her voice barely above a whisper. "I know I've been less than cooperative, but I'd rather stick with you...if you don't mind." She plucked at the fabric on the leg of her pajamas.

"Better the devil you know, than the one you don't?" Swede asked.

"No." She glanced up at him, though seeing through the moisture pooling again in her eyes was difficult. "I trust you. I know you really do have my best interests in mind." She leaned into his shoulder. "I promise not to take off without you."

"You won't have to put up with me much longer. The

wedding is the day after tomorrow. Then you'll be on your honeymoon in the Cayman Islands."

Yeah, that was the plan. If she chose to follow it. She reached for Swede's hand. "Thank you for rescuing me in that cave today."

Swede turned, his knees touching Allie's. "I think the real hero today was Ruger."

Allie swiveled toward the dog at the same time as Swede. She let go of Swede's hand and ran her fingers over Ruger's soft fur. "He was amazing. Did you have him specially trained?"

Swede scratched behind Ruger's ear. "He's a rescue from the pound. I picked him up because he was on death row. And to tell the truth, he rescued me."

"How could anyone leave their dog behind when they move on?" Allie shook her head. "How did he rescue you?"

"Since the attack that ended my career in the navy, I've had nightmares. Ruger helps get me through them."

Allie looked up from the dog to his master. "How so?"

"Just by being there. When he senses my distress, he nudges me with his nose. It brings me out of the dream world into the real world. Before Ruger…well, I wasn't coping well."

"He is a hero." She patted the dog's head and pushed to her feet. The more she learned about Swede, the more she wanted to know. With another man's engagement ring on her finger, she had no business learning more about Swede. The personal details only made her see him as a man. An interesting man. One with a love for dogs, which put him way up there on her list of great guys.

No, she needed to see Damien, and end her engagement, or go through with the wedding. Until she did that, she had no right to daydream or night dream about another man.

As she stood, she teetered on the edge of the step and would have fallen if Swede hadn't leaped to his feet, grabbed her arms and pulled her against him.

Allie's hands touched his chest, the hard muscles flexing beneath her fingertips. She had the wild urge to run her hands beneath his shirt and feel the skin stretched over those fabulous muscles.

Jerking away her hands, she got her footing and climbed the remaining steps to the porch. "I'd better go to bed. We have another load of hay to haul tomorrow."

"I'd say stay here and let me handle it, but I need you close, so that I can keep an eye on you. We'll do it the same as last time?"

Allie nodded.

"Allie?" Swede reached for her hand and laced his fingers with hers.

She stared at where their hands entwined, her heart racing, her mouth dry.

"Today scared me more than I've ever been scared in my life." He snorted. "And I've been in some pretty hairy situations." He lifted her hand to his lips and pressed a kiss to her knuckles. "I'm glad you're okay."

Electric currents raced up her arm and down her body to pool low in her belly. This couldn't happen. She couldn't be sexually attracted to a man she'd only known a few days. But she was, and it made her feel more alive than she'd felt…ever. An admission which shook her to the core. Using every bit of control she could muster, she pulled her hand from his, anxious to leave him, before she threw herself into his arms and made a fool of herself.

Swede's hand dropped to Ruger's head. "I'll see you in the morning."

SWEDE WAITED on the porch several minutes after Allie went inside, afraid that if he followed her, he'd stay with her all the way to her bedroom. Once there he'd convince her to make love with him.

Wrong, wrong, wrong!

He stood beside Ruger, the dog nudging his hand, sensing his turmoil.

"Sometimes I wish I were you, Ruger," he said. "Life as a dog is so much less complicated."

The dog whined and licked his hand.

"Yeah. Until you find yourself on death row and a broken-down veteran saves you from the gas chamber." He ruffled Ruger's neck, made a pass around the exterior of the house, looking for anyone lurking, unwilling to presume Will Franklin was the only one stalking Allie. When nothing moved and Ruger didn't snarl or growl in warning, Swede made his way inside to his room on the second floor. Knowing Allie was in the room on the other side of the wall reminded him of how close she was, yet how far she was out of his reach.

He stripped out of his shirt and jeans and lay on the

sheets, naked. The heat he'd felt burning inside when he'd touched her hand and kissed her fingers clung to him, making it difficult to go to sleep. For a long time, he stared up at the ceiling, willing his lust to subside. Time and fatigue finally won the fight, and he fell to sleep.

What could only have been minutes after he'd closed his eyes, Swede was awakened by the sound of quiet sobbing.

Ruger nudged his hand and trotted to the door. Thinking he might have been imaging the noise, Swede listened.

There it was again. The soft sobs were coming from the room on the other side of the wall. He leaped to his feet, dragged on his jeans and hurried out of his room. When he stood in front of Allie's door, he hesitated. If he went in, he wasn't sure he could walk out without touching her. And touching her wasn't all he wanted to do.

Another sob was the deciding factor. He tapped on the door and, careful not to wake her father, called out softly, "Allie."

Continued sobbing made him grab the door handle and twist. It opened easily, and he stepped inside, closed the door behind him and crossed to stand beside her bed before the next sob shook her body.

"Oh, darlin'," he said, his heart clenching inside his chest.

Tears stained her cheeks and her bottom lip trembled. Her legs thrashed, trapped in the sheets. Whatever she dreamed was either breaking her heart or terrifying her. Maybe both.

Swede couldn't stand by and do nothing. He scooted her over on the mattress and slid onto the bed beside her, pulling her into his arms. "Wake up, Allie. You're having a bad dream."

She rolled onto her side, burying her face into his bare chest, her hand resting against his skin.

The strawberry scent of her hair was almost his undoing. He couldn't stay long, or he'd be tempted to kiss her.

She took a shuddering breath, her fingers flexing and curling against him.

Swede tried again, his power of resistance waning with every passing second she lay in his arms. "Sweetheart, you need to wake up. You're dreaming."

"If I'm dreaming, please…don't wake me," she said, her voice low and gravely, spreading over him like melted chocolate.

With a groan, Swede clutched her tighter, his groin tightening, the blood rushing from his brain to parts farther south. He was losing it, and he had no way of letting go.

Allie's hand slid down his chest to his abdomen and lower still to where he'd only half-buttoned his fly.

Swede sucked in a breath, afraid to move lest he encourage her to keep going. This wasn't what he'd come to do. But he couldn't deny the magnetic attraction he had for this woman.

Her fingers slipped beneath the waistband of his jeans.

He covered her hand with his. "Allie, you have to know what you're doing. You can't be asleep on this."

"I'm awake," she said, opening her eyes.

From the little bit of moonlight edging its way through a gap in her closed curtains, he could see her staring up at him. "I should go," Swede said.

Her hand flatted against him. "Please, don't. Stay with me."

"I can't stay and not touch you."

She took his hand and slid it up under her pajama top to the rounded swell of her breast. "Then touch me."

His fingers slowly curled around her breast, weighing the fullness of it in his palm. Swede groaned. "God, you feel amazing."

She reached for the hem of her pajama top and pulled it up over her head, tossing it to the side.

"What about your fiancé?"

"It's over," she said. "I can't marry him."

Swede froze, his thumb and forefinger arrested in pinching her nipple. "Why?"

"After all that's happened, I've learned that I don't love him. I was in love with the idea of getting married, not with the man I was going to marry."

Swede leaned over and kissed the corner of her mouth, then her lips. "But your wedding is in two days," he said against her lips.

"Not anymore. I'm not going through with it," she said. "I'm telling Damien tomorrow."

Knowing he should wait until after she officially called off her engagement, Swede couldn't stop fondling her breast or kissing her lips. What had started as a means to comfort her had become an entirely different scenario he was ill prepared to fight against. This internal battle was one he was all too willing to concede.

The question was, could he live with himself the next day?

CHAPTER 11

The moment Allie felt Swede's arms around her, she knew she couldn't let him go. Her dream had shaken her. She'd been hiding in a dark cave, while a man with a gun stood silhouetted in the light, pointing at her. Her feet had felt cemented to the floor, her heart pounding so hard she couldn't catch her breath.

Then Swede's arms wrapped around her, and more than that, his voice penetrated the dream, bringing her to the surface of consciousness.

Wrapped in his embrace, she turned to him, running her hand across his warm skin, inhaling the light, musky scent that belonged only to him. This was where she wanted to be.

Only she wanted to be closer. Skin to skin. Allie wanted him inside her, filling her, making her complete. What started as a rescue from a dream quickly transformed into an aching need to be with him. A need so strong, she couldn't deny it a moment longer. "Please, stay with me," she repeated.

She laid her hand over his as he fondled her breast, the tingling sensations sending shocks of electricity throughout her body. At a touch of his lips, she opened to him, thrusting her tongue between his teeth, meeting him halfway in a long, sensuous caress. Allie pulled her top over her head, desperate to be with him, to feel him against her, their hearts beating together.

Swede's lips brushed across hers, kissing a path down the side of her neck, stopping long enough to tongue the wildly beating pulse at the base of her throat. As he moved downward, he nipped her collarbone, kissed the top of her breast and sucked a nipple into his mouth, pulling gently, tapping the nipple with the tip of his tongue until it hardened into a tight little bead.

Allie arched off the mattress, wanting him to take more.

He obliged, drawing more of her into his mouth, flicking the tip, again and again.

Taking momentary control, Allie guided him to her other breast. "Please," she moaned softly.

And he did please, nibbling the peak, rolling it around on his tongue and laving it until Allie thought she would come apart.

Swede moved his lips across her ribs, past her belly button and onward to the elastic waistband of her pajamas. Inching the fabric down her legs, he paused to kiss the tuft of hair over her sex. Then again to lick the inside of her thighs, and finally to nip her ankle as he tossed the garment to the floor.

Allie parted her legs automatically, making room for him to slide between.

Swede lifted her knees, positioning them beside his head and then slipped his finger through her curls. He parted her folds, touched his tongue to that little strip of flesh packed with what felt like thousands of nerve endings, sizzling with heat, sending messages to her brain and back to her core, making Allie slick with desire.

Just when she thought it couldn't get better, he pressed a finger to her entrance and swirled.

"Oh, God," she said, digging her heels into the sheets, pushing her hips upward. "Oh, God."

He pushed two fingers into her and licked her nubbin in a long, slow stroke, pushing Allie to the very edge of sanity.

She teetered on the brink until he flicked and teased her there, thrusting his fingers in and out at the same time. The combination rocketed her to the heavens, flinging her past the stars. She held onto his hair, riding the wave all the way, her core pulsing, her breath lodged in her lungs until she finally drifted back to earth and sucked in a lungful of air. Then need drove her to tug on his hair, drawing him up her body.

He leaned over her, pressing his lips to hers for a brief second.

"You're overdressed," she commented.

"I'm working on it." Swede rolled off the bed onto his feet and shucked his jeans, retrieving his wallet from his pocket as he did.

He was beautiful in a purely male way, with shoulders impossibly broad, narrowing to a trim waist. Firm, six-pack abs and…yes…his shaft jutted out straight and proud.

Allie's channel convulsed, liquid sliding through, dripping onto the sheet. "Hurry," she said, her belly tight, her lungs dragging in air in spasms.

"Protection." He pulled a foil packet from his wallet.

Allie leaned up, snatched it from his hand and applied it, rolling her fingers down his length. She fell back against the mattress. "Oh, sweet Jesus. Please. I can't wait another minute."

"Beautiful, and impatient." He spread her legs, running his hand up the insides of her thighs to the apex where heat radiated. Swede pulled her bottom to the edge of the bed, hooked her legs over his arms and pressed his cock to her entrance.

"Now," she urged. "Take me now."

He thrust into her, driving all the way to the hilt before he stopped. Her channel was so slick with juices inspired by all the foreplay, he slid right in, filling and stretching her deliciously.

Allie grabbed his ass and held him there, letting her body adjust to his length and girth. Then she eased him away and back in again.

Swede took over from there, moving in and out, gradually accelerating until he pumped in and out like a piston on an engine.

Raising her hips to match his every thrust, Allie urged him on, the friction causing the heat to build.

Swede's face tensed, his jaw tightened, and he threw back his head. If they'd been alone in the house, Allie was sure he'd have shouted or called out her name.

Instead, he slammed into her one last time and remained buried deep within, his cock pulsing, his muscles tight, his face set. Then he scooted her back on the bed, crawled up beside her and pulled her into his arms.

Allie nuzzled his chest, finding a little brown nipple. She touched it with her tongue, loving the taste of this man. Pressing closer, she basked in the skin-to-skin contact, her heartbeat slowing, her breathing returning to normal. Gone were the residual effects of the nightmare. In its place was the utterly poignant satisfaction of great lovemaking with an amazing man.

As she drifted to sleep, a nagging twinge of guilt made her stomach churn. Tomorrow, she'd break off her engagement. Tomorrow, she'd call off the wedding. Even if nothing came of her relationship with Swede, Allie knew in her heart, she didn't love Damien. A marriage between them would never have worked.

She wished he had been home earlier that evening so she could have made the break then. Tomorrow would have to be soon enough.

Swede lay for a long time, loving the feel of Allie in his arms, her soft body pressed up against his hard one, the smell of strawberries wafting beneath his nose. This must be what heaven felt like. He couldn't imagine anywhere else being as wonderful.

But the longer he lay there holding the woman he found himself falling for, the more that kernel of guilt grew into a sour wad in his gut. He'd made love to his client's fiancée two nights before their wedding. Not only had he broken the first rule of being a bodyguard, he'd betrayed Hank's trust and risked the reputation of the company his friend was trying to build. With Hank's sister.

Allie slept, seemingly dream-free.

After a while, Swede slipped from the bed, disposed of the condom, pulled on his jeans and left her room, closing the door behind him. From now until Allie called off the wedding, Swede vowed to keep his hands to himself. Touching Allie was strictly forbidden.

He returned to his room and lay on top of the covers, his hand reaching for Ruger's head and the calming influence of a dog who didn't judge. For a long time, he stared up at the ceiling, counting the minutes before sleep finally claimed him again.

Morning came too soon, the sound of Mr. Patterson clomping down the hallway in his cowboy boots waking Swede without need for an alarm. Groggy and with a slight headache pressing against his temples, Swede rose from the bed, dressed, brushed his hair and teeth and went downstairs to the kitchen.

"Eddy and Mr. Patterson already had breakfast." Georgia plunked two plates full of food on the table. "They're gearing up, and said for you and Allie to join them when you're ready."

Allie appeared, her hair pulled back in a ponytail, her face scrubbed clean. No makeup masked the simple beauty of her complexion and eye color.

Her cheeks were naturally blushed and her gaze didn't actually meet his.

"Did you sleep all right?" she asked.

"Yes," he answered. "And you?"

She nodded and took her seat across the table.

They spent the rest of the meal eating, not talking, the atmosphere strained. For such an amazingly close connection the night before, he felt like they were miles apart that morning, even though he could reach across the table and touch her face.

Having only pecked at her food, Allie got up, took her plate to Georgia and gave her a wry smile. "Guess I'm not very hungry. Could you save that for my lunch?"

"Sure can." Georgia's brows dipped. "Are you feelin' okay?"

Allie nodded. "Just a little tired."

"Maybe you should stay in and let me do the driving today."

"I think the fresh air will do me good." Allie kissed Georgia's cheek. "But thanks."

Swede carried his half-eaten plate of food to Georgia. "Thanks for breakfast. You're a great cook." He, too, kissed Georgia's cheek and winked. "See you later."

Georgia touched her cheek, her gaze following Allie out the door. "Look out for my girl out there."

"I will." Swede wouldn't let her out of his sight for a minute. He refused to allow anything to happen to her. His heart was riding on it.

The day flew by in a rush to get all the hay from the second pasture baled, loaded onto the trailer and unloaded into the barn.

Allie drove, not saying much to anyone. Not that the men were in the mood to talk. All of their energy was channeled into the work. By the time the sun crept toward the horizon, Eddy tucked the last bale onto the top of the stack in the barn. "Done."

"What say we have a beer to celebrate?" Lloyd draped a sweaty arm over his daughter's shoulders.

"Thanks, Dad, but I'll pass." Allie lifted her father's arm off her shoulders. "And you smell."

"Good, honest sweat."

For the first time since Swede had met Mr. Patterson, he saw the older man grin.

"That's right, you have a wedding to get ready for." His eyes narrowed. "Aren't you supposed to go out on the town for a bachelorette party or something?"

"No, Dad."

"Why not?"

"I don't feel like it." She turned toward the house.

"What about a rehearsal?"

"Damien and I opted not to do a rehearsal." She gave a weak smile. "I'm headed for the shower."

Swede hesitated before following her.

"Go on," Mr. Patterson said. "Eddy and I will take care of the animals."

"Thank you, sir." Swede hurried after her.

She was up the stairs and in the shower before he caught up.

If he expected any acknowledgement for the best night of sex he'd ever had, he wasn't getting any. He wondered if she really was going to break it off with

Damien. Swede's gut tightened. If not, he'd been played for a fool.

But the more he thought about it and everything he'd seen of Allie, she wasn't the kind of woman to play games. That woman was a straight shooter. The more likely reason for her silence today was that breaking her engagement was heavy on her mind. Because she was a straight shooter, she was probably feeling a crap load of guilt for having slept with her bodyguard.

At least that's what Swede hoped.

CHAPTER 12

Allie showered the dust and itchy hay off her skin, telling herself she'd feel better making the call she had to make with a clean body, if not a clean conscience. After she'd toweled dry, she dressed in shorts and a T-shirt and crossed the hallway. Her gaze drifted to Swede's bedroom, part of her hoping he'd open the door and give her an encouraging smile. She'd need all the encouragement she could get to make that call.

With no one stopping her to engage in conversation, Allie entered her room like she was walking to her doom. Taking a deep breath, she squared her shoulders, lifted the phone and dialed Damien's cell phone number, fully expecting to get the voicemail.

He answered on the second ring. "Alyssa, dear. I'm so glad you called."

"I thought you would be back by now," she said, startled into saying the first thing that came out of her mouth.

"I'm sorry, sweetheart. Business delayed me. I'll be back tomorrow morning."

"The wedding is scheduled for tomorrow, or had you forgotten?" she said, with a little snap in her voice.

"I know. I can't wait for the ceremony that will make you Mrs. Damien Reynolds. Then we leave immediately for our honeymoon."

"About the wedding—" she started, then had to swallow.

"Don't worry, darling. I'll be there on time. Until then, sweet dreams."

"But, Damien—"

The connection ended.

What the hell?

She dialed his number again and the connection went straight to his voicemail. She hung up and redialed, repeating the process four times until she finally gave up. Mad as hell and ready to end their engagement, she was tempted to do it by voicemail. But she couldn't. No matter how aggravating the man was, he deserved to be told to his face that she wouldn't marry him.

She stared at the clock on the nightstand. As late as it was, she wouldn't have time to contact everyone to tell them not to come to the wedding. What she'd tried so hard to avoid would come to pass. She'd jilt her groom at the wedding.

She stretched out on her bed, fully expecting to lie awake all night long, dreading the next day's confrontation with Damien. And she did. For a while, going back and forth on whether she'd marry him just to save face, and then have the marriage annulled a week later. Of course, she wouldn't go on the honeymoon. But Damien could at least enjoy the time on the beach. The Cayman Islands had been his idea of the perfect honeymoon. Not hers.

Allie would rather have gone to a mountain cabin where they could be alone, making love into the wee hours of every morning. Now, she couldn't picture making love to Damien at all. In her heart, it was Swede. And she couldn't go to him that night because, though she'd gone against her own code of honor and slept with him the night before, she couldn't do it again until she'd made a clean break from Damien.

So she lay in bed, irritated that she couldn't talk to Damien, and so sexually frustrated she thought she might explode.

Finally, she fell to sleep and woke the next day with dark circles under her eyes and a splitting headache. Which fell in line with the expected wedding day from hell.

SWEDE TOSSED and turned all night long, getting up several times with the full intention of marching into Allie's room and kissing her until she was completely convinced Damien Reynolds was not the man she should marry. Each time, he talked himself out of doing it. Swede was afraid she'd change her mind and marry the bastard anyway.

Allie needed to come to a decision on her own. She said she was going to call it off, but she hadn't come to him to let him know the deed was done.

By morning, Swede assumed it wasn't. Which meant his final duty as a bodyguard was to get Allie to the church on time that morning. He scraped the stubble from his chin, combed his hair, and dressed in pressed black trousers and a white button-down shirt. Strapping on his shoulder holster, he tucked his nine millimeter pistol in place and shrugged into his black suit jacket. Like it or not, he was going to a wedding.

In his best boots, he walked down the stairs, hating that he was taking the only girl he'd ever considered worth the trouble of settling down with to marry another man. He'd talk to Hank and hand over the job of protecting his sister to him. He lifted the phone on the table in the hallway and dialed Hank's number.

"Hello," a female voice answered.

"This is Swede; I'd like to speak to Hank."

"Hi, Swede. This is Sadie. How's Allie holding up?"

"Okay. I guess. She's still in bed as far as I know."

Sadie laughed. "She'd better get moving if she's going to make it to the church on time. Oh, wait. Here's Hank."

"Swede, Bear just walked in the door. Sadie and I are heading to the church as soon as he's debriefed me. I'll see you there." Hank hung up before Swede could ask him to take over his bodyguard assignment. Swede would have to deliver her to the church after all. *Great.*

Footsteps on the staircase made him glance up as he set the phone in the cradle.

Allie descended, wearing her usual jeans and a T-shirt, her hair pulled back in a simple ponytail. She carried a long white garment bag and a pair of white satin shoes. Dark circles beneath her eyes stood out against her pale face.

"Hey," Swede said, reaching for the bag. "Let me."

She held it against her chest, refusing to hand it over. "I can carry it." Allie glanced around him. "Have you seen the others?"

As if on cue, Georgia appeared in the kitchen door. "I've made some muffins you can eat on the way to the church."

"I'm not hungry, but thank you," Allie said.

"You can't get married on an empty stomach," Georgia said. She held up a brown lunch sack. "I packed them for you. You better get going, or Sadie and I won't have time to do your hair. Eddy, your father and I are following you in my van. I have decorations loaded in the back. Eddy's going to help put them on the pews. We'll see you in a few minutes." Georgia disappeared back into the kitchen.

Swede glanced down at Allie. "Ready to go?" He'd wanted to say anything but that. But Allie looked like she had a lot on her mind, and he couldn't make himself bring up the subject of the elephant in the room. Was she going through with the wedding, or would she call it off at the last minute? Swede prepared himself for the former, praying for the latter.

Allie led the way out to her truck. "I'll drive," she stated, climbing into the driver's seat.

On the thirty-minute drive into Bozeman, hardly a word was spoken between them. Swede studied the road ahead and behind, looking out for any signs of trouble. His gut told him Will Franklin wasn't the only one involved in the threat against Allie. And until they found out who was behind it all, he wouldn't consider her safe.

Allie parked in the church parking lot and carried her dress inside. Once through the door, she turned to the right and entered an anteroom where Sadie was waiting with a smile and an assortment of brushes and curling irons. "There you are," she exclaimed excitedly. "Let's get you ready for a wedding."

Swede made a sweep of the room, checking all doors and where they led. He made sure they were locked and secure. "I'll be in the vestibule. If you need me, yell." Swede left the room, not waiting for an answer.

Georgia sailed past him, carrying a veil. "See you fellows in a few minutes."

Swede went in search of Hank, his heart heavy. Hank wasn't in the vestibule so Swede entered the sanctuary.

"There you are." Hank approached him, his face tense. "I have news from Bear."

"Shoot."

"Three more soldiers from that same unit have been attacked since they'd gotten home. All of them were more or less gutted. Those three weren't as fortunate as Baker. They died before anyone could get to them."

Swede swallowed the bile rising up his throat. Three men who'd served their country, killed at home. "Anything stand out other than that they were in the same unit?" he asked.

"Bear talked to the commander and found out the four soldiers had been invited to a party on the last night of their deployment. They came back so intoxicated, they couldn't remember anything about the party the next day."

"Intoxicated? In Afghanistan?" Swede shook his head. "I didn't think they were allowed to bring booze into the country."

"They weren't, but the contractor who threw the party must have smuggled in some. My guess is, that because they couldn't remember anything from the night before, they were slipped some kind of date rape drug."

"Why?"

"Why would they all be cut open when they returned to the States?"

A horrible thought came to Swede, making his belly churn. "They were being used as God damned mules to smuggle something out of the country."

"Bear dropped by the Medical Examiner who processed one of the men. He didn't find any traces of drugs around the incisions or in the intestines."

"Where did Baker say their unit was stationed?"

"He didn't. But Bear found out from the company commander that they were on the edge of the Badakhshan Province."

"Isn't that province known for the lapis lazuli gemstone mining?" Swede asked, glancing around to make sure they weren't overheard.

Hank's eyes widened. "It is. And for the rampant smuggling of gemstones out of the country."

Swede closed his eyes, anger burning in his gut. "Who was the contractor?"

Hank's face grew taut. "RM Enterprises."

"Aren't they the contracting company that won the majority of the bids to rebuild or construct much of the Afghan infrastructure?"

Hank's lips pressed into a thin line. "Guess who one of the partners in that company is?"

Swede's heart slipped into his belly. "Damien Reynolds, the R in RM?"

"You got it," Hank confirmed. "His partner is a Frenchman by the name of Jean-Claude Martine. From what Bear found out, Martine has a wicked temper. Afghanis who crossed him had been rumored to disappear."

Swede headed for the door. "We need to tell Allie. ASAP. Where's Bear now?"

Hank followed. "He's contacting the FBI, the local police and anyone else he can get on short notice. This place will be lit up like the Fourth of July when everyone gets here."

"In the meantime, we need to keep Damien from making a run for it," Swede said.

"Right. Bear will also have them on the lookout for Martine."

Swede exited the sanctuary and entered the anteroom where Georgia and Sadie were helping Allie prepare for the ceremony.

Georgia was tucking a strand of hair into an updo on Sadie's head when the men barged in.

"Where's Allie?" Swede asked.

Sadie smiled. "She excused herself to go to the bathroom one last time before she put on her dress."

"How long ago?" Hank demanded.

"Not more than five minutes." Sadie's brows furrowed. "Why?"

His pulse racing, Swede responded, "She might be in trouble."

ALLIE KNOCKED on the door of the room the groom should be dressing in.

"Yeah," came the answer.

Still dressed in her jeans, her hair hanging down around her shoulders and no makeup on her face, Allie entered, dread churning her belly.

Damien stood in the middle of the room in front of a long mirror.

Miles stood behind him, brushing his hand over the crisp white shirt, smoothing away imaginary wrinkles.

Allie's gaze swept from the top of his neatly combed dark hair to the tips of his shiny black, patent leather shoes. Damien Reynolds turned heads no matter where he went. Why he'd asked Allie to marry him was beyond reason.

Damien glanced her way. "Darling, I'm not supposed to see the bride before the ceremony."

Allie smiled at Miles. "Could we have a moment?"

Miles nodded and left the room.

"What's wrong?" Damien took her hands and stared down at her clothes, his brows dropping into a frown. "You're not even ready."

"Damien, I can't marry you."

"What? Nonsense. Of course you can. You're just getting cold feet. It happens. Once the ceremony is over, you can relax on our way to the islands." His hands tightened on hers. "You did bring the case I had Miles give you?"

"It's on the back seat of my truck, but I'm serious." She pulled her hands out of his and reached for her engagement ring. "This week, I had time to think about us and I...I'm sorry, Damien." Now that the initial declaration was made, she felt only relief. Allie slid off the ring and tried to give it to him. "I don't love you. I don't think I ever did. I was more in love with the idea of getting married than being married to you."

He held up his hands, refusing to take the ring. "You can't back out on me now. We're getting married in a few minutes."

"I am backing out." She set the ring on a nearby table and moved a few steps away. "I tried to tell you last night, but you hung up on me. I tried calling you all week, but you didn't answer. I would rather have told you all of this before our wedding day. I'm sorry it had to be this way. But our marriage wouldn't have worked."

Damien's face changed from shock to anger. "You can't leave. We're getting married. Go get into your dress."

Allie shook her head and turned to leave.

Damien grabbed her arm in a painful grip and yanked her around. "Look, you can't jilt me. We have to get to the Cayman Islands today. Do you hear me? We're getting married, and that's the end of it."

Throwing up her hand like she'd learned in self-defense class, Allie knocked Damien's grip loose. "Don't touch me ever again. You don't need me to go to the Cayman Islands. Go without me. Goodbye, Damien. Oh, and I hope you figure out who destroyed your barn." Allie stepped out of his reach and hurried for the door.

"Damn you, Allie!" he yelled and made another grab for her.

She'd done what she'd come to do. Allie ran out of the room and down the hallway to the exit. Now that she'd called off her engagement to Damien, whoever was threatening him would have no need to torment her. Footsteps pounded on the tile floor behind her. She glanced over her shoulder at Damien chasing after her.

Allie burst through the side door of the church leading to the playground. She ran around to the front where she'd parked her truck. She could have gone back inside and asked her father or Eddy to drive her home, but right now, she couldn't face them. And Damien was going all whacko on her. She dove into the driver's seat and shut the door just in time.

Damien body-slammed into the side of the truck and slid to the pavement.

For a moment, Allie thought he'd hit his head and hurt himself. She opened the door and got out, stepping over his body.

"Damien?" She bent to shake his shoulder. That's when she saw a bright red stain on the back of his shirt, spreading wider with each second.

As her brain registered that it was blood, she heard a

sharp popping sound followed by the window behind her shattering. *Damn*. Someone was shooting at her. Allie threw herself to the ground beside Damien's inert body, glancing all around for the source of the gunshots.

A man ran toward her, his gun held out in front of him.

Allie rolled beneath the truck and out the other side. Before she could get her feet beneath her, someone grabbed her by her hair and slammed her head into the side panel of her pickup.

The blue sky of Montana went black.

CHAPTER 13

Swede ran toward the room Damien was supposed to be dressing in for the wedding. He was met in the hallway by Miles, Damien's butler.

"They're gone," the older man said, his face paler than usual.

"Who's gone?" Swede demanded.

"Mr. Reynolds and his fiancée." He pointed to the exit at the end of the hallway. "They ran out that door."

Swede pushed past the man and sprinted for the exit. Outside, he found himself near a playground. A scream sent him running toward the front of the building, Hank close on his heels.

A man in black trousers lay face down on the ground next to Allie's truck, blood staining his white shirt.

"Allie!" Swede shouted, drawing his Glock from the holster beneath his jacket.

"Swede! Be careful! He's got a gun!" she shouted from the other side of the vehicle.

A man who looked like the picture Hank had shown him of Jean-Claude Martine stood, dragging Allie by her hair, a gun with a sound suppressor pointed at her head. "Move, and I'll kill her."

"I'm not moving." Swede held up his empty hand. "Just don't hurt the girl."

"Where's the damned suitcase?" the man said, pulling back hard on Allie's hair. "I want that damned suitcase."

Her face was red, her neck extended back. "What suitcase?" she breathed.

"The one Reynolds gave you. I want it now." He pressed the gun into her temple.

Swede glance around, searching for a miracle to get Allie out of the situation. "Martine, let her go. You're not going to get very far."

"Shut up!" He fired into the air and then put the gun to Allie's head again.

"The police and the FBI are on their way. They know you and Reynolds are behind the killings of the soldiers."

"They won't take me. Not as long as I have her." He turned Allie so that her body was positioned in front of him. Again, he spoke next to Allie's ear. "Where is it?"

"In the truck," she said, gasping. "Take it. I didn't want it in the first place. I intended to give it back."

"It wasn't Reynolds's to give in the first place. I made all the sacrifices. Reynolds didn't have the stomach for it, once we started."

"Let go of the woman," Swede said. "Take the suitcase and the truck. Just leave the woman."

"No way. She's my ticket out of here. I'm going, but I'm taking her with me. Make any moves toward us, and I'll kill her. Just try me." He opened the passenger side of the vehicle and tried to shove her inside.

"Swede, don't worry. He's nothing but a rattlesnake." Allie started to climb in, stumbling, her head tipped back so far she probably couldn't see. Then she fell, slipping down to the ground, bringing Martine's hand down.

Swede had only one chance. He had to make it count. He raised his weapon and squeezed the trigger before Martine could jerk Allie back in front of him. The bullet left the chamber.

For a long moment, Martine stood there, his eyes widening. The gun he held to Allie's head slipped from his fingers and dropped to the ground, discharging a round. Then he slumped like a rag doll slipping from a child's hands. His body landed on top of Allie.

Swede ran toward them. "Allie!" Fear knifed through him. Had the bullet from Martine's gun hit Allie?

He rounded the hood of the truck, grabbed Martine's arm and dragged him away from Allie.

She lay still for a heart-stopping moment, her eyes closed, a bruise on her forehead rising into a goose-egg-sized lump. Then she blinked her eyes open and stared up at Swede. "Is he dead?" she whispered.

A huge wave of relief brought Swede to his knees. "Oh, sweet Jesus, Allie. Yes. He's dead."

Hank rounded the truck and stared down at his sister. "Oh, thank God, she's all right. The cops and the fire department are here. I'll bring them over." Hank left them alone, hurrying over to the emergency vehicles gathering in the church parking lot.

Allie smiled and raised a hand to her forehead, touched the bump and then winced. "That's going to leave a mark."

Swede laughed, gathered her into his arms and held her for a long time, his heart so full he thought it might explode. Allie was alive, the bad guys were dead and all was right with the world, again. His eyes stung with tears, and he blinked them away.

She reached up and cupped his face, her finger tracing the scar on his cheek. "Are you okay?"

He choked on a laugh, his throat constricting. "I'm okay."

"Thanks for killing that rattlesnake."

"You're welcome."

"And for the record, I'm glad you're my bodyguard."

He swallowed against the constriction in his throat. "I am too. You've got a pretty darned amazing body to guard."

She held up her ring finger. "I broke off our engagement before…before that man shot Damien. I'm a single woman."

"That's a good thing, because I'm planning to ask you out on a date."

"What's stopping you?"

"Not a damned thing." He bent to press his lips to hers in a tender kiss. "Allie Patterson, would you go out with a washed-up old navy guy?"

She tilted her head, pausing for a long moment.

Swede held his breath, searching her sweet face until she finally responded.

"No."

His heart skipped several beats and he frowned. "No?"

"No." Her brows dipped low. "But I would consider going out with a highly skilled bodyguard who can shoot like nobody's business." Her smile flashed. "I figure I'll never have to worry about rattlesnakes again."

Swede laughed and hugged her to him.

She pushed away enough to look him in the eye. "I have one condition."

"What's that?"

"Ruger comes along with us."

"Deal."

Then he kissed her, believing for the first time he might just have found his place in the civilian world, on a path to that happy ending he never thought could happen to him. If he played his cards right with Allie, he might be heading in that direction, starting with their first date.

Two weeks later

Swede leaned against the stone fireplace at the White Oak Ranch, a long-neck beer in one hand. He studied the group of men gathered in Hank's house.

Besides himself and Bear, a SEAL from their old unit had joined their ranks, along with another soldier from D-Force who'd worked with them on one of their joint operations back on active duty.

Hank stood in the middle of the room, never more in his element since he'd left the navy. "Brotherhood Protectors is growing fast. Apparently, there's more of a need for personal security services than I'd originally anticipated, and word is spreading fast. I'd like to welcome you aboard and thank you for giving this organization a chance."

Bear shook his head. "No, Hank, thank you. We're just glad to have jobs."

Hank dipped his head. "You all come highly recommended, and have special training and weapons skills."

"Yeah. For what it's worth." Former D-Force soldier, Carson 'Tex' Wainright rocked back on the heels of his cowboy boots.

Ben 'Big Bird' Sjodin, sat in a leather armchair, his long legs stretched out in front of him. "We're highly trained in combat skills, but there aren't too many opportunities as a civilian to use that training."

"Exactly," Hank agreed. "The challenge is to remember our clients aren't all familiar with the military way of thinking. We need to be open to learning about our clients' lives and what it will take to keep them safe."

Swede chuckled, thinking of Allie and how she'd taught him a few things about ranching. He was getting better at horseback riding and caring for livestock. And he'd taught Allie a few things about shooting she didn't already know. That had been their second date.

"The assignments can be more dangerous than we originally expected," Hank said. "So, don't let your guard down." He nodded toward Swede. "Swede's first assignment was protecting my sister Allie from some seemingly unexplainable attacks. We found out her fiancé was involved in smuggling gemstones from Afghanistan to the U.S., using soldiers as mules. Five people died in that operation. Three American soldiers, Allie's fiancé and his partner."

"His point is, don't think this will be a cakewalk," Swede said.

Hank picked up a handful of file folders. "The good news is we have work. Plenty of it." He glanced in the folders and handed them over to each man, one at a time. "Look over your clients' portfolios and requests. If you have questions, ask now."

The men studied their folders and compared notes, asking various questions about locations and protocol.

After the formal part of the meeting was over, Sadie joined Hank, her hand on her belly, which had begun to show a bit of a baby bump.

"Anyone need another beer?" Allie entered the room, carrying five long-necks. She made her way around the room, dropping them with the men, and coming to a stop in front of Swede. "Who'd you get?" she asked, leaning over his shoulder.

"An older woman afraid her neighbor is planning on taking over the country," he said, liking that she was interested.

Allie's eyes narrowed. "Older woman?"

Swede shrugged. "Really old. Thirty-six."

She crossed her arms over her chest. "I'm not so sure

I like the idea of you being a bodyguard to another woman. How do I know you won't fall in love with her?"

"Jealous?" Swede pulled her into his arms and brushed his lips across hers.

"Maybe." She lifted her chin. "You're growing on me, and I don't want to lose you to a cougar."

"We've been out together on fourteen dates, one for each day of the week since we started dating. You're not losing me to a cougar, bobcat or any other kind of feline." He nuzzled her neck. "I have my own little Allie cat. Sweetheart, I'm in this for the duration."

She wrapped her arms around his neck and kissed him back. "Good thing, or I'd have to hire you as my permanent, personal bodyguard."

Swede kissed her long and hard, convinced he'd found the woman for him. Two weeks wasn't a long time, but he knew in his heart he wouldn't find another woman like her. "Babe, I'll guard your body any time you want. How about now?"

Allie threaded her hand in his, glanced around at the others in the room, and, with a wink, tipped her head toward the door. "I'll show you where the teenagers go to neck."

"A woman after my own heart." He chuckled and followed her out of the house. She hadn't been after his heart, but she sure as hell had it in her capable hands.

. . .

THANK you for reading Bride Protector SEAL. The Brotherhood Protectors Series continues with Montana D-Force. Keep reading for the 1st Chapter.

Interested in more military romance stories? Subscribe to my newsletter and receive the Military Heroes Box Set.

Subscribe Here

MONTANA DOG SOLDIER

BROTHERHOOD PROTECTORS BOOK #6

New York Times & USA Today
Bestselling Author

ELLE JAMES

MONTANA
DOG SOLDIER

BROTHERHOOD PROTECTORS

NEW YORK TIMES BESTSELLING AUTHOR
ELLE JAMES

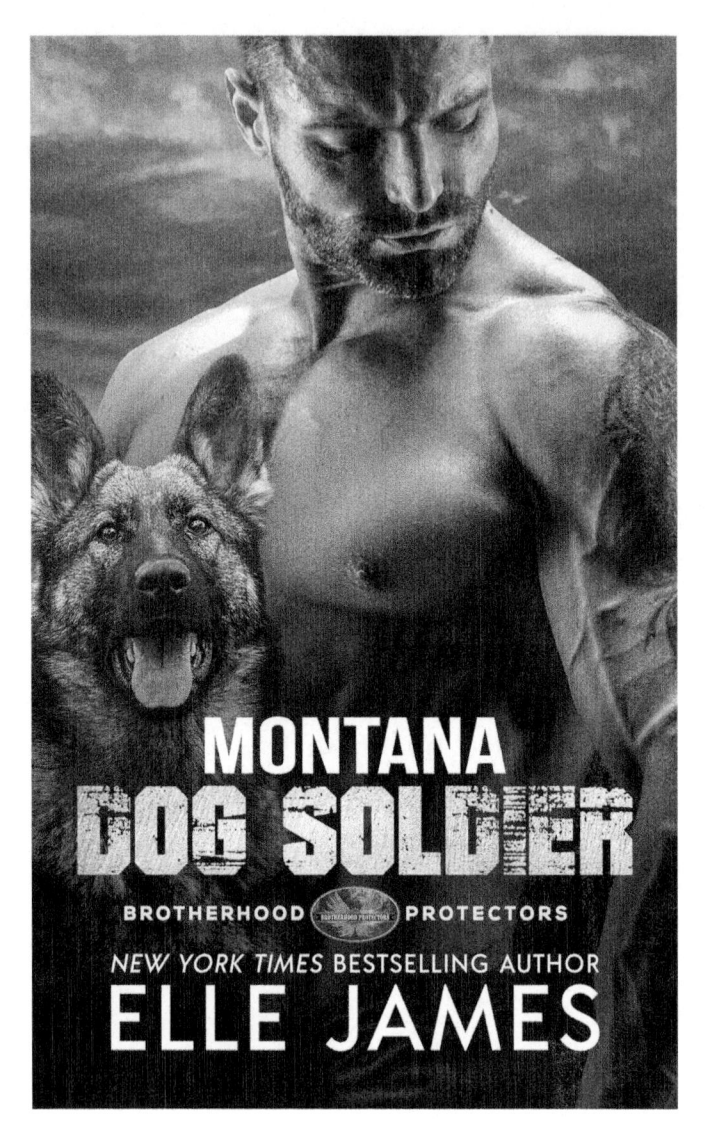

This story is dedicated to our military service dogs and their handlers, putting their lives on the line to save others.

Elle James

CHAPTER 1

"Kujo, you're up." Bear stood at the door to the Black Hawk helicopter waving at him to step forward.

Joseph "Kujo" Kuntz stood, snapped the O-ring onto Six's harness and moved toward the door. He locked into the cable that would lower him and his dog to the ground into enemy territory.

Their mission: rescue two female soldiers being held by the Taliban in a remote Afghan village. Al Jazeera television had released videos of the women trussed up like animals, their faces bruised and battered, Taliban soldiers pressing rifles to their heads.

During his unit's briefing, the intel guys had replayed the video, displayed the satellite images of where they'd determined the women were being held and gone over and over the village layout.

Kujo's gut clenched every time he thought of the captives. He knew what Taliban men did to foreign women. If they didn't outright kill them, they tortured them until they wished they were dead. The looks in those two women's eyes were of beaten resolution. They were prepared to die. Perhaps praying for an end to the pain.

The video had the desired effect on the extraction team. They wanted to get in, rescue the hostages and put the hurt on the bastards who'd tortured the American women.

Yeah, he'd be just as determined to free them if they were male soldiers. Kujo didn't discriminate with his need to help any American in trouble. But he couldn't push aside an image of his sister or his mother in a similar situation. Those captured women could be someone's sister or even mother.

Rage roiled in his gut, churning, burning its way through his veins and firing up his adrenaline. He wanted to make those murdering, cowardly Taliban men pay for what they'd done.

Standing at the door of the aircraft, he channeled his rage into tightly strung control. First, his unit had to find the women and then safely get them out. That was his job. His, along with the aid of Six, his sable German Shepherd that had been trained to sniff out explosives.

The information the intelligence guys had received originated from one of their Afghan spies. After verifying the data via satellite, they'd formulated their plan. That's when Kujo and Six had been called in.

The commander had a bad feeling about the entire operation. The fact the women had been paraded on Al Jazeera led him to believe it was a setup, a potential trap. But they couldn't leave the women to the machinations of the Taliban. They wouldn't last much longer. If they were even still alive.

Thus, the quickly formed extraction team of available Delta Force and SEALs who'd performed similar operations over the past six months. The integrated team members had proven their abilities. They trusted every operator to have their backs.

The helicopter slowed and hovered behind the hill blocking the view of the village. They'd fast-rope to the ground and move in on foot.

In Kujo's case, he and Six would be lowered to the ground by cable. Once they were there, they'd slip into the village, Six taking point to sniff out the danger of IEDs or other types of explosives the enemy might have set out to welcome their insertion.

Kujo briefly rested his hand on Six's head. The dog nuzzled it, and then waited patiently for their cue to step out.

"Go!" Bear said.

Kujo grabbed Six's harness, stepped out the door of the aircraft and dangled from the cable as they were quickly lowered to the ground.

Six didn't whine. He hung in his harness beside Kujo, his gaze fixed on the darkness below.

The dog had been whelped in Germany and spent the first year of his life there. He still responded to many German commands.

When he had been assigned to Kujo for training in the United States at Lackland Air Force Base, Kujo had called him by the last number of the tattoo on his left ear, ẞ826. The number just happened to coincide with the number of dogs Kujo had worked with in his career with the Army. He'd learned through the loss of the first five animals not to get too attached. They belonged to the Army.

His first dog, Fritz, had been a Belgian Malinois. He'd saved countless lives before he'd stepped on an IED and died in Kujo's arms. His second and third dogs had been German Shepherds whelped in the United States by a trusted breeder. They'd been retired after they grew skittish over the sounds of explosions.

The fourth, another Malinois, had developed a tumor in her face and had to be euthanized. The fifth, Rambo, had been a very smart black Labrador who'd saved many lives sniffing out IEDs, but he'd been too close to an explosion and lost his hearing. A retired Brigadier General and his wife in Colorado Springs had adopted Rambo and given him a great retirement home.

For five intensive months of training, Kujo had worked with Six, getting him ready to deploy. The animal had responded quickly, learning what he needed to know to help save lives in war-torn countries.

As soon as Kujo's boots touched ground, he unclipped his harness from the cable, reached for the O-ring, and released Six. The dog knew his mission and took off.

Other members of the team were already on the ground, having rappelled from the aircraft.

The Black Hawk lifted and swung away from them. The pilot would be far enough away to be out of range of RPGs and small arms fire, but the help would be quick to respond should the team radio for extraction.

Six led them over the hill and up to the village, sniffing his way through brush and the rocky terrain. So far, so good.

Perhaps, too good. No resistance, no guards perched on the rooftop.

The hairs on the back of Kujo's neck rose.

The team's weapons were fixed with sound suppression. Moving through a village, they relied heavily on stealth. For each mission, they strove to get in and get out, undetected. Their sound-suppressed weapons allowed them to fire a shot in one room of a building without being heard from another.

Kujo carried an HK MP7A1 submachine gun. The lightweight weapon allowed him to be more mobile and deadly, without announcing to the world or the village he was there.

As they approached the village, Kujo and Six moved ahead of the team. In the dead of night when most people slept, nothing moved but the team.

They paused just outside the village in a jumble of large boulders and scanned the buildings using night vision goggles, or NVGs, searching for heat signatures—the shadowy, green silhouettes of enemy soldiers perched on rooftops.

"Cover me," Kujo said.

"Gotcha," Bear replied into his headset. "Go."

Kujo sent Six forward several feet before he followed, hunkering close to the earth, moving swiftly toward the stick and mud wall surrounding the village. As soon as he arrived, he waited, providing cover for the others as they traveled the same path cleared by Six.

Bear knelt at the base of the barrier.

Kujo stepped onto his back and pulled himself up to the top of the wall and scanned the immediate surroundings through his NVGs. When he was certain the area was clear of enemy personnel, he motioned for Six to follow. Six leaped up on Bear's back and over the wall, dropped to the ground below and went to work.

Kujo slipped to the ground behind him and directed the dog down an alley between buildings toward their target. According to the satellite images in their briefing, the intel folks believed the women were being held in the largest of the mud and brick structures at the back of the village where it hugged the base of a rocky cliff.

At one corner, Six paused and waited for his handler to catch up.

Kujo stopped beside the dog, and sneaked a peek around the corner. Nothing moved. The town was too quiet. His gut tightened. He spotted the target location. "Building in sight."

"We'll cover," Bear said. "When you're ready, go"

"Roger," Kujo whispered, careful not to give away his position. To his partner, he gave the signal for the animal to move forward, nose to the ground, quietly sniffing, doing the job he'd been trained to do, search for explosives ahead of the humans.

Kujo could see the green outline of Six as the dog rounded the corner, his nose to the ground.

First into the village, members of the dog handling team had to be on their toes, whether two or four-legged. Their job was to warn the others of potential explosive hazards.

Kujo and Six had graduated top of their class during concentrated training at Joint Base Lackland in San Antonio. They'd received additional Tactical Explosive Detection (TED) training in southern Afghanistan before they'd been attached to the Delta Force unit where Kujo, a trained Delta Force soldier, reconnected with a couple of men he'd served with, Bear and Duke, prior to being trained as a dog handler.

He was glad to be back among men who'd shared some of the most intense missions of their lives. They'd survived because of their attention to detail, dogged preparation and dedication to teamwork, and all of them had come back alive.

Six moved through the narrow walkways between the buildings. Every so often, he would return to Kujo for instruction, and Kujo would send him back out.

They worked their way toward the target, coming to a halt twenty feet short, across the road and at the edge of a squat structure. Six returned to Kujo's side and sat, staring ahead, his head raised, ears perked high, ready and alert.

Bear moved in behind Kujo and waited for the rest of the small team to catch up.

"Too quiet," Kujo stated, his voice soft, barely enough to register on a radio. "Be alert."

Bear nodded, his face grim. He glanced back at the team. "Ready?"

Everyone nodded.

Three men took positions on either side of the alleyway to provide cover.

Kujo gave the signal for Six to search for explosives.

The dog set out in the dark, moonless night, with nothing but starlight to guide him.

Kujo watched, waiting for Six to indicate the presence of explosives.

A trickle of sweat slipped down the side of his neck. The earth retained much of the heat from the oven-baking, one-hundred-twenty-degree temperature of the day. Loaded with weapons, his vest and steel plate, Kujo carried an additional fifty pounds of gear.

A minute later, Six returned, tail wagging, anxious to please.

Kujo patted his head. "Let's go."

Kujo, Bear and Duke took the lead, with the others as backup. They approached the building at an angle, running in a low crouch toward the entrance.

Six arrived at the door first and sniffed the ground and doorframe, but he didn't sit, which would have indicated the presence of explosives.

While Bear and Duke flattened their bodies against the side of the building, Kujo pushed the door. It didn't move. He pulled a Ka-Bar knife from the scabbard on his side and slid it between the door and the frame, applied a little force and the door opened.

He toed it open and stepped aside. If someone had been on the other side, he wouldn't have an immediate target.

Kujo signaled to Six. The dog trotted through the entrance.

Figuring Six would have growled or tensed if someone had been inside, Kujo concluded the room was unoccupied and entered behind the dog, keeping low, and shifting quickly out of the doorframe.

Six made a quick survey of the room, nose to the ground, and headed for a hallway.

"Clear," Kujo whispered into his headset.

Six continued his search, one room at a time.

Bear and Duke followed Kujo down the hallway. The rooms were empty except for discarded cardboard boxes and empty cans and bottles. A wad of blankets was piled in the corner. Kujo nudged the blankets, praying he wouldn't find the dead bodies of the women beneath. He released the breath he'd been holding when he realized they were only rags.

He moved on, bounding past Duke to check the third room along the hallway, and then moved on to the doorway at the end.

Six was already there, sniffing at the gap beneath the door. He glanced up at Kujo and then sat.

Holy hell. Kujo's gut clenched.

The dog had identified the scent of explosives. The door wasn't closed all the way; it hung open a good four inches, and the room beyond was shrouded in darkness.

Kujo glanced back at Bear and Duke as they exited the rooms they'd cleared and waited for further instruction.

"We have a problem," Kujo said, hoping the others would hear his softly spoken words.

He didn't have to spell out the problem. Bear and Duke would deduce the issue, seeing Six sitting on his haunches, proud of his find and awaiting his next command.

Without a doubt, some kind of explosive device awaited the team behind that half-opened door. The only question remaining was whether the women were also inside the room.

A noise came from the darkness, sounding like a muffled sob.

Kujo's initial instinct was to step forward, toward the sound. He reached out, but paused before pushing open the door. If it were wired to the explosives, he would end up killing the women, the dog and himself. Instead, he pulled a shiny piece of metal from his pocket and squatted beside the door. Holding the metal mirror in his hand, he pushed his hand through the opening and angled the mirror so that he could see what was inside.

A small glimmer of light glowed in a far corner. Using the mirror's reflection, Kujo scanned the room until he found what he was looking for.

His hand froze and a lead weight settled in the pit of his gut. The women were there, and they were alive. But they wouldn't be for long.

Gagged and bound together, they were also equipped with vests of explosives of the kind suicide bombers wore beneath their robes.

Anger rose in Kujo's chest. The door wasn't rigged. The women were.

He slowly pushed the door wider but didn't enter. Instead, he slid his NVGs up onto his helmet and beamed a tiny flashlight toward the female soldiers.

The women blinked their swollen eyelids open and spotted him. Their eyes rounded, and they started shaking their heads, grunting through the wads of cloth in their mouths.

His gut told him not to enter the room, so he hesitated and motioned for Six to back away from the door. He studied the explosives from a distance, but he couldn't locate the detonator from where he stood. About the time he considered entering, a blinding flash burst around him and the world exploded.

The half-open door was blasted off its hinges and slammed into Kujo, knocking him off his feet. He landed on his back, his ears ringing, pain knifing through his knee and his head, his chest feeling as though a weight pressed down on his ribs. The air quickly filled with dust. If he could have breathed, he was sure he'd have choked.

Before he completely lost consciousness, he felt something sharp dig into his arm, and then he was being dragged across rubble. Before he could glance sideways at his rescuer, darkness closed in, burying him in a bottomless abyss.

CHAPTER 2

Three years later...

Kujo stood on the front porch of the log cabin, staring out at the snow-capped Rockies and scratching the beard he hadn't bothered to shave since he'd been medically boarded out of the Army three years before.

Why bother? He wasn't wearing the uniform, he didn't have a job, and he didn't even have to get out of bed in the morning.

He walked to the end of the deck and stretched in the cool mountain air. Though he'd been out of the military for a few years, he still worked out to keep his knee from stiffening. The operation to replace the torn ligaments had left him with a limp, but he refused to be a burden on anyone. So, every morning, he got his ass out of the bed and worked through the pain until he could walk. He was recovered enough he could even run again. But his knee wasn't the same, nor was his head.

Traumatic Brain Injury sucked. For the first few months after the explosion, he'd had blinding headaches at least once a week, and sometimes more. As time had passed, the headaches had eased and he was getting around better. He'd moved from his apartment outside Ft. Bragg, North Carolina to the mountains of Colorado to get away from the crowds and his old buddies, who'd drop in to cheer him up while they felt sorry for his suffering.

God, he hated pity. So, he wasn't in the military any more. So the fuck what. He had enough money coming in from his disability to survive. Barely. He'd been fortunate to rent this log cabin in the woods, too far off the beaten path to appeal to tourists. Without internet or cell phone coverage, not many city folk wanted to stay there. He'd worked a deal with the aging owner to live there at a very low rent as long as he fixed up the place.

He'd lived up to his end of the bargain and repaired everything that needed it, to the point he had nothing left to do. Now, he considered building a shed behind the cabin to house a four-wheeler he kept under a lean-to. He'd even dressed in a pair of jeans without holes and put on his least offensive boots for the trip into town in his old pickup.

About to step off the porch, he spotted a shiny, black four-wheel-drive Jeep climbing the rutted road up to the cabin.

Kujo frowned. He liked his privacy. When people wandered near, he gave them the stink-eye and told them they were trespassing on private property. If the look and the verbal warning didn't work, his glare, thick beard, shaggy hair and scarred face were threatening enough to scare them off.

Standing with his arms crossed over his chest, he frowned fiercely and waited for the Jeep to come to a standstill in front of the cabin. He hoped the people would get the hell out of there quickly. He had work to do, and he wouldn't leave the cabin while strangers wandered around the property.

As soon as the Jeep came to a halt, two men climbed out.

Kujo's frown deepened. The sunlight bounced off the windshield, blinding him. All he could tell was that the men were big, with broad shoulders and thick thighs. They wore leather jackets and cowboy hats, and carried themselves like men with a purpose.

"You've come far enough," he said, squinting against the glare. "You're trespassing. If you're lost, head back the way you came."

The men drew closer, moving out of the glare from the Jeep's windshield. They tipped their heads to stare up at where he stood on the porch.

"Kujo?" one of the men said in a familiar baritone. "Is that you?"

"Shit, dude, what the hell have you done to yourself?" the other man said.

A flood of emotions washed over Kujo. No one had called him Kujo since he'd left his unit in Afghanistan, extracted from the Afghan village on Bear's back. From there, he'd been transported to the nearest field hospital where they'd stabilized him then shipped him to the rear and out of the area of operations to the hospital in Landstuhl, Germany. Doctors had relieved the pressure on his brain and monitored him there for a couple days, and then evacuated him stateside to Walter Reed. All the while, he hadn't awakened. Not until the swelling subsided had he surfaced from the darkness that had claimed him. He hadn't remembered the explosion, and he barely remembered his name.

Two weeks had passed since the operation in Afghanistan before he learned of the deaths of the women. The explosives had been remotely detonated.

Someone had to remind him that he'd been a dog handler. He'd become distraught, asking about Six and the other members of the team.

Thankfully, Bear, Duke and the others had survived. If not for the door and the walls deflecting most the explosion, they all could have died. Aside from the deaths of the females who'd been rigged with the demolitions, Kujo was the only one seriously injured. Even Six had only minor shrapnel wounds. He'd been treated and assigned a new handler.

After his knee operation and physical therapy, Kujo had seen the writing on the wall. He'd never get back to the same physical condition he'd been in before the explosion. And, because of the TBI, the Army didn't want to risk putting him back in dangerous situations where others would rely on his mental acuity.

Thus, he'd lost his military family, his dog and his

career in one fell swoop. By the time his physical therapy was complete, he had nothing left of his former life. Living near Ft. Bragg had only reminded him of all he'd lost. So, he'd packed his duffel bag, sold his furniture and left.

He'd driven all the way to Colorado before he stopped, exhausted, his knee hurting and his head aching. Up in the mountains, he felt like he could breathe again, away from his memories.

Until now.

Standing before him, on the mountain he'd come to think of as his own, were two of the best friends a man could have. Two men who had risked their lives for him on multiple occasions. He should have been happy to see them. For a moment, he felt that old joy of seeing his long-lost friends, but just as quickly the joy was gone. They were part of what he was trying so hard to forget.

"Why are you here?" he demanded, his voice brusque.

Bear's jaw hardened. "Because we care."

"Do you know how hard it was to track you down?" Duke grunted. "If it weren't for the man at the hardware store in town, we might never have found you up here."

Kujo shrugged. "I like my privacy."

Bear shook his head. "We all like our privacy, but this takes it to an entirely new level."

Kujo wasn't much for talking. "Again, why are you here?"

"We got word from your former trainer at Lackland that Six is there. He was injured in an IED explosion and has been retired from active duty," Bear said.

"He's up for adoption," Duke finished.

Kujo's gut twisted. He'd spent the past three years trying to remember the details of what happened on his last mission, and to forget about the people and the dog he'd more or less lost. He couldn't go through that again. Forcing a nonchalance he didn't feel, he shrugged again. "So?"

Bear glanced at Duke and back to Kujo. "We thought you'd want to know and that you might consider taking him."

Something inside Kujo's heart pinched so tightly that, for a moment, he thought he might be having an attack. He pressed a hand to his chest in an effort to relieve the pressure. "He was a good dog. Why wouldn't he find a good home?"

"He's been available for months. He's had two foster families take him, but they couldn't handle him and returned him. Because of his injury, he limps. No one else has stepped forward to take him. Your former trainer contacted us, thinking you might want him."

"No." Kujo turned and walked away. "That part of my life is over."

"Yeah, but here's the deal," Duke called after him. "If you don't take him, he's scheduled to be put down in three days."

Kujo whipped around. "Put down?"

Duke nodded. "He's on death row. No one wants him, and you're his last hope."

"Why don't you take him?" Kujo shot back at his former teammates.

Duke shrugged. "We don't know how to handle him.

He's got issues. Since you left the service, he's been through four different handlers and been injured. He's punchy. The dog needs a stable influence."

Bear squinted up at him. "Your trainer thinks he doesn't trust anyone. No one sticks around."

Kujo grimaced. It wasn't like he'd wanted to leave Six. The dog belonged to Uncle Sam. Just like Kujo once had. The powers that be in the military had the say regarding where a soldier or a war dog went.

The Army had dropped Kujo. Now they wanted to drop Six.

His gut clenched, and his throat tightened. "I can't," he said.

Bear raised his brows. "So, you're willing to let him die?"

No! But he couldn't put his heart into another dog. The pain of loss had taken a toll on Kujo.

"Look, think about it." Bear glanced around at the cabin. "In the meantime, are you going to invite us in?"

With all his thoughts focused on Six, Kujo stared at Bear for a moment until his words sank in. Slowly, he nodded. "It's nice outside. You want to have a seat on the porch? I'd offer you a beer, but I'm all out. How's coffee."

"That would be good," Bear agreed and stepped up onto the porch.

"I'll take a cup, too," Duke said, climbing up the steps. He walked to the end of the porch and stared down at the valley surrounded by snow-capped peaks. "What a view. I can see why you like it here."

Kujo's gaze followed Duke's. He'd felt the peace as

soon as he'd driven into the valley and up to the cabin. No other place had that effect on him at a time when he needed to calm the anger and still his jumbled thoughts.

"I'll be back."

He disappeared into the house, a dull ache forming at the base of his skull. He hadn't seen familiar faces in so long, he wasn't sure how he felt. On one hand, he was glad to see Bear and Duke. They'd been as close, if not closer, than any blood brothers could be. Yet, they brought with them all the memories he'd tried too hard to forget.

Kujo went through the motions of making coffee, while getting his shit together. A few minutes later, he emerged from the house.

"I think Hank would agree," Bear was saying.

"Me, too." Duke said. "Let's do it."

The two men had taken seats on the only two seats on the porch—rocking chairs faded from the weather, but sturdy and comfortable.

As Kujo stepped out onto the deck, carrying two steaming mugs he asked, "Do what?" He handed a mug to each of his Delta Force comrades, and then leaned against the rail, folding his arms over his chest. By their cagey looks, they'd been discussing him.

Bear sipped the hot brew then glanced up at Kujo. "What are you doing up here in the mountains?"

Kujo stiffened. Where was Bear going with his question? "I've been working on this cabin."

Bear studied the structure for a moment. "I take it you don't have a real job."

Kujo's back stiffened. "I take my work seriously."

"The place looks great. How much acreage do you own with the cabin?"

Kujo's teeth ground together. "I don't own the cabin."

Duke's brows rose. "You're working on a cabin you don't own?"

"Yeah." Kujo frowned. "So?"

"What do you do for a living?"

"I have my medical retirement from the Army." He pushed away from the rail, his eyes narrowing. "Why do you ask?"

Bear shot a glance at Duke. "We have a proposition for you."

Kujo turned away and stared out at the mountains, willing the craggy peaks to bring him the peace he'd always expected from them. "Not interested."

"At least hear us out before you decide," Duke said. "Bear and I are out of the Army, too. We weren't sure what kind of work we could do after being Delta Force. The transition was rough."

"Until Hank Patterson offered us a job," Bear added.

Kujo half-turned. "Who the hell is Hank Patterson?"

Bear grinned. "A SEAL who left the Navy to help his father on his ranch in Montana."

Kujo frowned. "I don't know anything about ranching."

Bear arched an eyebrow. "I'm not saying you'll be ranching."

Duke blew on the coffee and took another sip. "Hank set up an organization in the foothills of the Crazy Mountains of Montana."

Kujo shook his head. "I'm not interested in being a survivalist or prepper, or whatever they're calling them now."

Duke grinned. "No, it's nothing like that. He started a service called Brotherhood Protectors. He hires the best of the best of former active duty military."

"SEALs, Marines, D-Force," Bear continued. "We provide protective services to clients who need them."

"He's given more than a few former fighters the chance to make a difference outside of the military." Bear tipped his head toward Duke. "We both work for Brotherhood Protectors."

"What does this have to do with me?"

Bear leveled his gaze on Kujo. "We think you'd be a good fit for the team."

Well, I don't. They don't know me anymore. Still, he couldn't help asking, "Why me?"

"For one," Bear said, "we don't have any dog handlers among us. I believe there's a need for one."

"I don't have a dog," Kujo reminded them.

"You don't have one *now*," Duke corrected.

Kujo straightened. "I'm not going to adopt Six."

Duke's lips thinned. "That dog is a highly decorated hero, just like you. I think he could be of use to the organization."

"But he needs someone who can handle him," Bear added.

Duke nodded. "He needs you."

Bear leveled a stare at Kujo. "*We* need you."

Kujo held up his hands. "I'm not interested."

"What do you have holding you here?" Bear asked.

"I have a life here," Kujo insisted.

"Are you happy?" Duke asked.

"Who says you have to be happy?" Kujo turned away. His thoughts tumbled, his stomach roiled and his head pounded. "I just want to be left alone"

"Really?" A hand descended on his shoulder. Bear stood beside him. "You used to like to hang with the team. Have a beer. Work out with the guys. Do you really like being here? Alone?"

That hollowness he'd felt since he'd left the service had intensified. Three years on his own and all the forgetting and pushing memories to the back of his mind meant nothing. Everything seemed to flow back into his thoughts, into his head.

Memories of his buddies sitting around his apartment, drinking beer and watching football, filled his mind. The times they stood at the door to the helicopter, adrenaline flowing, ready to punch out and do their jobs in an enemy-infested landscape. Sharing the camaraderie only men who'd faced death and survived could relate to.

The hand on his shoulder seemed to burn through his shirt, the heat penetrating to that cold hard organ that used to be his heart.

Bear tucked a business card into Kujo's shirt pocket. "Think about it, will ya?" he said. "We need men like you."

And Kujo needed *them*.

The thought surfaced before he could shove it to the far reaches of his consciousness.

"And Six needs you," Duke said. "Please, don't let him become yet another casualty to a thankless war."

Out of the corner of his gaze, Kujo watched Bear step down from the porch.

His former teammate said, "You have a lot to think about, so, we'll be going now. If you want to join us for a beer, you can find us in town until eleven o'clock tomorrow when we check out of our hotel."

Duke and Bear climbed into the Jeep and left, kicking up a trail of dust in their wake.

Kujo followed the vehicle's progress until it disappeared through the trees.

Up until that moment, he thought he'd been holding his own pretty well and had come to grips with his new normal.

The visit from his old teammates dispelled that fallacy. As the dust settled on the mountain road, Kujo didn't think he could feel more alone in the world. An awful, empty feeling threatened to overwhelm him. The longer he stood there, the tighter his gut clenched.

Ten minutes later, he entered the cabin and trimmed the shaggy beard, and then shaved his face clean. He packed his duffel bag with everything he'd brought with him when he'd moved into the cabin.

He didn't think too much, just followed his gut, moving like an automaton, not willing to overthink the situation—afraid that if he did, he'd completely fall apart.

Maybe he and Six could provide some value to Hank Patterson's Brotherhood Protectors...if the organization needed two broken-down soldiers. All he knew was Six needed him. Kujo hadn't been able to save the female soldiers, but he could do something about saving the dog soldier.

CHAPTER 3

MOLLY GREENBRIAR GOOSED THE THROTTLE ON THE ATV, sending it bumping over the rocky road up into the hills beyond the small town of Eagle Rock. With only a few minutes of instruction from the man she'd rented the vehicle from, she wasn't as confident as she'd like to be handling the four-wheeler on the dangerous mountain roads and trails. She wasn't in a hurry to get up to the top, nor was she in a hurry to go plunging off a cliff.

Taking the ascent slowly, she eased up the hill, keeping her gaze peeled for potential threats from man or beast. She was on a mission and had no intention of failing because she hadn't taken sufficient precautions.

As she neared the top of a ridge, she slowed to a stop, switched off the engine, dismounted and pulled off her helmet. As she stared out across the Crazy Mountains of Western Montana, she couldn't help feeling she was as close to Heaven as any mortal could be. If she weren't working, she'd be exploring these mountains, anyway. Unfortunately, though the scenery was beautiful and the mountains were breathtaking, they could potentially be harboring a deadly faction bent on harming innocent people.

She wrestled the drone out of the basket on the back of the four-wheeler and laid the parts on the ground. Then kneeling beside them on the rocky terrain, she assembled the pieces and adjusted the settings. She'd practiced with the device with the help of an instructor back in D.C., but flying it solo was an entirely different undertaking.

She didn't have the backup of the instructor. If she lost control of the drone and crashed it into the side of a cliff, she'd have a lot of explaining to do to her boss back at FBI Headquarters in DC. She straightened with the controls in her hands.

With her first opportunity to prove herself in the field, failure wasn't an option. She'd begged her boss, Pete Ralston, to let her come out to the Crazy Mountains, chasing a lead on a terrorist training camp in the vicinity of Eagle Rock.

A tip from one of the FBI computer gurus had landed on her desk at headquarters, indicating a growing concern over what appeared to be tactical training activities underway by individuals connected to some of the most dangerous ISIS sympathizers on US soil.

After investigating the lead, Molly had studied satellite photos of the area, spotting certain anomalies that indicated a suspicious concentration of people in the mountains, and they appeared to be conducting some sort of military-style maneuvers. The images set off alarm bells in Molly's mind, so she presented her findings to her boss. Unfortunately, she'd approached him at the same time a terrorist had plowed a truck into a crowd of tourists near the front of the White House. Her boss hadn't had time to review her research.

So sure of her findings, she'd asked to go to Montana to investigate with boots on the ground.

At first her boss had told her no. She didn't have experience as a field agent. He'd been buried in responding to calls from the press and House and Senate committees about the White House incident, as well as bombarded by the POTUS and his staff to give them answers about the man responsible for the White House incident.

In a weak moment, her boss had approved her assignment and the use of a drone for surveillance. "Strictly surveillance," he'd warned. "You are not to engage without backup. Get the information and get it back to me."

Thrilled, Molly had rushed home to pack a bag. Not only would it be her first time in the field, it would get her out of DC and away from everything that reminded her of Scott and the shambles of their failed relationship.

Molly adjusted the controls, and the drone lifted off the ground, hovered twenty feet in the air and then rose, moving out across a valley.

The time was long past for her to leave DC. When she completed this assignment, she'd put in for a transfer to a field office, anywhere but in the nation's capital, far enough away from Scott and his new fiancé that she'd never run into them again.

When he'd moved out of their apartment, he'd said he needed time to think. What he'd really meant to say was that he'd fallen in love with someone else. Within a month of moving out, he'd proposed to one of the secretaries from an office several doors down from where he and Molly worked.

Yes, Molly had been hurt when he'd left. But not devastated. She'd been more humiliated than anything else. As was the usual case for the spurned woman, she hadn't seen it coming. They'd been living together for over a year. Sex had become routine, and not anything to write home about. In fact, for the last two months they'd lived together, Scott had worked later and later. By the time he'd come home, Molly was asleep.

Molly shook her head over her own stupidity. In a convoluted way, losing Scott had led her here to this remote mountain pass. If she hadn't thrown herself into work, she might have missed seeing the clues. So, her personal life was in shambles. So the hell what? She'd prove herself ready for fieldwork and never look back.

The drone whirred across the valley, bringing Molly back to the present. She maneuvered it lower, while she scanned the digital screen, studying the terrain through the drone's camera.

She'd established herself in the nearby town as a nature and history enthusiast in Eagle Rock to film footage of the Crazy Mountains for a documentary she was working on.

She'd met with the local sheriff's department and

representatives from the forestry commission and the national parks, as well as the county commission, to study the local land survey maps. She'd needed a better understanding of who owned the land up to the edges of the national parks and forests, and where she could legally ride the four-wheel-drive ATV she'd rented.

All the research and preparations had taken a few days, but finally, she was out in the mountains, armed with her GPS, the drone, a backpack of survival gear and her personal 9-millimeter pistol. She wasn't supposed to engage, but she was prepared. Not only did she have to worry about being discovered by terrorists, she had to be bear aware. She was in grizzly country, and the area was also known for the wolves that had been reintroduced to the region.

Molly hoped the pistol was enough. She'd considered bringing a rifle as well. Perhaps she needed something even more powerful to stop a grizzly in its tracks.

At the moment, she was alone on a hilltop. The only wildlife she'd noticed was the occasional bird flying overhead.

She maneuvered the drone lower, toward a small river burbling through the valley. Molly had a lot of territory to cover. If there was a training site in the mountains, the people conducting and attending would have to be able to get into the area.

Molly was armed with topographical maps indicating all roads, paved and dirt, leading into the mountains along with the elevations and landmarks. As vast as the range was, she might be searching for a needle in a haystack. She had to think like the people leading the effort to train terrorists on US soil. She had to find where they had moved their encampment between multiple satellite images.

The FBI's computer guru had been unable to trace the tip to the source. Molly figured it had to be someone in the Eagle Rock area since the tip had specifically mentioned the mountains west of the small town.

Part of her investigation would be to find her informant. In the meantime, she'd do her best to locate the training site using the drone.

She'd drawn quadrants on the maps she'd acquired, and set about using the drone to scan each for any signs of suspicious activities.

Today was her first official trek into the mountains after the few days of preparation. The weather had been sunshine and blue skies all week, with the glorious backdrop of snow-capped peaks. This morning had been no different. But as soon as she rode her four-wheeler up the trail into the hills on the outskirts of Eagle Rock, clouds had slipped in from the west, blocking out the cheerful sunshine.

Molly didn't let it slow her down. She kept watch on the weather situation, knowing the trail would become treacherous should it start raining or, God forbid, snowing.

She'd positioned the drone at the western end of the valley and moved it slowly over the terrain, heading east toward the western fence line, surrounding land belonging to Bert Daniels, a cattle rancher who'd inherited his property from a long line of Daniels'. Molly had yet to meet the man, but she planned on talking to as many of the locals as possible, as casually as she could, without giving away her real purpose for coming to Eagle Rock.

Her first pass through the valley yielded nothing out of the ordinary. The only movement had been from a herd of antelope grazing on the grasses near the river. She'd observed no signs of manmade structures or roads leading in or out that appeared to have been heavily travelled.

She retrieved the drone and drove farther south along a narrow road that could have been an old mining road, or a logging road placed there years ago by a logging company when they'd still been allowed to harvest trees from the national forest. She took up a position at the top of another ridge and turned the key, killing the engine.

A noise behind her made her spin around. An animal burst from the tree line and barreled toward her.

Molly tensed and reached for her weapon. She'd been warned to be on the lookout for wolves and bear. At first, she thought wolf, but the animal didn't have the thick fur of a wolf. It appeared to be a German Shepherd. What a German Shepherd was doing out in these wild hills was another question.

If the animal was feral, it could be as dangerous as a wolf. As she watched, it bounded toward her, its gait not as graceful as most dogs. When it slowed, it settled into a limping trot.

Molly raised her weapon, not willing to take chances that the dog was friendly. If it growled or bared its teeth, she'd shoot first, ask questions later.

When the animal was within ten feet of Molly, she called out. "Sit!"

The German Shepherd stopped in its tracks and sat.

Molly frowned. "Are you a good dog or a bad dog?" she said aloud.

The shepherd's tail swished back and forth in the dirt.

"Here, boy," she said, calling it closer. Molly held the pistol in one hand and extended her other hand with her fingers curled under for the dog to sniff—and it did.

A long pink tongue snaked out and licked her hand.

"Ah, you're just a big sweetie." Molly holstered her weapon beneath her jacket, squatted on her haunches and ruffled the dog's neck, scratching behind his ears. "What are you doing out this far? Are you lost?" She looked the animal over. He appeared to be in good health, except for a scar on his leg and being a little thin. Had another animal attacked him? The wound appeared to be an old one. Though the hair had not grown back over the wound, it had healed long ago, the scar gray instead of the pink of a newer injury.

"What about a collar?" Molly felt around his neck and found a thick, leather band but no identification tag. However, he had a tattoo in his ear, ß826. "No dog tags but a tattoo? Are you a working dog, perhaps? Where's your master?"

As if in answer to her question, a movement caught her attention, and a man emerged from the same direction the dog had come. He wore jeans and hiking boots. A short-sleeved, black T-shirt stretched over impossibly broad shoulders, and his biceps bulged beneath the sleeves' hems.

Shaggy dark hair and dark stubble shadowing his chin gave him the appearance of a rugged mountain man, or a badass biker dude.

Molly caught her breath.

"Six," he said in one short, sharp command.

The dog leaped to his feet, ran back to the man and sat at his feet, looking up, ready to execute the next command.

His master stared at Molly through narrowed eyes.

She straightened, though standing up didn't make her feel any more in charge. The man towered over her. He could take her down with one hand tied behind his back. He could easily snap her neck in one twist.

Was he one of the people she'd come to Montana to find? A shiver rippled down the back of her neck. Unwilling to show even a small sign of fear, Molly squared her shoulders and tilted up her chin. "Is this your dog?"

He nodded. "He is. I hope he didn't scare you."

Her chin lifted a fraction more. "Not at all. I just wondered what he was doing out here, all alone."

His eyes narrowed even more, giving him a dark and dangerous look. "I could ask you the same."

"I'm enjoying the scenery," she stalled.

He held out a hand. "I'm Joe."

She hesitated before taking his hand. "Just Joe?" she challenged, narrowing her own eyes.

"Just Joe." He cocked a brow and waited for her to reciprocate. "And you are?"

"Molly," she said, not giving any more than he'd given. If he wanted his surname to remain anonymous, so be it. She could play the same game. A man like him would be easily recognized in town.

His lips twitched, and the slight crinkling at the corner of his eyes gave away his humor. "Just Molly?"

She gave the barest of nods, and then glanced down at the dog. "Yours?"

The little bit of laughter in his face died and a mask slid in its place. "Yeah."

"He's beautiful and friendly."

A frown pulled his brows together. "You touched him?"

Molly nodded. "Yes. Is it a crime?"

"Do you always pet strange dogs?"

"Only ones who let me."

"Ever consider they might bite?"

Oh, she'd considered it. She'd almost shot the poor animal. "Yes. But he sat when I told him to, so I figured he had some manners." *Unlike his master.*

"Did you ever consider their owners might not want you to pet them?"

Her brows shot up. "You don't want me to pet your dog?"

He shrugged. "Six is a highly trained dog. In order to keep control over him, it's best for only one person to give him commands."

She raised her hands in surrender, anger pushing to the surface. "Excuse me. The dog didn't come to me with instructions. But he did come to me." Molly crossed her arms over her chest. "And what the hell kind of name is Six?"

"None of your business," he muttered. "Why are you out in the mountains alone?" He looked over her shoulder at the four-wheeler and the drone.

Molly stood taller, as if in an attempt to block his view of her equipment. "None of your business."

He gave a curt nod and turned his attention to the dog. "Six, come." Without another word to her, the man departed, his dog trotting alongside. Both had a bit of a hitch in their gaits, both on the same side, as if they had received matching injuries.

For a long moment, Molly stared after them. Then she shook her head, climbed on her ATV and drove along the ridge in the opposite direction as the man had gone.

Rude. The man was completely rude.

On the other hand, the dog was sweet and well-mannered. "Joe" could learn a thing or two from his dog.

Following the directions to the locations she'd programmed into her GPS, she drove down an old mining trail into another valley and up to the top of the next ridge where she stopped, got out the drone and surveyed the next valley that featured a sheer rock wall lined with caves.

She fought to push the odious man to the back of her mind, but she couldn't help looking around every so often, as if half-expecting Just Joe to appear again.

Again, she sent the drone into the air, maneuvering it

slowly across the valley, pausing it in front of the caves to give her a chance to peek inside. She had her head down and was staring at the video imaging when a loud bang rang out, echoing off the hillsides. The view on the screen jerked to the side, bounced then began to spin.

Molly looked across the valley to the last location she'd sent the drone. The device had disappeared altogether and no amount of fiddling with the joystick brought it up again. Her drone was down, and based on the sound prefacing its crash, someone could have used it as target practice.

"Damn." Over a thousand dollars' worth of electronics had just crashed into the valley below.

Though she wasn't supposed to make contact, Molly had to know if a terrorist or a redneck poacher had shot down the drone.

She tucked the controls into her jacket, and pushed the four-wheeler into the bushes. Then she headed down the trail into the valley, hugging the shadows.

If the shooter were willing to take down a drone out in the middle of nowhere, would he also be willing to shoot a living, breathing human? Even if that person wasn't part of the terrorist training camp, he might not want to be caught shooting down an expensive piece of machinery. He might shoot at the owner of the drone rather than take the blame and possible financial repercussions of replacing the device.

Molly slowed to a stop and listened. The sound of an engine was heading in her direction.

Her pulse rocketing, she raced back up the trail, pulled her ATV out of the bushes and started the engine. Then she spun the vehicle around. But not fast enough.

She looked back in time to see another four-wheeler careen around the bend in the trail, the rider dressed all in black, wearing a black helmet, barreling straight for her.

Fear pinched her gut as she thumbed the throttle, sending the four-wheeler shooting forward and upward along the rocky trail, bouncing like popcorn in a kettle. She held on to the handgrips as her bottom left the seat again and again.

The ATV behind her slowly closed the distance.

At another bend in the trail, Molly risked a glance back. The rider had stopped in the middle of the trail, pulled a handgun and was pointing it at her.

She had two choices, continue on her way up the trail, in full view and range of the man's gun, or throw herself off the vehicle and down the side of the trail, tumble down a steep hill and risk breaking every bone in her body, but possibly living to see another day.

Molly released the handles, kicked off and away from the vehicle, and lunged toward the edge of the trail. She flew through the air for what felt like a very long time before she hit the side of the steep hill and tumbled, cartwheeled and slid down the rocky hill to the bottom where a huge boulder broke her downward trajectory.

With only moments to spare, she hauled her aching body up to her hands and knees and crawled behind the boulder where she collapsed, the light dimming around the edges of her vision and finally blinking out.

CHAPTER 4

Kujo had only been in Montana for two days. After Bear and Duke's visit to him in Colorado, he'd driven to San Antonio, where he'd spent a week filling out paperwork and convincing the trainers at Lackland he was fit to adopt Six, and that the dog and he were still a good match.

When he'd arrived at the kennels where the dogs were kept, he'd been hard pressed to keep his shit together. Since leaving the Army, he'd had nothing to do with dogs or the people who trained them. Nor had he been around men in uniform.

The range of feelings washing over him had kept him glued to the seat of his truck. He'd taken several minutes sitting in his pickup, gathering the courage he needed to face the very things he'd worked so hard to forget—the career he'd trained for, the dogs he'd loved and the only life he'd ever known.

When the sergeant in charge led him back to Six's kennel, no amount of mental coaching prepared him for the rush of emotion that nearly brought him to his knees.

As they approached, Six sat at the back of the kennel, his tail curled beneath him, his shoulders slumped and the light completely drained from his eyes.

"He's been like this since the people at his last foster home returned him," the sergeant said. "Nobody can reach him. He's non-responsive and completely shut down." The man pointed to the full bowl at the corner of the cage. "He hasn't eaten anything in three days."

Kujo had to swallow hard several times before he could voice a command. When he finally could squeeze air past his vocal cords, all he could manage was, "Six, come."

The dog's ears twitched, and his nose lifted slightly as if sniffing the air.

Kujo waited, afraid to say anything for fear of revealing just how devastated he was by the appearance of the dog that had saved his life.

For a long moment, the dog sat, sniffing the air. Then he rose up onto all fours, his tail drooping, and took a step forward.

Kujo opened the gate, stepped inside and pulled out of his pocket the old tennis ball he'd kept with his gear all those years. He squatted on his haunches and repeated, "Six, come."

Six sniffed the air, his ears now standing straight, his body tense. One step at a time, he eased toward Kujo, limping slightly.

"He took a hit from shrapnel on his last deployment," the sergeant offered.

Kujo barely heard the man. His attention remained on the dog, his gaze meeting Six's, silently urging him to close the distance between them.

When at last he did, Six sniffed at the ball, took it from Kujo's hand, and then he collapsed against him, whining, wiggling and cuddling until the weight of his body pushed Kujo over, forcing him to sit on the concrete.

Since then, Six had stuck to him like flypaper, refusing to leave his side.

From San Antonio, he'd driven all through the night, stopping only to put gas in his truck and to let Six out to stretch and do his business. Normally, he would have kept Six in a crate, like he had when he'd been in training or transporting him. But he figured they were both retired. To hell with the crate.

Six lay on the seat behind Kujo and occasionally stuck his nose over Kujo's shoulder and licked his face.

The dog had picked up bad habits over the years he'd been away from Kujo, but it didn't matter. All that mattered was that he and Six were a team once again.

When he arrived in Eagle Rock, Montana in the foothills of the Crazy Mountains, Kujo had driven straight up to Hank Patterson's house, introduced himself and asked if the job offer was still good.

Hank had welcomed him, given him a bed to sleep in for the night and briefed him the next morning about the work they were doing and his expectations of the people he hired to provide protective services.

At the moment, Hank was negotiating with a client who was coming to Montana in a few weeks and would need someone to work as a bodyguard. As all of his men were currently assigned, that job would be the one he'd assign Kujo. In the meantime, he could either stay with Hank, his wife and baby, or find a place of his own.

Kujo had gone out the next day and found a cabin in the mountains to rent. It wasn't much more than one room with a bed, small kitchen area and an outhouse. He suspected it was someone's old hunting cabin. The isolation suited him. The only drawback was the lack of telephone or cell phone reception. He figured he could rent the place for a few weeks while he waited for his assignment. It would give him time to acclimate to the town of Eagle Rock and the people in the community. Once a day, he'd visit town and check in with Hank.

The solitude would give him time to work with Six.

After moving into his cabin, Kujo had gone hiking in the mountains to work out the kinks of his long road trip, when Six had finally run ahead of him instead of clinging to his legs, refusing to leave his side.

The dog had separation anxiety from having been passed from one handler to the next, and then one foster home to the next. As far as Kujo was concerned, Six was now settled with his last owner. And Six seemed to know it. He'd finally left Kujo's side and raced ahead on the mountain trail, circling back to make sure he was still there and then running ahead again.

When the dog hadn't returned after a period of time Kujo was comfortable with, he'd picked up his pace, until he was jogging, trying to catch up to Six.

When he'd emerged from the tree line to find Six

with a woman squatting next to him, he'd been both relieved and a little angry. And he'd taken his anger out on the woman.

He didn't want to admit to himself she'd awakened in him something he hadn't felt in a long time. Attraction. When she'd given him just as much trouble as he'd given her, he couldn't help but admire her gumption.

At first, he couldn't understand why a lone woman would be out in the wilds of the mountains alone. But then he'd noticed she was probably packing a pistol beneath the leather jacket she wore. The telltale bulge around her waist had nothing to do with the gentle swell of her breasts above.

Her green eyes had sparkled when she'd been angry with him for being less than forthcoming with his reasons for being so high up on the trails, wandering the mountain, just him and his dog.

If he was still the same man he'd been before the explosion that got him medically boarded out of the Army, he might have teased her, or cajoled her into giving him her number.

But what good would that have done? He'd been out of the dating scene for three years. What woman wanted a washed-up Delta Force soldier with a limp? What did he have to offer to a relationship when all he'd done for the past three years was to bury himself in the woods, refusing to take part in life? All he had to show for all that lost time was a fixed-up cabin he couldn't even call his own.

His friends had been right. He owed it to himself and Six to get on with his life. Patterson had given him the opportunity he needed to make a new start, hopefully doing work he was still cut out for.

Dating and women would have to wait on the backburner until he had something to offer in a relationship.

As he'd continued along the path through the woods, down into a valley and up to the top of the next ridge, he'd pushed himself physically. During his years in the Colorado Rockies, he'd climbed rocky hillsides, increasing his lung capacity and the muscles in his bum leg.

Deep in his heart, he'd harbored a dream of regaining enough of his old physical abilities to convince the medical board to reinstate him in the military.

He snorted and paused at the top of the ridge.

Like the Army would ever want a broken-down soldier among able-bodied men. He and Six had outlived their usefulness for the Army, their injuries sidelining them from doing the jobs they were trained to do. The sooner they both accepted their new normal, the sooner they could get on with the business of establishing new lives for themselves.

As he stood looking out over a valley, a movement caught his attention. Below him, something flashed and moved in a straight line along the valley floor.

He squinted, trying to make out what he was looking at. Finally, he realized the flying object was a drone, hovering in front of several caves in the side of a rocky escarpment.

At the moment he identified the drone, a shot rang

out. The drone tilted sideways and then dropped out of the sky, crashing into a stand of trees.

An engine roared to life at the top of the ridge opposite from where he stood. A dark smudge moved across the terrain and away from the valley. It appeared to be an ATV much like the one the woman called Molly had been standing so close to when Kujo had confronted her about petting Six.

Another engine fired up from a different location, deeper in the valley.

Kujo assessed the scene. One vehicle turned around on the mountain trail, a second ATV raced upward to meet the other. He assumed they were working together, until he saw the rider of the lower vehicle stop and raise both arms as if aiming at the person on the other ATV.

All of the sudden, the rider on the upper ATV flew through the air and over the edge of what appeared to be a cliff.

Kujo tensed and started running across the ridgeline toward the scene of the accident. The second vehicle came to a halt, the rider leaped off and stood at the side of the trail, looking down and holding something in his hand.

What was he doing?

Kujo wished he had a pair of binoculars. He narrowed his eyes, focusing on the man standing at the edge of the cliff. As he moved closer, he could make out the shape of the object in the man's hand.

It was a handgun.

Now running all out and doing his best to ignore

pain flaring in his bum leg, Kujo knew he had to get to the driver who'd gone over the edge before the man with the weapon fired.

The sharp report of gunfire echoed off the hillsides. Five rounds were discharged before the man with the gun climbed onto his ATV and headed over the top of the hill, disappearing out of sight.

Kujo ran as fast as he could, Six by his side, but the rough terrain slowed his progress as he slipped and slid in the rocks and loose gravel. When he got to the point on the trail where the abandoned ATV had come to a halt against a tree trunk, he stopped, sucked in deep breaths, and stared over the edge.

When he peered downward, he couldn't see signs of anyone below. At the bottom of the steep slope were several giant boulders.

Six sniffed the ATV, the ground, and then lifted his head. Before Kujo could stop him, he leaped over the edge and half-slid, half-loped down the slippery, steep hillside to where it bottomed out in front of the boulders. Then he ducked out of sight, behind the huge rocks.

Kujo waited for the dog to reappear. When he didn't, Kujo had no choice but to follow.

He stepped over the edge and started slowly down the hill. But the ground was nothing but loose rocks and gravel. Once he started sliding, there was no stopping until he reached the bottom. At first, he skied, balancing on both feet. Eventually, he sat, using his bottom as a sled, taking him all the way to boulders.

Fortunately, other than a sore tailbone, he arrived

relatively unscathed and leaped to his feet to follow the direction Six had gone. Behind the boulders, he found a dark lump lying against the ground. Six stood over the mass, licking something.

As Kujo moved closer, dread knifed through him as he realized the lump of black was the woman who'd introduced herself as Molly, and Six was licking her face. *Jesus, don't let her be dead.*

"Six, sit," Kujo commanded.

Six gave the woman one last kiss and sat back on his haunches, his eager brown eyes shifting from Molly to Kujo. He let out a worried whine, and then waited for Kujo's next command.

Molly laid still, not a muscle moved and her eyes were closed.

Kujo squatted next to her and felt for a pulse at the base of her throat. His gut clenched when he didn't feel the reassuring thump of a heartbeat against his fingertips. He shifted his hand and let go a sigh of relief when he located the strong, steady rhythm. She was alive but had suffered quite a fall.

Although afraid to move her, he knew he couldn't leave her where she was long enough to get off the mountain and call for help. Her attacker could return, or some scavenging animal might find her.

He shot a glance at Six. He could leave the dog and return with help, but he hadn't been with Six long enough to know whether he'd stay until Kujo returned.

No, he couldn't leave the woman. He touched her shoulder gently. "Molly."

She didn't respond.

He spoke louder. "Molly, wake up."

She stirred and moaned.

"Molly, you have to tell me what hurts."

For a long moment she didn't respond, but then she whispered, "Everything."

He chuckled. "Could you be more specific?"

"No," she said.

He had to lean close to hear her response.

"Can you move your fingers and toes?" he asked. Kujo stared at her hand, lying on the rocks beside her face. The digits moved slightly. He glanced at her feet, but boots covered her toes. If she moved them, he couldn't tell. "How did that feel?"

"Not bad," she said. Still her eyes remained closed.

"Did you feel your toes?"

She started to nod, but winced and then stilled, emitting a pathetic whimper. "Head hurts."

"Tell me if anything I touch causes you pain." Kujo wrapped his hands around her arms and squeezed gently, moving from the shoulder down to her wrists. "Anything hurt?"

"No."

"Could you feel my hands?"

"Yes."

"Good." He repeated the technique on the other side with the same reaction. Then he moved to her legs. Starting at her thighs he swept his hands down one leg. "Can you feel my hands?"

"Mmm."

His lips quirked. "Is that a yes?"

"Yes. Feels good," she said, and her eyes opened,

rounded and then closed again. "Did I say that out loud?"

He let go of some of his tension in muted laughter. "Yes, but you probably won't remember tomorrow, so don't worry about it."

"But you'll remember," she said, laying her arm across her eyes. "And you don't like me."

"I didn't say that."

"I could tell," she said, her voice fading.

"Molly, do you think you can sit up?"

"Sure," she said. As if to prove her words, she pushed herself to a sitting position with a little help from his arm supporting her.

"How's the back? Any pain?"

"I feel like I was run through a rock tumbler." She swayed and would have fallen over if he hadn't placed his hand behind her and held her upright. "I'm all right," she said. "I just need a little help standing."

"Are you sure you can?"

She nodded and winced again, then pressed a hand to the back of her head. "I can do this."

"If you're sure."

"Please, just help me stand so that I can assess the damage." She gripped the front of his shirt.

He wrapped an arm around her back. "On three. One...two...three." He stood, more or less pulling her up with him.

When she was upright, her fingers curled into his shirt, and she smiled. "See? I'm fine." Then she passed out, going completely limp in his arms.

Molly almost slid back to the earth. If Kujo had not

held on, she would have ended up back on the ground, possibly injuring herself even worse.

Six whimpered and leaned against Kujo's leg.

"You don't know the half of it, buddy. At least you don't have to carry her back up the hill."

He scooped her legs up and cradled her against his chest then emerged from behind the rocks. A quick evaluation of the slippery hillside had him formulating another plan. If he walked along the base of the hill, he'd come to a less vertical slope. Then he might stand a better chance of climbing while carrying an inert woman.

He started out, keeping a cautious watch out for the man who'd chased her down and shot at her after she'd fallen down the hill. If he showed up again, Kujo needed to be ready.

Something between him and her dug into his ribs, he glanced down and noticed the shoulder holster beneath her jacket and the 9-millimeter pistol.

He smiled. As he'd suspected, she'd come to the mountains packing. If the shooter returned, he could defend them. He wondered why she hadn't stopped and set up a defensive position, instead of falling over a cliff. She must have been as surprised as he was by the attack. Only someone desperate to avoid being shot would have chosen throwing herself off a cliff as a viable alternative.

His leg ached with the additional weight, but he trudged onward, slowly climbing through the trees and boulders. At a point when the slope grew steeper, he stopped and laid her over his shoulder, freeing one of his arms to better balance himself as he climbed. By the time he reached the old mining road, he was breathing hard, and his legs felt like they were on fire. Before he stepped out of the shadows, he checked both directions, held his breath and listened for the sound of an ATV engine.

He heard nothing but the wind stirring the lodge pole pines. Kujo and Six backtracked along the trail. Having walked more than five miles into the mountains, he knew he couldn't carry the woman all the way back. He had to get her out on the four-wheeler she'd ridden.

The ATV was wedged against the trunk of a tree. Though the handlebar was bent, the vehicle appeared to be intact.

He laid Molly on the ground, dragged the ATV away from the tree and hit the starter switch. The engine turned over and died. Kujo hit it again, and the motor roared to life. Shifting into neutral, he set the brake and returned to Molly's prone body.

Six stood guard beside her, refusing to move until Kujo lifted her into his arms and carried her to the ATV. How he was going to drive the ATV and hold onto the woman was an entirely different challenge. He straddled the seat and draped her body over his arm, resting her bottom across his thighs. It wasn't the most efficient way to get a person out of the mountains, but it would have to do.

Now, where to take her?

She had to have come up from one of the roads leading to the highway.

Unfamiliar with the trails, his best bet would be to take her back to his cabin, load her into his truck and drive her into Eagle Rock and the nearest medical facility.

Balancing Molly against his chest, Kujo shifted the ATV into gear and set off at a sedate pace back the way from which he'd come.

The five miles back to the cabin took over an hour. Six trotted alongside with his uneven gait. By the time he reached the cabin, Kujo's arms ached with the effort of maneuvering the four-wheeler and keeping Molly from slipping off his lap.

Six climbed the porch and flopped down, tongue lolling. He didn't move as Kujo dismounted the ATV and carried Molly toward the truck.

When he arrived there, he stood her against the truck, his body pressed to hers to hold her in place, and fumbled with the handle.

"Where are we?" she asked, blinking her eyes open.

"At my cabin about to get into a truck to take you to the hospital." He opened the door and would have laid her on the front passenger seat, but her hand shot out to grip the truck's door, blocking him from sliding her into the truck.

"No."

Tired, achy and past cranky, Kujo frowned down at the woman in his arms. "You need to see a doctor. You could have a concussion, maybe even swelling on your brain. And Lord knows if you've suffered any spinal cord injuries."

"Don't take me to town."

"Why?"

Her head lolled against his chest, and she closed her eyes again.

"Molly, I need an answer."

"Please, don't take me to town."

"Where else would I take you?"

"I don't know. But if the man who shot at me finds out I didn't die, he might not be happy about it."

"All the more reason to get you to a hospital, and then call the sheriff to report what happened."

She gripped his shirt. "Please, don't."

"I don't understand. A man shot at you. Do you want to ignore that fact? What if he targets another person?"

"I can't let him know he wasn't successful. It's better if he thinks I'm dead."

"I'm taking you to the doctor. You're delirious and not making any sense." He started to slide toward the open door again, but her hand on the doorframe put a crimp in his effort. "Woman, you've been a thorn in my side since we met."

"You're not a bundle of happiness, yourself," she whispered with her eyes still closed. Then she opened them and stared up into his gaze.

Those green orbs pierced him to the heart.

"Please."

Well, damn. When she put it that way, with the plea in her eyes as well as in her voice, how could he say no?

He sighed. "Where do you want me to take you?"

"Can't go back to my room in Eagle Rock," she mumbled. Then she shot a glance toward the old hunting cabin and the surrounding wilderness. "This place looks deserted. How about here?"

Kujo shook his head. "No way."

"Why?" she asked.

"Because it's *my* place, and I don't share it with women."

"For a couple days?" she pleaded, her voice fading as her body seemed to lose all the muscles holding it together. "I promise not to be a pain—"

"Sweetheart, it's too late for that kind of promise. You've been nothing but a giant pain in my ass since I ran into you on the ridge earlier."

Since she'd already passed out again, he had no choice. Lifting her in his arms, he marched across the clearing to the porch steps and climbed up to where Six lay, taking it all in as if he'd known all along the woman wasn't going anywhere.

"Traitor," Kujo said as he kicked the door to the cabin open and carried Molly inside.

Six slipped inside before the door swung shut.

CHAPTER 5

Molly faded in and out of consciousness. One moment she was being held in the arms of her rescuer, bouncing along a mountain trail. Dust kicked up around her, but she didn't have the will to cough. She knew she should sit up and get herself off the mountain, but she didn't have the energy. So, she rested her cheek against the solid wall of Joe's chest and gave herself permission to go back to a very disturbed sleep where she couldn't quite rest because her bruised body was being jolted until her teeth rattled in her head.

When the vehicle finally came to a halt, her head cleared long enough for her to think. Whoever had been shooting at her probably assumed she was dead. Which might be a better position to be in to continue her investigation. She'd have at least a few days to recuperate and lay low, giving the B&B time to report her missing. The missing person report would support her cover of being dead. The person who'd shot at her wouldn't be concerned she'd mouth off to the authorities, and she'd have time to find the camp before the terrorists scrambled to leave the area.

Convincing "Just Joe" that she didn't need to go to the hospital had been exhausting. Once he'd agreed, she'd faded out again.

How long she'd been out, she didn't know. When she opened her eyes again, she had to blink several times. The room was so dark she'd thought she might have dreamed opening her eyes.

A dim light shined in the far corner of the dark room. As her vision cleared, she noted a potbellied stove glowing orange through a cast-iron grate.

She turned her cheek against the coarse fabric of a wool blanket and a damp nose bumped into her skin.

Molly jerked back and grinned when Six placed a paw on her arm and again nudged her with his snout.

"Hey, boy," she said, her voice hoarse. When she tried to move her arms and legs, a shadow crossed the room and hovered over her.

Joe sat on the edge of the bed, slipped a hand beneath her shoulders and helped her rise up just a little.

Again, she groaned. "If this is being alive, death might have been preferable."

"Take this." He held out a capsule.

She frowned. "What is it?"

"A painkiller."

Her frown deepened. "How do I know it's not some date rape drug?"

"Lady, if I'd wanted to rape you, I could have done it any time in the past twenty-four hours."

"Twenty-four hours!" She sat up straight and immediately regretted the sudden movement. Her strained muscles and bruises joined forces across her body to hurt all at the same time.

She collapsed against his arm, biting hard on her bottom lip to keep from crying out.

He shook his head. "Ready to take the pill?" Joe held it to her lips.

Obediently, she opened her mouth and took the offering, her lips touching his rough hands in the process.

He reached behind him for the tin cup on the nightstand beside the bed and held it to her lips. "Drink. You're probably dehydrated after being out for so long. I was going to take you into town if you didn't wake up soon."

Molly swallowed the pill and drank several more sips before leaning back. "I'm sorry to be so much trouble."

"I don't understand why you don't want to see a doctor. The kinds of injuries you sustained could kill you or leave you paralyzed for life."

"I can move." She raised her arm and winced at the number of bruises marring her skin. Then she noticed she wasn't wearing the shirt she'd had on when she'd fallen down the hill. Frowning, she shot a glance at Joe. "This isn't my shirt." Heat blossomed in her cheeks when she moved her legs against the coarse wool blanket. The prickly fabric abraded her skin. She grabbed the edge of the blanket and pulled it up to her chin. "Where are my clothes?"

Joe's lips twitched. He turned toward the potbellied stove and pointed at a line strung from one wall to another in the cozy room. On it hung her jeans, shirt, jacket and shoulder holster.

"My pistol?" she demanded.

"It's on the table by the stove. You can have it when you can hold it up."

"Did you…undress me?" she asked, her voice dropping to a whisper.

He straightened, set the cup on the nightstand and went to the stove. "Since you refused to go to a doctor, I had to make sure you didn't have any other injuries that needed attending. Removing the clothing allowed me to check you all over. After I cleaned your wounds, I couldn't put dirty clothing back on you." He nodded toward her drying shirt and pants. "I washed them. They should be dry by now."

So, the big T-shirt that enveloped most of her body was one of his. She should have known. It smelled like him. A hint of musk and the woodsy scent of the outdoors. Despite the aches and pains from sliding halfway down a mountain, her body responded to the man, her core tightening. Her lips still tingled where they'd touched his hand.

Heat burned her cheeks at the thought of those big, rough hands touching her skin, brushing across her thighs as he'd pulled off her jeans. After a little wiggle, she could tell she still had on her panties and bra. God, had he removed them and put them back on her? She felt completely exposed and at his mercy. "You shouldn't have removed my clothes without my permission."

"You didn't give me much of a choice. I would gladly have handed you over to the doctors and nurses at the emergency room and let them tally the wounds."

She bit down on her lip. Yeah, she should be grateful he'd carried her down from the mountain and taken care of her. He didn't have to. She wasn't his responsibility. She wanted to be mad at him, but she couldn't, since he'd gone to all the trouble to make certain she'd lived. "I suppose I should thank you," she said, reluctantly.

He nodded. "As it is, I'm not equipped with enough bandages and supplies for someone with as many cuts and scrapes as you have. I need to make a run to town. I could drop you off anywhere you would like. Even the hospital, if you've changed your mind."

Even before he finished the sentence, she shook her head. "I'd rather not go back until I figure out what exactly happened."

"I can tell you what happened. I saw it all from the opposite end of the ridge." His brows dipped into a fierce frown. "You jumped off your four-wheeler and fell to the bottom of a very steep hill. Then the guy on the other ATV shot at you. I take it you don't know who he was?"

Molly nodded. "I have no idea who would want to shoot at me."

"And then there's the matter of the drone he shot down first."

Molly's eyes widened as the reason she'd been out

there in the first place finally came back to her. "Oh, dear Lord." She flung back the scratchy blanket and started to swing her legs over the side of the bed. The pain of movement, made her cry out. Then she glanced at her legs, appalled at the huge cuts and bruises making her skin look like the canvass of an angry painter.

Joe stood in front of her, blocking her from getting out of the bed.

Not that she could. Her muscles screamed and some of the bruises and cuts throbbed.

"Where do you think you're going?'

"I need to find my drone and the controls." God, her boss was going to kill her. She had to get to the device and see if there was anything to salvage.

"The drone crashed in the trees. More than likely it's nothing more than scrap metal or plastic now."

"Yeah, but I need to collect all of the pieces. There was a camera on it too."

"It'll have to stay where it went down until you're well enough to climb around in the mountains."

When she tried to rise again, he laid a hand on her shoulder and applied the slightest pressure. "Stay."

Molly glared. "I'm not your dog to be trained and fed treats." As soon as the words left her mouth, her stomach grumbled as if to prove her wrong. She'd gone more than twenty-four hours without food. Her belly was reminding her of the fact. She also realized it wasn't fair for this man to have to feed, clothe and care for a stranger. "I should leave. You've done more than enough to help me."

"Where will you go?"

"Back to the bed and breakfast in town."

"And as soon as you do, the shooter will know you're still alive. Not that I have a stake in this situation, but you seemed to care a lot about hiding the fact you're still alive, thus the reason for your insistence on staying here." He walked to where her clothes hung on the line near the fireplace and lifted a gadget from the table. "I found this in the four-wheeler's basket. He held it out.

Molly stared at the device. "Oh, thank God." The controls had a built-in recording device. "I don't suppose you have a television or computer here?"

Joe snorted. "There's not one for at least a five-mile radius. We don't even have radio or cell phone reception out this far."

She chewed on the tip of her fingernail. "Electricity?" For the first time, she noticed the cabin didn't have a single light fixture—unless she counted the candles and oil lamp on the table.

"No."

"Holy hell, how do you live?"

Joe burst out laughing.

Six's ears perked, and he stared from Molly to Joe.

Up to that moment, Molly hadn't considered Joe that handsome. He'd been too serious and stone-faced to be considered traditionally handsome. However, he was ruggedly attractive, and when he smiled and laughed, he was stunningly gorgeous. The dark hair falling over his forehead and the twinkle in his brown eyes made her heart flip in her chest and her nipples tingle.

Damn, she should have better sense than drool over a man she'd just met.

He's seen me nearly naked.

Which didn't count since she'd been unconscious at the time. Still, this man knew more about her body than any other stranger off the street.

Joe held up his hand. "Look, stay here one more day, and I'll take you anywhere you want to go."

Molly frowned, trying to think of reasons she couldn't, but the bottom line was that she could only go back into town and, once she did, her attacker would know he hadn't killed her. Then it might become a race to see who could get to the downed drone first.

It had to be her. Until she was ready to go back into the woods, she'd be smarter to remain off-grid. That would give her time to recover from her injuries before she headed back out to that valley to retrieve the drone.

"Fine. I'll stay one more night. As long as you promise not to take advantage of me in the meantime."

He held up two fingers, Boy Scouts style. "I promise not to molest you, unless you want me to." With a wink, he lowered his fingers. He turned to Six. "Stay."

Six faced Joe, his tail sweeping the floor in rapid swipes.

Then Joe was gone, leaving Molly and Six alone in the dark cabin with only the light from the potbellied stove. The view through the door indicated it was light outside, though it was murky and dreary as if clouds covered the sun.

For a long time, Molly stared at the door through which Joe had disappeared. She knew nothing about him, but somehow she felt in her heart she could trust him.

Her glance went to the gun lying on the table. And apparently, he trusted her, especially since he'd convinced her to stay another day, instead of throwing her out on her injured ass. She could always get up, grab the gun and be out of there before he returned. She moved again and was reminded how badly movement hurt. The pill he'd given her was just beginning to take effect.

Molly yawned and lay back on the thin mattress.

Six laid his paw on her hand.

A chill settled over Molly, and despite the blanket wrapped snugly around her, she couldn't get warm enough. Once the shivers started, she couldn't stop them, and every tremble caused more pain, disturbing her stiff muscles and battered body.

The dog sniffed at her trembling body and whined quietly.

Molly patted the mattress beside her and said, "Up."

Six glanced toward the door and back to her. Then he crawled up on the mattress beside her, sharing his warmth.

She needed rest to allow her body to recover. Molly fell asleep, cuddling up to the German Shepherd. When she woke, she'd get that gun and be on her way.

CHAPTER 6

Kujo drove his truck into town and headed straight for the little pharmacy on the corner beside the grocery store. Not only was he out of bandages and disinfectant, he needed food for supper.

Molly would probably be better off with soup or something easy to eat or drink, but after his workout, Kujo needed a heartier meal.

For the past three years, he'd spent his life as a hermit, barely going to town for much more than the bare necessities. He still wasn't sure he was the right man for Hank's job. Guarding people would mean he'd have to actually interact with more and more *people*. Thankfully, his assignment wouldn't start for a little bit longer, which would give him time to acclimate himself back into society with all the noise and drama that accompanied so many people.

Kujo collected the medical supplies from the pharmacy then entered the grocery store to purchase enough food for the night. The cabin didn't have electricity, thus no way to refrigerate food. He'd have to shop on a daily basis. Yes, his choice of accommodations had given him a little transition time. He'd get his peace and quiet while at the cabin. At the same time, he'd be required to be more social when he came into town every day to get enough food for the day.

Inside the grocery store, he headed straight for the butcher counter where he selected a couple of thick steaks. Then he gathered potatoes and some broccoli. He topped off his basket with canned chicken soup, aluminum foil, salt and pepper.

The woman at the checkout stand smiled. "You must be new in town. I'd remember a handsome man like you." She held out her hand. "Mrs. Prichard. My husband and I own the grocery."

He took her hand and shook it, feeling uncomfortable with the attention when all he wanted was to pay for his purchases and get the hell out of this little burg. "Joe. Nice to meet you...ma'am."

"Joe? Do you have a last name, Joe?"

"Kuntz." Joe placed his items on the counter, hoping the woman would get on with adding up his total.

The older woman tipped her head and touched a finger to her chin. "I used to know some Kuntzs who lived up near Cut Bank. Are you related?"

Kujo shook his head. "My family is from Texas."

She brightened. "Oh, well. You never know." Mrs. Prichard rang up the items, bagged them and waited for Kujo to count out the money from his wallet. "Are you staying long?"

"Don't know," he answered noncommittally.

"Working yet?"

He shook his head.

Mrs. Prichard smiled. "I hear they could use more people at the Blue Moose Tavern. If you have ranching skills, there are plenty of people in these parts who need ranch hands. All you have to do is ask around."

"Thanks." Kujo held out his hand for the change, gathered his bags and left the store. He almost bumped into a big burly guy dragging a skinny woman with lanky hair by the arm, outside the door.

"Damn, woman, I told you I didn't want to be in town long. Move." He shoved her toward the grocery store hard enough she fell to her knees, and her purse flew across the sidewalk, spewing its contents.

"Goddamn it, now look what you've done." He grabbed her by her arm and jerked her to her feet. When she tried to bend back down to gather her purse and belongings, he shook her. "Leave it. It's just a bunch of junk anyway."

"Ray, that's my purse. It was a gift from my mother."

"Your old lady's dead. She won't know if you tossed it in the trash." The woman pulled her arm free and dove for the purse and the items rolling across the sidewalk.

The big burly man snarled and kicked the woman in the backside, sending her flying across the concrete.

Kujo carefully set his bags on the ground then grabbed Ray by the arm and spun him around. "Leave her alone."

"You know what? Maybe you should mind your own

business." The big guy cocked his arm and threw a hard punch straight for Kujo's jaw.

Kujo ducked to the side, caught the man's wrist, then twisted and pulled his arm up between his shoulder blades. "Maybe you should reconsider how you're treating that woman," he said, his voice low and threatening.

"Let me go, goddamnit!" Ray rolled his shoulders in an attempt to dislodge the man holding his arm.

Kujo kept his voice dead even. "I'll let go when you promise to be nice."

The woman laid a hand on Kujo's arm. "Sir, please don't."

Kujo shot a glance at the woman whose eyes were wide and round. "No man should treat a woman like he was treating you. Are you all right?"

"Martha's my bitch, so back off," Ray roared.

Kujo shoved the bastard's arm higher up his back. "Apologize to her for calling her names and abusing her."

"The hell I will," Ray grumbled.

"No, really, sir," Martha pleaded. "Let go of Ray. He doesn't mean to hurt me." Her voice shook. Apparently, she was terrified.

Kujo shook his head. "He shouldn't treat you that way. You don't have to put up with it."

"He's my husband."

"Yeah, but it doesn't give him the right to hit you. He's breaking the law."

"No, no, it's not like that. I wasn't hurrying fast

enough. I promise to be better next time, so he won't be angry."

"Seriously?" Kujo didn't understand the woman. "He has no right to hit you or throw you around like a rag doll. You can have him arrested on assault charges."

Ray snorted. "Tell him you love it," he said. "Tell him you beg me to treat you that way."

Martha shot a nervous glance toward Ray then nodded. "I do. I like it when he's…when he's mean to me."

Kujo's heart clenched when he noticed the yellowing bruise on her cheek. This woman had been abused on more than this occasion. She probably had been beaten enough to know to keep her mouth shut or she'd get it again when she reached home.

"Martha," he said, his voice softer. "I can go with you to the sheriff's department. You can file a complaint. They have shelters for women who are abused."

Ray bucked beneath Kujo's hold. "Don't be tellin' my woman she has to leave me. I married her fair and square. She's my property. She belongs to me."

"No one owns another person, asshole," Kujo said, pushing Ray's arm higher up his back.

The man stood on his toes, his face turning red from the effort to relieve the pain in his arm. "You might have me in a pinch now, but when you let go, I'm gonna kick your ass."

Kujo snorted. "Big words for a man who can't get out of a simple arm hold."

"Hey, what's going on here?" a deep voice called out from across the street.

Martha ran to the man crossing the street, wearing a law enforcement uniform. "Sheriff, you have to make him let go of Ray. You have to."

"Okay, okay, break it up." The sheriff stepped up to the two men, his hand resting on his service weapon, nestled in the holster at his hip. "Ray, have you been causing problems again?"

"I didn't do anything wrong when this man attacked me," Ray said.

The sheriff faced Kujo. "Sir, you'll have to let go of him."

Kujo didn't move. "After his wife tells you what Ray was doing to her when I stepped in."

Martha wrung her hands and shot glances from the sheriff to her husband "He wasn't doin' anything. I promise."

The sheriff looked from Martha back to Kujo. "Mister?"

"I stopped him from kicking and shoving his wife," Kujo said. "When I did, he took a swing at me. I merely defended myself."

Resting his hand on his service weapon, the sheriff said, "Well, I got you covered if you'd like to let go of him now."

Kujo gave the man a little shove before he released him, putting some distance between them in case Ray came out swinging.

Then he stepped back and turned to the sheriff while keeping an eye on Ray as the man rubbed his shoulder.

Martha slipped her hand through Ray's arm and clung to him.

"I'm Sheriff Barron." The sheriff held out his hand. "New in town?"

"I am." Kujo took the sheriff's hand in his. "Joe Kuntz. Just arrived."

"Wanna tell me what happened?"

"Yeah, right," Ray grumbled. "Get the story from the outsider. You should arrest him. He tried to break my arm."

"I'll hear both sides," Sheriff Barron said, focusing his attention on Kujo. "Start at the beginning, Mr. Kuntz."

Kujo told him what he'd observed and of the abuse Martha had suffered at her husband's hands.

"Martha?" The sheriff turned to Martha.

"I don't know what Mr. Kuntz is talking about. Ray's been a perfect gentleman." The woman ducked her head, refusing to look the sheriff in the eye.

"Sheriff," came a warbling voice from behind them. Mrs. Prichard stood in the doorway to her shop. "The newcomer had it right. I saw everything from my cash register. Ray was being an ass to poor Martha. This man had the balls to stand up to him."

Ray glared at Mrs. Prichard. "Stay out of it."

"Like hell I will." Mrs. Prichard planted her fists on her hips. "You've been badmouthing and picking on Martha since she agreed to marry your sorry ass. It's about time someone gave you what for."

"Is that right, Martha?" the sheriff asked.

Martha stood with her head down, tears trickling down her cheeks. "He doesn't mean anything by it."

"But he's hitting you and hurting you, isn't he?" the sheriff asked.

"Don't answer him, Martha," Ray warned. "You don't have to say anything. Don't let them put words in your mouth."

The sheriff glared at the big bully. "Ray Diener, you're under arrest for assault. You can come with me willingly, or we can do this the hard way."

"You can't arrest him," Martha cried. "I don't want to press charges. He didn't hurt me."

Mrs. Prichard slipped her arm around Martha's shoulders. "Honey, look at your knees and hands. They're all scraped from him shoving you to the ground and kicking you. He treats you worse than he treats his dogs."

"No, please, don't take him," Martha sobbed. "He's all I have. How will I live?"

"We'll get you settled," Mrs. Prichard said. "Don't you worry. That sorry excuse of a man won't hurt you ever again."

"Martha, if you go with them, we're over! You hear me?" Ray's brows dipped low on his forehead, and his gaze burned with hatred.

He swung a hand toward her, but Kujo stopped the meaty fist from making contact by blocking his arm with his.

Martha flinched and cowered.

Mrs. Prichard pushed Martha behind her. "Does it make you feel like more of a man to abuse someone half your size? The big bad man can hit a woman. Oooo, I'm so scared."

"You'll regret this," Ray warned, his gaze encompassing Mrs. Prichard, Martha and Kujo. "All of you. No one comes between me and what I own."

"You don't own Martha," the sheriff stated.

"She's wearing my ring, isn't she?" Ray demanded.

"That doesn't mean you own her. Everyone has a right to protection, even if it's protection from her own husband." The sheriff glared at Diener.

Mrs. Prichard hugged Martha. "Come on, sweetie. I know someone who can help you." She led Martha into the grocery store.

"Ray, hold out your hands," the sheriff said.

"This is bullshit," Ray yelled. "You're going to arrest me all because some outsider son-of-a bitch stuck his nose in where it doesn't belong?"

"No, Ray, I'm arresting you for assault. You can't beat Martha just because you're married."

"She's my wife!" The man lunged at Kujo.

Kujo had expected the man to do something stupid. He stepped aside.

Ray's momentum carried him past Kujo. He tripped on the curb and crashed to his knees, ripping his denim jeans. Stupid with anger, he staggered to his feet, spun and charged toward Kujo.

Sheriff Barron raised his hand and shot a stun gun at the big man. It hit him square in the chest, and he dropped like a bag of stones.

The sheriff shook his head, a smile curling his lips. "Always wanted to try that to see how it worked on someone besides my deputies." He nodded. "Glad to see it's effective." He switched the device off and slipped it into his pocket. Then he rolled Ray onto his stomach and cuffed his wrists behind his back.

"I'll need you to stop by the station and give your statement," the sheriff said.

Kujo nodded. "Will do."

A sheriff's deputy pulled up in a large SUV and jumped out. Together, Sheriff Barron and the deputy hauled Ray into the back seat and took him away, leaving Kujo standing in front of the grocery store, tense and ready to get back to his cabin in the wilderness. A hand touched his arm, and he spun in a low crouch, his fists clenched, ready to defend himself.

"Hey, slugger." Bear held up his hands. "It's just me."

Kujo dropped his hands and straightened. "Sorry, I just had a run-in with one of the locals."

"Oh, yeah? Anyone I know?"

"Ray Diener?"

Bear held up his hand at about Ray's height. "About this tall...dark and mean?"

"That about sums him up." Kujo gathered his grocery bags from the ground and walked to his truck.

Bear strode beside him. "I'm glad you decided to take Hank up on his offer. He said you showed up with a German Shepherd." Bear grinned. "I bet Six was happy to see you. How's he doing?"

"His injuries gave him a limp, but he compensates and gets around pretty well." Kujo shook his head, recalling how he'd gone running ahead of him and allowed Molly to pet him. "He needs refresher training, but I think he'll respond quickly."

Bear pounded him on the back. "Glad to hear it. I hated to think of that dog being put down because no one could handle him. He saved our butts enough times he deserves to live the rest of his life high on the hog."

"Yes, he does. But he still has some good years left in him. And he likes to work. No use retiring him just because he has a limp."

"Agreed." Bear glanced across the street. "I'm meeting some of the team at the Blue Moose. Care to join us?"

"I'll take a rain check. I have to get some things back to the cabin I'm renting and check on Six."

Bear glanced around. "That's right. He's not with you. I thought you'd took him everywhere you went."

"I do, for the most part." Kujo didn't want to lie to his friend, but he didn't feel like he could tell him about the woman in his cabin. Not yet. Molly said she wanted to keep her presence a secret from everyone. As long as no one saw him carry her into his cabin, no one knew she was there. He hoped she didn't plan on staying for days. Kujo had done his share of sleeping on the cold, hard ground. He didn't plan on doing it for long, if he could help it. Sleeping on the ground played havoc with his bad knee. "I'll join you another night."

"Hank said you're in an old hunter's cabin until you can find a place closer to town."

Kujo nodded.

"Is it true, no phone or electricity?"

Again, Kujo nodded.

Bear shook his head. "Better you than me. Mia wouldn't like it much if she couldn't blow-dry her hair in the morning."

Kujo eased his mouth into a smile. "That's right, you're married now. When do I get to meet Mia?"

"We're staying in the house her folks left to her here in town. But she's in Hollywood for the week, meeting with her agent about one of the scripts she wrote."

"Do you ever go with her?" Kujo asked.

"Depends on my assignments. I'm starting a new one in two days. I'll be providing protection to a Hollywood star while he's on vacation on his ranch in Montana."

Kujo shook his head. From the hills and dust of Afghanistan to the fancy ranches of the rich and famous in Montana, the Delta Force soldiers had come a long way. He arched an eyebrow. "It's a tough job."

Bear nodded. "But someone has to do it. And what better way to make a living outside the Army?"

Bear seemed to have come to terms with his role in the civilian world. Kujo hoped he'd find peace and a sense of purpose in his new job, too.

In the meantime, he had a hungry woman waiting for him in his cabin and a dog he needed to retrain practically from scratch. He had some bad habits, like licking pretty women.

Not that the idea hadn't slipped through his own consciousness. Molly had a beautiful body. One he'd had the pleasure of viewing as he'd stripped her out of her clothing to check her for any life-threatening wounds. "Bear, tell the others I'll meet up with them soon. I have to get back for now."

"I'll tell them. And for the record, you're welcome to stay in our house until you find a better location. You don't have to rough it out in the woods."

"Thanks. I'll keep that in mind."

Kujo loaded his groceries into the back seat of his pickup and climbed in.

Bear waved, crossed the street and entered the tavern.

In the past, back when Kujo had been part of the Delta Force team, he'd been eager to join his teammates for a drink after work.

Three years away had created distance between them. Kujo wasn't quite sure how to close that distance, or if he even wanted to. He hadn't realized how truly lonely he'd been until Bear and Duke had shown up on his doorstep. But fitting back into the social dynamics of a team might be something he could do slowly.

He drove past the tavern and the sheriff's office, where the sheriff and a couple of deputies struggled to move Ray from the back of the SUV and into the jailhouse.

Kujo didn't have time to worry about the bully who treated his wife like a doormat. He needed to get back and check on Six and Molly.

As he drove out of town and through the countryside to the road leading up to the hunting cabin, he wondered if the man who'd shot at Molly could have followed them back to the cabin. Kujo had been so focused on not dropping the unconscious woman, he couldn't be sure. He'd been moving slowly enough it wouldn't have been hard to trail them.

The more he thought about it, the more worried he became, until he was pushing his truck to go faster and faster. By the time he reached the narrow road leading up through the woods, he was flying over the bumps and ruts. He skidded to a stop in front of the cabin and hopped out of the truck.

When he unlocked and pushed open the cabin door, he nearly collapsed with relief.

A beam of light from the setting sun trailed across the floor to the bed where Six lay on the mattress.

Kujo didn't have the heart to be mad at the dog. Not when he moved closer to discover Molly on the other side of the big shepherd. Her eyelashes lay in dark crescents against her pale cheeks, and her full, luscious lips were parted as if in a sigh.

Six glanced up and started to move.

Kujo held up his hand in a motion to still the dog. "Stay," he said.

Six settled again, laying his head on his paws, his gaze following his master around to the other side of the bed.

Molly was pretty when she wasn't being a smartass. She had the face of an angel, but what had she been doing out in the mountains with a drone? And why would someone shoot down the drone, and then try to finish off the woman?

Perhaps the drone and the video footage captured by the camera would be the answer.

In the meantime, Kujo had a houseguest. A very pretty houseguest, who was full of sass. Hell, he didn't need these kinds of complications. With a new boss and a new job, he needed the opportunity to prove himself. Instead, he was stuck babysitting a woman who'd more or less invited herself into his cabin for who knew how long. And now, she was taking up his bed. He'd be damned if he slept on the floor for very long.

CHAPTER 7

The delicious scent of grilled steak woke Molly's stomach before it actually woke her. A day and a half without food had that effect. Her belly rumbled loudly. Eventually, Molly opened her eyes and looked around the dark room for the source of the heavenly smell.

"Hungry?" a deep, rich voice asked from the other side of the small room.

The reassuring weight of the German Shepherd was gone, and the cool air made her shiver.

"Do I smell food?" she said, her voice cracking.

"Steak and potatoes. My cooking skills are limited."

"Sounds wonderful." She pushed up on her elbows, the movement waking up all the battered and bruised parts of her body. Still, the pain wasn't nearly as bad as the first time she'd made the same attempt. The pill she'd taken earlier must have given her some relief.

He loaded a plate and carried it over to her.

"I can eat at the table." Molly tried to get out of the bed, swinging her bare legs over the edge. The chilly, mountain air made her immediately regret her decision to get up. "You don't have to serve me," she muttered. Molly's independent streak, the one that got in the way of most of her relationships couldn't be ignored. Well, maybe just this once.

She glanced at the smooth planks on the floor and imagined they would be icy cold. Her bare toes curled at the thought of touching the wood.

Joe set the plate on the nightstand, scooped her legs up and tucked them back under the covers. "Stay in the bed until I have a chance to put something on your cuts and scrapes."

"I can do that myself. You don't have to do anything else for me." She wasn't used to having anyone wait on her.

"I haven't done much," he said.

But he had carried her out of the woods, up and over the mountain and cooked dinner for her. Molly inhaled deeply, drawing in the heavenly scent of charbroiled steak.

Joe reached for the plate, handed it to her and went back to get his. He grabbed a chair and stood it next to the bed and sat beside her.

Six curled up on the floor nearby.

Leaning against the wall, Molly rested the plate on the blanket in her lap, cut off a slice of the juicy steak and placed it in her mouth. The juices danced across her taste buds. As she chewed, she closed her eyes, leaned back her head and moaned. "Sweet Jesus, that was amazing."

A quick glance at her rescuer revealed his lack of

agreement and a positively frowning countenance. "Are you always this emotional about your food?"

She sighed. "Only when it's orgasmic. This is better than sex," she said before thinking and popped another bite of the steak in her mouth, hoping he'd let the comment pass.

He didn't. "Apparently, you haven't had good sex." Joe took a bite and chewed before speaking again. "What were you doing out in the mountains yesterday that would warrant someone shooting at you?"

And so started the interrogation... Molly didn't have the clearance to tell Joe about her operation. A twinge of guilt knotted her gut as she opened her mouth prepared to lie.

"Don't say anything if it means you have to lie."

She blinked. "You don't know I was going to lie."

"You hesitated, looked away and gathered a whopper of a story before you opened your mouth. It was going to be a lie." He shook his head. "I'm good at reading people."

She pressed her lips together and glared at him. "Oh, yeah? What am I thinking right now?"

He chuckled. "That you hate me for outing you before you could concoct your story. That you'd like to throw your plate at me, but you're too hungry to waste the food. And you're wondering if sex with me could possibly be as good as that steak." Joe shoved another bite of steak into his mouth and chewed.

Molly opened her mouth and closed it again. The man had been spot on. Damn him. "I wasn't thinking what sex would be like with you. And you're being all creepy, talking about it when you have me at your mercy."

He shrugged and polished off the steak on his plate. "Finish your meal. I'm going out to get more wood for the stove. Don't get dressed yet. I got ointment and bandages that need to be applied."

He stood, laid his plate in a tin pail and opened the door to the cabin, letting in a cool breeze.

Molly shivered.

Outside, darkness had wrapped its mystery around the man and the mountain, cutting them off from the rest of the world and making the setting even more intimate than in the daylight.

Six trotted out onto the porch.

Joe followed and closed the door behind them.

Inside the relative warmth of the cabin, tucked into the rough woolen blanket, Molly stared at the door, her pulse pounding against her ribs. The man was entirely too cocky. To think she would be interested in anything sexual with him was ridiculous.

So what if he had incredibly broad shoulders, arms that could lift her up as if she weighed no more than a child, and a smile that turned her knees to noodles. Molly had to remind herself he'd been rude and less than forthcoming with information about himself. Much like herself.

His name was Joe. Just Joe. First thing she had to do was get his full name and have her contacts back in DC run him against the National Crime Information Center database to see if they found a match. Of course, he could give her a fake name, which might result in a bogus hit. For all she knew, the man could be a serial killer.

"Doubt it," she said out loud. "He has a nice dog." Yeah, the conclusion wasn't scientific, but she liked Six, and Six liked both of them. Dogs, for the most part, were good judges of character.

But it wouldn't hurt to run him through NCIC, just to be safe.

He could have killed you by now, she reminded herself. Joe could have left her for dead out in the mountains. No one would have found her until the scavengers had picked her bones clean—if anyone found her at all.

Molly chewed on that and another piece of the amazing steak. The man had talent when it came to cooking beef.

Minutes later, Joe entered the cabin, carrying an armload of wood. He set the load beside the stove then grabbed the pail and left the cabin again.

Six stayed inside this time, taking up a position beside her bed.

"He doesn't talk much, does he?"

Six stared up at her with soulful brown eyes.

Molly glanced at the door, cut off a bite of steak and had it halfway to Six's mouth when the door opened, and Joe returned.

He frowned when he spotted her hand held out with the piece of steak. "Don't."

"It's just one piece."

"He's on a strict diet. Anything foreign might create problems in his digestive tract."

Six stared at the chunk of steak, and drool slipped out of the corner of his mouth.

"I'm sorry, boy," she whispered. She popped the steak into her mouth and chewed, her brows dipping as she glared at Joe. Once she'd choked down the offending morsel, she set the plate to the side. "One piece of steak?"

"One. I told you, he was a highly trained working dog." Joe set the pail on the stovetop and cleaned his plate and the skillet in which he'd cooked the steak. He collected her plate and made quick work of it as well.

After he stacked the plates on a shelf, he carried the pail back outside, tossed the water and returned with fresh, clean water. Joe wiped his hands, wet a washrag, and grabbed a towel and the bag, bearing the label of the local pharmacy, then sat in the chair beside the bed.

When he reached for the blanket covering her legs, he stopped short. "Do you mind? We need to treat some of those cuts and abrasions before they get infected."

Molly hesitated. The thought of Joe's big, coarse hands on her legs sent shivers all across her body and heat coiling at her core. Her tongue knotted in her mouth, so all she could do was nod.

Without preamble, he flung the blanket aside and stared down at the cuts, bruises and abrasions. Joe smoothed his hand over her thigh and down to her ankle, and then he went to work, cleaning the wounds and applying antibiotic ointment. When he'd completed the tops of her legs, he looked up. "Lie on your stomach. I'll take care of the backs of your calves and thighs."

"No, really. I can do that." She held out her hand for

the ointment, knowing perfectly well, she couldn't see all the damage and would botch the job. But having him stare at her backside for any length of time was just... just... Another shiver rippled through her body. The tops of her legs where he'd cleaned and treated her scrapes tingled everywhere his hands had been. How the hell was she supposed to play it cool and unaffected?

"Roll over," he commanded.

Six immediately complied.

Molly laughed, nervously.

Joe raised an eyebrow. "If Six can do it, you can, too. Come on. Some of these wounds had dirt ground into them. The sooner we get it out, the better."

Gathering the long T-shirt around her bottom, Molly rolled onto her stomach, her core tightening, and her sex aching.

This time, he started at the ankles and worked his way up the backs of her legs to her thighs. With the washcloth, he gently wiped the dirt out of the wounds. He smeared salve over the abrasions and applied bandages over the deeper cuts.

"Can't do anything about the bruises. When you get back to town, I recommend ice for the swelling.

The whole time Joe ran his hands across her legs, Molly couldn't stop the heat building inside. What would happen if he slid his hand between her legs and brushed against her center?

She swallowed hard on the moan rising up her throat. How could she have sexual fantasies about a man whose name she didn't know?

"What's—" Molly's voice squeaked. She cleared

her throat and tried again. "Joe, considering your know more about me than I ever thought possible, perhaps you could tell me your last name. Unless of course, it's a secret and you're in the witness protection program, in which case, you will likely tell me and then have to kill me." Holy shit. She was babbling. His touch was doing crazy things to her insides.

"Kuntz," he replied. "Do you always talk so much?"

"Only when I'm nervous."

"Nothing to be nervous about. I won't take advantage of the situation, if that's what you're concerned about."

Oh, hell, she wasn't worried about Joe taking advantage of her. She was worried he wouldn't. Or that he would, and she'd embarrass herself by begging for more.

He'd reached the tops of her thighs just short of the T-shirt hem. "I know you scraped your back in your fall. I need to get to it. Do you mind?"

"Hell, you've come this far and seen me practically naked when I was unconscious—what's the difference?" Except now, she was awake, and her body was reacting to his ministrations to the point she might orgasm before he finished.

"Exactly." He slipped her shirt up her back, his knuckles skimming across her skin, setting off an array of fireworks blasting along her nerve endings.

This is a very bad idea. Despite the fact he was treating stinging cuts, his touch felt so good, she couldn't say no, or stop, or anything any rational woman should say when nearly baring her all with a virtual stranger.

He wrung out the washcloth in the pail of water. "This is going to sting a little." Joe pressed the damp cloth to the scrapes on her back.

Molly hissed. More because of the brush of his knuckles against her skin than the stinging sensation created by rubbing the abraded skin.

"I cleaned these wounds last night, but I didn't have anything to put on them and no bandages."

"Thank you for taking care of me. I would have died had you not found me when you did," she said softly.

"Actually, I didn't find you. Six did," He said, leaning close enough, his warm breath stirred the hairs along the back of her neck.

She turned her head toward the dog and held out her hand.

Six nuzzled her fingers until she reached up and scratched behind his ears. "Aren't you going to tell me to stop touching your dog?"

"I'll work on his training later. He's still trying to readjust to me."

Molly frowned. 'Readjust?"

"He's been passed around from trainer to trainer and then to foster families. He needs time to settle, to feel like he's home to stay with one owner, one trainer." Joe continued to work on her back, cleaning and applying ointment.

"Sounds like he's had a rough time of it." Molly said.

Joe unclipped her bra.

Molly gasped and brought her hands up to the sides of her breasts. "What are you doing?"

"Dressing your wounds. I'll hook it back when I'm done."

"I certainly hope so."

A low chuckle rumbled close to her. "Relax."

"Easy for you to say," she grumbled. "You're not the one at the mercy of someone twice your size and strength."

His hand stilled. "Look. I don't know what kind of men you've been hanging out with, but I don't abuse women. Have I hurt you in any way?"

"No," she mumbled.

"And I won't. I don't need to hurt women to get off."

Molly's cheeks heated. The man had been more than a gentleman in his dealings with her, and she'd given him nothing but hell. "I'm sorry. I'm judging you without getting to know you." She cleared her throat. "Hi, I'm Molly Greenbriar." She couldn't turn her head far enough to look up at his expression.

"Joe Kuntz, but you already know that." He smeared ointment into the scrape across her back. "My friends call me Kujo."

Molly snorted. "I was okay with Joe and Kuntz, but Kujo isn't making me feel all warm and fuzzy."

"It worked when I was in the military."

"I can imagine. What were you, a Ranger or Special Forces?"

"Delta Force," he responded, his tone low, almost too hard to hear.

"I'm impressed." She stared at Six. "And Six?"

"He was my battle buddy. He and I led the way into enemy territory."

"Is he trained to attack?"

"No. He's a bomb-sniffing dog."

Molly reached out to touch Six's scar. "Is that how he got this?"

Joe applied a bandage over one of the deeper scrapes across her back. "That's what it says on his record."

"You weren't with him when it happened? I thought handlers stayed with their dogs?"

"That's usually the case, unless one or the other is injured."

Molly leaned up on her elbow, realized she was exposing her breasts, and covered them with her hands so that she could turn far enough to face Joe. "I'm confused. Obviously, Six was injured."

His face was a mask of stone, the only movement a muscle twitching in his jaw. "Six was injured three years after I was released from active duty."

Molly stared at the man, her eyes widening. "You were injured first?" She swept him from head to toe, lingering on his legs. "You were limping when I first met you. Was that what got you kicked out?"

Joe stared at her for a moment then dropped his gaze to the bandages on her back. "Yes."

"And you didn't get to take Six with you?"

"He wasn't injured as badly."

"But you were his handler." Molly couldn't imagine the two being apart. *How cruel.*

Joe shrugged. "He belonged to the Army. He still had good years left in him. A lot of time, money and effort went into his training." Again, Joe's jaw hardened. "He still had a job to do."

Joe didn't say the words *Even if I didn't*, but Molly heard them. The man had been injured and kicked out of the military, losing his friends, his dog and his job all at once.

"But you have Six now," Molly reminded him. She smiled. "And he seems happy to be with you. Are you going to train him to work in an airport or for the police department?"

"No." Joe hooked her bra together and pulled her shirt down over her back and bottom.

She tugged it over her thighs and pushed to a sitting position. "What kind of work are you doing now?"

"I've answered my quota of questions. It's your turn."

Molly closed her mouth on the next words she'd been about to say. She'd expected him to spill his guts, but she wasn't at liberty to reveal the real reason she was there.

"What is Molly Greenbriar doing in the mountains flying a drone?"

Feeling guilty over the fact she couldn't be honest with him, she lowered her eyes. "I'm filming footage of the mountains. I'm attempting to create my own documentary on the Crazy Mountains and the history surrounding them."

Joe's eyes narrowed. "Who are you working for?"

She'd practiced her answers to the point she could recite them without thinking. But something in Joe's countenance made her suddenly forget. "I…uh…" As her gaze met his, she couldn't look away and her mouth couldn't seem to form the words.

He cocked an eyebrow. "Is the question that hard?"

Heat rose up her neck and suffused her cheeks. "No. Of course, not. I'm...I'm freelancing. I was gathering information and footage I planned to look at later during the editing process. Which reminds me, I really need to recover the drone and see if it can be salvaged. It's key to my work here."

Joe didn't respond. Instead, he held her stare long enough to make her feel even more uncomfortable. He wasn't buying her story.

Molly fought to keep her face set and her body still. She refused to squirm under his scrutiny. This was her first assignment in the field. If she proved herself here, she might be considered for future field assignments. If she blew her cover in the first few days, she'd be back at a desk, performing background checks.

"I'm feeling a little better," she said, shifting her gaze from his.

"Liar," he countered.

Molly frowned. "I'm not lying."

"It's all in your body language." He reached out to brush his finger along her cheek. "Every time you say something untrue, you glance away."

"I do not!" She stared straight into his eyes, even as she fought the urge to look away.

"It's okay. I figure you have a reason for lying to me. Keep your secrets; I'm not interested. As long as they don't come back to bite me in the ass."

"Look, I can go back to my room in town. I don't want to inconvenience you."

"Too late for that." He chuckled. "You've been an inconvenience since I ran into you on that mountain trail."

Molly slid her legs over the edge of the bed. "Seriously, if you could give me a ride back to town, I'll be out of your hair. No. Never mind, I'll take the ATV."

He pressed a hand on her shoulder. "Don't get your panties in a wad. You're not up to riding a damaged ATV seven miles back to town in the dark. And as much as I'd like to have my cabin and bed back, I wouldn't feel comfortable leaving you alone in town. Not until we figure out who shot at you and left you lying out in the mountains for buzzards to pick through your bones."

"Now who's being overly dramatic?" Her lips curled upward. The man had rescued her. He deserved her gratitude. "Thank you for saving my life and treating my wounds."

"Don't thank me, thank Six." Joe tipped his head toward the dog.

Six had settled beside the bed with his chin on his paws. When he heard his name, he lifted his head, his ears perked.

Molly reached out to stroke his neck. "Thank you, Six. And despite being a bit cantankerous, your master isn't so bad himself." She faced Kujo again. "If you like, I can sleep on the floor. You shouldn't have to give up your bed for the second night in a row."

"Stay. You're still recovering. Besides it's cold on the floor. With your injuries, your body's immune system might be compromised." Again, he lifted her legs and tucked them beneath the blanket. "Get some rest. We'll figure everything out in the morning."

"Where will you sleep?" she asked.

He gave her a twisted grin. "In a chair or on the cold, hard floor."

Molly shook her head. "No way." She hesitated for only a moment before saying, "If you promise not to do anything, you can sleep in the bed. It's big enough for the two of us." Her cheeks heated at the thought of Joe slipping beneath the blanket, his long legs brushing against hers, his broad shoulders taking up most of the space. She'd been stretching the truth that time. The bed was big enough for Joe. Alone. "I sleep on my side, anyway."

She scooted to the far side of the mattress, turned her back to him and twisted around to nod at the space she'd created. "See? There's enough room if you sleep on your side."

Joe's brows dipped. "I'll be fine on the floor."

She shrugged. "Have it your way. But if you change your mind during the night, the offer's still open. I'll leave room for you." Molly settled on her side, resting her head on half of the pillow. She laid for a long time, feigning sleep, her ears straining to hear every sound coming from Joe.

He moved about the room, the floor creaking, marking his progress. She heard the clank of the cast-iron stove door opening and closing.

A cold breeze blew through the cabin as Joe opened the door, making Molly shiver. The click of toenails on the wooden floor indicated Six heading for the door for one last visit to the great outdoors before he settled in to sleep.

Molly dared to turn and look.

Joe stood for a moment in the door before following Six out onto the porch and closing the door behind him.

Molly didn't know much more about Joe than when she'd run into him on the mountain trail, but she knew she trusted him.

Her body ached, but she could handle it better. Sleep eventually claimed her, though she shivered in the cool cabin.

Sometime during the night, she dreamed of a dark stranger firing at her, of falling off a cliff, falling…falling…into a bottomless abyss. She cried out, afraid she would hit the ground and break into a million pieces.

Strong arms caught her and held her close. Half asleep, she snuggled up to the heat and slipped into a deep, deep sleep, finally feeling safe.

CHAPTER 8

Kujo held off as long as he could. He cleaned the dishes, stoked the fire and took Six out to do his business one last time before calling it a night.

No matter how long he stayed away from Molly, he returned, stared down at her sleeping form and spent time talking himself out of taking her up on her offer to share the bed.

But when Molly started thrashing, her arms and legs flailing in the air, he couldn't ignore her for a moment longer. Whatever dream she was having had to be bad, and it would be really crappy of him to ignore a woman in need, wouldn't it? And she might worsen her injuries, if she kept it up.

Kujo understood dreams. For the past three years, he'd woken in the middle of the night, sweating and reluctant to go back to sleep. His dreams consisted of the last few minutes before his life had changed and the lives of the two female soldiers had ended.

He could still imagine those women's faces, the

desperation in their eyes, and hear the explosion as it rocked his world forever.

Yeah, he understood dreams.

Six stood beside the bed, staring at Molly, his ears perking with every moan from the woman. He glanced back at Kujo and whined softly.

"It bothers you too, doesn't it?" Kujo crossed to Six and ran his hand over the dog's head and down his neck.

Six nuzzled his hand, and then used his nose to nudge Kujo toward Molly.

Kujo sat on the side of the bed and touched Molly's arm.

She moaned again and reached out to cover his hand with hers, her fingers gripping his like a lifeline.

Now what? He couldn't disengage and leave her hanging. Too late for second thoughts about touching her, he toed off his boots and slipped onto the mattress. As soon as he did, she rolled up against him.

The bed really was too small for two people. To keep from falling out, he turned on his side, facing her and spooned her body with his.

Molly sighed and turned toward him, resting her hand and her cheek against his chest. Her calf slid over his and hooked him from behind.

Kujo swallowed a groan. This was the reason he hadn't wanted to share the bed with her. Molly Greenbriar was entirely too pretty and sexy. A man had to be made of stone to ignore a body like hers pressed against him.

Kujo wasn't made of stone. Although his cock was

making a damned good imitation. He lay perfectly still, trying not to rub anything that would make him even harder and more uncomfortable. Being still didn't make a difference.

Molly's fingers curled into his shirt, her nails scraping his chest through the fabric. Her hair smelled of peaches, and her breath warmed his neck.

He gave up any pretense of sleep and stared at the woman in the fading light from the potbellied stove.

How had he gone from being a hermit in a Colorado mountain cabin to having a job and a woman in his bed, in such a short time?

His pulse pounded, and his staff stiffened. Perhaps that was the problem. He hadn't had a woman in over three years. His desire wasn't just directed at Molly. She could have been any woman, and he'd have reacted the same.

Or would he? Molly had been sassy on the mountain trail. And she'd been very convincing about not calling in the authorities. She was strong and determined.

He could almost bet she'd have found a way off the mountain without his help. Still, he was glad that theory hadn't been tested.

Kujo closed his eyes, hoping that by not staring at the beautiful woman, he could almost forget how close their bodies were.

Ha! Closing his eyes only made him more aware of the softness of her curves and the peachy scent of her hair.

The night promised to be a long one. As he lay awake, sleep the furthest thing from his mind, he thought through Molly's responses to his questions. He knew she was lying, but he couldn't figure out why.

As soon as the sun came up, he'd go after the drone. Perhaps he could see what the camera had recorded to know better what Molly was really up to, and what someone didn't want her to find.

The longer he lay with Molly curled against him, the sleepier he got and his desire slowly ebbed.

When he opened his eyes again, the gray light of pre-dawn filled the windows. He tried to move his arm, but couldn't and turned to see why.

Molly lay in the crook of his arm, her cheek resting on his chest. Her auburn hair spread out in wild abandon, the fiery strands tickling his nose.

The blanket had slipped behind her, leaving her legs bare, one silken calf curled over his leg, her knee resting against his crotch.

His usual morning erection sprang to attention.

Sweet Jesus, he had to get up quickly or risk frightening the poor woman with a monster boner.

He edged away, slipping his arm out from under her, in such a hurry, he rolled out of the bed backwards and landed on the ground on top of Six.

The dog yelped and skittered out of the way.

"What the hell?" a groggy voice said from above.

Kujo pushed to his feet. "Sorry, I was trying not to wake you."

"I'm not awake," she assured him. She blinked her eyes and pushed the hair out of her face. "Are you okay?"

Hell, no. He was hard and had no way to relieve the

need. No, he wasn't okay. "Yeah. I have some beef jerky, if you're hungry, and a can of beans."

"I'll pass." Molly stretched and winced. "I found some more sore spots. I don't suppose you have another one of those pain pills."

"I do. But you should eat something before you take it."

"Jerky, then. And water." She licked her lips.

The movement made his stomach flip crazily. Kujo turned away before his arousal became evident. He reached into his duffel bag for the snack, tore the package open and handed a strip of dried beef to Molly.

She accepted his offering, ripped off a piece with her teeth and chewed with her eyes closed. "I feel like I was put through a meat grinder."

"You took a pretty serious tumble." He handed her a bottle of water he'd had in his bag.

She leaned up on her elbow and drank deeply. When she'd slaked her thirst, she capped the bottle and sat it on the nightstand. "I need to find the drone." Molly swung her legs over the edge of the bed and winced again.

"You need to stay put," Kujo said. "You aren't up to dodging bullets, just yet."

"I'm not going to be ready to dodge anything by lying around being waited on."

"Seriously, I saw your drone go down. I'll find what's left of it and bring it back. Besides, there's only one four-wheeler, and the handlebars are bent."

Molly bit her lip. "I wonder what that's going to cost me when I turn it into the rental place." She shook her head. "If you were able to steer it and carry me back, I should be able to manage it." She sat up and pressed a hand to her ribs. "Did you see the mule that kicked me?"

A smile tugged at the corners of his mouth. The woman was far too independent for her own good. "You're not going anywhere. It wasn't easy getting you here on that four-wheeler. I don't relish doing it again should something happen out there."

"I can take care of myself." She gave him a sheepish grin. "For the most part. But thank you for taking care of me." When she tried to get out of the bed, Six stood in front of her.

"See? Even the dog doesn't want you to leave."

"Look, I can't leave that drone out there. It's an expensive piece of equipment."

He held out one of the pills he'd given her the night before. "Take this. It'll help with the aches and pains."

"I'm not changing my mind." Molly bent forward, determined to get up. As soon as she leaned toward him, her face creased in a grimace, and she eased back. "Seriously, did you get that mule's number?"

"Will you stop acting tough and take the damned pill?" He took her hand and placed the medication on her palm.

"What is it, anyway?" she asked and then placed it on her tongue and washed it down with the water.

"It's one of the painkillers my doctor gave me."

"Strong stuff."

His jaw tightened. "Needed to be."

"Do you still take it?" Her gaze slipped down his body to his legs.

Kujo didn't want pity. He could get around almost as well as before the injury. Yes, it was more painful, but he didn't let that stop him, and he didn't rely on the drugs. Too many of the wounded warriors lost their lives to drugs, alcohol and suicide. He wasn't going to be one of them. "Not often. I didn't want to get hooked."

Molly nodded. "Well, thanks. But I have a feeling you gave me that pill to keep me here. The last one knocked me out." She bit into another piece of the jerky and chewed.

"You almost died. Give yourself time to recuperate." He turned and opened the door for Six.

While the animal was outside, Kujo slipped on his boots and stoked the fire to chase away the chill of the morning air.

"Joe?" Molly called out.

"Yes?" He looked over his shoulder at her, sitting with her back to the wall, the blanket covering her sexy legs. He wanted to crawl back into the bed with her. In the light of day, he was almost positive she would put up a fight.

"I had a dream last night." Her cheeks reddened.

His heartbeat sputtered and sped up. "Yeah?"

"I dreamed I was falling down that hill again."

"I'm sure you did." He closed the door on the stove. "Something like that is hard to get over."

"Joe?"

He had nothing else to fiddle with and was forced to face the woman lying in his bed, her wild hair and makeup-less face not at all detracting from her appearance. In fact, she looked like a woman who'd just had sex.

Holy shit. Where had that thought come from? He sure as hell didn't need to think down those lines. He'd just gotten his hard-on under control. Further, she'd be out of his cabin and out of his life as soon as they figured out who shot at her and her drone.

The red in her cheeks deepened, and she looked down at where her fingers were pulling at the fabric of the blanket. "When I was falling…in my dream… someone caught me."

Kujo's gut clenched. "And?"

Molly glanced up at him. "It was you, wasn't it?"

His groin tightened, recalling how she'd felt snuggled up against him throughout the night. He forced a casual shrug. "I don't know. I wasn't in your dream. I don't read minds."

"No, but you held me in the night, didn't you?" Her brows pulled together. "You were my dream catcher, weren't you?"

He couldn't lie. "You were having a bad dream and moaning. All I did was hold you until it was over." Okay, that last part might have been stretching the truth. He'd held her all night, until he fell out of the bed.

Molly nodded. "I thought I was still dreaming. Not the nightmare, but a good dream. And you were warm when I was cold." She smiled. "Thank you."

He turned away and opened the door for Six to come in. "No problem. And don't worry, I didn't do anything to violate you." Oh, he'd wanted to, but he wouldn't have. Not without her consent.

Her warm chuckle filled the interior of the little cabin. "It's nice to know chivalry is alive and well in the Crazy Mountains."

"I prefer my women conscious," he said.

She arched an eyebrow. "And I'd like to think I'd remember it if you'd tried something. But last night was a little foggy to me." Molly ran a hand through her hair, pushing it back from her face.

The movement drew Kujo's attention to the T-shirt as it stretched across her breasts. He could see the black lace through the white fabric and wanted to unclip the back again and do more than rub ointment into her wounds.

Molly stared at Kujo, noting the way his nostrils flared whenever she moved. The man was a complete stranger. He could have done anything to her during the night, and no one would have been the wiser.

But he hadn't.

She was at once delighted to know she could trust him, while disappointed he hadn't even tried to squeeze one of her breasts or cup her sex.

Her core tightened, and an ache grew between her legs. She pulled the blanket up a little higher to cover her from the waist down.

The man couldn't help he was hot and sexy. She found it hard to believe he'd been in the bed with her and she hadn't been awake enough to do anything about it. She wanted to ask for a do-over so she might snuggle even closer and maybe taste his skin and touch him in some of his naughty places.

Heat filled her cheeks and rushed all the way out to the tips of her ears. She had to pull her mind out of the gutter, and quickly. The man was a loner, and she was invading his space. As soon she felt up to leaving, she would.

She yawned, covering her mouth with her hand. "Damned pills knock me out."

"Then sleep. I'll be back in a little while."

"I want to..." she yawned again, "come with you."

"You'll fall off the four-wheeler if you do."

She tilted her chin. "Not if you hold onto me."

He shook his head. "No. It's too dangerous—even when you're not drugged."

She yawned again and tipped over onto the pillow. "If you insist. But don't let anyone shoot at you. I kinda like having you around." Molly closed her eyes. "I'll only be asleep for a little while. When I wake up, I can help..."

"Rest." His warm, rich voice coated her like chocolate syrup. "I'm leaving Six with you."

"That's nice," she muttered and patted the side of the bed. "Come here, boy."

Molly registered the sound of the dog's toenails clicking across the floor. Six nudged her hand, pushing his head beneath it.

Molly scratched him behind his ears, and then patted the mattress beside her.

The dog eased up into the bed and stretched out, resting his furry body against hers.

"Traitor," Kujo said.

Molly peeked from beneath her heavy eyelids. "He likes me."

"You're going to be hell on my retraining efforts."

"Dogs were meant to be loved," she said, wrinkling her nose and slipping her arm around Six's neck.

"I'll be back as soon as possible. Don't go anywhere."

"Oh, I'm not. And when I wake up, I'll be as good as new," Molly promised.

The door creaked open, sending a cool blast of mountain air into the warm cabin. As quickly as it opened, it closed again, leaving Molly and Six in silence.

"I hope he'll be all right," Molly said and snuggled against Six, falling into a deep sleep.

CHAPTER 9

For a long moment, Kujo stood outside the cabin, hesitant to leave Molly alone, but unwilling to take her with him when she was still in pain from her injuries. Besides, she'd slow him down if he had to beat a hasty retreat.

He had no idea how he'd ended up in the same place at the same time as she had two days ago, but his gut told him he'd been there for a reason. He was glad the reason was to save Molly. She was bright, strong and beautiful. When he got back from searching for the drone, he'd get the truth out of her. If not by force, then by other, more pleasurable means.

With a sense of urgency, he climbed onto the four-wheeler, started the engine and roared away, back the direction he'd come when he'd held an unconscious woman in his arms, trying not to drop her while steering the damaged vehicle.

The bent steering wheel took some getting used to

again, but he didn't let it slow him on his quest to find the drone.

As he approached the ridge, he slowed the four-wheeler to a stop and killed the engine. He'd go the rest of the way on foot. Whoever had been in the valley might still be there, and he intended to find out who it was.

After hiding the four-wheeler in the brush, he slipped through the woods and up to the top of the ridge, clinging to the shadows of the trees and underbrush. He stood for a long moment, scanning the valley below. As far as he could see, nothing moved. The caves dotting the cliffs on the opposite side stared back at him like gaping maws, so dark he couldn't see into them. A single, narrow road led in from the eastern end of the valley. If he hadn't been studying it so carefully, he might have missed it.

Before he started down the ridge, he studied the area where he recalled the drone had gone down. Aiming for that location, Kujo slipped over the edge of the ridge and down through the trees toward the valley floor. He moved as quietly as he could on the steep slope, stepping over twigs and taking care not to slip on the gravel.

When he reached the bottom, he slipped through the woods, shadow to shadow, until he came to an opening, bright with sunlight and green grass. A creek ran through the valley, burbling over rocks, reflecting sparkles of sunshine. Nothing about the setting screamed danger, but Kujo didn't let down his guard. He studied the forest glen, hoping to spot something white or shiny, like parts to the drone Molly had been operating.

On the opposite side of the creek something glinted on the gravel banks. He focused on the spot. The wind shifted, tossing tree branches over the banks, allowing another patch of light to hit that area. Again, something bright shined in the dull gravel.

His pulse quickening, Kujo made his way along the banks of the creek, searching for a crossing point that wouldn't leave him exposed for very long. He found a point where the stream narrowed and the trees formed an arch, shadowing the banks and the water. After studying both directions and glancing up at the dark cave entrances, he hurriedly leaped over the water and ducked back into the shadows.

Moving quickly, he reached the spot where the shiny object lay. It was part of the drone. He left it where it was for the moment and searched the surrounding area. Piece by piece, he located the rest of the drone. The main body of the device was still intact; two of the arms had snapped off in the crash landing. A hole through the center marked the spot where a bullet had gone through the motor.

Kujo doubted the drone would fly again, but he'd carry it back and see if they could salvage the camera or the disk that stored the video data. He piled the parts in one location against the base of a tree, hiding it in the brush, and then looked up at the caves.

Part of him wanted to get back to the cabin in a hurry, fearing someone could have traced him and

Molly there. But something about the caves made him stay. What was someone hiding in the valley? He hadn't seen anything other than trees, boulders and the stream on the valley floor. The narrow road leading in could have been an old mining road used back in the days when men mined the mountains for gold and silver. Hunters might still use it during hunting season. The road ran the length of the valley following the base of the cliffs with the caves.

Someone with a need to keep things on the downlow could have used the road to run people or supplies into the valley. Perhaps they'd used the caves to store supplies.

Or teenagers could have used the road and the caves for campouts and parties where they'd be out of sight and range of concerned parents.

Either way, Kujo felt the need to explore the caves before he left the valley.

Choosing the least revealing path up to the largest and most accessible cave entrance, he crossed the road and eased up the side of the rise. He didn't know what he would find, man, beast or nothing at all, but he'd be prepared for anything. Except maybe a bear. For a bear, he'd need a bigger gun.

The last few yards up to the entrance were traversed in the open. He had no other choice but to make a run for it, up the hill and into the darkness, without knowing what to expect. Taking a deep breath, he sprinted up the incline, his bad leg aching with the effort. He ignored the pain and ducked into the shadows, then stood with his back to the cave wall. Listening, he stared into the darkness, his heart thundering all the while. God, he'd missed the game of hide and seek with the enemy. Pitting his strengths against the Taliban or ISIS had always been an adrenaline high.

Slowly, his vision adjusted to the dimly lit interior. It appeared like any other cave with a stone floor and a damp, earthy smell. Since nothing moved, Kujo ventured deeper inside. At the very back, he had to use the tiny flashlight he kept in his pocket. He shined the narrow beam along the walls and floors. In a corner, he found what appeared to be the remains of a wooden crate with military identification markings on it.

Kujo frowned, broke off the part with the writing painted on it and hurried back to the entrance. Again, nothing moved that he could see. The valley was almost eerily silent. Even the birds paused in their songs.

When he was certain the coast was clear, Kujo climbed down the trail to the road below and hurried to the next cave. It wasn't as deep, but it had a small scorched area where someone had set up a campfire. Based on the charred remains, it appeared to have been in the recent past with a fresh stash of tinder tucked in the driest area of the cave. From this cave's position, he could see across the entire valley. It was a good vantage point for a lookout, or a machine gunner.

The next two caves proved to be smaller still and barely cut back into the mountain. By the time he finished exploring them, he'd been gone from the cabin for over two hours. He didn't like leaving Molly that long. As far as he could tell, the valley was empty. Which led to the next question. Where was the shooter?

Kujo jogged across the valley floor to where he'd left the drone parts, gathered them in his arms, along with the board from the crate, and hurried up the hillside and over the top of the ridge. He made it to the ATV without running into anyone or being the target of a shooter.

Though he was glad he'd been danger-free, he couldn't help feeling he should be back at the cabin by now. His gut was telling him to hurry.

He piled his collection into the basket on the front of the four-wheeler, slung his leg over the seat and started the engine. It sputtered and died.

Sweet Jesus! Not now. He held his breath and hit the starter switch again. The engine chugged, and then caught and roared. Letting out the breath he'd held, he raced back toward the cabin.

SUN SHONE through the windows of the cabin when Molly opened her eyes again. She pushed to a sitting position, only mildly discomfited by the twinge in her ribs. The additional, dreamless sleep had left her refreshed and ready to face the world.

Six yawned, stretched and stepped down off the bed where he continued to stretch, until he ended his routine with a hearty shake.

Molly wished she could do the same and be ready to rock and roll. Instead, she swung her legs over the edge of the bed and stood. Aches and pains made her stiff, but the painkiller Joe had given her dulled her suffering to a manageable level. She stretched carefully, babying her ribs. She needed to relieve herself and find some water to splash on her face.

Six stood beside the door, expectantly.

"You, too?" She opened the door for the dog and stepped out onto the porch.

The mountain air hit her legs and forced her back inside where she slipped into her jeans. She didn't try to put on her shirt, noticing it was shredded on the back where she'd slid down the hillside. Joe's shirt would have to suffice for the time being. She lifted the fabric to her nose and sniffed. It still smelled like him, clean, fresh and woodsy.

She sat in one of the two wooden chairs the cabin sported and pulled on her boots. Her 9-millimeter lay on the table where Joe had left it. She slipped the holster over her shoulders and gingerly settled it in place over the cuts and scrapes Joe had so carefully bandaged.

As much as she liked to think she could take care of herself, she couldn't have treated her own wounds. Joe had been a perfect gentleman when he'd cleaned them, smeared ointment and applied the dressings. What if he hadn't been so platonic? What if he'd smoothed his hand over her unaffected skin and twisted his fingers in her hair?

A tremor rippled through Molly. The man was every woman's dream: tall, dark and ruggedly handsome with broad shoulders and thick muscles. Lying against him through the night had left her feeling safe and protected.

Of course, that wasn't what a good FBI special agent should need. So far, her first field assignment was an unmitigated disaster. She didn't have any more information than she'd started with, and she'd crashed a very expensive drone. Molly dreaded the call she'd have to make to her supervisor when she got back to town. He'd likely order her to return to DC and her desk job.

As far as Molly was concerned, the threat of returning to boring background checks was all the more reason to hold off on that call until she could dig a little deeper and find where the ISIS training was being conducted. What a coup that would be. If she could pull that off, maybe her boss wouldn't be so angry about the drone. And she might get more field assignments.

If she proved herself a competent field agent, she'd request a transfer out of DC to one of the regional offices. She wondered if they had one in Montana. She was quickly falling in love with the mountains and the wide-open plains. And the male scenery wasn't so bad, either.

Not that she was in Montana to start a relationship. Her track record in that department sucked. Still... Joe was a temptation she might not be able to resist. Perhaps a fling was in order to tamp down her desires and hold her for a while.

Her core tingled at the thought of giving in to a little mattress dancing with the former soldier. Based on how gently he'd treated her wound, Molly bet Joe would be an amazing lover.

In the meantime, she had to pee. Six stood by a tree with one leg hiked. Seeing him relieving himself, made

Molly's needs even more urgent. She rounded the cabin hoping to find an outhouse. No such luck. The cabin had to have been built for male hunters with no regard to a female's requirements. Hiking out into the trees, she found a spot in the shadows and took care of business. The gurgling sound of running water lured her deeper into the woods.

Six caught up, passed her and led the way to a pretty stream, nestled in a copse of trees. Molly followed the stream a little way and found where it widened into a pool, big enough to swim in. What a heavenly place, and what a change from the city streets and traffic of her home back on the east coast. Why would anyone want to leave the Crazy Mountains of Montana?

The air was cool, but the sun found its way through the trees to the pool, making it shine like glass. Molly turned in a three-hundred-sixty-degree circle. She would bet there wasn't a soul within miles of where she stood.

Before she could change her mind, she shucked her boots, stripped out of her clothes and peeled off the bandages she could reach. After sliding down a hill, she was still covered in dirt. A dip in the pool would go a long way toward reviving her spirit and washing away the dirt.

When she was completely naked, she dipped a foot into the water. *Holy moly!* It was icy cold. Knowing there was only one way to get clean, she dove in and surfaced, her breath frozen in her chest. Wow, it was cold.

Six stood on the bank, lapping at the water.

Molly laughed. "Now who's the more intelligent species?"

Six looked up and sat, prepared to wait for her to get out of the water. He stood guard while Molly worked the dust out of her hair and off her skin. At first the water stung her wounds, but after a minute or two, the cold numbed them, as well as her feet and toes. She finished quickly and climbed the banks, refreshed and feeling almost normal.

The cool air felt warm after the chill of the water. She stood in the sunshine, squeezing the excess water from her hair and shaking her arms and legs until they dried enough for her to dress. Still damp, she slipped into her jeans and Joe's shirt, pulled on her boots and slipped her holster in place.

When she straightened, a breeze blew through the trees, bringing with it the acrid scent of smoke.

Six paced in front of her as she buckled her shoulder holster and pulled on her jacket. The smoke seemed to be coming from the direction of the cabin.

Molly took off running. Her ribs hurt with every footfall. She ignored the pain and raced through the woods, emerging in the clearing to find the cabin in flames.

Had she left the door open to the potbellied stove? How could it be so consumed in flames when she'd only been gone for less than half an hour?

A movement caught her eye around the side of the building. A man wearing a ski mask slung liquid at the side of the cabin from a red jug. The pungent scent of gasoline filled the air as flames licked at the wooden sides of the structure.

"Hey!" Molly yelled and raced toward the man.

The bastard was pouring gasoline on the cabin.

Six streaked past her and reached him first to sink his teeth into the man's arm.

The man yelled and kicked at the dog in an attempt to free his arm.

Six refused to let go, his body swinging around with the man's movements.

Molly pulled her weapon and aimed at the man, but was afraid to shoot and injure the dog.

Finally, the man's shirt ripped off his arm, and Six fell to the ground. Before the dog could latch onto him again, the man ran around to the other side of the cabin.

Molly raced after him, but didn't catch up before he sped away in an old red and white pickup. She ran down the road after it, hoping to get the license plate number, but the vehicle didn't have one.

Six chased the truck around the bend in the dirt road, leading toward the highway.

"Six!" Molly yelled. She didn't want the dog hurt by the arsonist, or for him to get hit on the highway. She sprinted after him, her heart pounding against her chest. As she reached the curve in the road, Six appeared, trotting toward her.

Molly slowed to a stop and bent over, breathing hard. The fire raged behind her. Once she filled her lungs, she went back to see what she could do to contain the damage.

The cabin was completely engulfed in flames, and

the heat intense. Molly couldn't get inside to salvage any of Joe's belongings.

Embers flew into the air, landing on pine straw and starting up smaller fires in the immediate vicinity.

Molly hurried to stamp down the flames of the smaller fires, afraid the blaze would spread to the woods beyond and set that whole damned forest on fire.

CHAPTER 10

Halfway back to the cabin, Kujo topped a hill and froze.

A plume of smoke billowed into the air from the direction of the cabin.

Damn! He knew he shouldn't have left Molly alone in the cabin. And he'd given her a painkiller.

His heart in his throat, he raced down the hill and through the woods as fast as the damaged four-wheeler would carry him. Every horrible scenario he could imagine raced through his mind. Molly could be trapped in the cabin. By the time he reached her, there'd be nothing left but her charred remains. And Six...

Fuck! Why couldn't the ATV move any faster? As it was, he nearly crashed into a boulder at one bend in the trail and narrowly missed a tree trunk at another. When he finally emerged into the clearing around the cabin, his heart sank to his knees. The cabin was a complete loss, the flames licking the sky, smoke chugging into the air in billowing puffs.

If Molly hadn't gotten out…

Kujo brought the ATV to a skidding stop, leaped off and ran around the side of the building, racing for the entrance.

The porch roof had collapsed blocking the door. Even if he'd wanted to go inside, he couldn't.

He stood staring at the inferno, his chest squeezing so tightly he couldn't breathe.

A hand touched his arm, and he nearly jumped out of his skin.

"Joe?"

He spun to find Molly standing behind him with Six at her heels. "Oh, dear God." He pulled her into his arms and crushed her to his chest. "I thought you were still inside."

She wrapped her arms around his waist and leaned her cheek against his chest. "We're okay, but I'm afraid your cabin is toast."

"I don't give a damn about the cabin." He buried his face in her hair for another long moment before he lifted his head.

Molly looked up at him, her brow furrowed. "We should probably move away from the fire, before we become a part of it."

Without releasing Molly all the way, Kujo walked her away from the blaze and bent to scratch Six's ears. He cleared a lump in his throat before he spoke. "I though you two were inside," he said, his voice hoarse.

"We were in the woods when it started." Molly touched a hand to his cheek. "We're fine, but Joe, someone set this fire."

"What do you mean?" He jerked his head up and looked around. "Who?"

"I don't know. He wore a ski mask and took off in an old red and white pickup. He used gasoline as an accelerant."

"Bastard," Kujo said.

"No kidding." Molly shook her head. "Six tried to stop him, but he got away. He should have some significant bite marks on his right arm. Six was amazing."

Kujo ruffled Six's neck, and then hugged Molly close again. "I'm just glad you weren't inside."

Molly stared up at him. "You were really worried?" She stepped back and stared at him. "Joe, you're shaking."

He closed his eyes, the images of those soldier's faces permanently etched in his mind as the world exploded around them. "I couldn't go through that again," he whispered.

She cupped his cheek. "Through what?"

The sound of sirens gave Kujo the needed distraction from confessing his own nightmares. "That will be the fire department. You need to hide if you want to remain missing."

Molly shook her head. "Whoever set the fire knows I'm here. There's no point remaining in hiding."

"Good, then as soon as they have the blaze under control, I'm taking you to my boss."

"Your boss?" She stared up at him, her brows dipping.

A short fire truck bumped up the road toward them, followed by a longer one and a tanker truck filled with water. Pickup trucks lined the drive as volunteer firefighters pulled in and jumped out, ready to assist and put the flames out before the flames spread and created a forest fire.

Kujo moved the four-wheeler out of the way. Then he and Molly loaded the drone parts into his pickup and parked the truck farther along the road, out of the way of the firefighters.

Within the hour, they had the fire contained in a smoldering pile of ash that once was a hunting retreat in the woods.

Kujo stood with Molly in the curve of his arm, watching as the experts dealt with the fire. The sheriff showed up with a couple of his deputies to ask questions.

Molly told him what she'd witnessed.

"You didn't see his face at all?" the sheriff asked as he made notes on a pad.

"No, sir," Molly answered. "He wore a ski mask and took off in an ancient red and white pickup."

The sheriff's eyes narrowed. "Not many red and white pickups around these parts anymore."

One of the deputies leaned toward the sheriff. "Doesn't Old Man Donovan have an antique hunk of junk pickup?"

The sheriff nodded and scribbled a note on the page. "Notify dispatch to send someone out to check on Donovan and his truck."

The deputy hustled toward his vehicle to do the sheriff's bidding.

The sheriff locked gazes with Kujo. "You know, Ray

Diener blames you for his wife leaving him. You sure you didn't see him?"

Kujo shook his head. "Molly was here alone. But whoever did it will have a nasty dog bite on his arm."

The sheriff shot a glance at Six. "He's not dangerous, is he?"

"He's a trained war dog," Kujo said. "But Six was mostly used for bomb sniffing."

Sheriff Barron reached down to scratch Six's ears. "Hopefully, he won't have much bomb sniffing to do around here."

"He's retired from service." Kujo glanced toward the men rolling up hoses. "Are you done with us?"

"For now," the sheriff said. "Will you be in the area for long?"

"Yes, sir. Now that the cabin's gone, I'll have to get a place in town."

"Good. I might have more questions as we get further along in the investigation." The sheriff stared at the smoldering heap. "Could have been worse. You're lucky no one was inside when he lit the place."

Kujo's chest tightened all over again. "Yes, sir."

Sheriff Barron's gaze swept the surroundings. "And had the fire burned out of control, it could have wiped out thousands of acres. We'll do what we can to put the arsonist away."

"Thank you, sir," Molly said.

Kujo cupped her elbow and led her away from the firefighters as they cleaned up. When he reached his truck, he helped her up into the passenger side and opened the back door for Six. After the dog jumped into the back seat, Kujo closed the door, rounded the front of the vehicle and slipped into the driver's seat.

"Where to?" Molly asked, fastening her seatbelt.

"To Hank Patterson's place."

"He's your boss?"

Kujo nodded.

Six stuck his head between the seats and stared out the front window.

"What kind of work do you do?" Molly turned to pet Six.

Kujo shrugged. "Security work, from what I can tell."

"You don't know?"

"I just signed on. I haven't had my first assignment. You can ask him when we get there."

Molly settled back in her seat. "Is he prior military as well?"

"SEAL."

Molly's brows rose. "And you're former Delta Force?" She smiled his way. "The best-of-the-best. Does he hire all former spec-ops-trained personnel?"

"As far as I know."

"Interesting. I look forward to meeting him. Where does he live?"

"On White Oak Ranch. His wife is Sadie McClain."

Molly shot a glance his way. "*The* Sadie McClain? Hollywood phenomenon?"

Kujo frowned. "I suppose."

"Now, I'm really interested in meeting them." She shook her head. "Wow, I came to Montana thinking I'd just meet backwoods and small-town folk. I didn't expect to meet Sadie McClain."

The rest of the trip to White Oak Ranch passed in silence.

When they pulled up to the ranch house, Hank, Duke, Bear and three other men rose from chairs on the porch and came down the steps to greet them.

"Kujo, I'm glad you're here. I was just about to send someone out to get you from that hunting cabin." Hank held out his hand. "You have to move to a place with phone service. In the meantime, I'll equip you with a satellite phone and a GPS tracker."

"Hank, Bear, Duke." Kujo shook hands with the men he knew and turned to the others.

Hank clapped his shoulder and turned to the other men. "Men, this is Joseph Kuntz, or more affectionately known as Kujo. Kujo meet Axel Svenson, Brandon Rayne and Vince Van Cleave. Alex Davila is on assignment. Actually, all these men are on assignment, but came in for a brief meeting."

Kujo held out his hand to the big Viking of a man with blond hair and blue eyes.

Axel grinned. "They call me Swede."

Kujo nodded, and then shook hands with a broad-shouldered, man with black hair and gray eyes.

"My parents named me Brandon, but my SEAL team called me Boomer."

"Which do you prefer?" Kujo asked.

Brandon lifted his chin. "Boomer."

Molly chuckled. "Do any of you go by your real names?" She turned to Kujo. "I'll have to remember that. Cujo was a killer dog, right?"

He shook his head. "Nothing that impressive. It's

short for Kuntz, Joseph." He cupped her elbow and guided her forward. "Hank, this is Molly Greenbriar."

Hank grinned. "So, *you're* Miss Greenbriar." He held out his hand.

Molly took it, her brows furrowing. "Should I know you?"

"Not at all. I got word from a buddy of mine in the FBI that you'd be in the area. Pete Ralston. Know him?"

Kujo shot a narrow-eyed glance at Molly. "FBI?"

She gave him a sheepish half-grin. "I was supposed to be flying under the radar. You know, incognito." She shook her head and faced Hank. "Pete's my supervisor."

"He asked that I keep an eye out for you. That you were doing some surveillance work."

Anger roiled in Kujo's gut. He didn't like it when he was left out of the information loop. "Apparently, she was doing surveillance work—until someone shot her drone out of the sky and tried to kill her."

Hank's brows rose. "Is that so?" He studied her. "Is that why you're covered with soot? Are you all right?"

"We just came from Joe's cabin," she said. "Someone torched it."

Hank shook his head. "Okay. You two need to fill me in on what's going on." He climbed the stairs and entered the house. "Sadie? We have more company!"

Kujo let Molly go first. As she passed him, he whispered, "Thanks for letting me in on the joke."

"No joke. Just what my supervisor ordered," she said. "Apparently, the cat's out of the bag. At least with Hank and his organization."

He followed her, and Six trailed behind them,

entering the house with the big group of Brotherhood Protectors.

Molly's words didn't make Kujo feel any better about being left out of the loop. He'd have a long discussion with her later and get all the pertinent facts.

"Oh!" Sadie McClain stood in the middle of the large living area, a baby on her hip. "I didn't realize you had *female* company. What a pleasant change."

Molly stood in awe of one of her favorite actresses.

The woman graced the silver screen in multiple movies that had shot to the top of the ratings. She could demand any salary she wanted, and there she stood in faded blue jeans, her gorgeous blond hair up in a casual, messy bun and baby spit up on the shoulder of her T-shirt.

She laughed, her blue eyes twinkling as she looked down at her mussed appearance. "Pardon my mess. I was awake most of the night with Emma. She's teething. We just got up from a much-needed two-hour nap."

"Don't let me interrupt. I'm sure you have plenty to do without playing hostess to an army of people in your living room," Molly said. She stepped up to the woman and baby. "I'm Molly Greenbriar."

"Are you another one of Hank's new recruits?" She nodded toward Kujo. "I've met Kujo and Boomer. I didn't know he'd hired a female. I think that's awesome."

"No, no. I have a job. I just happened to…run into Joe—Kujo, in the woods a couple days ago."

Kujo stepped up beside her. "Could I?" he held out his hands for the baby.

"Sure." Sadie handed him the baby then bent to scratch behind Six's ears. "Hey, Six." She glanced up. "Oh, be forewarned, Emma just ate, and she tends to burp with projectile vomit."

Kujo held the baby away from him, raising her up and down without holding her against his body. "On second thought, you'd better take her." He handed the baby back to Sadie.

"Don't have the stomach for baby vomit?" Sadie grinned. "No worries. Neither did I before I had Emma. It's amazing what you learn to tolerate when you love someone as much as we love this little pooping, puking machine." She rubbed noses with Emma, making her giggle.

"No, I just remembered I smell like smoke," Kujo said. "I didn't want to share that with the baby."

Sadie frowned. "Camping out?"

Molly snorted. "I wish that were the reason."

Hank joined them. "The hunting cabin Kujo was staying in burned to the ground."

Sadie's eyes widened. "Wow. I hope no one was hurt." She stared from Kujo to Molly. "That would explain the smudged look. I wondered if it was a fashion statement." She balanced Emma on her hip, grabbed Molly's hand and said, "Come with me. I can fix you up with something clean to wear until you can get to your own clothes."

"I'm fine for now. I won't be here very long." She gave Hank a questioning look.

"Stay for as long as you need to. You're welcome to spend the night if necessary."

"No. I have a room at the B&B in town. And my clothes are all there." She tipped her head toward Joe—she'd never get used to calling him Kujo. "Kujo's the one who lost everything in the fire."

Hank eyed Kujo. "I have some jeans and shirts you can borrow until you can stock up on what you need. And you can stay with us until you find a place of your own."

"I'll stay at the B&B in town," he said. "If they have a spare room…"

Molly's heart fluttered at the news. She'd see more of Joe than just the past two days. "I would like to use the facilities in the meantime to wash my hands and face. I promise not to leave a mess."

"Honey, don't worry about it. I can't believe you two have been through the trauma of a fire." She turned. "Follow me."

Molly fell in step behind the gorgeous actress, pinching herself inside, when all she wanted to do was fangirl all over Sadie McClain.

Sadie showed her to the bathroom on the main level and left her with a fresh towel. "Think you can find your way to the kitchen when you're done? I'm sure the men will be gathered around the table in there. Just follow the noise."

After scrubbing her face and hands, Molly finger-combed her hair and grimaced at her reflection in the mirror. So much for swimming in the pool earlier. She was a wreck. The sooner they made it back to the B&B, the better.

Taking a deep breath, she left the bathroom and followed the sound of deep, male voices to a huge kitchen equipped with state-of-the-art appliances. At one end was a table large enough to seat twenty people. With the seven men seated around it, Molly could see how useful it was.

The men quieted when she entered.

Kujo stood and pulled a seat out between him and Hank at the head of the table.

Molly sat. "Don't stop talking on my account."

"We were just chewing the fat while we waited for you to discuss what's happened since you came out to Montana." Hank laid his palms on the table. "Shoot."

Molly told him her side of what happened, and Kujo recounted his recollection.

Hearing his side again reminded her of how she owed her life to this man. Joe had saved her from hypothermia or being scavenged by animals.

"And just what is it you're looking for in your surveillance?" Hank asked. "Pete hinted at terrorists without coming right out and spilling the beans."

Molly stared around the room at the men before her.

Hank touched her arm. "If it makes you feel any better, we've all been involved with special operations so secret, even the President of the United States didn't know about them."

"Every man in this room has had a top-secret clearance. You can trust us," Duke said. He elbowed Bear in the side. "Well, maybe not Bear. After all, who can trust a bear?"

Bear punched him in the shoulder before facing Molly. "If you want our help, you have to trust us."

"Yeah." Kujo crossed his arms over his chest and held her gaze.

Molly nodded. "I got a tip from one of our computer hackers back at headquarters in DC that there might be a terrorist training camp in the mountains near the town of Eagle Rock. I'm here to determine if there's any credence to that intel." She drew in a deep breath and let it out. "I was to observe and report back. I'm not cleared to engage the target."

Kujo dropped his arms to the table. "They sent you out here alone?"

"Apparently not." She nodded toward Hank. "My supervisor called for backup with the Brotherhood Protectors. In case you've been disconnected with the news, there was another ISIS attack in DC. They're working that now. I got this gig because they didn't see it as a big threat."

Joe's eyebrows lowered in a fierce frown. "Holy crap, Molly. If there's a terrorist training camp here, that's a huge can of worms that could have gotten you killed, and no one would ever have found your body."

Molly lifted her chin. "I can take care of myself."

Kujo snorted. "Like you did when you threw yourself over a cliff to save your ass?"

"The shooter didn't hit me with his bullets," Molly argued, though she knew she didn't have a leg to stand on. She sighed. "I know. I wasn't expecting to hit pay dirt the first day out." Which clearly demonstrated her lack of experience. Perhaps she wasn't ready for field assignments, after all.

"At the very least, you should have had a partner," Hank said. He glanced past her to the man seated beside her. "Kujo, consider Molly your first assignment. You're to keep her safe while she performs her mission. And under no circumstances are you to engage the enemy."

"What if they start shooting at us first?" Kujo asked.

Hank nodded. "Correction: no circumstances except being fired on. In the meantime, I'll work with your guy back in DC to see if we can track down the source of your intel. Perhaps they can trace the IP address to a street address or a name."

"Good luck," Molly said. "The guy in our office couldn't, and he's an expert, dark web hacker."

Hank's lips curled on the corners. "I've got people."

Kujo pushed to his feet. "The day's still early. I want to hit a few stores. Much as I appreciate the loan of your jeans and T-shirts, I'd rather have my own."

Hank stood. "I understand. If you can't find what you need, you're welcome to raid my closet." He turned to Molly. "How many people know you're in town?"

"The B&B owner, and the guy I rented my four-wheeler from." She shrugged. "It was my attempt at a low profile."

"Kujo, you're still pretty new. Maybe you two can go undercover as a couple looking for a place to live. That would give you the perfect excuse to look all over the county and surrounding mountains."

Molly shook her head. "I don't know... I have my

room at the B&B. I didn't tell the lady I had a boyfriend or anything." The idea of pretending she and Kujo were a couple made a swarm of butterflies take off in her belly.

"You can tell her he just arrived in town to surprise you," Hank said. "Think about it. It might save you some trouble and give Kujo a plausible reason to stick around."

With a flutter in her belly, Molly nodded. "Now, if we're done here, I could use a shower and change of clothes. The day's still young, and I have a job to do."

"Not without me," Kujo reminded her.

"Much as I'd like to do this on my own, I'll gladly accept your help." She held out her hand to Hank. "Thanks."

"Don't thank me." Hank took her hand and held it in his. "Kujo happened to be in the right place at the right time. Be careful in the Crazy Mountains. They say you can get lost in there. And by lost, I mean someone can bury a body that'll never be found."

Joe glanced at Molly then turned to Hank. "While we're out searching for a training camp, could you get one of your people to look at the camera on the drone Molly was flying?"

Molly nodded. "I'd send it back to DC, but that would take too much time and it might get more damaged in transit."

"There might be some footage to explain why someone felt the need to knock it out of the sky."

"I'll see what I can do. Show me whatcha got." Hank and the others followed them out to Kujo's pickup.

Kujo handed them the pieces of the drone, pointing out the bullet hole through the motor.

Hank swore. "Not only did they hit it, they hit it where it counted. Dead center. I'll have my guys look at it. If there's any video to be salvaged, you and Molly will be the first to know."

"And while you're at it, I found a piece of a crate in a cave close to where the drone went down. It appears to have government nomenclature painted on it. Perhaps you can trace it back to its origin."

Molly stared at the slat. "You didn't tell me about that."

"I was a bit preoccupied by a fire," he reminded her.

She'd cut him some slack this time. After he'd nearly come unglued when he'd found her alive, she figured the board was the last thing on his mind until now.

Having discharged their findings, Kujo held the door for Six, then Molly and helped her into her seat. He shook hands with Hank, got in beside her and started the engine. As he shifted into gear, he shot a glance her way. "Ready to find a terrorist training camp?"

She nodded. "Hell, yeah."

His brows drew together. "Are you feeling up to it?"

"I'm sore, but I'll live." She squared her shoulders and stared at the road ahead. After nearly dying on her last trip into the mountains, she was even more determined to find the person who'd shot down the drone and to locate the training camp. Having Kujo along would be a bonus. He'd cover her six.

But pretending to be a couple? That might push her comfort level a little too far.

CHAPTER 11

"Where to first?" Kujo asked as they entered Eagle Rock.

"I would think you'd want to replace your personal items as soon as possible. I don't recall seeing a department store, but the feed store might carry denim jeans and shirts."

They stopped at the feed store. Just as Molly said, they carried a selection of jeans and chambray shirts. Kujo purchased three pairs of jeans, four chambray shirts, a white dress shirt, a dozen pairs of socks and seven T-shirts. He added a camouflage duffel bag to the pile and a pair of binoculars. After he paid for everything, he stuffed the items in the duffel bag.

"You'll have another T-shirt available after I wash the one I'm wearing," Molly pointed out.

"Keep it. You lost a shirt in that fire," he reminded her.

"I brought enough to last a couple weeks. I'll be fine."

They stopped at the grocery store and picked up

toiletries, a case of bottled water and a box of microwavable popcorn.

"The B&B serves breakfast and has microwaves in the rooms. Most of our meals will be eaten out," Molly warned.

She gave him directions.

"The B&B is a big house that's been converted into several rooms for rent, operated by Mrs. Kinner. She's a seventy-year-old woman who has the energy of someone half her age. And she insists on being called Mrs. K."

"Sounds like a real ball-buster."

"She is." Molly smiled. "With a heart of gold."

Molly entered the house first. "Mrs. K?"

A diminutive woman, who couldn't be over five feet tall, pushed through a swinging door into a large dining area equipped with bistro-style tables. "Molly, I'm so glad you're here. I was going to call the sheriff since I hadn't seen you in two days. Where were you?"

Molly smiled. "I'm sorry. I should have called to let you know that my…fiancé came and carried me out to a hunting cabin in the woods for some alone time." She winked, her smile fading. "Unfortunately, the cabin burned to the ground this morning."

"Oh, dear Lord." Mrs. K clutched Molly's arm. "You two weren't in it when the fire started, were you?"

"No, thank goodness. But since Joe is in town, do you have a room he can rent while he's here? He's also got a dog with him."

"Oh, honey, I'm not so old that I'm offended when

young couples sleep together before they're married. He's more than welcome to share your room."

Molly's eyes widened. "But—"

"Dog, you say?" Mrs. K looked past them. "Where is it?"

"He's on the porch," Kujo said.

"Well, let me see him. I love dogs, though Mr. K never let me have them in the house." She gave them a sly smile. "Since he passed, I allow guests to bring their dogs. It gives me the chance to enjoy them without committing to one. I have so much work to do around here, I doubt I'd have time to give to another being."

Kujo opened the front door. "Six, come."

The German Shepherd entered the house and sat at Kujo's feet.

Mrs. K stood back. "My, he's a big fellow." She looked up at Kujo. "Is he friendly?"

"You can pet him. He won't bite, unless I tell him to."

"Oh, I'm not certain I'm reassured." Mrs. K reached out to pet Six and smiled when he nudged her to keep it up. "Oh, he is a sweet fellow. He's more than welcome. Just let me get another towel. It's a good thing you two can share a room. With the cattle auction in town, I'm booked through the rest of this week until next Sunday." She talked as she headed up the stairs.

Kujo almost laughed at the stunned and slightly desperate expression on Molly's face. But he didn't. Instead, he hooked her elbow like a good fiancé and guided her up the stairs.

Mrs. K fished a fresh towel out of a linen cabinet.

"You'll want to freshen up, I'm sure. I'll leave you two alone."

"Thank you, Mrs. K," Kujo said to fill in Molly's silence.

The older woman started for the stairs.

"Oh, Mrs. K?" Kujo called out.

She turned. "Do you need some shampoo and soap?"

"No, thank you," Kujo gave the woman one of his killer smiles. "We like the Eagle Rock area and the surrounding mountains, so we'll be out a lot searching for a place to live. Just in case you get worried."

She grinned. "Thank you for the notice. And if you're looking for a land agent, David Perez is the most knowledgeable agent in the area. And I wouldn't go stomping around on other people's property without an appointment. Some people around here would just as soon shoot first and ask questions later."

"Thank you," Kujo said. "We'll check him out and get lined up for appointments."

Molly stuck her key into the lock and pushed open the door. Once she and Kujo were inside, she closed it and shook her head. "We have to find somewhere else for you and Six to stay."

"You heard Mrs. K. She's booked."

"Then we'll find another B&B."

"If this one is full, the others will be as well." Kujo took her hand. "Besides, I'm your sidekick, your partner. How can we work as a team when we're staying in two different places?"

"I don't know, but we can't sleep in the same bed."

He chuckled. "Why not? We did last night, and I didn't hear any complaints."

Molly opened her mouth, but nothing came out. Then she snapped it shut. "I'll be first in the shower. You can unpack. There's room in the closet and the bottom two drawers of the dresser." She grabbed a shirt and jeans from hangers in the closet, and panties and a bra from the drawer and scurried into the connecting bathroom.

Kujo's lips curled. If the flush of color in Molly's cheeks was any indication, she was worried about sleeping with him. He wondered if she was worried he'd take advantage of her this time, or if she was attracted to him and afraid to act on that attraction.

No matter what the case, he wasn't leaving her alone in the B&B. After coming back to the burning cabin, he couldn't leave her alone anywhere. His chest had hurt so badly, he'd felt like he was having a heart attack as he'd stared into the blaze, thinking Molly was trapped inside.

He pulled the jeans and shirts from the duffel bag and ripped the tags and stickers off, tossing them in the wastebasket. He preferred to wash clothes before wearing them, but that would take too much time. Molly would be ready to hit the ground running again as soon as she'd showered and dressed.

He hung the jeans and shirts in the closet for the moment, unwrapped his toiletries from their packaging then looked out the window at the main street running north and south through Eagle Rock.

In a community this small, he found it hard to

believe it could harbor an ISIS training camp. Who were they recruiting? Ranchers? Farmers? Businessmen or women?

His stomach rumbled, reminding him they hadn't had breakfast or lunch. The local diner would be a good place to kill two birds with one stone. They could eat and gather information from the locals.

Molly entered the room, carrying her dirty clothing. She'd dressed in a clean pair of dark jeans and a white button-down blouse. Her hair was brushed back from her forehead, the damp tresses lying in a neat sheath over her shoulders and down the middle of her back.

The woman didn't need makeup or high heels to appear sexy. The natural glow of her skin and the bright green of her eyes made her more appealing to Kujo than any other woman he'd ever dated.

"Your turn," Molly said. "I left some hot water for you."

"Thanks." He nodded toward her. "How are your wounds?"

She smiled. "Healing nicely, thanks to you."

He didn't offer to medicate them again, knowing he would be pushing his own limits if he did. Kujo entered the bathroom, shucked his clothes and ducked into the shower. He spent the next few minutes standing under the spray, washing the soot off his body and hair while trying not to think of Molly in the same shower, naked with the water running over her breasts and down her belly to the juncture of her thighs. He groaned and switched the water to cold.

"Are you all right in there?" Molly asked, her voice muffled by the door.

"I'm fine." Just fine, with a boner and desire he couldn't slake. He was working with Molly, not dating her. Giving in to lust would only complicate their task and take the focus off the real issue.

Despite the use of cold water, Kujo spent several minutes freezing before his erection dissipated. Quickly, before he could start thinking of a naked Molly again, he turned off the water, dried his body and dragged on the stiff jeans and shirt and headed out of the bathroom.

Molly wasn't in the bedroom and neither were Kujo's new jeans and shirts, nor his soot-covered clothing. When had she come into the bathroom to collect his soiled clothes?

The door to the room opened and Molly appeared. "I hope you don't mind, but I took your clothes to the laundry room. I got them started in the washer. Mrs. K offered to switch them to the dryer while we're out."

"Thanks." He pulled on the new socks and his boots. "I'm ready when you are."

"I'd like to stop at the realtor's and set up some appointments to see property in the area," Molly said.

"We can do that on the way to the diner. I don't know about you, but I'm hungry enough to eat a side of beef. And while we're there, we can ask the locals what people do for work around here."

Molly's brows scrunched. "Are you already looking for a new job? You just started with Hank."

Kujo shook his head. "No, I need to give this one a

chance before I start looking again. I'm looking for reasons a community would condone such a thing as a terrorist training camp. Some people must know it's here—at least, ones the group has recruited."

"Most people recruited into such organizations have issues," Molly agreed. "Low self-esteem, being fired from a job, trouble with the law and more. You're right, the job situation around here might have contributed to brainwashed targets." Molly's belly growled and she pressed a hand to her midsection. "And yes, stopping to eat would be good."

They left the room, Six trotting along behind them.

"The diner is only two blocks away," Kujo said. "Do you feel well enough to walk?"

She nodded.

Kujo took her hand. He liked the feel of her soft warm hand in his.

Molly glanced up.

"Our cover, remember?" he whispered. "Might as well look like we're together." She might not be on board with the idea, but Kujo was liking it all too much.

Molly's pulse hammered through her veins. Holding Joe's hand shouldn't have had that effect on her. Could he feel the rapid beat of her heart through her fingertips? Would he think she was excited by his touch? Well, she was. Far more than she should have been, having only known him for such a short time.

And they'd share a bed that night, unless Joe slept on

the floor. If not him, she could. Joe. Kujo. She was having a hard time calling him by his nickname.

Good Lord, she didn't need the distraction of lust getting in the way of her first field assignment. This was her job. The career she'd chosen, trained for and loved. She'd be damned if she sabotaged it due to a fling with a handsome Army veteran.

For the sake of their cover, she forced a smile onto her face and pretended to enjoy being with him. That part wasn't hard at all. The man had proven brave, gentle and solid. And those muscles…

There she went again!

She walked the two blocks in silence, afraid if she opened her mouth, some of her tumultuous thoughts would spill out, and she'd make a fool of herself.

Other than holding her through the night and holding her tight in front of the burning cabin, he hadn't shown a desire to go any further. Perhaps he wasn't all that into her. And she shouldn't care.

Outside the diner, Kujo gave Six a one-word command, "Stay."

Six sat beside the entrance, his gaze on Kujo as his master held the door for Molly.

The diner had a retro-fifties appearance, with checkered black and white tile flooring, chrome finishes and checkered tablecloths.

"Welcome to Al's Diner," a waitress called out. "Pick a seat, I'll be with you in a minute."

Molly chose a table in the middle of the room, the better to eavesdrop on other patrons. She sat with her back to the door, allowing Kujo the seat facing the entrance, so that he could have her back.

He held her chair until she sat then took the one across from her.

"Hi, I'm Daisy, I'll be your server." The waitress brought menus and two glasses of water and laid them on the table. She took their drink orders and disappeared. When she came back with coffee for them both, she smiled and set them on the table. "You two are new in town."

Molly nodded. "Yes, we are."

"Passing through or looking to stay a while?" Daisy pulled an order pad from her apron pocket and a pencil from behind her ear.

"We're looking for a home in the area," Kujo said. "I'm Joe, and this is my fiancée, Molly."

"Joe and Molly, so glad to see people my age moving into Eagle Rock, rather than leaving."

"Are young people leaving?" Molly prompted.

"Oh, sure. Most kids graduate high school and leave for the bigger cities to go to universities or find jobs." She stood with her pen poised over the pad. "What can I getcha?" Daisy took their orders then glanced up. "Oh, hi, Mr. Perez. Find a seat. I'll be with you in a minute." She looked back at Molly and Kujo. "If you need a good real estate agent, Mr. Perez is one of the best in town. He knows everything about every piece of property in the county."

"Now, Daisy, that's an exaggeration." A dark-haired, dark-skinned man, dressed in neatly ironed slacks and a polo shirt, stepped up to the table where Molly and

Kujo sat. "Hi, I'm David Perez."

Kujo stood and held out his hand. "Joe Kuntz." He nodded toward Molly. "My fiancée, Molly."

Molly's tummy did a backflip when Kujo called her his fiancée. She liked the sound of it too much. Pushing the thought aside, she squared her shoulders and took Perez's hand. "Is it true you're a real estate agent?"

"I am." He pulled a card from his pocket and handed it to her. "Are you looking for a place?"

"We are," Kujo said. "We're considering moving to Eagle Rock, but we'd like to see all it has to offer."

A big man with shaggy hair and a beard turned on his stool at the counter. "If you're coming for the job opportunities, you're in the wrong place."

"What do you mean?" Molly asked.

"Coal mines are laying off workers. Pipeline work is on hold, and we got more people out of work than there are jobs in ranching."

"I'm sorry to hear that," she said.

The bearded man's eyes narrowed. "You ain't looking for work, are you?"

Kujo held up his hands. "No. I'm an independent contractor and do most of my work out of state."

"Then why live here in Eagle Rock?"

Kujo shrugged. "Why not? I travel most of the time, and my fiancée is into photography. She likes it here." He smiled. "Don't worry. We're not here job hunting. Just property shopping."

The grizzled man continued to frown but turned his back to them, mumbling, "Damned outsiders with more money than brains are driving the prices of property up around here."

Perez shook his head and smiled at them. "Don't let George discourage you. Most people in the area are friendly."

"Yeah, most of those who didn't lose their jobs," George muttered, still with his back to them.

"If you want to look around the area, I have time this afternoon. It'll only take me an hour to set up some appointments," Perez said.

Molly beamed like a new bride. "Could you?"

"Of course." Perez pulled out his cell phone. "I'm here for lunch, then I'll head back to my office. You can meet me there. Anything in particular you're looking for?"

"Your office is fine." Kujo glanced at Molly. "My fiancée is an avid photographer and has fallen in love with the Crazy Mountains. We'd like to look at acreage up against the national forests near there."

Perez made a note on his cell phone. "Got it. I'll see you in an hour." He left them to sit at a table with another man whose back was to them.

"Okay, we have an agent." Kujo sat in time for Daisy to bring out their plates of sandwiches and fries.

"What George said about people being out of work…" The waitress shook her head. "It changes people."

"How so?" Molly asked.

Daisy looked down at her hands. "My boyfriend—I should say, ex-boyfriend—lost his job working the oil pipeline. One day, Tanner was making good money, and we were thinking about getting married, building a house and having kids." She looked out the window of the diner. "Then he was out of a job with no prospects and no other skills than what he'd learned on the pipeline. He looked for work, even took a job at Pinion Ranch doing manual labor."

"Wasn't *any* work better than none for him?" Molly asked.

Daisy shook her head. "They only pay Tanner a quarter of what he was making on the pipeline. He can't make the payments on his new truck nor afford the house he's renting. He hates that I make more money in tips than he does for all the backbreaking work he does all week. He gets so angry." She rubbed her arms, staring past Molly and Kujo as if reliving the past. Then she shook herself and pasted a smile on her face. "I'm sorry. I shouldn't have said all that. Forget it. I broke up with him, anyway. Enjoy your meal." The young woman spun and scurried away.

Molly's heart squeezed in her chest. "That really sucks for her."

"Yeah. When life throws you curve balls. You have to learn how to swing at them." Kujo's gaze followed Daisy to the swinging door to the kitchen.

"Is that what happened to you? Is that why you're working for Hank, now?" Molly stared across the table at the man.

Kujo's lips firmed into a tight line. "The army was all I knew, all I trained for."

"Like Daisy's boyfriend."

He nodded. "When that was no longer an option, I was lost and angry."

"What did you do?"

His lips formed a crooked smile. "I lost myself in the mountains of Colorado."

"Lost yourself?"

"Figuratively speaking. I became a hermit in a cabin in the mountains."

Molly touched his hand. "I'm beginning to see a pattern."

His smile grew softer. "I stayed there for three years, until Bear and Duke came to tell me Six was up for adoption."

Molly studied the strong, vibrant man sitting across from her and marveled at how he had felt lost when he'd left the military. If he could be that angry and disappointed about losing the life he'd come to know, others might feel the same.

"Your friends threw you a lifeline," she said.

He nodded. "That lifeline was Six."

Molly's chest swelled. She'd liked the dog from the first moment they'd met. Now she had even more of a reason to appreciate the animal.

"Six had been injured in his last assignment, and fostering wasn't working out for him. If I hadn't come along, they would have euthanized him."

Molly gasped. "You saved each other."

His lips quirked up on the corners. "I guess we did. Now we have a chance at a new life." Kujo stared at the door to the diner as if he could see Six sitting outside so patiently waiting for them to come out.

Kujo smiled across the table like a man in love.

Molly's heart flipped. What would it be like to have this man's love?

"In the military," he said softly, "we had annual suicide prevention and operations security briefings. In each of the sessions, we were trained to look for signs in our peers and subordinates of depression or extreme stress. Studies showed when things aren't going well at home, either with relationships or financial disasters, good men can be turned bad more easily. They might sell information to the enemy or join the other side to get out of the situation they find themselves in."

"Or commit suicide," Molly added.

"True. The people around here who've lost their jobs are in similar situations. They've become desperate and do stupid things or lash out."

"Like Tanner, Daisy's ex."

He nodded. "I'll bet he isn't the only one who's angry and willing to find an outlet for his anger."

Though they spoke softly, Molly couldn't resist making a casual perusal of the diner to see if anyone was paying attention to them, possibly eavesdropping into their discussion.

Everyone appeared to be concentrating on the people sitting at their own tables, not Molly and Kujo's.

Molly ate the rest of her meal in silence, while listening to the conversations around their table, hoping to glean more information about the layoffs and subsequent relationship issues.

One woman talked about substituting in the local elementary school to a friend who thought it was a good idea. A man complained about the price of feed for his horses to another man who tried to one-up him with the rising cost of fuel for his tractors. None of them appeared to be angry enough to be terrorist recruits.

Except maybe the cranky, bearded man at the counter. Only he didn't look like he was in any condition to run obstacle courses or storm buildings with high-powered machine guns.

Then again, it only took a man driving a vehicle into a crowd to create chaos and fear. Her intel had mentioned an ISIS training camp, not what kind of training they were conducting.

Kujo finished his meal and leaned across the table to grasp her hand. "Penny for your thoughts." He entwined her fingers with his.

Molly's thoughts flew out the window as soon as he touched her. "I wasn't thinking about much," she stalled. "What about you?"

"I was just thinking about how lucky I am to be sitting with the prettiest woman in the diner."

Her cheeks heated, and that kaleidoscope of butterflies took off once again battering her insides with their soft wings. "Be serious," she said, her voice a little breathless.

"I am." He lifted her hand and pressed a kiss to her knuckles. "We have a few minutes before we meet with Mr. Perez. Want to window shop and see what Eagle Rock has to offer?"

Molly practically jumped from her seat, anxious for

any movement that would require Kujo to release her hand.

When he did, she felt the loss immediately and could breathe normally again. Why did this man have such a profound effect on her? "Give me a minute. I want to visit the ladies' room," she said, her heart pounding.

"Take your time."

Molly hurried to the back of the diner where a hallway led to the restrooms. She entered the ladies' room and stood at the sink, staring into the mirror at her flushed face. What was wrong with her? She never reacted to men the way she was reacting to Kujo. If she weren't careful, she'd lose focus on her mission.

Hell, if she weren't careful, she'd fall in love with the former Army soldier.

Molly splashed water on her face, telling herself to snap out of her growing infatuation with the big guy. So, he'd held her hand. He was doing it for their cover. He'd said she was beautiful. Again, for their cover.

She dried her face and straightened. "Now, don't be a fool. Get out there and do your job."

The door to the restroom opened, and Daisy stepped in.

Molly moved aside, but Daisy didn't pass her. Instead, she stopped in front of Molly. "I'm sorry about unloading on you in the diner."

"It's quite all right." Molly touched the young woman's arm. "It's hard breaking up with someone you thought you had a future with."

"I guess it was so new, I couldn't help it. I kicked him

out of my apartment yesterday. I had my apartment manager change the locks while he was away."

Molly gave her a twisted smile. "I bet he wasn't happy when he came back to find that his key didn't work."

"I warned him, but he didn't think I'd do it. I packed all his clothes into bags and set them outside the door. The only thing of his I didn't put out was his laptop. I figure if he wants it enough, he'll have to ask nicely. I put it in the back of my Jeep so I won't have to let him back into the apartment to get it." Daisy looked up, her eyes pooling with tears. "Was I wrong to kick him out? When he hit me, should I have been more understanding?"

Molly's heart hurt for the woman who couldn't be more than twenty-one or twenty-two. She wrapped her arms around Daisy. "Oh, sweetheart, you did the right thing. No man has the right to hit a woman."

"My friend, Martha—her husband hits her all the time. And she just takes it." Daisy shook her head. "Am I weak? Should I stand by my man like Martha does when times are tough?"

"Was her husband laid off like your boyfriend?"

Daisy nodded and swiped at a tear leaking out of the corner of her eye. "They worked together. They still do on the Pinion Ranch. But they're frustrated and not making enough to live on. That's why my boyfriend moved in with me. He couldn't afford an apartment on his own, and now I feel guilty about kicking him out."

"That's his problem. You shouldn't feel guilty. Especially if he's abusing you."

"That's what I keep telling myself. But at the same time, isn't a woman supposed to stand by her man, through good times and bad?" She leaned back and stared into Molly's eyes.

"Not that kind of bad. A guy has to be man enough to handle the bad times without taking it out on the ones he's supposed to love. You're smart. You knew it wasn't right and got out before it got worse. Some women don't figure that out until too late."

Daisy hugged Molly. "I'm so sorry to dump all of this on you. But you seemed so nice, and you aren't related to anyone in Eagle Rock. I knew you'd give me an unbiased opinion."

"Daisy, I'm glad to help. You deserve better, and you're doing the right thing to cut it off before you're hurt badly."

Daisy squeezed her one last time then stepped away, adjusted her apron and wiped the tears from her cheeks. She gave Molly a watery smile. "Thank you."

"If you need me for anything, I'm staying at Mrs. K's B&B. Day or night." Molly took the pad from Daisy's pocket and the pen from behind her ear and wrote her cell phone number on one of the pages. She handed the pad and pen to the woman. "Anytime. I mean it."

Daisy and Molly left the restroom at the same time. Daisy entered the kitchen, while Molly weaved through the tables to where Kujo sat.

He stood as she approached. "Ready to go?"

Kujo paid at the counter, left a tip on the table and called out, "Thank you, Daisy."

Daisy had just walked back through the swinging

kitchen door. She smiled at Kujo and then at Molly. "Thank you."

Molly liked Daisy and hoped her ex-boyfriend didn't try to seek vengeance on the girl.

Before they left the diner, Molly had one thing she wanted to do.

"Hold on," Molly said. She stepped up to the grouchy man at the counter and held out her hand. "Hi, I'm Molly. I thought I'd introduce myself and thank you for your insight on the job situation."

He frowned at the hand held out to him as if it might bite him. Finally, he took it in his meaty palm and practically crushed her fingers.

"And you are?" she asked and smiled brightly through the pain.

"George Batson."

"Mr. Batson, I look forward to running into you again. Thank you for taking time to talk with us about Eagle Rock."

His face turned a ruddy red. "Ain't nothin'. Eagle Rock's a nice place to live, if you have work."

"We think so, too. I hope things improve soon for you and all of those people who lost their jobs."

"Oh, I didn't lose my job. But my sons did, and their friends. Most of them left. The ones still here are making peanuts hauling hay and mucking stalls part time at Pinion Ranch."

"I see." Molly smiled again. "Well, it was a pleasure to meet you." She hooked her arm through Kujo's and left the diner.

"What was that all about?" Kujo asked.

"Your boss, Hank, has connections, right?"

"Yeah. So?"

"Between mine and his, we should feed them names of people we come across who could possibly be involved with terrorists."

Kujo glanced back at George Batson through the windows of the diner. "And you think Batson might be one of them?"

"Maybe. Or his sons." She shrugged. "I'm throwing noodles against the wall, hoping something sticks." She leaned into him, hugging his arm. "Work with me."

Kujo dropped his hand to the small of her back. "Good point. As soon as we get to somewhere private, we can call in the names of the people we just spoke with."

Molly laughed. "You think Daisy might be involved in covert activities?"

"Some say the really bad ones are the folks you least suspect."

Molly nodded. "Well, Daisy would be the least likely candidate in my book. Now, her boyfriend might be someone we consider as well."

"Names, sweetheart," Kujo said. "We need first and last names."

"I didn't get Tanner's last name." Molly had been so wrapped up in Daisy's story, she'd forgotten to ask for the name of her boyfriend. Then she relaxed. "I know someone who can help."

"Who?"

"Mrs. K at the B&B. She said she's been in Eagle

Rock all her life. She's proud of the fact she knows everyone."

Kujo grinned. "A busybody."

"Of the best kind," Molly agreed.

"What about Perez?" Kujo asked. "Should we add him to the list of potential suspects?"

"Wouldn't hurt to run his name through some criminal databases to see if we come up with a match." She held up her cell phone. "I even snapped a photo of him while his attention was on George."

Kujo leaned back, his eyes wide. "Damn, woman, you really are in it to win it."

"You bet I am. I have a lot riding on this investigation," she whispered, the smile dropping from her lips. "This is my first field assignment. If I screw it up, I'm back at a desk." She sighed. "I hate paperwork."

CHAPTER 12

They walked to the end of Main Street and a little farther, out of range of the houses and any nosey neighbors. At the end of town, Molly called her supervisor, Pete, gave him Batson and Perez's names and asked him to scan the criminal data bases for any hits.

While Molly talked to her boss, Kujo placed a call to Hank, giving him the same information. When they ended their calls, they turned and headed back into Eagle Rock. They were halfway back to the diner when they saw Perez enter one of the buildings. It appeared to be the one they'd passed with pictures of houses posted on the insides of the windows.

"Give him another fifteen minutes to set up appointments, then we'll step in. In the meantime, let's go in here," Molly steered Kujo into the first store they came to. Six sat outside the door and waited patiently.

It just so happened the store was filled with baby and maternity items.

"Oops." Molly fought the smile threatening to spill across her face. "Guess I should have looked first."

"Hello. Welcome to First Comes Love." A petite and very pregnant woman waddled toward them. "Can I help you find anything?"

Molly shot a glance at Kujo and nearly burst out laughing. "We're just browsing right now."

"Oh, please. Take your time," the young lady said. "When are you expecting?"

Molly laid a hand over her flat belly. "Not for a while," she said, choking down a giggle.

"I'm Simone. If you have questions, feel free to ask." She rubbed a hand over her belly. "Don't worry. This isn't my first baby; I have three more with the sitter. I can tell you just about anything you might want to know about having babies."

"Thank you. I'll keep that in mind." Molly dragged Kujo deeper into the store. "What do you think about this crib?" Molly stopped by one painted white. "Or do you prefer the darker one?"

"I actually hadn't thought about either." Kujo tugged at the collar of his T-shirt, a fine sheen of sweat breaking out on his forehead. "Isn't it a little soon to be looking at cribs?"

"It's never too soon. You'd be surprised at all of the furniture and equipment available to make your baby more comfortable." Simone appeared beside them. "Do you know if it's a boy or a girl, yet?"

Kujo coughed. "Absolutely not."

"Oh, are you going to be surprised, then?" Simone smiled. "I was surprised with my second one. They told me it was a girl, but his little thingy was hiding every time we did the ultrasound." Simone made a motion with her finger, indicating the baby's penis. "We welcomed him into a pink baby room. Oh, my husband painted it within a week, but we're very happy to have our little Robbie. He's three now."

"Uh. I think I need some air," Kujo bolted for the door.

Simone stared after him. "Is he going to be all right?"

Molly laughed out loud. "I don't think he's quite ready for all of this."

Simone smiled. "Are they ever? My husband always turns a little pale when I tell him I'm pregnant again. I'm just thankful he has a good job with the sheriff's department, what with so many people out of work lately. But he loves every one of our babies, and he's a good father."

If she weren't on a mission, Molly would have spent more time with the woman. "I'd better catch up with my fiancé before he runs clear to the next county. Thank you for your assistance." She hurried out of the store, chuckling all the way. When she caught up with Kujo and Six outside, she couldn't wipe the grin off her face. "I'm sorry." She touched his arm. "That was unfair of me."

"I was good up to…" He crooked his finger like Simone had.

Molly grinned. "I liked Simone. She's very passionate about her job."

"That's not the only thing she's passionate about. Three kids and another on the way?" He shook his head.

Molly fell in step beside him. "How many children is the right number?"

"I don't know…2.5?" He shoved a hand through his hair.

Molly almost felt sorry for him. But not quite. "I always pictured having four children like Simone. I grew up an only child. I wouldn't wish that on any kid."

"I'm one of five. I'm not sure I'd wish that on any kid."

"Did you like your siblings?"

"For the most part. My mother didn't see fit to give us a sister to tone us down, so we fought, wrestled and broke things."

"And I bet you'd fight to your last breath for any one of them."

Kujo didn't say anything for a moment. "Yeah. I'd give my life for them."

"How long has it been since you've visited your siblings?"

He shrugged. "Four or five years."

She stared at him with a frown puckering her brows. "Are you kidding me? If I had siblings, I'd make it a point to visit them more often."

"We all went our separate ways after high school. I went into the Army, two of my brothers joined the Marines. Another went to college and is an engineer working for one of the big aircraft manufacturers. The other stayed on the ranch down in Texas to work the horses and cattle my father raises."

"And you haven't been back to Texas?"

Kujo shook his head.

"Why?"

He turned away and stared up at the mountains. "It doesn't matter."

"It must or you'd have gone back to visit. Do you and your parents get along?"

"Sure. It's not like that."

"It's about losing yourself in the mountains, isn't it?"

"Yeah. Pretty much."

"I'm glad you found yourself." Molly wanted to wipe the grim look off his face. "And it's a good thing. If we're having children together, I insist on them knowing their grandparents."

He whipped his head around to stare at her in alarm.

She grinned and hooked her arm through his. "Don't sweat it. I guess I'm jealous of your family and wanted to live vicariously. I'm sure your reasons are good." She leaned her head against his shoulder. "We should go look at property. I hope we find what we're looking for."

David Perez met them at the door. He had a list of properties to show them and had called ahead to warn the sellers they would be coming.

"Do I need to take my dog back to the B&B?" Kujo asked.

David glanced down at Six. "Is he friendly?"

"He's well-behaved," Kujo said.

Perez seemed to think about it then shrugged. "He can ride in the back."

They loaded into Perez's SUV and set off on the hunt for property.

After the first three places proved to be small acreages, not nearly close enough to the area Molly had hoped to explore, she took the matter into her own hands. "I was really hoping to get closer to the mountains. Is there any property for sale in that direction?" She pointed to the hills she'd gone into two days before. "All of what you've shown us is too small. Think bigger. And we don't mind remote."

David's brows dipped. "Have you ever been in Montana during the winter? Remote can be the difference between accessible and cut off."

"We're from Wisconsin," Molly said, coming up with the first cold state she could think of. "We know how to deal with snow."

"Wisconsin doesn't have the mountains Montana does."

"Like I said, my fiancée is an avid photographer," Kujo said. "She wants to live as close to nature as she can. Her photographs can be seen in all of the nature magazines."

"Could you drive that way and tell us a little about the larger tracts of land?" Molly asked. "Who owns them? Are they friendly? Would they mind an outsider moving in next door?"

Perez turned the SUV around and drove in the direction Molly had pointed. "I haven't called any of the property owners," he said.

"Can we drive up into some of the hills and find a vantage point where we can look out over the area from higher up?" Kujo asked.

Molly clapped her hands. "Great idea. That might

give us a better understanding of the terrain and available properties."

"There isn't any place like that."

"No?" Molly blinked up at the realtor, giving him her most innocent look.

"Most views are blocked by tall trees." Perez shook his head. "I'd take you up into the mountains, but it'll be dark soon, and I wouldn't want to get us lost finding our way back out."

"Understandable," Kujo agreed. "Maybe tomorrow."

Molly recognized the dirt road she'd turned off on the day she'd gone out on the four-wheeler. "I adore this area. The trees are so tall and lush. Is this property for sale?"

Perez snorted. "Not hardly. It's a three-thousand-acre ranch owned by Paul Tilson."

"Oh, my." She pushed out her bottom lip in a pout. "I know we can't afford that much land, but do you think we could ask him to sell off a small corner?"

"No," Perez said, his tone unbending. Final.

Molly studied Perez.

His face was firm, unyielding. She found it intriguing. Perhaps he'd asked Tilson on previous occasions and been rebuffed.

Still, she persisted. "Can't we even ask?"

"He rarely visits the Pinion Ranch, and he's even harder to get in touch with. He contracted me with the authority to hire people to maintain the house and fences, but asked not to be troubled otherwise."

Molly frowned. "That's strange. With such a pretty place you'd think he'd be here all the time."

"Well, he isn't," Perez said, his voice curt.

"What about on the south side of his place? Is there anything available?" Kujo asked.

"No, that property is part of the National Forest."

Perez stepped on the accelerator, skimming past the rest of the countryside, headed back into town. "Drop you off somewhere?"

"At the diner would be fine. We can walk from there, thank you," Molly said.

"I'll look at the MLS system and see if I can come up with anything else for tomorrow."

"Have you always lived in Eagle Rock?" Kujo asked. "I wondered, because you know so much about the town and the surrounding countryside.

"My parents moved here when I was just shy of my fourteenth birthday. I've been here ever since."

"And your parents?" Molly asked.

"They moved on to California."

Molly tilted her head. "I imagine real estate gets you around."

"True. I know just about every property in this county and many of the surrounding counties."

The sun was on its way toward the horizon as they neared town.

Red and blue lights flashed as emergency vehicles crowded the streets. Molly leaned forward and peered through the windshield. "What's going on at the diner?"

"I was wondering that myself." Perez parked several blocks away. "This is as close as I can get."

"That's fine," Kujo said. "We can walk." He leaped out and let Six out of the back.

Molly glanced across at Perez. "Thanks for your assistance. We'll be in touch when we're ready to look some more."

Perez had turned away and had his cell phone pressed to his ear as he hurried toward his office.

Kujo and Six joined Molly. "Ready?"

She nodded. "Let's go."

As they neared the emergency vehicles, a sheriff's deputy stepped in front of them. "I'm sorry, but you'll have to take another road through town. They're conducting a crime scene investigation."

"What crime?"

"Someone set off an explosion at the diner. Several people were injured."

Molly's pulse quickened. "An explosion? Was Daisy, the waitress, one of the injured people?"

The deputy held up his hands. "That's all I know. The EMTs are working it, and the state police crime lab is on its way."

Kujo cupped Molly's arm and guided her down a street to one block over that ran parallel to Main Street. They reached the B&B a couple minutes later.

Mrs. K was in the dining area sitting beside a police scanner. When she saw them walk in the door, she leaped to her feet and hurried toward them. "I was worried about you two. Someone blew up the diner."

"We heard." Molly hugged the older woman. "Any news on who was hurt in the explosion?"

"I've only heard the names of a few. Al was knocked

off his feet in the kitchen. He might have a concussion. And Daisy Bishop was taken to the trauma center in Bozeman."

"Any idea why the diner was targeted?" Molly asked.

"Someone saw Tanner Birge running from the scene." Mrs. K's eyes rounded. "The sheriff has a BOLO out for him. I knew that boy wasn't good enough for our Daisy."

"Daisy's ex-boyfriend?" Kujo asked.

Mrs. K nodded.

Molly's fists tightened. *The bastard.* "He's mad because she dumped him."

Mrs. K's brows rose. "She did?"

Molly nodded.

"About damned time. He didn't treat her right."

The police scanner crackled.

"I better go and listen." Mrs. K spun and ran across the dining room to where she'd been sitting when they'd entered.

Molly was already halfway to the stairs when Kujo and Six caught up to her.

"Are you thinking what I'm thinking?"

She shot a glance back at him. "Probably. Where would a country boy learn how to set explosives?"

Kujo's lips firmed into a straight line. "At the local terrorist training camp."

CHAPTER 13

As soon as Kujo entered the room he shared with Molly, he pulled his cell phone from his pocket. Just as he was about to hit Hank's number, the phone rang. Hank's name came up on the viewing screen.

Kujo answered. "Hank."

"I guess you've heard."

"About the explosion?" Kujo asked.

"Yeah. I'm listening on the police scanner. They've cornered a guy named Tanner Birge."

Kujo gripped the phone tighter. "Wow. He's the ex-boyfriend of Daisy Bishop, a waitress at Al's Diner."

"The sheriff's department says the explosion wasn't the typical Molotov cocktail or fertilizer, home-made job."

"Are you thinking he had some training?"

"It's possible," Hank said. "I'll see what I can do to get a ring-side seat at the interrogation when they bring him in." Hank paused. Voices and the staticky noise of a radio sounded in the background. "Hold on, Kujo. We're getting more information."

Molly stood beside Kujo and tilted her head close to his hand holding the cell phone. "What's going on?"

"They've cornered Tanner Birge," he whispered.

She nodded and leaned closer, her hair brushing across his skin. The peachy scent of her shampoo invaded his senses.

"What a cluster-fuck," Hank said when he came back on the line.

"What's happening?"

"He was headed north toward Canada, when they forced his truck off the road. He had his hands up, getting out of the vehicle, when some trigger-happy son-of-a-bitch fired a shot. In the confusion, Birge got away."

"Who fired the shot?" Molly asked.

"They don't know. They're checking everyone's weapons. Wait…" More voices and static sounded through the receiver.

Kujo tapped the phone, engaging the speaker option, and held it between himself and Molly.

She captured his gaze and held it.

"Are you still there?" Hank asked.

"We're here," Kujo responded.

"It appears none of the deputies discharged their weapons."

Molly shook her head. "How can that be?" As soon as the words were out of her mouth her eyes rounded.

Kujo's jaw tightened. "Sniper."

"I'm running Birge's name through my people," Hank said.

Molly tipped her head over the phone and spoke, "I'll contact my supervisor and get the folks back in the office working it, too."

"Someone didn't want Birge talking about where he got those explosives," Kujo stated.

"Do you think his ex-girlfriend could be in trouble, too?" Molly asked.

"If anyone thinks she has information about who Birge hung out with, she might be the next target," Kujo added.

"Taz is back from assignment. I'll put him on her. He can provide the protection she might need, and also question her when she's able to answer. Whatever he finds out, I'll pass on to you.

"Good."

"In the meantime," Hank continued, "hang tight until we know something."

Kujo nodded. "Will do."

"Out, here," Hank said.

"Out, here." Kujo ended the call and lowered the phone. "We need to know as much about Tanner Birge as we can find out." He paced to the end of the room and back. "Who are his friends? Where do they hang out, and what he might have stored in his apartment?"

Molly shook her head. "I can't believe he moved on Daisy so quickly. Poor Daisy." She stared across the floor at Kujo. "I bet he was so mad he nearly hit the roof when he found his stuff outside her apartment and the door locks changed." Her eyes widened and a grin spread across her face. "I know where we might get some information on him."

"Yeah? Where?"

"His laptop."

"I'm sure the sheriff's deputies and crime scene investigators have confiscated his laptop by now, since he had all his belongings in his truck."

Molly's grin widened. "Not all of his things were in his truck. His laptop is in Daisy's Jeep." Molly strode to the closet, pulled out a long-sleeved black turtleneck shirt and tossed it on the bed.

"Why would it be in her car?"

"She didn't want him to have a reason to enter her apartment again. She was going to give it to him one day when he was in town and being reasonable." Molly pulled her shirt up over her head and tossed it beside the black one.

Kujo's heart flipped, and his groin tightened. He stood like a statue, all the blood in his head, rushing to his dick. "Uh..." he cleared his throat, "Don't you think we should go get the laptop?"

She laughed. "That's what I'm doing. Don't you have dark clothing you can wear? It's dark out, now. We don't want anyone to see us, do we?"

Kujo's cheeks heated, and he pulled his brain out of his pants. "Right." He dug in his duffel bag for a long-sleeved black T-shirt he'd purchased at the feed store and stripped out of the blue chambray shirt he'd worn all day.

When he glanced across at Molly, she stood with her

lips parted, her gaze traveling over his chest and downward to the waistband of his jeans.

"Like what you see?" he joked, his smile fading as he studied her in her bra and jeans. "Because I sure as hell like what I see."

He closed the distance between them and took her hands in his. "We could wait for it to get darker, and for the streets to empty before we hunt for Birge's laptop." He raised her hands and laid them on his chest. "You're not resisting. I'll take that as a good sign you won't coldcock me for doing this." He bent and brushed his lips across hers.

Molly pressed her hands to his chest, her fingers curling into his skin, her nails digging into the flesh.

Sweet Jesus, he couldn't let go of her. The laptop would wait while Kujo drank his fill of the beautiful FBI agent.

He slipped his hands down her naked back, careful of her cuts and bruises, stopping at the stiff cotton of her denim jeans.

Molly lowered one of her hands to his and guided his fingers beneath the waistband of her pants and panties.

Kujo's cock strained against the confines of his zipper. He wanted to toss Molly over his shoulder and carry her to the bed where he'd plunge deep inside her.

Instead, he skimmed the line of her lips until she opened to him on a sigh.

Go slowly. A woman didn't want a man pawing her. Besides, he wanted her as hot and ready for him as he was for her.

He thrust his tongue between her teeth and caressed her in a warm, wet slide. With his hands, he cupped her ass and kneaded the flesh, loving how her muscles flexed and released.

She wrapped her calf around the back of his leg, and pulled herself closer until her sex rubbed against his thigh, with only the layers of denim in the way.

Molly slipped her hand between them, flicked the button on his jeans and eased the zipper down.

Immediately, his cock sprang free, nudging the backs of her knuckles.

She captured him in her grip, holding him firmly, her slim hands making him even harder than steel.

Molly looked up into his eyes. "I don't need foreplay this time. I want you now. Inside me, don't pass GO, don't think you have to get me there. Trust me...I'm so hot, I think I'll spontaneously combust if we don't do it now."

"Damn, Molly. If you're not ready..."

"What did I just say?" She pushed his jeans over his hips and down his legs.

He toed off his boots and stepped out of them and his pants.

She stared at him, her gaze traveling from his chest down his abs to stop at his jutting erection. Her eyes flared, and her tongue swept across her bottom lip. "What are you waiting for?"

"First things first." Kujo lunged for his wallet in the back pocket of his jeans, scrounged for the condom packet he always kept there and held it up, relief flooding through him. He tossed it on the nightstand.

Then he scooped her in his arms, fused her lips with his in a scorching kiss and then laid her on the mattress.

He pulled her legs over the edge of the bed, stripped off her jeans and panties, parted her thighs and stepped between them. "I'll show you romance." He bent over her, nudging her entrance with his cock. But he wasn't going for the gold yet. Despite her words to the contrary, he wanted her to orgasm before him.

Kujo reached behind her, unclipped her bra and slid the straps from her shoulders. He cupped her breasts in his palms and gently squeezed them. Then he captured one perky nubbin with his lips. Sucking gently, he pulled it into his mouth, tongued the nipple and rolled it between his teeth.

She arched her back off the mattress. "I want you, now," she moaned.

He rolled his face to the side and gasped. "Patience, I'm not ready."

"The hell you aren't. I saw the evidence," she protested. "Please…"

Ignoring her entreaty, he moved his mouth to claim the other breast, flicking her nipple with his tongue and rolling the tip between his teeth. When she was squirming beneath him, he moved down her torso, tonguing and kissing a gentle path over each rib to her bellybutton and lower to the tuft of hair covering her sex.

She weaved her fingers into his hair and urged him even lower. "Now that you've started along this path…*finish*." She widened her legs.

Kujo traced a finger down her center, over her clit to

her damp entrance, where he swirled in her juices. A large, work-roughened finger poked inside her, then another and another, until he stretched her opening and pushed inside.

Molly moaned, her bottom twisting against the comforter, her fingers tightening their hold on his hair.

Kujo parted her folds with his thumbs and blew a stream of air across her nubbin.

"Oh, sweet heaven, do me already," she cried.

Kujo chuckled. "As you wish." He flicked his tongue against her clitoris.

Molly's back rose off the bed, and her fingernails dug into his scalp. "Again!" she begged.

He obliged. This time he dragged his tongue across that strip of nerve-packed flesh, swirled and ended on a flick.

Molly lifted her knees. "Joe, this is absolute torture."

He lifted his head. "Do you want me to stop?"

"Hell, no!"

Knowing he had her where he wanted her, he bent to the task of taking her over the top by tonguing, nibbling and sucking on her until she bucked beneath him, her body stiffening to the point she stopped breathing altogether. She raised her hips even closer to his mouth, her body trembling with her orgasm.

Kujo didn't stop until Molly lowered her bottom to the bed and tugged his hair.

He moved upward, repeating his downward journey in the opposite direction, kissing her torso, nibbling her nipples and finally claiming her lips.

Molly wrapped toned legs around his waist and locked her heels behind him.

He slipped an arm beneath her back, lifted her up onto the bed and lay down between her legs. "Say no now and I'll back away."

She lifted her head. "Are you kidding me?"

He laughed. "I didn't say it would be easy, but I wanted to give you the chance to stop."

"Don't be a tease. I want it all." She tightened her legs around him and pulled herself up to where his cock pressed against her pussy.

"Okay, okay." He unwrapped her legs from around him and pressed her head against the pillow with a long, soul-defining kiss. He leaned away from her, grabbed the foil packet and tore it open.

Impatient fingers took the condom from him and slipped it over his cock. At the base, she paused long enough to fondle his balls, squeezed him, and then guided him to her entrance. "Now, don't tease me anymore." She swirled the tip of his dick in her moisture. "I'm ready for whatever you've got. The harder and faster, the better."

With permission granted, Kujo let loose, driving into her like a sword into its scabbard—hard, deep and sure. He didn't stop until he was buried to the hilt, his balls slapping her buttocks. Once inside, he stopped, allowing her to adjust to his thickness and to allow him to remember how to breathe.

Then he settled into a slow, steady rhythm, pulling out, thrusting in, coating his shaft in her juices and enjoying the tightness of her grip on him.

She dropped her feet to the mattress. Each time he pulled out, she rose, digging her heels into the mattress, following him. When he pressed back inside, she met him at the end of each thrust.

His tension increased and, with it, his speed, until he hammered in and out of her, moving faster and faster.

Molly sank her fingers into his ass, clutching him, guiding him to slam even harder until he rocketed to the edge and over, his orgasm sending him into the stratosphere. He dropped down on her, holding himself just above her, his cock buried deep, his breathing as ragged as a marathon runner's pushing through to the finish.

He could have stayed there forever, but if he lowered himself more, his weight would crush the air from her lungs and add pain to her already bruised ribs. Kujo rolled to his side, taking her with him. He lay there for a long time, strumming his fingers from the swell of her breasts, down the curve of her waist to the flare of her hips and back.

Molly lay back against the pillow and raised an arm over her head. "Wow."

"Agreed," Kujo said. "If I had it in me, I'd say let's do that again. Now."

"I've never felt anything as intense," she whispered into the air. "Ever."

"Nor have I," he said, and meant it. None of the women he'd slept with in the past had brought him that close to heaven before "We have to do that again."

Molly nodded. "Damn right." She lay for a long time, one hand tangled in his hair.

The last thing Kujo wanted to do was leave the bed, but duty called. He leaned up on his elbow and stared down into her eyes. "Well?"

She nodded. "It's that time, isn't it?"

He nodded. "Let's go find a laptop." He kissed her hard, thrusting his tongue into her mouth.

She wrapped her arm around his neck and kissed him back, coming up for air at the same time.

His cock thickened, but he couldn't put off what they had to do any longer, and he didn't have another condom. He rolled to the edge of the bed, disposed of the condom and pushed to his feet. Grabbing his jeans, he jammed his legs into them, before he changed his mind and made love to Molly again.

She rolled out of the bed and stood before him naked, more beautiful than he could have imagined, her auburn hair cascading around her shoulders in a shiny mass.

He gripped her arms and gazed into her eyes. "This isn't over by a long shot. You know that, right?"

She grinned up at him. "I certainly hope not. If we didn't have a job to do, I'd have gone for another round."

Kujo laughed, feeling lighter and happier than he had in what seemed like forever. He slapped her bare bottom and squeezed it. "Get dressed, or I might throw you back on the bed before we get out the door."

She found her jeans across the room and slipped her legs into them. "Promises, promises."

He couldn't stop looking as she put on her bra and the black turtleneck shirt.

Kujo dressed in dark clothing and found the dark

knit hat he'd purchased in the store, pulling it down over his ears.

When he faced Molly, he was amazed at the transformation. From naked siren to sexy alley cat, she was as stunning in her stealth clothes as she was without. He pulled her into his arms and kissed her again. "Ready?"

Molly smirked. "For what? To strip naked and climb back in the bed with you?" She nodded. "To go sneak into a woman's car for a laptop that might point to the leader of the ISIS training effort in the area?" She shrugged. "Sure. Let's do this." She glanced down at Six. "What about our friend?"

Kujo gazed at the animal that had lain quietly in a corner during their sexual encounter. The dog had manners. "He can come. He's dark enough he won't be easily seen in the shadows. But first, we need to locate Daisy's Jeep."

"It's probably at the diner since she was at work when the explosion happened." Molly reached for his hand and held it in hers. "Or it could still be parked at her apartment, depending on how close it is to her job."

Kujo liked that she'd reached for his hand and reveled in the warmth of hers. He wanted more of her than just her hand. He wanted her mind, her body and her heart.

Oh, hell, where was he going with this infatuation? They barely knew each other. He had to stay focused on the task at hand. He could sort through his feelings after they found the source of the terrorist training effort. "Any idea where Daisy lives?"

"No, but I bet I know someone who does." She led him downstairs to the dining room where Mrs. K was listening intently to the conversations going on with the police band radio.

"Mrs. K, I'd like to run by Daisy's apartment building and let the manager know what's going on with Daisy. Do you know where she lives?"

Mrs. K jumped up and turned down the scanner. "She lives in the apartment building two blocks south of the diner." The B&B owner's brows furrowed. "Is there anything I can do to help?"

"Pray." Molly said and hurried out the door, dragging Kujo behind her and with Six bringing up the rear.

Once outside, Molly paused.

"Walk or drive?" Kujo asked.

"Walk. If anyone else has the same idea and knows where that laptop is, we could have some competition."

CHAPTER 14

Molly chose to remain in the shadows as they passed from house to house via back alleys to within view of the diner. If someone else was after the laptop, she wanted to see them, not the other way around. If they managed to get to the laptop first, she didn't want anyone tracing it back to her and Kujo. That would put them at risk until they learned whether or not there was any information worth hacking off the machine.

The fire department had long since rolled up their hoses and driven away. A sheriff's deputy's patrol car stood guard on the street in front of the diner. The state crime lab would be there the next day to sift through the rubble to determine the source of the explosion, even though the fire chief had given his findings. The state crime lab folks might be able to trace the parts and pieces back to the source. Molly doubted it.

"I don't see a Jeep. Daisy said she put his laptop in her Jeep."

"If it suffered any damage, the sheriff could have had it towed to an impound lot."

"In this small of a town?" Molly shook her head. "I would think everything would have to remain in place until the crime lab arrives. Let's check her apartment."

They slipped away, traveling through a back alley the two blocks away from the diner to the apartment complex Mrs. K had indicated. In the parking lot was an older-model Jeep with a daisy flower decal on the back windshield.

Kujo chuckled. "Could she have made it easier to identify?"

Six sat at Kujo's feet, looking up at him, waiting for a command.

They stood near bushes. The moon shone down from overhead, casting a bright glow over the parking lot and Daisy's Jeep. They'd have to step out into the open to reach the vehicle.

"I'll go." Molly pulled her stocking cap down over her face and tucked her hair beneath it.

"No, I should go," Kujo insisted.

"Is your gun loaded?" Molly asked.

"Yes, of course, it is."

"Then stay here and provide cover."

He shook his head. "I should go, and you should provide cover."

"Six responds to you. If you go, he might follow."

"Six will do as I tell him." Kujo's jaw firmed in the limited lighting.

"Look, this is my job. Let me do it."

"I don't know where in the FBI training manual it

says breaking into a vehicle is part of your job description."

She pulled what appeared to be a long flat file out of her sleeve and held it up. "I won't be breaking anything. But I know how to use it, and you don't." Molly grinned. "Now, stay with Six while I do what we came here for."

Kujo didn't appear to like it, but he stood stoically in the shadows and drew his weapon from the holster beneath his jacket. "Okay, but don't be long. If you don't get it open on the first couple of tries, come back."

"I'll get in," she promised.

Just as Molly was about to step out of the shadows into the light, a hand caught her arm and yanked her back hard against a wall of muscles.

"What the—" she started.

Kujo's hand clamped over her mouth, and he whispered in her ear. "Shh. Watch." He dropped his hand from her mouth and motioned to the dog.

Molly held perfectly still and scanned the parking lot and apartment building. A movement alerted her to the fact they were not alone.

A dark figure detached itself from the shrubbery on the far end of the lot and hurried toward the apartment building and up the stairs to one of the doors. A light shined down on the figure. Like Molly and Kujo, the figure was covered in dark clothing, with the addition of a ski mask. He tried the door, but it wouldn't open. Then he cocked his leg and kicked the door. The sound echoed against the walls of the other units, but no one came out to investigate.

Again, the burglar kicked the door. The sharp crack

of wood splitting could be heard all the way out to where Molly and Kujo hunkered in the shadows.

"We have to get to the Jeep before he discovers the laptop isn't in the apartment," Molly whispered.

The intruder disappeared into Daisy's unit.

"What if he has a sidekick covering his back?" Kujo asked.

Molly shook her head. "It's a risk we have to take. "I'll stay low and use the Jeep for cover." She didn't wait for his response. Molly ducked low and ran for the Jeep. She didn't slow until she reached the passenger door, where she paused to catch her breath and will her pulse to slow.

When she had her heart rate under control, she raised her hand, slipped the flat file between the window and the door and slid it down inside the panel. Moving it closer to the door lock, she raised it slowly, searching for the mechanism. She engaged nothing but air. Pushing the file back down, she moved it over a little and tried again. As she pulled it up, she glanced toward Daisy's apartment door.

The file engaged with metal. As she dragged it upward, the lock disengaged. Her heartbeat speeding, she glanced up again to reassure herself no one was coming down the stairs.

Then she lifted the handle on the door and opened it. As soon as she did, the overhead light blinked on.

Damn. She'd forgotten about the automatic lights. Too late, she didn't have time to find the switch to turn it off. Molly checked the front seat and floorboard, without finding a computer or case.

She hit the lock mechanism, unlocking all the doors and closed the front door softly. The overhead light blinked out. Molly glanced at the apartment. Again, no one had emerged. Moving to the back door, she eased it open. Again, the light clicked on.

There, on the back floorboard was a black case the size that would fit a laptop. She lifted it. It was heavy enough to be a laptop. Taking the time to check, she looked over the top of the back seat into the back of the vehicle. It was empty, as was the rest of the back seat.

Molly slipped out of the vehicle and carefully closed the door. The light blinked out. A movement out of the corner of her eye caught her attention. Someone emerged from Daisy's apartment and ran down the stairs.

Sure the intruder hadn't spotted her in the moon shadow of the Jeep, Molly lay flat and rolled beneath the vehicle, clutching the laptop to her chest. She lay still, holding her breath. Footsteps sounded across the gravel and stopped beside her, within two feet of where she lay.

She prayed Kujo didn't get trigger-happy and start shooting. If the person were looking for the laptop in Daisy's Jeep, he'd have easy access with the doors unlocked. He wouldn't find anything inside, and he would go away, none the wiser of the woman who hid beneath the chassis.

The moon had risen higher in the sky, beaming down on the gravel parking lot. It glinted off something shiny near to where Molly hid.

Damn! Her heart stopped and shuddered, and then

beat a thousand beats a second. The file she'd used to trigger the lock lay within inches of her face. If the intruder bothered to look down, he'd see it. If he bent to pick it up, he'd see her lying beneath the vehicle.

A vehicle drove by the apartment building. The man turned toward it, his feet pointing away from the Jeep and the file.

Molly reached out, grabbed the file and pulled it to her chest. The file bumped against the under carriage making a clanking sound. Molly froze.

The feet spun toward her again.

A light shone into the parking lot. Her intruder ducked down low enough, Molly could see his knees. She closed her eyelids to keep him from seeing the whites of her eyes and waited for the next move. A scuffle of gravel indicated someone was moving away.

Molly opened her eyes and watched the intruder running for the bushes close to where Kujo and Six waited for her.

Holy hell. Molly slid the laptop and file off her chest, pulled the H&K pistol from the holster beneath her jacket and aimed at the man's back. If he tried to hurt Kujo or Six, she'd take him down without hesitation.

The bushes parted, and the man disappeared.

A woman and a man got out of a car nearby, talking about their visit to his mother's house and plans for the following day. They entered one of the ground-floor apartments, and the world returned to silence.

Molly lay for a long moment, waiting for the reassuring sound of crickets chirping.

When she was certain no one else was moving

about, she started to roll from beneath the Jeep only to find a nose poking beneath the side, sniffing.

Six.

Behind him, Kujo squatted beside the vehicle. "Are you all right?" he asked.

"I'm fine. Are you?" Molly handed him the file and the case with the laptop, and rolled clear of the Jeep. "I was afraid you'd shoot that man," Molly said, her voice shaking slightly.

"I almost did. I was afraid he was going to shoot you. He had a gun in his hand."

Molly shook her head. "I couldn't see that, or I might have shot him when he ran toward you."

Kujo pulled her into his arms. "We're a pair. It's a good thing we didn't pull the triggers."

She leaned into him for a moment, enjoying his strength and outdoorsy scent. Finally, she pulled away. "We have to see what's in this."

"You know we're tampering with evidence, don't you?"

"Yes, but if we get in and figure out what's on there, we can get it back into her car before anyone knows it was ever missing."

"Let's get it to Hank." Kujo grinned. "He's got people."

"We can also get Daisy's permission to enter her vehicle, if she's conscious. After being blown up, I'm positive she'll give it." Molly led the way back to the B&B where Kujo had parked his truck earlier that day.

Six jumped into the back seat.

Kujo drove, and Molly sat back in the passenger seat,

thinking through all that had happened in less than twenty-four hours and all that could happen in the next twenty-four.

Hopefully, the laptop would give them the information they needed to locate the ringleader of the ISIS training camp.

Kujo phoned Hank as soon as he got into the truck, giving him the heads-up about the apartment break-in and the computer they'd confiscated. "We'll need a computer guru, ASAP."

"Got it," Hank said. "And I'll let the sheriff know about the break-in."

"Good," Kujo said. "Have you heard from Taz? Is Daisy conscious?"

"I have, and she was. She's given her statement to the sheriff, but it won't help. She didn't see anything. Al, the owner, is in critical condition. He suffered a heart attack along with the injuries due to the explosion."

Kujo's lips pressed together. "Text Taz's number to me. We need to talk to Daisy."

"Texting now."

"Thanks." Kujo ended the call as a ping sounded on his cell phone. He slowed near the edge of town and pulled to the side of the road to read the message.

"What's going on?" Molly asked.

"Daisy's awake."

"Do we need to drive to Bozeman to interview her?"

"I think Taz can handle it." He placed the call.

Taz answered on the first ring. "Yeah."

"This is Kujo, one of Hank's new guys."

"Oh, hi. Welcome to the team. What can I do for you?"

"Is Daisy awake?" he asked. "I need to ask her some questions."

"The sheriff's been in and questioned her, but she didn't see anything."

"I know. I have some different questions to ask her."

"I'll check." Taz paused. A few moments later, he came back online. "She's awake. I have you on speaker."

Kujo handed the phone to Molly.

"Hi, Daisy, it's Molly from this morning. How are you feeling?" Molly asked.

"I've been better," she said, her voice sounding small. "The doctor says I can go home tomorrow."

"You might want to stay with family until you're back to one-hundred percent," Molly warned her.

"I will," Daisy agreed.

"Daisy, I work with the FBI."

"Seriously? You're being here…was it a coincidence?"

"No, Daisy. I've been conducting an investigation. I'm really sorry you got caught up in all of this. I had no idea where my investigation was leading."

"It's not your fault. My ex…" she paused to take a deep breath, "what he did… I still can't believe it. My poor boss…" She cleared her throat. "How can I help?"

"Daisy, you said you had Tanner's computer in your Jeep. We think we might get information off of it that can help us find any others who might have helped him with the explosives. Will you give me permission to get that computer out of your vehicle?"

"Sure. Help yourself. From what they told me, Tanner's on the run from the law. He won't be using it." Daisy's voice shook as she finished the statement.

"I'm sorry about what happened with Tanner." Molly said. "I'm sure it must hurt."

"I shouldn't be sad. The man tried to kill me." Daisy sniffed and began to cry. "And to think, I would have married him, if everything hadn't gone to hell."

"I understand." Molly waited for the sobs to slow. "Daisy, one other thing. Do you know the password for Tanner's computer?"

"I don't…wait…I think it's my birthday." She gave Molly the month, day and year. "If you need anything else, just ask. I hate to think someone else helped him. Al's in the ICU, and they say he might not make it."

"I'll keep Al in my prayers. Now you worry about getting well. We'll let you know what we find, if we do find anything." Molly handed the phone to Kujo.

"Hi, Daisy. Let me speak with Taz." He waited a moment and then asked, "Taz, everything going okay there?"

"All's well. I won't let anyone get past me to Daisy."

Kujo ended the call and put the truck in motion. Minutes later, they pulled up to Hank's house on the ranch.

Hank stepped out on the porch, wearing a T-shirt and sweats. "Swede's my tech guru. He's on his way. He and Allie were at the Blue Moose Tavern when I called.

They should be here momentarily." He grinned and nodded his head toward the drive.

Kujo turned to see lights coming toward them.

"That will be them."

A truck pulled up beside Kujo's, and the tall blond man Kujo had met before stepped out and rounded to help an auburn-haired woman down, but she'd beat him to it and let herself out, dropping to the ground. She took Swede's hand and joined Hank, Kujo and Molly.

"Hi, I'm Allie, Hanks's sister." She smiled and held out her hand.

Molly shook her hand. "Nice to meet you. I'm Molly."

"Joe Kuntz." Kujo held out his hand. "Call me Kujo."

Allie shook it, her brows raised. "Should I be afraid of your bite?"

Hank laughed. "Kuntz…Joe. Ku…Jo."

Allie nodded. "I get it. Nice to meet you. And this is?" She went down on her haunches to pet Six.

"Six," Kujo said.

She looked up. "That's his name?"

"It's the last number on his tattoo," Kujo explained and turned to Swede. "Need your help hacking into this." He held up the computer case.

"Let's do this inside." Hank held open the door.

Swede took the laptop case and followed Hank inside.

Molly gave him Daisy's birthdate. While Swede opened the computer and entered several combinations of Daisy's birthday numbers, Molly and Kujo filled

Hank in on the details of what had happened at Daisy's apartment.

"Apparently, someone is worried about the information on Tanner Birge's laptop," Kujo said.

"Daisy said Tanner's been working out at Pinion Ranch," Molly said. "Can you show me where that is on a map?"

Hank's brows furrowed. "Pinion Ranch butts up against the National Forest and the Crazy Mountains."

He led them into another part of the house and a large office with a huge mahogany desk in the middle. In the far corner of the office was a storage cabinet with wide, shallow drawers. Hank pulled one out, pushed it back in and slid out another. He lifted a huge square map from the drawer. "I got copies of all the survey maps available in the area around Oak Creek Ranch, my current home, and Bear Creek Ranch, my family's home. The Pinion Ranch borders Bear Creek on the southern border."

He pointed to the map. "On its eastern border is the highway, and the western edge backs up to the national forest." Hank hurried back to a drafting table and returned with a crumpled contour map.

"I recognize that map." Molly stepped forward and helped Hank flatten it. "This was the map I was using to search the surrounding areas."

"You were really close to the Pinion Ranch when you were flying your drone."

"Were you able to recover the footage on the drone's camera?" Kujo asked.

"Sadly, no," Hank shook his head. "The bullet hit the video storage device."

Molly sighed. "I still have to explain that one to my supervisor."

"Already have. He's more worried about having sent you here without a partner. I assured him we've got you covered."

Molly's cheeks bloomed with color. "I appreciate that."

Kujo's body warmed at the words. She was covered all right. He wondered what his new boss would think about just how well-covered Molly was. He changed the subject. "Did you get anything from the nomenclature on the board?"

"I hadn't before dinner. I sent it off to a friend of mine in procurement at the Pentagon earlier today." Hank turned to a computer monitor on a desk against the wall and wiggled the mouse. The black screen flooded with color. He clicked a few keys and brought up his email.

After scrolling through a couple screens, he stopped. "Wait. He responded." Hank leaned closer, his brows lowering. "Huh. Apparently, that box was a crate of M4A1 rifles that went missing from a warehouse near Ft. Drum, NY. They conducted an investigation of the warehouse employees. One went missing before they could interview him. He was found dead a couple days later."

"So, we might be dealing with some illegally acquired military weapons appropriated by people who aren't afraid to kill to keep anyone from spilling the beans," Kujo summarized.

Hank stood and faced Kujo and Molly. "Based on the sniper activity around Tanner Birge's arrest, I'd say the same type of people are at work here. Anxious to keep their secrets."

Molly nodded. "What can we do now?"

"Until Swede finds more information on that computer, not much."

"We need to look everywhere Tanner Birge has been. I want to get boots on the ground on Pinion Ranch," Molly said. "I'd say let's go tonight, but we wouldn't see much in the dark." Her gaze shot to Kujo. "Tomorrow? We can be there early in the morning."

He shook his head. "If it's truly a terrorist training camp, they will be on guard and watching for intruders. If they're planning anything soon, security will be even tighter. Especially if one of their trainees has gone rogue."

Hank nodded. "I can gather four or five members of the Brotherhood Protectors team, and we can stage a recon mission into the ranch."

"How soon?" Kujo asked.

Hank glanced at his watch. "Tomorrow." He held up his hand. "Depending on what we find on that computer, if anything."

Kujo nodded. "I like the plan."

Molly frowned. "You are including me on this mission onto the ranch, right?"

Hank glanced across Molly to Kujo.

Kujo tilted his head. "She's the reason we're even contemplating it. I say she's in."

"I'll gather the equipment we'll need," Hank said. "Be here at O-five-hundred in the morning. We'll need to brief the team regarding the communications devices and protocol for the mission."

Kujo's pulse hummed in anticipation. This was the kind of work he'd been trained for, the type of job he was good at. Though he'd included Molly, he wasn't sure she had as much cover and concealment training and tactical experience as the rest of Hank's team. Lack of training and experience got people killed. He'd talk to her on their way back to the B&B. Maybe he could talk her out of going.

Ha. Fat chance. The woman had a stubborn streak almost as long as his.

"In the meantime, you better get some rest." Hank glanced around at Molly. "You two are welcome to stay here for the night since you'll need to be here at the crack of dawn."

Molly shook her head. "No, thanks. We can be here that early." She didn't meet Kujo's gaze, and her face flushed pink.

Could it be she wanted to be alone with him through the night to pick up where they'd left off?

Kujo's groin tightened. "We'll be here at O-five-hundred. If you find anything tonight, call. We'll be available at a moment's notice."

Molly nodded.

They left Hank's office and passed Swede banging

away on the keyboard of the laptop. He didn't even glance up when Kujo and Molly walked by.

Allie lay on the couch nearby, her feet tucked beneath a blanket. "Hope to see you two soon," she said.

"Are you staying the night?" Molly asked.

"I haven't decided. I might leave him here. I have animals to take care of on Bear Creek Ranch in the morning. Dad can't do it all himself, anymore. We'd love it if you stopped by sometime. The gate's always open to friends of Hank's."

Hank held the door for Molly and Kujo. Six trotted out and went straight to Kujo's truck where he sat and waited for his master.

The trip back to the B&B passed in silence, Kujo thinking about what they'd learned, and the night ahead, potentially spent holding Molly in his arms. God, he hoped she was thinking along the same lines, or he'd spend a long time in a cold shower.

CHAPTER 15

Molly was first in the door at the B&B. Her heart raced, pounding an irregular beat against her ribs. She and Kujo had already had sex once. It wasn't as if it was an all-new experience for her.

Then why did she feel like a teen on her first date?

Kujo held the door for her but didn't follow her inside. "I'm going to exercise Six for a few minutes. I'll be in shortly."

Molly's excited heart slipped like a hunk of lead into her belly. She schooled her face to an indifferent mask in an attempt to hide her disappointment.

"Yeah. Sure." She nodded. "He's been patient with all of our running around all day. I'm sure he could use some exercise. I'll just go up." God, she sounded pathetic.

"We won't be long." Kujo caught her hand and tugged gently, pulling her up against him. "I promise." Then he pressed his lips to hers in a warm, hard kiss, before he let go.

Molly spun away, her cheeks flushed, her body on fire. All due to one single, tongue-less kiss. She might have burst into flames if he'd done more. She skipped up the stairs, a sense of joy in her heart and anticipation sending electrical impulses across her nerve endings.

She slipped into the shower for a quick rinse, rubbed soft-scented lotion on her body and scrounged through her suitcase for a pretty nightgown, remembering at the last minute she'd only brought T-shirts and shorts to sleep in. She'd planned a mission, not a seduction.

With a sigh, she pulled a soft gray T-shirt over her head. It hung down past her thighs, covering everything that needed covering, including the fact she hadn't put on any panties.

She creamed at her own naughtiness and couldn't wait for Kujo to discover her secret.

She glanced at the clock. Eight minutes had passed and still no Kujo. Molly bit her bottom lip. Should she go look for him? What if someone had come after him? What if he and Six were lying in the street bleeding out?

Molly jumped into a pair of jeans, tugged on her boots and ran for the door. As she reached for it, the handle twisted, and Kujo appeared with Six at his side, panting.

"Sorry, I didn't mean to keep you up. Six was more than happy for the exercise and didn't want to come back inside." Kujo stared down at her in her big T-shirt, jeans and boots. "Were you worried?"

"Of course, I was worried. After being shot at and having a cabin burn to the ground, I'm a little punchy. I thought maybe my bad luck had rubbed off on you and

Six." She let out a long breath and stepped aside, allowing them to enter the room.

Kujo's mere presence made the room seem smaller. His broad shoulders filled the space and stole the air. Suddenly, Molly couldn't breathe. Her body quickened at his nearness, and her sex grew damp in expectation of what could come.

Six weaved his way through their legs and flopped onto the wooden floor.

Kujo stepped across the threshold, closed the door behind him. He laid his weapon on the dresser.

Molly handed over her pistol.

Kujo laid it beside his. Then he took Molly into his arms and kissed her.

Molly melted into his embrace, her body pressing against his. She curled her hands around his neck and pulled him closer, opening her mouth to his insistent tongue. For a long moment, they stood frozen in that kiss, tongues caressing, hearts beating in sync.

When at last Kujo lifted his head, Molly remembered to breathe. But not for long.

Kujo scooped her up and strode for the bed.

"Don't trip on Six," Molly warned.

The dog saw them coming and moved out of the way.

Kujo set Molly on her feet, instead of the bed, ran his hands down her arms and grabbed the hem of her shirt, tugging it up her torso.

She raised her arms over her head and gazed into his eyes until he pulled the shirt over her head and tossed it onto a chair.

His lips curved into a smile when he saw she wasn't wearing a bra. He cupped her breasts in his palms. "Beautiful."

Molly laughed, her breath catching. "I'm up here," she joked.

Kujo raised his gaze to hers, and he gave her a slow, heart-stopping smile. "Yes, indeed, you are." He dragged her against him and kissed her, melding his mouth to hers. He gently ran his hands down her naked back, avoiding her injuries, and slipped his fingers beneath the waistband of her jeans.

The urgency of her need made her push him away.

He frowned down at her. "What's wrong?"

"You're wearing too many clothes. I'm wearing too many clothes, and we're wasting time." She pulled his shirt up over his body, admiring the defined muscles of his torso. Maybe she stared a little too long. He took over, ripping the garment over his head and dropping it to the floor.

"You're right. Too many clothes between us." His voice was a low, sexy growl. He stared up at her hungrily as he knelt to remove her boots and unbutton her jeans. Then he slid the denim over her hips and down her legs, taking his sweet time, as he touched her, brushing his knuckles across her skin, torturing as he descended to her ankles.

Once she was completely naked, he stood and Molly took control. She flicked the button loose on his jeans.

Kujo toed off his boots.

Hooking her thumbs into the waistband of his jeans, Molly dragged them down his thighs. She dropped to her knees to ease the fabric all the way down to his ankles.

Kujo stepped out of the jeans and kicked them to the side. He gripped her arms and attempted to pull her to her feet.

Molly shook her head, refusing to come up. Her eyes were on the prize.

She wrapped her hand around his engorged cock, amazed at how hard, long and thick he was. "Damn, Kujo, you're a freakin' stud."

He laughed out loud. "You do that to me."

Molly flicked her tongue across the velvety smooth head.

His shaft jerked in response and, a droplet of come emerged. "I'm not sure I have another condom," he said through tight lips. "But I'm clean of STDs."

"And I'm on the pill. So, what's the problem?" Molly took his dick in her mouth, clutched his tight ass in both hands, and sucked him in until he hit the back of her throat.

Kujo caressed the top of her head, weaving his fingers into her hair. "Keep that up and I won't last long."

Molly leaned back, letting his shaft slide all the way out of her, her hand replacing her mouth around him. "I take it you like that."

"You have no idea."

She squeezed him gently. "I think I have an idea." Then she took him into her mouth again, flicking the tip and gliding her tongue around the ridge.

Kujo fisted his hand in her hair and held her head as he thrust into her mouth.

Molly dug her fingernails into his buttocks and forced him deeper. His firm, velvety thickness in her mouth made her want him inside her, or at least touching her aching entrance.

"Much as I love what you're doing, I want to touch you, too." Kujo pulled out of her mouth, scooped her off the floor and laid her on the bed.

When he climbed onto the bed, she moved toward the center

"I wasn't finished," she complained.

"And I haven't started." He straddled her head with his knees and bent over her body to part her folds with his thumbs. "Now, we're on equal footing."

"Mmm." She sucked his cock into her mouth as he came down on her and licked her clitoris, sending her into waves of ecstasy. She raised her knees, planted her heels in the mattress and rose to meet his glorious tongue.

While she sucked him, he flicked her nubbin until she was squirming beneath him, her body stiffening until that excruciatingly moment when she exploded into an orgasm that rocked her world.

Kujo continued the attack until Molly had wrung every last little bit of sensation out of her release. But it wasn't enough. She had to have him inside her, down there, filling that empty space so exquisitely sensitive after he'd brought her to the brink of sanity and back.

Molly pushed him away, forcing him to lie on his back. "My turn to do the work."

"I thought you were."

"Baby, I've only just begun." She climbed on top of him, straddled his hips and positioned her entrance over the tip of his cock. "Are you ready?" She lowered herself just enough to wet the tip of his shaft.

"Yes!" He raised his hips, dipping in.

Molly came down on him and rose back up. She repeated the motion, moving faster and faster.

Kujo gripped her hips and brought her down harder as he thrust upward. Then he lifted her off him and set her on the bed beside him.

She frowned. "But you weren't there, yet."

"I want to go deeper, harder and faster."

Her pussy creamed, and she smiled. "I'm all for it."

"Good." He rose on his knees and flipped her onto her stomach.

Molly hadn't expected the movement, but understood when he gripped her hips and raised her bottom into the air.

Then he kneed her legs apart and settled on his behind her. He leaned over her back and cupped her breasts, squeezing gently. "I want to fuck you hard and fast. Any objections, tell me now."

His rich, rough tones slid over her like melted butter, sliding into every part of her being. "Please," she said and rose on her hands.

Kujo thrust into her. As good as his word, he fucked her hard and fast, again and again.

The friction and pounding sent Molly back up that peak, until she was teetering on the edge.

She dropped her chest to the mattress, freeing one of

her hands to touch herself. She flicked her own clit as Kujo filled her inside. The combination shot her over the top, and she climaxed, her body shaking with the intensity.

Kujo slammed into her once more and held her hips tight, his cock buried deeply inside her, throbbing with his release.

After many long moments, Kujo eased Molly onto her belly and rolled with her to his side, spooning her body, his cock still rock-hard within her. One of his hands circled around her, toying with her breast.

Molly lay nestled against him, her backside warmed by his front, their intimate connection incredibly reassuring. "Joe?" she whispered.

"Yeah, babe."

"Are you thinking about tomorrow?"

"I'm thinking about how beautiful you are, and how good you feel." He squeezed her breast and pinched the nipple between his thumb and fingers.

"Mmm," she murmured. She let her thoughts leave her for a moment, but they came back to haunt. "When we find the ISIS training camp, then what?"

"We bring in the big guns to close them down." Kujo leaned close and nibbled her ear. "Then we celebrate by doing this." He pumped into her with his still-hard cock.

She covered his hand with hers and pressed her bottom backward, taking more of his length. God, he felt good inside her. But she couldn't shake her dread of the future. "What about after we close them down? What then?" She hadn't asked him for commitment when they'd first made love. And she wouldn't ask him now.

"I'm sure Hank will assign me to another client."

"And I'll be on my way back to DC," she murmured.

His hand on her breast stilled for a long moment. Then he palmed her breast. "I hadn't thought that far ahead."

"I hadn't either, until now." What did she expect him to say? Did she want him to declare his undying love for her, after knowing her for so short a time? A dull ache grew in the pit of her belly. No. Love was too soon. And they wouldn't get the opportunity to find out.

Her throat thickened, and she swallowed hard before saying, "I need a glass of water. Can I get you anything while I'm downstairs?"

"I'll go," he said.

"No, please. I need to stretch my legs." She slipped from his arms, his cock sliding from her body. When she stood, she grabbed for her T-shirt, pulled it over her head, and jammed her legs into her jeans.

Kujo swung his legs over the side of the bed. "I'll come with you."

"No, please. I need some…space," she said.

He frowned. "Is it something I said? Because, if it was, I don't know what it could be. Please. Come back to bed, and I'll make it up to you, whatever it was that's made you unhappy."

She smiled at him, her eyes burning with tears she wouldn't let fall. To hide them from him, she turned away, pretending to search for her shoes. "No, no. I'm not mad, or anything. It's just that everything is moving so fast, and I just don't want to do anything I'll regret." She gave him a sideways smile. "I'll be right back."

She gave up on the shoes and headed for the door. As she passed Six, the dog rose from the floor to follow her.

"Six, stay," Kujo commanded.

The dog immediately lay on the floor between Kujo and Molly and rested his chin on his front paws, staring at Molly as she neared the door. Six rolled his eyes toward Kujo, his face seeming to plead with his master.

Molly would have laughed if she weren't already struggling to breathe past the tightness in her throat. "Oh, please, if he wants, I can take him out for one last time before we call it a night."

Kujo shrugged. "If you're sure he won't bother you."

"Not at all." Molly held the door open for the dog. "Six, come," she said with the same amount of force she'd heard from Kujo.

The dog remained where he was, his gaze darting from Molly back to Kujo.

Kujo nodded. "Six, go."

Six leaped to his feet and ran for the door, his butt and tail wiggling so fast he could barely stand still.

No matter how sad Molly felt, Six's happiness wouldn't let her be down for long. "You're a good boy, Six." She scratched behind his ears, cast a glance at his owner and sucked in a deep breath.

The man rose from the bed, naked, and so damned gorgeous, he brought more tears to Molly's eyes and heat throughout her body.

"I'll be back," she choked out, turned and ran down

the stairs barefooted, Six right behind her. She hurried out of the B&B into the chilly, night air, the concrete sidewalk cool against her toes.

Six bounded outside, ran for the nearest post and relieved himself.

Molly sucked in deep breaths, willing her pulse and her core temperature to calm. She stood for a long time until she shivered, her bare arms and feet reminding her of how cold the nights could be in the Crazy Mountains.

"Six, come," she called out.

Six immediately returned to her side, sat and stared up at her, his tongue lolling to one side, his eager gaze fixed on hers.

Molly opened the front door to the B&B and held it for Six to enter.

The dog leaped inside and turned looking at her for a moment.

Molly hesitated, suddenly nervous and shy about returning to the bedroom she'd share with the man who'd wrung the most intense orgasm out of her body ever.

She'd told him she needed space. Hell, what if he thought she wanted him to get lost? That was the last thing she wanted. If anything, she wanted to tell him she would give up everything to be with him. Even her job with the FBI, if only he wanted her as much as she wanted him.

Molly also knew that if she said anything like that, he'd run in the opposite direction as fast as his sexy legs would carry him. Nothing sent a man running faster than a declaration of love so soon after a woman met him.

Six stared at her, standing in the doorway.

"Yeah, I know. I'm completely irrational," she said aloud to the dog.

In response, Six emitted a low, threatening growl.

"What's wrong, Six?" Molly asked. A shiver trickled down her spine. She leaned toward the doorway when an arm snaked out and wrapped around her trunk, trapping her arms against her sides. A meaty hand clamped tightly over her mouth. She was yanked backward. The B&B door hinge, which hung on a spring, retracted, slamming the door shut, Six trapped inside, with a finality that made Molly's heart slip into her belly.

She tried to scream, but nothing more than a desperate murmur made it past the thick hand covering her mouth.

On the other side of the door, Six barked and scratched in an attempt to get to her.

Molly fought, kicked and wiggled, but the arm around her was strong. She stomped on the man's instep. He grunted and slammed an open palm against her temple, knocking the sense out of her head and sending her into a gray and black spinning vortex that sucked her into an ever-darkening hell.

CHAPTER 16

Kujo dressed in jeans and a T-shirt and pulled on his boots. He clipped the satellite phone onto his belt. If Molly wanted space, he could go for a walk with Six.

He paced the room several times, counting the minutes until Molly's return. How much space was enough? And how did that translate into time? Was she rethinking their microburst of a relationship? Did she regret making love with him? Shit, had she faked her orgasm just to get it over with?

He shook his head. *No way.* Her body had been as tense as his, and her tremors had appeared uncontrolled.

With a glance at his watch, he tucked his pistol into the waistband of his jeans and stared at the door, willing Molly to enter. Five minutes had passed since she'd left the room. As far as he was concerned, that was long enough. Kujo's hand was on the doorknob when Six started barking.

Kujo's heart thudded against his ribs. He yanked open the door and ran to the head of the stairs.

Six was at the screen door, tearing at the mesh with his paws, frantically trying to break through to get outside.

By the time Kujo made it to the bottom of the staircase, Mrs. K had emerged in her bathrobe with her hair up in sponge curlers, blinking the sleep from her eyes. "What's going on? My Lord, why is Six destroying my door?"

He didn't respond, just powered past her, opened the door and ran outside.

Six shot ahead of him, racing down the street after the disappearing taillights of what appeared to be a truck turning onto Main Street.

Kujo could think of only one reason Six would be chasing the truck.

Molly.

Mrs. K came out of the B&B behind him.

As he ran to his truck, Kujo yelled, "Call 911. Molly's been abducted. She might be in a pickup. I'm going after her." He jumped into the driver's seat and cranked the engine. He was halfway down the street in seconds.

Six cut through a yard, leaped over a low bush and ran like the wind.

By the time Kujo reached the corner, the taillights were near the edge of town. Six ran down the middle of the street, losing ground on the disappearing truck.

Kujo raced after them. When he came alongside the slowing dog, he flung open his door and yelled. "Six, come!" The dog shot a glance toward him and then back at the truck, so far ahead. As if making up his mind, he slowed long enough to jump up into the truck, clambering over Kujo to the passenger seat. Once there, he sat forward, his gaze on the road in front of them, his tongue lolling from his mouth as he gasped for air.

Kujo closed his door and slammed his foot to the accelerator. He'd have to push it to catch the other vehicle. And he didn't know for certain Molly was in it. What he did know was Molly had been taken. He knew in his gut she wouldn't have gone walking alone, leaving Six in the house.

He switched off his headlights and focused on the taillights in front of him, doing his best to catch up to the truck and yet, not be seen. He pulled the satellite phone off his belt and hit the numbers for Hank.

Hank answered after the second ring. "Kujo, what's wrong?"

"Molly's been taken. I'm following a pickup I think she might be in. The B&B owner is putting a call through to 911. I might need help."

"I'm in the process of gathering the team. Which way are you headed?"

"East, into the Crazy Mountains." He told him the highway number and the direction. "I'm flying in stealth-mode with my lights out. I don't think he knows he's being followed.

"As I said, I was in the process of gathering the team, anyway, and I was about to call you," Hank said.

"Why?"

"Swede found a social media group Tanner Birge belonged to called TA for Take America. On the page, we found images of weapons, political statements against the current administration and more."

"That doesn't mean they're plotting a coup."

"No, but there were several passages that seemed to be encoded messages. I had Swede and Molly's boss, Pete, work on decoding. It didn't take long. Apparently, they're planning something big in the next couple of days. They put out a call to all their disciples, as they call themselves. And they end the messages in AA."

Kujo's blood ran cold. "Allah Akbar." The cry most jihadists called out as they killed non-believers of Islam. *God is greatest.*

"That's not all. The owner of the ranch has been missing for several months. Supposedly, he left on a vacation to Mexico. He hasn't been heard from since."

"Great. A missing woman, a missing ranch owner and ISIS training leaders calling their forces together for a big operation." Kujo laughed, humor absent from the sound. "Any more good news for me?"

"Four of the team members are on their way out to the ranch now. We can be at your location within fifteen minutes."

"I'm not waiting. If they're planning something big, they might not let Molly live long enough for the team to get in there and free her."

"Do what you have to, but don't get yourself killed. We'll be there as soon as we can. I'm mobilizing now. I'll meet the team on the road. Do you still have your GPS tracker on you?"

"I do," Kujo said.

"Good. If you get to a point you can't communicate,

we'll follow your blip on the screen. Kujo, we've got your back."

Kujo felt the sense of belonging he'd missed since he'd been cashiered out of the military. That feeling of family, a community of people who understood him and his way of thinking. "Thanks."

The brake lights on the truck ahead of him blinked red as the vehicle slowed and turned off the highway onto a side road.

Though the darkness changed his perspective, Kujo could tell this road was the one leading onto Pinion Ranch.

They should have gotten out there sooner, uncovered the ISIS training activities and shut them down before Molly was taken.

Now, he had nothing but his wits to guide him through what might happen. The team wouldn't be there before he had to ditch his own truck and follow on foot.

He prayed Molly was all right. If they hurt her, he'd make them pay with their lives.

His fists clenched around the steering wheel as he neared the turnoff onto the dirt road leading across a cattle guard onto the ranch with the missing owner.

Kujo couldn't be sure the entrance wasn't being monitored. He pulled past the turnoff. When he reached a bend in the road, he waited until he was past it to apply his brakes to keep anyone watching from the Pinion Ranch entrance from seeing his brake lights flare.

He pulled the truck off the road, hiding it behind

bushes and trees. Then he snapped a lead on Six and got out. Kujo reached into the back of the cab for the rifle he kept in a case behind the back seat. Shoving boxes of bullets into his pockets, he straightened and closed the door. From this point, he'd be on foot.

He just hoped he could cover enough ground fast enough to be there in time to help Molly.

Kujo took off at a jog, carrying his rifle and encouraging Six to find the truck he'd been chasing.

Molly came to when her head bounced against what felt like a rubber mat. She opened her eyes and stared around at what appeared to be the cab of a pickup truck. She lay jammed between the front and back seats on the floorboard. The scent of dust and diesel fuel filled her nostrils, making her want to sneeze. She wiggled her nose, willing herself to hold off long enough to figure out an escape plan. If her captor knew she was awake, he might hit her again.

She lowered her eyelids and, peering through her lashes, looked around the interior, searching for a quick exit. If she could reach the door handle above her, she could open it, do a flip and roll out the side.

The likelihood of success was minimal. She'd have to be a contortionist to flip over backward while jammed between the front and the back seat on the floorboard.

Her head pounded, her left temple aching from where the man had hit her, but she couldn't give up, nor could she let him win. When she got the chance, she'd give the bastard what he deserved and more.

Molly used every time the vehicle bumped over a big rut to shift her body until she lay on her belly. If she played her cards right, she could use the next bump to shift her knees beneath her. The driver might see her bottom rise from the floorboard, but by then she might be able to get her hands on the door handle, shove it open and propel herself out of the truck. Then all she had to do was to survive the landing, pick herself up and run into the woods. Being lost in the woods wasn't nearly as concerning as being in the clutches of someone who'd knocked her unconscious and carried her away from the B&B and Kujo.

Another bump gave her enough momentum to lunge for the handle. She grabbed it and shoved the door open, pushed hard and flung herself out onto the ground.

She fell hard, landing on her shoulder. Pain shot through her arm. Molly couldn't worry about it, she had to keep going. Rolling away from the truck and the tires, she pushed to her feet.

The truck ground to a halt behind her. A door opened and a man jumped down. "Goddamn, bitch. You'll be sorry."

He caught her before her vision cleared, and she could take ten steps. Grabbing her by her hair, he dragged her backward.

Instead of trying to run and risk losing a hank of hair, she backed into him, fast and hard, knocking him off balance. He let go of her hair and fell on his ass.

Unfortunately, so did Molly, landing in the middle of the man's belly.

Air blasted from his lungs.

For the moment, he lay there. Molly struggled to get her feet beneath her and shot to a standing position.

A hand clamped on her ankle.

She tried to raise her foot, but the hand around her ankle kept her from going far.

Molly turned and slammed her heel into the man's face. "Take that, you son of a bitch." She heard the satisfying crunch of cartilage breaking in his nose.

The man jerked his hands back to cover his face, spewing curse words muffled by his hand.

Once again, Molly turned to run but hit the brick wall of someone's chest, bringing her up short. Hands gripped her arms and a familiar face stared down into hers. "Why the hell did you bring her?"

Molly gazed into the face of David Perez, the real estate agent who'd shown her and Kujo around the county, searching for properties for sale.

"I don't understand," she whispered. "What are you doing here?

"That's not as important as your reason for being here," He grabbed the front of her shirt and pulled her up against him.

"Trust me, I don't want to be here. That man hit me and shoved me into his truck. Ask him why." She glanced around at the view in the darkness. Several electric lanterns had been lit, but it was the tents beneath the camouflage netting that made her pulse quicken.

Men stood beside trucks loaded with wooden crates. One by one, they handed out weapons, in many sizes and shapes. Most appeared to be military-grade rifles and machine guns. Another man passed around vests, and yet another distributed hand grenades.

From what Molly could tell, they were gearing up for war. Only they weren't US military forces. They appeared to be a bunch of bearded bubbas, some younger, angry looking men of a variety of ethnic backgrounds and a few men Molly had seen in Eagle Rock recently.

Perez nodded to the bearded man who'd gotten out of the truck. "Diener, why is she here?"

"I owed her boyfriend for making my wife leave me."

Perez's mouth twisted into a snarl. "You realize what bringing her here means?"

Diener smirked. "It means she can't leave. She'll have to die. Serves that Kuntz fellow right."

"It also means her fiancé will be searching for her. You've raised the chances of being discovered before we've completed our mission." Perez nodded to one of the men standing nearby. "The penalty for revealing our location to outsiders is clearly outlined in the training."

"Hey." Diener raised his hands and backed away, his eyes widening. "I did you a favor by bringing her here. She's the one who was snooping in the valley the other day." He shouted to another man. "Birge, tell 'em."

A clean-shaven younger man stepped away from his position handing out grenades to others. He carried one of the grenades in his palm as he approached Perez and Diener. "What are you talking about?"

Diener glared at Birge. "Tell Mohammed about the

person you thought you shot in the valley. The one who was flying the drone."

Birge shrugged. "I shot down a drone in the valley and chased someone on a four-wheeler. So?"

"So? You thought it might be her, the woman who was shackin' up with the stranger in the old DeLong hunting cabin in the woods."

"Again." The younger man stared at Diener with a deadpan face, no emotion nor expression in his eyes or anywhere else. "I don't know what you're talking about. I figured whoever was flying that drone shouldn't be snooping in the valley when we were still moving supplies. So, I took care of it."

Molly stared into the eyes of Daisy's ex-boyfriend and struggled not to let a shiver shake her entire body. The man appeared to have no soul whatsoever.

Diener's eyes narrowed. "That's not what you told me. And I suppose you didn't bother to tell Mohammed it was you who set that explosive at Al's Diner."

Molly couldn't see Perez's expression, but she felt him stiffen behind her.

"Birge, were you the one behind the explosion in town earlier today?" Perez demanded.

Birge shook his head. "Why would I start something that could bring in the ATF, the FBI and the National Guard? That would undermine our mission. I'm not that stupid."

"You lying bastard." Diener lunged for Birge and slugged him in the face.

Molly clenched her fists. Birge was lying and deserved to be slugged. He'd almost killed Al and his ex-girlfriend was in the hospital. If she could Molly would have put a bullet between the jerk's eyes.

Birge staggered backward, clutching at his jaw. "I'm not the one interested in revenge. I didn't burn down a hunting cabin to kill the man who broke up a fight between my old lady and me."

Diener pointed at Birge. "No, but you planted the explosives to take out your girlfriend who worked at the diner."

"From what I heard, the man who broke up the fight between you and your wife was inside that diner when the explosives went off. I have no interest in hurting Daisy. We've been done for a long time. She just did me a favor by moving all of my stuff out of her apartment."

Perez's grip tightened on Molly's arm. "And by all your stuff, are you referring to furniture and clothing? What about your computer? Can you tell me where your laptop is at this very moment?"

In the light from the open door of the truck, Molly could see Birge's face pale. But he raised his chin. "It's in my vehicle."

"Liar!" Diener shouted. "Daisy had it. When you went to get it, someone got there before you."

Birge's lip curled back in a snarl. "You don't know that."

"I was there. I saw you go into her apartment. I also saw someone sneak into her car and take the computer bag."

"Since your vehicle is here, Birge," Perez said, his tone low and threatening, "be so good as to show me your laptop."

Birge turned and started to walk away. He took only five steps and then broke into a run, veering toward the woods.

Diener raised the pistol in his hand and shot Birge in the back.

Birge staggered and fell, face first, to the ground, where he lay still.

"I told you he was lying."

Molly's heart thundered, but she had to play it cool. She was in enemy territory and the man holding her wasn't the friendly real estate agent she'd thought he was. Apparently, she'd found an ISIS training camp, and he was their leader, a man they called Mohammed.

So much for not engaging the enemy. *Now, would be a good time to come up with a backup plan.* She had to get out of the camp, back to town, and call for reinforcements.

The arm around her tightened. "Bind her," Mohammed commanded.

Diener smirked. "I told you she was worth capturing."

"You've caused enough trouble with your petty desire for revenge. Don't give me a reason to do to you what you did to Birge." He shoved Molly toward Diener, who caught her in one of his thick arms, crushing her against his side.

Molly cocked her elbow, ready to plant it in Diener's gut, but stopped when she stared down the barrel of a nine-millimeter Glock.

"All I have to do is pull the trigger and take care of

two thorns in my side." Mohammed's eyes narrowed into slits. "Go ahead. Tempt me."

Molly lowered her arm. She could fight people, but a bullet wasn't as easily overcome.

Perez's hand never wavered, but he raised his gaze to the man behind Molly. "We're moving our mission in Bozeman and Helena up a day."

Diener shifted his weight. "But we can't move all the supplies by morning."

"Then we'll take what we can and destroy the rest." Mohammed stared at Molly. "And by the rest, that includes you."

CHAPTER 17

Kujo ran through the woods, paralleling the road the truck had taken into Pinion Ranch, all the while ignoring the pain in his bum leg. The physical ache would eventually go away. The emotional anguish of Molly's death wouldn't be eased by putting his feet up. He had to reach her before her captor did anything to harm her.

Six ran alongside him, his unsteady gait not slowing him one bit. The dog had found a friend in Molly and seemed as concerned about her wellbeing as Kujo.

After what felt like miles, Kujo glimpsed a flicker of a light ahead, between the trees and brush.

He slowed, pulling Six to a stop. If what he was nearing was the ISIS training camp, there could be sentries guarding the perimeter.

Kujo knelt on the ground beside Six, unhooked the lead from the animal's collar and spoke quietly, but firmly near the dog's ear. "Heel."

Six sat on his haunches and waited for Kujo's next

command, his attention completely focused on his master. At that moment, he appeared to be the dog Kujo had partnered with in battle all those years ago.

He tested the theory by taking several steps through the woods.

Six trotted beside him, matching his pace.

With no time to waste, Kujo ducked low and worked his way toward the encampment then circled the area. The only guards he spotted were at the entrance, on either side of the road.

The site was nestled into the trees. Tents had been erected and covered with camouflage netting to blend into the foliage, making it difficult to spot from above. He counted twenty-eight men moving about, loading items into the backs of pickup trucks with short camper shells on the back. What didn't fit, they stacked in a pile at the center of the area between the tents.

Kujo wished he had his satellite phone to call Hank and warn him about the number of men in the camp. The four or five men his boss could round up from the Brotherhood Protectors would be no match against the number of men he was counting. And all Kujo had was his rifle and Six.

A man shouted, drawing Kujo's attention. Three men stood near the open door of a pickup. The interior light shining behind them made silhouettes out of their bodies. One of the men seemed thicker than the others until Kujo realized he was holding a body against him.

More shouting made Kujo strain to make out the words. But he was too far away. Then one of the men started to walk away. He didn't go far before he broke into a run.

The sharp report of gunfire sounded, and the running man dropped to the ground.

The man holding the body shoved it toward the one who'd fired the shot and walked away.

The shooter spun the person around and appeared to bind the figure to the pile of boxes and debris growing in the middle of the camp. With the headlights of a vehicle backlighting the figure, Kujo couldn't see a face, but he knew by the feminine shape, that person was Molly.

A twig snapped nearby.

Six growled low in his chest and hunkered down, ready to spring.

Kujo spun and dropped to a prone position, his arms out in front of him, his weapon pointed in the direction of the noise.

"Kujo," a voice whispered in the darkness. "Don't shoot me." Bear low-crawled to Kujo's position.

"Are you trying to get yourself killed?" Kujo gritted out.

"I was more worried about Six ripping off my face." Bear handed him a headset. "The gang's all here. Seven, counting you."

He didn't know how the hell they'd arrived so quickly, but he was glad they had his back.

"Hank checked with the sheriff. They're mobilizing and on their way here."

Kujo shook his head. "Can't wait for them. See the pile of boxes in the middle?"

"Yeah," Bear acknowledged.

"Molly's somewhere near that pile. They're loading the trucks. It looks like the pile is what they're leaving behind."

Bear stared at the center of the camp. "And they won't leave that much evidence intact."

Kujo's gut knotted. Bear's conclusion was what Kujo had come up with. Which meant when the trucks moved out, they'd set fire to, or detonate, what was left. "We have to get her out of there before that happens."

"Enemy head count?" Bear queried.

Kujo settled the headset over his head and pressed it into his ear. "Twenty-eight tangos."

"Four to one," Hank's voice came over the radio. "The odds are in our favor."

Kujo had been in operations where they'd had ten-to-one odds. Hope flared. "If you all could take the rest, I'll get Molly."

"Yeah, take the sweet job," Bear said. "Leave us with the bubbas."

"Let's do it," Hank said. "Keep it quiet, and only use necessary force. We're not in Afghanistan or Iraq."

"Your definition of necessary?" Duke said.

Hank didn't answer. The team moved forward, slipping into the camp on silent feet.

His concentration on Molly, Kujo nearly missed a man lounging in the shadows, his back to the wheel of a truck, sound asleep.

Six alerted Kujo with a low growl.

Kujo hit the guy in the temple with the grip of his pistol. The man went down without a fight, never waking up. He'd likely rouse to a sheriff's deputy reading his Miranda rights as he dragged the traitor's ass into the back of his service vehicle. Just to make sure, Kujo pulled the man's shirt over his head and tied his arms together behind his back. He didn't like taking the time to do it, but he couldn't risk the man sneaking up behind him when he was getting Molly out of trouble.

Kujo couldn't hear the team as they dealt with the men in the camp, but he trusted they'd be there if he needed assistance. He prayed he wasn't too late.

Molly struggled to loosen the zip-tie Diener had used to bind her ankles and to secure her wrists behind her back. Then he'd dragged her across camp and shoved her toward the growing stack of empty crates and boxes. Unable to catch herself, she fell against a wooden crate, hitting it with her hip.

That's going to leave a bruise, she thought as she glanced off the crate and did a face-plant in the dirt. She rolled to her side and used her elbow to leverage herself high enough she finally managed to sit up.

"Hurry it up! If it won't fit, we'll destroy it," Mohammed called out. "Five minutes, and we bug out."

The sense of urgency grew more frenetic until the men were throwing what they could into the truck beds, running from tents to trucks.

Molly scooted back against one of the crates and rubbed the zip-tie against an edge of rough wood.

"Come on," she muttered, rubbing harder, taking

layers of skin off her arms and wrists with each pass. Skin would grow back. But if she didn't get out of there soon, they'd light her up with the debris they left behind. And she needed to get back to civilization to warn law enforcement that these men were planning assaults in Bozeman and Helena the following morning. If she didn't get away and warn someone, innocent people would die.

With lives hanging in the balance, Molly rubbed harder, and, finally, the zip-tie snapped and her wrists were free. When none of the frantic men were looking, she broke a board off a crate, and twisted it into the zip-tie binding her ankles until it broke. She sprang to her feet and started for the safety of the woods.

"Oh, no you don't." Someone grabbed her hair and yanked backward, nearly pulling her off her feet. The barrel of a pistol pressed against her temple.

Instinct kicked in. Molly pushed her hand up between them, knocking his pistol upward.

He fired, the shot going into the air.

The sound of the gunshot threw the rest of the men into a panic. Suddenly there were more people than before, some of them fighting. More shots were fired, and men yelled.

Molly didn't have time to wonder what the heck was happening around her. She wrapped her arm around her attackers and twisted his behind his back, forcing him to drop the pistol. He lurched forward, taking her with him and falling to the ground.

Molly fell on top of him, refusing to release her hold

on the arm she'd shoved up between his shoulder blades.

Perez, or Mohammed, as Tanner and Diener had called him, rolled over, crushing her beneath him, his weight pushing the air from her lungs.

A flash of fur streaked from the right and leaped onto Mohammed. Six's deep, vicious growl might have frightened some, but to Molly, it was the sound of heaven.

Six ripped into Mohammed's arm, tearing into the flesh.

Mohammed cried out then rolled, kicked and flailed, but Six wouldn't let go.

When Mohammed's body slipped off Molly's, she rolled away and pushed to her feet.

"I should have killed you in town." Ray Diener stood in front of her, his pistol pointed at Molly's head.

Half crouching, Molly shivered with rage. She'd been so damn close. "Go ahead, shoot me. But you won't get away with this. The sheriff is on his way. You won't get to the highway before they catch you. You might as well give up."

"Shut up, bitch!" He lowered his weapon and pointed at her chest, but before he could pull the trigger, a shot rang out.

Diener dropped where he was, the gun falling from his hand onto the dirt.

Molly looked in the direction from where the shot had been fired.

Kujo stood with his pistol held out, his hand shaking. "Holy shit, Molly. I thought you were dead."

Molly straightened and glanced to the side. Six held Mohammed pinned to the ground.

With his free hand, Mohammed reached for the weapon Diener had dropped. When his fingers closed around it, he raised it, aiming toward Six.

"No fucking way." Molly kicked his hand so hard, the bone snapped and the gun flew into the pile of boxes. Mohammed screamed in pain.

Kujo raced to her side and pulled her into his arms.

Sirens wailed as the fighting came to an end.

The Brotherhood Protectors emerged victorious, the ISIS-trained men lying at their feet, holding broken limbs or hands to the gunshot wounds that had maimed but wouldn't kill.

"How did you find me?" Molly asked, leaning hard against his chest.

"I was right behind the truck he took you in, up until he turned down the road to the ranch." He pulled her closer and pressed his cheek to her hair. "I couldn't let them hurt you. You're the best thing to happen to me since I got Six back."

She laughed. "I see where I rank. First Six, and then me."

"How about equal?" He tilted her chin up and pressed his lips to hers for a quick, hard kiss.

"I can live with that," she whispered into his mouth. "You both saved my life. My heroes."

"You're a brave, woman, Molly Greenbriar." He kissed her again while Six growled and shook Mohammed's arm.

The sheriff, and every deputy in the county arrived,

along with the fire department and emergency medical technicians.

While the sheriff's deputies cuffed and read the ISIS trainees their rights, Molly gave the sheriff the rundown on Mohammed's plans to wreak havoc on Bozeman and Helena. Hank told him about the information they'd hacked from Birge's laptop and promised to hand it over as evidence.

Hank gathered the Brotherhood Protectors and Molly in a half-circle away from the melee.

"You all did well tonight. I've cleared it with the sheriff to cut loose. He'll want to get statements from you, but we need to get out of here before the media descends on us."

"But that would be good advertisement for the team," Duke said.

"Yeah," Bear agreed. "You'd get more business."

Hank grinned. "I've got more business than I have men to work. Looks like we'll be hiring more people." He pounded Kujo on the back. "And you've more than proven yourself as part of this team." He held out his hand to Kujo. "Welcome aboard, Kujo. Glad you're part of Brotherhood Protectors."

Kujo shook his boss's hand. "Thanks, but Six gets the credit for saving Molly. He and I are a team."

"Absolutely." Hank dropped to one knee and held out his hand to Six, now that the dog had been relieved of his prey. "Welcome to the team, Six."

Six put his paw in Hank's hand and barked.

The team laughed and congratulated each other on a

job well done. Then they headed back to the highway where they'd left their vehicles.

Kujo insisted Molly get the EMTs to treat the wounds on her wrists and hip and check her for concussion. When they cleared her, he lifted her into his arms and carried her back down the road to where he'd left his truck.

"You know I can walk, right?"

He nodded. "I know." But he carried her all the way to the truck and settled her in the passenger seat.

They were back at the B&B twenty minutes later. Molly made the trip in silence, wondering what was next between her and Kujo. Before she was abducted, she'd wanted space to think, to get her mind around her growing attraction to the man.

After all that had happened, all she wanted now was to be in his arms.

Mrs. K met them at the door. "I've been listening to the scanner. I'm so glad you're all right."

"I'm sorry about the door, Mrs. K," Kujo said.

The older woman waved her hand. "Now, don't you worry about that. I'm just glad Miss Molly is okay." She hugged them both and promised a big breakfast in the morning to celebrate their return.

Molly climbed the stairs and entered their room. She waited for Kujo to close the door, and then she threw herself into his arms.

"Hey," he said, brushing the hair back from her face. "What's this? I thought you wanted space." He chuckled. "How's that going for you?"

"I'm done with space. I want you," she said. "I don't

know if you feel the same, but I'll take any scrap of attention you want to throw my way. If you feel the same, I'll make it work somehow. We can make a long-distance relationship work, can't we? I can fly out whenever I have time off. Better yet, I can transfer to the Montana office of the FBI. We can do this." She looked up at him, her eyes filling with tears. "Please say something. I know I'm making a complete fool of myself."

He cupped her cheeks in his hands and bent to kiss her forehead.

Molly's heart sank to her knees. A man didn't kiss a woman's forehead unless he was about to break up with her.

She braced herself for the pain, knowing it would be worse than any wound she'd ever received.

Kujo arched an eyebrow. "Now that I can get a word in edgewise, I want to say, I'll give you the space you need as long as it never exceeds five minutes again. I almost lost my mind waiting for you to come back to the room. I'd given up on waiting, and was about to beg you to come back, when Six started barking."

She stared up into his eyes, her heart swelling, tears tipping over the edges of her eyes and trailing down her cheeks.

He nodded. "I don't know how I went from a mountain hermit to falling in love with a woman in less than a week, but here I am, my heart in your hands. Give me a chance to show you how much you mean to me. Go on a date with me. Let me woo you the way you deserve. Will you let me love you?"

"Yes!" Molly stood on her toes and kissed him like there might be no tomorrow. And that had almost been the case.

Kujo held her close, loving her back as hard as she was loving him.

Six pressed his warm, furry body against them, making their joy complete.

EPILOGUE

Kujo stood on the porch looking out over his valley. The Crazy Mountains rose behind him, and the blue Montana sky was bright and clear above. Molly was in the yard, throwing a ball for Six to keep the dog's injured leg from getting stiff.

They'd found the cabin in the mountains a few weeks ago and made an offer. The owner, who'd moved to Florida, accepted. The timing couldn't have been better.

Molly's transfer to the FBI's regional office had been denied. Her boss, Pete, wanted to keep her and arranged for her to take field assignments from her new home in Montana.

Molly tossed the ball one last time for Six and climbed up to stand beside Kujo on the deck.

He slipped his arm around her waist and pulled her against his body. "The team will be here in a few minutes. Are you ready to host our first barbeque at our new place?"

She nodded. "I can't believe this is ours." She grinned up at him. "I keep thinking life can't get any better just being with you, but then it does."

"I know what you mean. But I can think of one more thing to make it better."

"Yeah?" She leaned up on her toes. "Like maybe a kiss?" She pressed her lips to his, but he only gave her a brief peck then set her back on her heels.

"Yes, to the kiss, but that wasn't quite what I had in mind." He dug in his pocket for what he'd gone all the way to Helena to find. When his fingers wrapped around the object, he took her hand and dropped down to one knee.

Molly frowned. "What are you doing?"

"Molly Greenbriar, we've known each other now for three months, four days, ten hours and thirty-seven minutes."

Her eyes rounded and filled with tears. "You're not—oh, hell—is this…?"

"Shut up and listen," he said. "I don't want another minute to go by that you aren't mine. Will you marry me?"

"Yes! Oh, yes. Please." Molly dropped down on her knees and curled her fingers around his.

He pried his hand loose and slipped the ring onto her finger. "The sooner we start the rest of our lives, the better."

IF YOU ENJOYED THIS STORY, you might enjoy others in the:

Brotherhood Protectors Series
Montana SEAL (#1)
Bride Protector SEAL (#2)
Montana D-Force (#3)
Cowboy D-Force (#4)
Montana Ranger (#5)
Montana Dog Soldier (#6)
Montana SEAL Daddy (#7)
Montana Ranger's Wedding Vow (#8)
Montana Rescue

ABOUT THE AUTHOR

ELLE JAMES also writing as MYLA JACKSON is a *New York Times* and *USA Today* Bestselling author of books including cowboys, intrigues and paranormal adventures that keep her readers on the edges of their seats. When she's not at her computer, she's traveling, snow skiing, boating, or riding her ATV, dreaming up new stories. Learn more about Elle James at www.ellejames.com

Website | Facebook | Twitter | GoodReads | Newsletter | BookBub | Amazon

Or visit her alter ego Myla Jackson at mylajackson.com
Website | Facebook | Twitter | Newsletter

Follow Me!
www.ellejames.com
ellejamesauthor@gmail.com

ALSO BY ELLE JAMES

Shadow Assassin

Delta Force Strong

Ivy's Delta (Delta Force 3 Crossover)

Breaking Silence (#1)

Breaking Rules (#2)

Breaking Away (#3)

Breaking Free (#4)

Breaking Hearts (#5)

Breaking Ties (#6)

Breaking Point (#7)

Breaking Dawn (#8)

Breaking Promises (#9)

Brotherhood Protectors Yellowstone

Saving Kyla (#1)

Saving Chelsea (#2)

Saving Amanda (#3)

Saving Liliana (#4)

Saving Breely (#5)

Saving Savvie (#6)

Brotherhood Protectors Colorado

SEAL Salvation (#1)

Rocky Mountain Rescue (#2)

Ranger Redemption (#3)

Tactical Takeover (#4)

Colorado Conspiracy (#5)

Rocky Mountain Madness (#6)

Free Fall (#7)

Colorado Cold Case (#8)

Fool's Folly (#9)

Brotherhood Protectors

Montana SEAL (#1)

Bride Protector SEAL (#2)

Montana D-Force (#3)

Cowboy D-Force (#4)

Montana Ranger (#5)

Montana Dog Soldier (#6)

Montana SEAL Daddy (#7)

Montana Ranger's Wedding Vow (#8)

Montana SEAL Undercover Daddy (#9)

Cape Cod SEAL Rescue (#10)

Montana SEAL Friendly Fire (#11)

Montana SEAL's Mail-Order Bride (#12)

SEAL Justice (#13)

Ranger Creed (#14)

Delta Force Rescue (#15)

Dog Days of Christmas (#16)

Montana Rescue (#17)

Montana Ranger Returns (#18)

Hot SEAL Salty Dog (SEALs in Paradise)

Hot SEAL, Hawaiian Nights (SEALs in Paradise)

Hot SEAL Bachelor Party (SEALs in Paradise)

Hot SEAL, Independence Day (SEALs in Paradise)

Brotherhood Protectors Vol 1

Iron Horse Legacy

Soldier's Duty (#1)

Ranger's Baby (#2)

Marine's Promise (#3)

SEAL's Vow (#4)

Warrior's Resolve (#5)

Drake (#6)

Grimm (#7)

Murdock (#8)

Utah (#9)

Judge (#10)

The Outriders

Homicide at Whiskey Gulch (#1)

Hideout at Whiskey Gulch (#2)

Held Hostage at Whiskey Gulch (#3)

Setup at Whiskey Gulch (#4)

Missing Witness at Whiskey Gulch (#5)

Cowboy Justice at Whiskey Gulch (#6)

Hellfire Series

Hellfire, Texas (#1)

Justice Burning (#2)

Smoldering Desire (#3)

Hellfire in High Heels (#4)

Playing With Fire (#5)

Up in Flames (#6)

Total Meltdown (#7)

Declan's Defenders

Marine Force Recon (#1)

Show of Force (#2)

Full Force (#3)

Driving Force (#4)

Tactical Force (#5)

Disruptive Force (#6)

Mission: Six

One Intrepid SEAL

Two Dauntless Hearts

Three Courageous Words

Four Relentless Days

Five Ways to Surrender

Six Minutes to Midnight

Hearts & Heroes Series

Wyatt's War (#1)

Mack's Witness (#2)

Ronin's Return (#3)

Sam's Surrender (#4)

Take No Prisoners Series

SEAL's Honor (#1)

SEAL'S Desire (#2)

SEAL's Embrace (#3)

SEAL's Obsession (#4)

SEAL's Proposal (#5)

SEAL's Seduction (#6)

SEAL'S Defiance (#7)

SEAL's Deception (#8)

SEAL's Deliverance (#9)

SEAL's Ultimate Challenge (#10)

Texas Billionaire Club

Tarzan & Janine (#1)

Something To Talk About (#2)

Who's Your Daddy (#3)

Love & War (#4)

Billionaire Online Dating Service

The Billionaire Husband Test (#1)

The Billionaire Cinderella Test (#2)

The Billionaire Bride Test (#3)

The Billionaire Daddy Test (#4)

The Billionaire Matchmaker Test (#5)

The Billionaire Glitch Date (#6)

The Billionaire Perfect Date (#7) coming soon

The Billionaire Replacement Date (#8) coming soon

The Billionaire Wedding Date (#9) coming soon

Ballistic Cowboy

Hot Combat (#1)

Hot Target (#2)

Hot Zone (#3)

Hot Velocity (#4)

Cajun Magic Mystery Series

Voodoo on the Bayou (#1)

Voodoo for Two (#2)

Deja Voodoo (#3)

Cajun Magic Mysteries Books 1-3

SEAL Of My Own

Navy SEAL Survival

Navy SEAL Captive

Navy SEAL To Die For

Navy SEAL Six Pack

Devil's Shroud Series

Deadly Reckoning (#1)

Deadly Engagement (#2)

Deadly Liaisons (#3)

Deadly Allure (#4)

Deadly Obsession (#5)

Deadly Fall (#6)

Covert Cowboys Inc Series

Triggered (#1)

Taking Aim (#2)

Bodyguard Under Fire (#3)

Cowboy Resurrected (#4)

Navy SEAL Justice (#5)

Navy SEAL Newlywed (#6)

High Country Hideout (#7)

Clandestine Christmas (#8)

Thunder Horse Series

Hostage to Thunder Horse (#1)

Thunder Horse Heritage (#2)

Thunder Horse Redemption (#3)

Christmas at Thunder Horse Ranch (#4)

Demon Series

Hot Demon Nights (#1)

Demon's Embrace (#2)

Tempting the Demon (#3)

Lords of the Underworld

Witch's Initiation (#1)

Witch's Seduction (#2)

The Witch's Desire (#3)

Possessing the Witch (#4)

Stealth Operations Specialists (SOS)

Nick of Time

Alaskan Fantasy

Boys Behaving Badly Anthologies

Rogues (#1)

Blue Collar (#2)

Pirates (#3)

Stranded (#4)

First Responder (#5)

Blown Away

Warrior's Conquest

Enslaved by the Viking Short Story

Conquests

Smokin' Hot Firemen

Protecting the Colton Bride

Protecting the Colton Bride & Colton's Cowboy Code

Heir to Murder

Secret Service Rescue

High Octane Heroes

Haunted

Engaged with the Boss

Cowboy Brigade

Time Raiders: The Whisper

Bundle of Trouble

Killer Body

Operation XOXO

An Unexpected Clue

Baby Bling

Under Suspicion, With Child

Texas-Size Secrets

Cowboy Sanctuary

Lakota Baby

Dakota Meltdown

Beneath the Texas Moon

Printed in Great Britain
by Amazon